Dim The Flaring Lamps

A NOVEL OF THE LIFE OF JOHN WILKES BOOTH

JAN JORDAN

PRENTICE-HALL, INC.
Englewood Cliffs, New Jersey

Dim The Flaring Lamps by Jan Jordan
Copyright © 1972 by Jan Jordan
All rights reserved. No part of this book may be
reproduced in any form or by any means, except for
inclusion of brief quotations in a review, without
permission in writing from the publisher.
ISBN 0-13-214411-5
Library of Congress Catalog Card Number: 72-167625
Printed in the United States of America T
Prentice-Hall International, Inc., London
Prentice-Hall of Australia, Pty. Ltd., Sydney
Prentice-Hall of Canada, Ltd., Toronto
Prentice-Hall of India Private Ltd., New Delhi
Prentice-Hall of Japan, Inc., Tokyo

To
HELEN COOPER JORDAN
Who gave me life, love and loyalty

AUTHOR'S NOTE

When the shadowy figure of John Wilkes Booth, assassin of Abraham Lincoln, raced away from Ford's Theater into the dark night, a curtain of government censorship was dropped over the famed actor's life Anyone is able to learn the most intimate details of the life of Lincoln because the record is intact. But whoever wants to know about the personal life and loves and hates of John Wilkes Booth, comes up against frustration and silence.

Secretary of War Edwin Stanton imposed a search and destroy policy on the life of Booth. He inflicted a reign of vengeance upon the Booth family, all innocent of the crime. He ordered all their family records, all letters, diaries, manuscripts, pictures, seized and destroyed. Even the ailing favorite sister of Booth, Asia Clarke, was subjected to Stanton's policy and her Philadelphia home entered by Federal Authorities who confiscated every personal paper and picture. Even a portrait of Wilkes was ripped from the nursery wall where Asia had it hanging over a crib.

Stanton, rightly or wrongly, nearly accomplished his aim of total removal of Booth's memory from the records of this nation. The items which did escape his policy are not voluminous, but they are sufficient, when carefully fitted together, to give the full story of the life of John Wilkes Booth.

There are private and public libraries which hold valuable references to Booth. The chase of facts is exciting and leads the researcher into a variety of places including our National War Archives, the Library of Congress, the New York City Library, universities, and even to Canada. However, thanks to Stanton's destruction of the major portion of the written record, the story of Booth's life may never be fully documented. Because this is true, *Dim The Flaring Lamps* has been written as a novel in order to round out the facts. The incidents related in the novel are all based on actual events in Booth's fascinating life.

There are places where known incidents have been accelerated or telescoped for the sake of the narrative; where I have drawn conclusions based on the record to link heretofore unrelated facts and events; where details and information have been eliminated due to sheer lack of space. But in general, I have made every effort to stick scrupulously to documented chronology and to highlight the factual story which history seems to have misinterpreted or overlooked. In this way, I hope, posterity—to which John Wilkes Booth appealed for compassion—can now reach an understanding of the man and his tragic destiny.

J.J.

One

"Junius, what name is this new son of yours going to use in the world?" Old Richard Booth sat hunched forward in a red velvet chair in the library of Tudor Hall, the Bel Air, Maryland, home of stage-famed Junius Brutus Booth. There was a hoarseness in the old man's voice this morning which was not entirely attributable to his advanced age: He was concerned, knowing that he was tossing his son a bitter question.

Junius Booth paced the room, his restless steps bringing him full circle to the silver tray of liquor that lay on a marble-topped table in front of his father. As he refilled his glass, Junius said firmly, "If it is a boy, you know that Mary Ann favors naming him Antony."

The elder Booth squinted up at his son through a watery haze that misted over his pale blue eyes. "You know damn well that's not what I'm talking about, Junius. You and Mary Ann are about to present the world with another bastard. When will your children receive the name of Booth? Or are they to carry the bar sinister all their lives?"

Junius lowered the glass from his lips. The rage which shook him was so fierce that he almost reached out to strike his father. Instead, he sat down on the couch opposite the old man, a sense of weakness overwhelming him.

In the spacious room above, Mary Ann was giving birth to their ninth child. They both hoped it would be another son, but legally there was not a Booth son or daughter among his children, nor did his adorable, loving Mary Ann have a right to his name.

Junius Brutus had married his wife Adelaide in London's St. George's Parish in May, 1815. He had deserted her years ago, but since it was he who had left her to elope to America with a young woman of London, she would not give him a divorce.

"I'm sorry, my son." Richard Booth leaned forward in the chair, lifting a sympathetic hand toward Junius. "Forgive this old Jew," he begged. "It's just that my heart cries for my grandchildren, and for you."

Junius smiled. Even in his declining years, Richard Booth was a noble person, and he was only expressing his deep love for his family. The Booths were all a highly emotional breed, as Junius well knew—erratic, talented, courageous. Each generation took its cue from its ancestor, Ricardo Botha, a Spanish Jew from whom the Booths received their superb good looks, their high-strung temperaments, and their daring.

A lawyer, Botha had written inflammatory pamphlets against the royalist government and, consequently, had to flee to Portugal for his life. His son, Roberto Botha, went on to England where he anglicized his name to Robert Booth. Then, in England, in time, the Booths and the famed Wilkes family were united through the marriage of Richard to the niece of John Wilkes, the English revolutionist and statesman.

"I know how you feel, Father," Junius muttered. He stood up again and started to pace the room. "God knows all I want in this world is to give my children my name. Do you know, I don't believe I really ever think about much else. Not even the theater helps. Sometimes, on stage, I forget my lines for just a moment." He shook his head. "I suppose the audience thinks I have been with the bottle a little too much."

"It's a habit I see growing," the old man said, "and you know it won't help."

"Ah, but it does, it does!" Junius went to the table and reached for the glass. "When I'm away from home and have long hours alone after the theater closes and not much to do but think—it helps!"

Richard Booth frowned. "There is one good thing in this miserable situation, Junius. The children are too young to realize their estate. And it may be they will never have to know."

"Adelaide hasn't any pride at all. We didn't have a marriage worthy of the name; only when I found a woman to love did Adelaide discover her precious wife's right to me and to my name. She's a mean, jealous woman. I'm afraid of her, of what she may do in time."

"Surely she would consider your children's innocence before she'd think about creating a scandal."

"I don't know. The younger children at this time would hardly be affected, but Rosalie's a very serious young woman at fifteen. I wonder if she could bear up if infamy were flung at her parents."

"Oh, I think Rosalie is the least emotional of all the children. Asia and Edwin are very healthy, too."

"We have done all we can to make a good life for our children," Junius said as he poured himself another glass of liquor. "Do you know, Father, my success is really quite tremendous? They tell me I am gathering the largest theater crowds ever seen in America. The theaters are sold out long before the opening dates of my appearances."

"And I am becoming known as the father of Junius Brutus Booth!" Richard Booth's eyes twinkled. "I'm very pleased."

But Junius suddenly held up a hand. "Listen!"

The cry of a newborn baby, muffled by the floor between them, hung in the air.

"He is here!" Junius put down the liquor glass and hurried from the library.

"It sounds to me as though he has lungs just made for the stage," Richard Booth called after him.

Rosalie opened the bedroom door in response to Junius' knock. Her young face was pale but smiling; the huge white apron she wore over her cotton dress was wet. "Oh Father, everything is all right! And it's a boy!" She pulled him toward the bed where Mary Ann lay. The baby was already wrapped in a white blanket and cradled in the crook of his mother's arm. Hagar, the dark maid who had attended at the birth of each child, backed away from the bed, her sweaty face bright with a smile.

"Sir," she advised Junius Booth, "You all has out-done yourselfs. This child is the most beautiful one I ever did see."

"Thank you, Hagar." Junius moved to Mary Ann's side.

"It's true," Mary Ann said, her exhausted voice but a whisper. "He is so beautiful."

Junius bent and kissed her, then sat down on the edge of the bed, his whole attention focused on her. He only glanced at the blanket-swaddled infant tucked into the security of her encircling arm. Again he bent and kissed the moist cheek of the woman he loved, and anxiously he searched her face for signs of distress—there were none. The dark, thick curls of her head brushed high off her forehead, she was at ease, and a pinkness was returning to her face.

"We have another son, Junius."

"So I understand." He smiled now too.

When Mary Ann pulled the flap of the blanket away from the baby's face, Junius stared, open-mouthed and speechless. The baby was indeed beautiful: black hair, startling white skin, charcoal-colored eye lashes, delicately arched eyebrows, straight nose, curved lips, flat, pearl-like ears. Every feature, perfect. The eyes, especially, held Junius' gaze. They were not blue like most infants' at birth. No, these were dark and luminous, with flecks of gold.

Mary Ann drew her husband's hand to her lips. "Shall we name him Antony? I would like to, very much."

Junius held out a hand to Rosalie. "Come here, sweetheart. You had a hand in this birth. What do you think we ought to name this baby? Do you agree with your mother?"

"Whatever Mother wants," she said. "I like Antony well enough."

Hagar folded a diaper and cleared her throat.

"All right, Hagar," Junius said, "your vote?"

The big black woman smoothed out the diaper on the table. "Oh, I ain't got no call to speak up, this being a family matter."

The Booth family exchanged glances, smiling. "Come, now, Hagar," Mary Ann urged, "speak your mind. We're listening."

"Well, Missy Mary, if you like. I only says when you pick a name for that young 'un, jest be sure it's a name to go with a wild nature an' a sure enough spirit of fight. You jest mark my words on that."

Junius frowned and looked at the baby, who chose that moment to become restless. Tiny hands thrashed out blindly and the pink mouth opened and closed in a sucking sound. Mary Ann caught the moving hand in hers, fondled it, and held it for the others to see.

"Look at this delicate hand, Hagar!" The mother kissed it

and smiled. "It's the hand of an actor. He's going to follow in his father's footsteps. We must give him a name which will be just right for the stage."

Hagar was stubborn. "No disrespect, Missy, but there's black magic in those strange eyes. He's gonna break a whole lot of hearts, one way or 'nother. He's a stormy one, all spirited. Give him a name fitten him."

Junius leaned over and picked the infant up from the mother's embrace. He had to hold him tightly for the infant seemed to arch his back and struggle to be left alone. "By God," Junius said to Mary Ann, "he'd be up and running, if I let him go."

"I thought we decided on Antony," Mary Ann said.

"There's another which will fit him better. I would like to name him after his grand-uncle of London."

Mary Ann was appalled. "But John Wilkes was an agitator. A malcontent, a disturber of the peace."

"Exactly. But because he was all of those things, my dear, he became a Member of Parliament, a British statesman, the Lord Mayor of London. Perhaps, the knowledge that he is named for such a man will always have its influence on the boy."

"Oh, but——"

"I'm sorry. Do you want to name him Antony?"

"John Wilkes. Johnny . . . " Mary Ann spoke the names slowly, tasting them, one by one. "You're right! John Wilkes he is, but I know I will call him 'Wilkes.' "

"Are you sure?" Junius prodded.

"Yes." She put a hand on the baby. "John Wilkes Booth."

Junius nodded. "Now before you get him back, let me show him a little bit of the world." Junius arose from the bed and carried the baby to the white-curtained window which gave on the front yards of the mansion. It was the tenth day of May, 1838, and the fields and orchards and woods of Maryland were green. Large white clouds were blowing swiftly across the spring sky. Flowers bloomed, and the ponds and waters of the land were warming under the returning sun.

Junius held the baby in his right arm, and with his left he pulled aside the organdy curtain to let the warm rays shine in on the child. The baby blinked against the glare and Junius stepped back a little to keep the direct light from the newborn's eyes. Then, pointing to the fields and woods beyond the trim lawns of Tudor Hall, he spoke to his new son as though every word would be understood. Mary Ann reached for Rosalie's hand, and the young girl sat down beside her mother on the bed.

"John Wilkes Booth, out there beyond the forest lies your native land—Maryland, Virginia, the South—your country. Be true to her and your name will never be dishonored. You receive a name of pride and patriotism in tribute to a man who knew how to battle for a cause. Carry it to new fame, my son!"

The baby opened his eyes and seemed to gaze up at his father in what seemed to be frowning contemplation. Junius grinned and hefted the child a bit as he moved back with him to Mary Ann.

"Here, he's due for a nap, and so are you, my dear."

When John Wilkes was six months old his parents took him to be baptized at St. Timothy's Church at Catonsville. That evening, upon her arrival home, Mary Ann took her new son with her to the rocking chair in front of her bedroom fireplace, where she sat and began rocking slowly. Taking his tiny right hand in hers, she held it up a bit so she could study its perfection. Tiny, innocent hand, she thought, what power is at your command, for evil, or good! Be slow to be sure, firm to resist, pursue, endure—God, let me see what this hand shall do in the silent years we are tending to. On this ghostly night, in my hungering love, I implore to know whether it will labor for or against Thee?

She held the hand tightly and turned her gaze to the fire in front of her, staring at the leaping, twisting, moving flames. Watching, she suddenly sat rigid in the rocking chair as there arose from the blaze a blood-red hand. As she observed it, petrified, she saw letters form on the back—*JWB*.

The vision slowly faded.

Mary Ann clutched her son. "No!" she whispered. "Oh, no!"

Two

In that May of 1838, a birth of a different nature was anticipated in Illinois. Abraham Lincoln, twenty-nine-year-old legislator in the state government, had conceived a bill which would
move the capital of Illinois from quiet Vandalia to growing
Springfield, where he himself was a new resident.

Lincoln's removal bill was an unpopular cause at first. He
heard himself referred to scathingly as a lobbyist for the rich
men of Springfield who would certainly benefit if the Illinois
capital were set in their affluent midst. But he stuck with it, and
he found friends and allies. The bill was passed by the Illinois
legislature, and it brought Abraham Lincoln his first real political victory.

While the baby in Bel Air, Maryland, thrived that year, the
attorney legislator in Springfield and Vandalia began his lifelong
crusade against what he believed was the ultimate crime: lawless
rebellion.

When Elijah Lovejoy wrote against slavery in 1837, the mob's
destruction of his printing presses caused Lincoln to object in
the halls of the Illinois legislature:

> Good men who love tranquility, who desire to abide by
> the laws and enjoy their benefits, who would gladly spill
> their blood in the defense of their country, become tired
> and disgusted with a government that offers them no
> protection . . . Whenever the vicious portion of population
> shall be permitted to gather in bands of hundreds and
> thousands, and burn churches, ravage and rob provision
> stores, throw printing presses into rivers, shoot editors, and
> hang and burn obnoxious persons at pleasure and with
> impunity, depend upon it, this government cannot last.

7

Three

Some theaters remained open during the hot part of the year, and traveling shows stayed on the northern circuit, but Junius Brutus Booth, the recognized leading star of the theater who had risen so high that he was now billed simply as "Mr. Booth," could afford to take his summer months at home. Upon his return in the fall, the stock companies throughout all the theater circuits would welcome him back with enthusiasm.

The first summer of Wilkes' life saw Junius a happier man than he had been in several years. He threw himself into the role he liked best, that of father and husband. "I'll be here until early October," he told his father, "so I want you to catch up on your reading and writing and sleep. You've had enough responsibility for a few months. Play with the children, go wading, and I'll do the work of running this farm for a time."

Richard put his booted feet on the ottoman in front of his chair and folded his hands over his stomach. "You'll get no argument from me. Robinson Crusoe's Island is all yours. But don't overwork, and watch out for your feet. You ought not to go around shoeless."

"Take yourself a nap and let me do the fretting."

In the next few months, Junius and his black help (freed slaves who remained at "Hall") devoted themselves to repainting the house and constructing a new room on the second floor. Two new houses were also built for the Negroes, and the barn was given a coat of paint. Junius and the blacks went about the work singing. In the evenings Junius gathered his family around him. When it was cool outside they sat beside the huge stone fireplace in the library and often they entertained each other with little skits. Junius read to them from books they could not really understand—the Bible, the Talmud, the Hindu teachings—but they listened, and the words became familiar and the sound of their adored father's voice held their attention. Most frequently he read them Shakespeare, repeating his favorite passages. When one of the children surprised him by quoting the words one night, Junius was bright-eyed with pride.

On the Fourth of July, Mary Ann packed a picnic dinner, and the family went to the springs in a shaded area of the fields. The dinner was spread out on a clean tablecloth and baby Wilkes was laid nearby on his own sheetings.

At dusk, when the remains of dinner were packed away in the hamper, Mary Ann held Wilkes to her breast to nurse. "He's the image of Henry Byron," said Junius, sitting beside her. "Have you noticed?"

Surprised, Mary Ann brushed Wilkes' hair back from his forehead. "I've noticed, but I wasn't sure I ought to say so."

"Well, I can talk about Henry Bryon now since God gave us Wilkes. It's all right."

She gave Junius her free hand and tears wet her face. She remembered how Junius had been on the evening they had met—he had come to her flower stall in Bow Street Market near London's Covent Garden Theater, where he was starring as Richard III. He had purchased a huge bouquet of pink roses and then given them to her, saying: " . . . because they match your cheeks." Then he had invited her to dinner and she had accepted, even though she knew he had a wife and son waiting at home.

From that evening on, she loved him so deeply that she was able not to think about Adelaide Booth very often. When she did, it was with a sense of pity that Adelaide had not been able to hold the man she had married. When Mary Ann and Junius had settled in Bel Air and their children began to arrive, Mary Ann almost never thought of Adelaide. Among the times she did were those tragic days which saw the deaths of four of their children. Each time, in an awful agony, Mary Ann had wondered if God were punishing her for her sin.

Grief-stricken as she was over each child's death, it had been Junius who had nearly perished in sorrow. She glanced at Junius now as he sat close to her, stroking the dark hair of little Asia. She had wondered if he ever again would be able to speak the name Henry: He had adored eleven-year-old Henry above all. Two years before, they had taken a trip with the children to

9

London, where Henry died of the smallpox. This was the first time since then that Junius had mentioned the boy's name, and his voice had broken. But the terrifying grief was gone, and he had accepted Wilkes in his heart in place of Henry.

Yet, had the deaths of the other three babies been any easier? She thought about bright, wonderful Frederick. She had sent word to Richmond where Junius was on stage that Fred was taken violently ill and was crying for his father. Junius had made a swift trip home, and when death took his son, he had rushed out of the house to wander the fields, screaming. She had brought him back and with the help of servants put him to bed. For some weeks, he was too sick with sorrow to return to Richmond, but at last he had packed his costumes and gone off again. Before he could reach Richmond, a servant overtook him on the road to tell him that three-year-old Elizabeth was severely ill. By the time Junius reached home, the little girl had died. Mary Ann remembered that though Junius had cried for hours, she could not cry at all.

Back on his feet at last, Junius took off for his stage commitment in Richmond once more, and while he was there tiny Mary Ann died without warning. Word was sent to Junius that he was needed at home—Mary Ann could not send word that the child was dead.

When Junius reached home, he did not fully realize that his daughter was dead. He ran to the small graveyard where half a dozen members of the family and a few slaves had been buried. The newest grave was piled high with dirt.

Seizing a shovel, Junius shouted, "Help me save my child. I've got to get her out of there."

Richard Booth came running with Mary Ann close behind.

Mary Ann, close to fainting, allowed the old man to lead her back to the house. But she remembered the terrible sight of Junius placing the small shroud-covered body of their daughter on the ground and tearing the shroud from the face.

"Breathe!" he had ordered. "Breathe!"

Servants watched as the crazed father struggled to warm the body back to life.

When the little grave again held the body of the child, prayers were said and flowers were laid and the new headstone was carefully placed.

10

Junius walked the house in silence for days on end. He drank steadily. The children, seeing him speechless and unsteady on his feet, thought he was ill. Their mother always told them this peculiar condition was "father's calamity," and so they accepted it as such. In the years at Bel Air it became all too ordinary for "father's calamity" to intrude upon the family life.

When Wilkes was two years old, Mary Ann gave birth to her tenth and last child—Joseph.

It really was no shock to his parents when eighteen-year-old Junius announced without warning at dinner one evening that he wanted to leave home and try his own fortune in the world. Mary Ann, just lifting Wilkes out of his chair at the table, gripped the baby all the more firmly. "I'd like any funds you might spare me, Father," Junius said. "I'm going to try my luck in New York. But if you can't afford anything, I'll go anyway. I've got some few dollars, you know. I want to leave this week."

They gave him ample funds and sent him off, Mary Ann holding back tears until he was gone. Undeniably proud of his son, Junius cajoled: "He'll be all right. He has a certain affinity with the world which I envy. We'll not worry about June, my dear. If he needs us we're here. Let him go."

Wilkes was not four years old when word came of June's marriage to Clementine De Bar, an actress eleven years his senior. And within several years—unbelievably to them—Mary Ann's and Junius' first granddaughter was born and was named Blanche.

June reported, too, that he was doing well enough as an actor, even though the world had not been startled at his arrival on the stage. Junius the elder thought he detected a leaning toward the management end of the business in his son's comments.

Wilkes regarded June as something of a stranger, or, at best, a distant relative. He grew up with only the most vague relationship with his grown brother and he really did not know him well enough to miss him. More and more Wilkes became the playmate of his sister Asia, and his brother Edwin. With teenage Rosalie watching over them, the trio took over the farm. Wilkes and Asia, however, shared their father's sensitivity for all living creatures. For several years, when the children were still very small, Junius had prohibited the eating of all meats, asserting that blooded animals and men were "distant relatives" and that the flesh of animals and fowls ought not to be eaten.

Junius found increasing joy in his son Wilkes. The boy was handsome and manly; obedient and affectionate; he learned to ride and shoot inanimate targets. Junius never came home from his travels without bringing the children gifts. When Wilkes was ten years old, and it was time for his father to return from his winter away on the stages of America, the boy had a surprise for him. All during the winter months, Wilkes had crammed Shakespeare, memorizing many portions of the plays. And as a special tribute to his father, he had totally memorized the role of Richard III.

The evening he recited it standing in front of the fireplace, Junius knew he was watching his stage heir. When Wilkes finished, giving his father and the rest of the family a sweeping bow, Junius rose to his feet and went to clasp Wilkes to him.

"My God, here is a Booth to seize the world!" he said and kissed his son's cheek.

"Father, will you take me with you on your next tour?" Wilkes' eagerness made his voice tremble.

Junius put an arm around his shoulder. "No. Not yet. You're still a boy. You've got enough to learn yet right here." Junius looked to Edwin who was staying quietly in the background, wholly upstaged. "I'll teach you many things this summer, but I'm going to take Ned with me in the fall. He's also earned the right to understudy me, and he's fifteen now. I want him with me this next season."

Edwin was on his feet. "You mean it, Father?"

Junius smiled from son to son. "You'll both carry the name of Booth to new glory, in time. It won't be easy, but I vow I'll do all I can to help you."

Junius held to his promise. All through the summer months he instructed Wilkes in how to handle himself on the stage. Wilkes drank in every word. He learned the importance of total preparation. "Don't ever step on any stage to speak so much as a word until you have made a study of the theater itself," Junius warned him. "Know exactly how many seats you are playing to. Test the strength of your voice—its carrying power—to the very last row of those seats. Determine which profile you want most to present to the audience, and make your entrances with that in mind. Never let anyone intrude on your role. When the play is in your hands, do not relinquish the attention of the audience to anyone else. And, above all, know your lines. There are actors who wait until the very last minute, who are actually standing in the wings waiting to go on stage, to learn their part. Don't you ever do that, but if you need to be prompted, don't show it. Look to the man in the wings who will be holding your prompt book. He will follow your lines as you speak them, and should you need to be reminded, he'll prompt you well."

Wilkes let out a breath. "There's a lot to remember, isn't there?"

Junius nodded. "There's the matter of lighting, too. The larger theaters in most of our cities are well equipped with gaslight, which is a vast improvement over the oil lamps they used when I first went on the stage—or the flares which gave off such a bad odor and an unreliable light. Remember that light and shadows are important to your role. So are colors. That means you must avail yourself of costumes which are bright and durable. Or dramatically dark, if the stage light is strong enough to allow it."

"Father, does anyone at the theater tell you what you must do? I mean, does a manager tell you how to act?"

Junius put a heavy hand on Wilkes' shoulder, and his face was red with anger. "Have you learned nothing? Any man tell Mr. Booth how to *act*? Oh, Wilkes, I thought better of you than this."

Wilkes bit his lip. "Sir, I only meant to ask, does a manager of a theater have the right to try to tell a star what to do on stage?"

"No man *lives* who can tell a Booth what to do on stage! A theater manager is the businessman of the enterprise. He conducts all the necessary work involving the star's appearance. He develops a regular stock company which is contracted to his theater and stands ready to support any star who appears on the stage of that theater in any play the manager and the star decide to present. He sees that everything runs smoothly and that everyone, from the callboy who gets you out of your dressing room to the prompter who stands by to assist you, is on the job. Never make an enemy of a manager, if you can help it.

They walk hand-in-glove with patrons, they are never fooled about a performance, and know when you are good and when you are not. In that sense, of course, they very well do tell a star what to do—they make him toe the line in terms of his contract."

Junius studied the boy's face. Wilkes sighed. "Well, I guess it's worth it all, though, isn't it, Father?"

"It is. And the proudest day of my life will be the day you take your first curtain bow."

"Father," said Wilkes, looking up into his face, "I'm awfully glad I'm a Booth. I hope I can be just like you."

Within a matter of a few hours of their conversation about the theater, Richard Booth was dead.

Junius and Mary Ann, returning to the house from the cemetery, stood together in the library, hand in hand, gazing at the chair where Richard had spent so many hours of his life. Junius tried to speak, but a lump of tears had caught in his throat and only a sob came out.

Mary Ann rubbed his cold hands and said, "I'll fix you a drink." It was the first one she had ever voluntarily offered him.

He sat down in Richard's chair and glanced at the oil painting of General George Washington over the fireplace. The painting had first hung in the drawing room of Richard Booth's London home, where all guests had to remove their hats and bow their heads to the General's likeness.

"You know," said Junius, "I believe Wilkes worships Washington quite as much as Father did. He calls him 'The Southerner,' you know. And I think when Wilkes is riding Captain he likes to pretend he is the General himself, riding to save his country."

Four

On the first afternoon of March, 1849, Wilkes rode his white pony, Captain, in from the woodlands where he and his playmates had again maneuvered through a hectic game of soldiers. Of all the friends he rode with—little Sammy Arnold, Michael O'Laughlin, and Johnny Yates Beall—Johnny was the closest to Wilkes in friendship. Because the Bealls' home was in Virginia, the boys saw each other only when school was in session, but they shared a room at the military academy and were inseparable. The affection between the two was actually stronger than that which Wilkes felt for his own brothers.

This weekend was the first time Johnny had ever come to visit Wilkes at the Booth home.

Wilkes reined Captain to a halt on the far curve of the driveway. A strange carriage stood at the front entrance of Tudor Hall. It was not a carriage common in the countryside, but a shining town rig, its polished black paint and gleaming silver trim dazzling in the sunlight.

Wilkes was puzzled. Obviously there was a visitor from afar at Tudor Hall. But who? His father was on tour, and his mother had not been expecting company. Was it a doctor's rig? His heart raced.

"Go home," he ordered Michael and Sammy. "I've got business in the house."

Sammy shrugged his shoulders and spurred his pony around. "Heck," Michael said, "I'm kind of thirsty. Can't I come in for some water?"

"You beat it, Mike. Get your water at home."

"Come on, Mike!" said Sammy, who knew Wilkes only too well. "He's said his piece."

Wilkes beckoned to Johnny to follow him. They rode to the stable, Johnny's freckled face reflecting Wilkes' own tension.

"Something wrong?" he asked, riding behind his friend and host.

"Maybe. Look, Johnny, will you take care of the ponies? If you need any help, call for Perry."

A tall, husky black man came out of the stable. "Master Wilkes, you want me to stable 'em? Or you goin' out again?"

"Stable them, Perry. Master Beall will help you. He wants the exercise." Wilkes dismounted.

Perry quietly grasped the reins as the young boy struggled with the heavy sword and scabbard he kept attached to his saddle. The weapon was almost as long as eleven-year-old Wilkes himself, but the slave shook his head and made no move to help. Perry had learned a long time before about this child's moods and pride. There were some things the young master expected to have done for him without question or delay; but then, there were other things, like the handling of a sword, which a soldier and a gentleman managed for himself.

The sword, presented to him in a ceremony by his father, was a veteran of the Mexican War, and Wilkes wielded it in play with all the fervor of a dashing officer. Also attached to his saddle was a small American flag, flying briskly into many a mock battle.

Advising Johnny that he would see him later at the house, Wilkes hurried away from the stable, carrying the sword in both hands, his feet scuffing the dust of the stable grounds into the clear cold air.

As he skirted the parked rig at the front door, he glanced up at the immobile Negro driver. The man bowed his head: "Good afternoon, young sir."

Wilkes gave him a responsive nod, but did not pause to speak or to inspect the carriage which ordinarily would have attracted his attention. Opening the front door, he heard the loud and angry voice of a woman he did not recognize.

He came quietly to the entrance of the library, where he stood, unseen by the two occupants of the room. A fire was burning in the fireplace; his mother sat in the old red chair near the fire. She was pale and her lips were stretched taut, but she held her head high, defiantly watching the woman across from her.

Wilkes looked at the visitor. She looked like an ugly queen.

Her posture was stiff, and her brown hair, parted in the middle and pulled tightly back from her round forehead to a mold at the back of her head, gave the effect of a giant toasted bun. Overweight, she was nudging obesity.

When she turned her back to the door, Wilkes noiselessly entered the room and stood beside his mother, slipping his hand into hers, his other hand still gripping the sword. Mary Ann gave his hand a squeeze, but with a look he understood. She urged him to leave the room. Instead, he tightened his hand on hers.

The woman turned, saw Wilkes, and stopped her frantic pacing. Hate and scorn came into her eyes.

Then, laughing like a jungle bird, raucous and mirthless, she said, "So! This is one of the nameless ones, obviously. He's every inch the image of his rascal father, yet he has not the right to call him Father. How very sad, my dear! Let me see . . . your name is Holmes, is it not? Yes, Miss Mary Ann Holmes. So then this is a Holmes, is he not?"

Mary Ann stood up, still holding onto Wilkes' hand. She was shaking with rage, and red spots burned on her cheeks. "Get out, get out!" Her voice rose and broke.

The woman made no move to leave, but drew her cape closer over her dress as though to avoid contamination. "What's your name, child?" she said to Wilkes.

Wilkes, feeling that his answer was very important, replied with dignity: "M'am, I'm John Wilkes Booth."

"Oh, no," the woman corrected him, "John Wilkes it may very well be, but you are not a Booth. Your mother is not married to your father. I am the only wife Junius Brutus Booth has ever had. My son, Richard, is the only legal son Junius Booth has. You, John Wilkes, are a bastard and nothing else."

Wilkes simply could not speak. He knew the meaning of "bastard"; it was a common term, used often in reference to the nameless Negro slave children whose parents were legally forbidden to marry. Was this woman saying he was no better than one of them? That he was not a Booth?

Mary Ann wept, her arm supporting Wilkes. Her words seemed hushed as he fought the faintness seizing him. "Get out of my house," he heard his mother say, "or I will have you thrown out."

This order to leave the home of her husband's common-law

wife filled Adelaide Booth with a new sense of outrage. Deliberately, she stood motionless and looked at John Wilkes. My God, what a handsome man he would be! How dared Junius produce a son such as this when he had deserted and ignored his only legal heir in London?

Wilkes handed his mother the sword, then stepped forward to bow stiffly. "M'am, my mother has asked you to leave Tudor Hall. I'll show you to the door."

So surprised was Adelaide by the boy's act that she instantly responded to it. Totally avoiding another look at Mary Ann, Adelaide Booth followed Wilkes to the front door.

As she drew on her long gloves, Wilkes opened the door and stood aside to let her pass. She paused, however, and looking down upon him with something which could have been belated compassion, she reached out to touch his dark curls, so like the thick ones she had admired on Junius Booth. The boy withdrew from her hand. "Well, I see you have something of the Booths. Pride. Probably a little madness, too. I——"

"Good day, M'am," Wilkes said, not wanting to hear or see any more of her. "Your carriage is waiting."

"Yes, so it is. Good day, then." She hurried out the door, and Wilkes closed it before she reached the carriage.

He went slowly back to the library, where his mother had remained. She came to him, her arms outstretched, but he turned away from her embrace.

"Mother?" It was a plea.

Mary Ann put a hand under the delicate-boned chin and lifted the young face higher so that she might look into the stricken eyes. There was no eluding any of it now, and Junius was not here to help her explain and console. Wilkes was waiting for the truth and with him there was never a compromise.

"Wilkes, dear. Sit down."

"If you don't mind, Mother, I'll stand."

Of course, she thought. A soldier stands straight, unflinching, to take his punishment, deserved or not. A Booth runs from nothing, hides from no one. She saw that he was as ready as he ever would be, and yet she begged for time. "Wilkes, it isn't—evil. It's not the way she made it seem."

He would not permit evasion. "Is it true, Mother? You and Father are *not* married?"

Mary Ann shuddered. "We did have a ceremony performed in London many years ago, before we came to America to make our home, that is." The words sounded wrong, and they did not fool Wilkes.

His throat was so dry he could hardly articulate. "But how could you have a ceremony if Father was already married to that woman? Was he, Mother?"

"Yes." She was defeated at last. "Your father was married to Adelaide Delonny. He couldn't get a divorce, Wilkes." She plunged on, "But he loved me enough to bring me here where we could be together as husband and wife. And, Wilkes, the ceremony was in a church. It was a very good thing."

Wilkes let his gaze go to the sword that lay on the floor where his mother had dropped it. His face was very white again. But his fists were clenched and his knuckles were white, too. Tears filled his eyes. He looked again at his mother, and he backed slowly away from her, a step at a time.

"Wilkes!" Her hands reached toward him.

"My name is not John Wilkes Booth. I am not a Booth." His voice rose hysterically. "I have no name at all."

"Oh, my God, Wilkes, don't say that!" Mary Ann, crying, tried to embrace him, but he pushed her away and ran from the room.

He fled to the haven of the deep woods, and there he flung himself on the damp ground near a stream. His body heaving with sobs, he vomited, and then lay exhausted, letting his hands into the icy water of the stream.

"Wilkes?"

Wilkes turned over onto his back and looked up at his friend Johnny Beall. "I've been sick," Wilkes said.

"Yes, I saw." Johnny sat down beside him. "I guess you didn't see me when you ran out of the house. I followed you but I didn't say anything when you were crying cause it seemed like your own business. But, I don't know, maybe it would make you feel better to tell me about it."

Wilkes sat up. "I'm not sure I should. I'm not sure about anything anymore." He hesitated and looked down at the ground. "Would you still be my friend, I mean like always, if you found out some things about me? I mean, suppose I'm not really a Booth at all."

"Don't guess a friend is worth anything unless he's a friend all the time, no matter what."

Wilkes explained what had taken place in the house, then stopped a moment and took a deep breath through trembling lips. "I hate him!"

"You mean your father?"

Wilkes' teeth were chattering from the cold and shock. "He only pretends to be my father. His real son lives in London. I wish he'd go live with him and leave us alone."

"Aw, come on Wilkes! Your father *is* your father, same as ever. You're talking crazy. Look we better get you up to the house."

The two boys left the woods and approached Tudor Hall, its windows reflecting the winter sunset.

Mary Ann met them at the door and took Wilkes into a silent embrace, tears wetting her face, as Johnny slipped past them and went upstairs to Wilkes' room.

"Oh, you're so cold! Come in by the fire." She hugged him close to her side as they walked into the library, and he was rigid in her arms, oblivious of her soft words.

He saw the sword on the floor where she had dropped it, near the old chair which had been Richard Booth's on his visits to Tudor Hall. It was a gentleman's sword; it could only be worn by a man of honor, a man with a name—it really was not his anymore. That woman and his father had taken not only his sword but his rights as a gentleman—his heritage, his pride, his name. Well, maybe he was only John Wilkes, but maybe that was enough. After all, he still had his mother and a friend, Johnny Beall—especially Johnny. He could tell Johnny things he could never even tell his mother.

Wilkes reached out and wiped his mother's cheek. "Don't cry anymore, Mother. It's all right. I love you."

And Mary Ann, who thought the crisis had come and gone and her son was unchanged after all, sank to her knees and held him close in her arms. Thank God, she thought, the things Adelaide Booth said to him have passed over his head!

Five

Junius Booth walked slowly back from the coach road connecting the carriage drive to Tudor Hall. He carried a large packet of mail in his hands, sorting it as he walked through the fields toward the big house. Coming up the narrow dandelion-strewn field path, Junius stopped in his tracks. There was one large envelope bearing a Baltimore postmark and marked: *Baltimore County Court*. Fearful, he ripped open the large envelope, pulling out a heavy-papered brief.

The Bill of Divorcement lay on the desk in the library. None of the other children had displayed more than a perfunctory interest in the announcement that all legal obstacles to their parents' marriage had been removed.

Sixteen-year-old Edwin understood their desire, but he told them calmly, "It doesn't really matter. A Booth is a Booth, and nothing ever has changed that fact, no matter what any law says. Still, if you feel you ought to have a legal ceremony, I suppose then it must be done."

Asia and Rosalie shared Edwin's complacence. After all, they *were* the Booths of Maryland, and it was just ridiculous that any kind of a ceremony could make them any more so. Even Joseph, the "baby" of the family, was satisfied.

It was Wilkes who eyed the divorce document curiously. Alone in the room, he stood at the desk and looked solemnly down at the paper. That odd hush prevailed which pervades any room lined with books and furnished with thick rugs and cushioned couches. It was so quiet he felt uncomfortable.

Cautiously, Wilkes picked up the document and held it closer to the lamp. The first part of the paper described the relationship of Junius Brutus Booth and Adelaide Delonny Booth and their children—a son, Richard Booth, and a deceased daughter. The words accused Junius Booth of abandoning Adelaide and her living child and stated that their separation was beyond any reasonable expectation of reconciliation.

"The said Junius Brutus Booth left the Kingdom of Great Britain and came to the United States as aforesaid in company with a woman with whom he had been in the habit of adulterous intercourse from that time to the present and that he has lived for many years last passed and now does treat and recognize said woman as his wife and that he has by her a large family of children. Your oratrix asks leave to state that in charging this fault she is impelled alone by the necessity for the vindication of her own rights (and not by any desire to add infamy and disgrace either to said husband or to the said woman whom he has professed to himself or to the children, the fruits of said adulterous intercourse)."

Infamy and disgrace! The words whirled in his head.

⌒

On the morning of Wilkes' thirteenth birthday, a knock on his door awakened him. "Come in," he called, stretching his arms over his head as he lay under the blankets. He expected it to be one of his sisters or brothers, and was surprised when his mother and father entered and closed the door behind them, smiling and happy. Mary Ann waited for Junius to say something, but he nudged her arm. "You tell him."

She went to the bed and gave Wilkes a kiss on the cheek. "Happy birthday, dear."

"Thank you, Mother." He sat up and reached for his robe.

His parents exchanged a glance. Mary Ann said happily, "Wilkes, your father and I are going to be having a marriage ceremony here today, just before your dinner party."

Wilkes got out of bed, went to his dressing table, and picked up a hair brush.

"I'm so proud to be able to make all of you my legal heirs," Junius said solemnly, "I——

Wilkes gave a short gruff laugh. "You aren't really going to do anything so silly, are you? The whole world knows you're not married. Why stir up anything now?"

Mary Ann gasped and pressed a hand against her mouth.

Anger swelled in Junius. "See here, I don't want to hear one more word from you such as you have just thrown at us. Your mother——"

Wilkes looked at her. "I'm sorry, Mother. It's not your fault, but you might as well know I don't see how you can go through with it. You ought to leave him, not marry him."

Junius stepped forward and slapped Wilkes hard, twice. "Now you behave like a man, and face what has to be faced with all the good grace you can muster. If you ever speak like that again, I'll disown you. Is that clear?" Mary Ann was crying. She started to go to Wilkes, but Junius caught her. "Let him alone!"

Wilkes was standing against the dresser, straight and defiant. He did not touch the flaming spots on either cheek.

"You are still a child," Junius raged, "and you shall do as I say. The ceremony is scheduled for four o'clock this afternoon. Following it, there will be a family birthday dinner for you. You will attend both events. And you will join this family and be a part of it for all time. You are to harbor no secret hates or show either of us any further disrespect. I planned at your birth for you to amount to something in this world and that you should make the name of Booth an honored one. And, by God, you shall! Now, you get dressed, come downstairs, and enjoy this day and all the others of your life yet to come. You understand?"

Wilkes saw the pleading in his mother's eyes, so he said, "Yes, Father. I understand."

"We'll see you downstairs." Junius led Mary Ann to the door so that she could not stay to soothe Wilkes. At the door, he turned and said, "You might keep in mind, Wilkes, that in spite of this reprimand I have had to mete out to you, I love you very much. In fact, that is why we want to go through a legal ceremony."

"Yes, Father."

The door opened and closed, and his parents left Wilkes alone. He heard their feet on the stairs. He waited a moment, then flung his hairbrush at the door with all his strength.

Mary Ann had selected the elongated front room with the cushioned window seats as the room in which she wanted the ceremony performed. The children helped gather mayflowers and apple blossoms which were brought in by the armful from the woods and gardens and placed in great abundance around the room.

The minister, who was right on time, maintained a solemn face throughout the ceremony, and officiated as though he spoke at a funeral. Graying Hagar stood quietly at the door of the room and observed the occasion with a similar solemnity, keeping her gaze on Wilkes. Poor boy! He could not even look at his parents as they took their belated marriage vows. He stood behind them, alongside Asia and Edwin, and kept his eyes cast downward.

Wilkes lifted his head and looked at his parents as they kissed at the end of the ceremony. His mother received a smile from him, but he moved away from her before his father reached them.

Edwin came and put a hand on his young brother's shoulder. "Wilkes, don't spoil everything with one of your moods."

"What does it matter? I tell you, it's useless for them to get married now. None of us was born a Booth. Personally, I'll only use my given name, John Wilkes. I won't use *his*. As an actor, he *is* the greatest in the world. I know that, and I hope he'll let me tour with him and learn everything I can from him, but he's not my father."

Edwin was appalled. "He *is* your father. And it's too bad you don't deserve him."

The two young brothers looked at each other in their first encounter out of childhood, and it was Edwin who turned away for lack of anything more to say.

Six

~~~~~~

In Springfield, Illinois, Abraham Lincoln was back at his law desk, retired from Congress after one term in which he lost the confidence of his constituents. He had dared contest the right of the President of the United States to send troops into battle in Mexico.

On the tenth day of May, as a young boy in Maryland stood in crushed silence at the wedding of his parents, Abraham Lincoln stood in dejection at the window of his office and looked out at the spring day on the prairie. The affairs of the nation were becoming enmeshed in the slavery problem of the South. Democrat Steve Douglas, the top statesman in Illinois, was rising to national prominence. The Missouri Compromise and Steve Douglas—one couldn't think of one without the other, really.

Lincoln thought of his two young sons at home. Robert was almost nine now and a very bright boy, Willie not quite two. Lincoln thought, as he so often did, of Eddie, his second son who had died at four years. There was one consolation: The child had never known anything but love from his father and mother.

At the age of forty-two, his political career seemed to be all behind him. He was just Abraham Lincoln now—and, he pondered, there were some folks who might even question his name. The talk, it came up every campaign: Was he the legitimate son of Tom Lincoln? Some dared to say no. Or, that other talk: Was Lincoln's mother, rest her soul, the legitimate daughter of Lucy Hanks? Others doubted that too.

Seven

Wilkes had always been a good student. With a rare instance or two of childish temperament, he had always conformed to the demands of the institutions in which his parents had placed him. There was no record of real trouble with him at Milton's Boarding School, a Quaker-endowed place of learning at Cockeysville, Maryland, but he had been very young then, and still inclined to accept the word of his elders, even if resentfully at times. And in the private school in Richmond, Virginia, where he first met John Beall, there was no mark against him—he had devoted himself to the rules and to his friendship with the young Virginian.

But when he was placed in St. Timothy's School near Baltimore, at the same place of his baptism, he was in his teens and was uncertain as to who he really was, what he really believed.

Why did his parents insist on sending him to St. Timothy's when they knew he wanted to go to military school in Virginia with John Beall? Wilkes sulked about that until his father threatened punishment and his mother explained, again, "But it's closer to home. I don't want you so far away, not this year. And besides, your father wants you to attend St. Timothy's." They promised him that when the time came he could go on to the University of Virginia, where John would also be, but it gave him no satisfaction.

The entire student body at St. Timothy's, seventy-five boys, found quarrel with the food they were served daily, but their demands for better food went unheard. Wilkes wrote to his mother that they would all rather go hungry than eat what was placed before them at each meal.

Concerned, Mary Ann wrote back that the food was no doubt plain, but probably very well prepared with thoughts of their health in mind. She begged him to try it just a little longer . . . if it did not improve, she would want to know.

One evening when all the lamps were supposed to be out in the big dormitory, the boys held a meeting. "We've got to see to it ourselves," Wilkes told them.

Michael O'Laughlin, who secretly thought the food was not so bad, chimed in: "Yeah, we sure got to do something to help ourselves."

"Sure, but what?" Sammy Arnold was sitting on Wilkes' bed, eager to follow his leader.

There was a certain worship of Wilkes Booth among his classmates. His famed father was known to them all, but even better, Wilkes was outstanding in all the things they liked most. His closest friends in school, Sammy and Mike, earned the envy of the others. And now as the three of them sat on Wilkes' cot, their white nightshirts pulled down over their legs against the chill, the other night-clad boys grouped around them.

Wilkes frowned as he contemplated what would it take to force the school administration to provide decent food. "I know!" he finally decided. "A hunger protest. We won't eat at all, then they'll have to do something."

The silence in the room told him the idea hadn't exactly been welcomed.

"Look," he explained, "if we don't eat, everyone in town's going to know it right away. Our parents will hear about it. And the school's got to do something. Don't you see?"

"Well, yeah." Sammy said, "But s'pose they just don't pay any attention? S'pose they just let us go hungry?"

"They'll have to pay attention to us if everyone in town knows what we're doing. Won't they?"

A boy who had sat on his own cot near the door asked, "Who's going to know what we do here, except the faculty?"

"Just let Wilkes tell you," said Sammy.

"Yeah, shut up," Mike agreed.

"It's easy. We'll just camp out in the woods and we'll wear our dress uniforms so everyone seeing us will know who we are. We won't be too quiet, either."

"Well," said one of the older boys, "maybe that's not as smart as it sounds. That means we're leaving classes and breaking all kinds of rules. We'll all go to prison."

"Yeah, and we just might starve to death," one of them added.

Wilkes stood up. "Well, I'm going to camp out and I'm not going to eat a thing until we're promised decent food. I'm getting dressed now and I'm leaving. Anyone coming with me?"

The entire student body went with him, dressed in their steel gray uniforms, and each carrying a blanket roll. They left the dormitory in the dark and padded silently across the green lawns into the woods which lay beside the road to Baltimore, where travelers were bound to see them. They were "discovered," as Wilkes knew they would be, and word of the strike at St. Timothy's spread rapidly. Sympathetic adults brought food to the woods, but it was refused.

"Golly, Wilkes, who's going to know if we take some of the food baskets?" asked Sammy. "After all, if we eat the stuff after regular meal hours at the school, isn't it our business?"

"Listen," said Wilkes, "we're cadets. We're supposed to be almost as good as regular soldiers. They go hungry lots of times. We can stand it for a day or so. Just think of the meal they'll finally serve us."

But others' hunger pangs were not to be quieted so easily. Some boys began to drift away from Wilkes, but this only gave him a strange new determination. Finally, the self-appointed chief of a newly formed opposition, a youth of fair hair and pouting mouth, stood with his booted legs apart, his hands on his slim hips, and defied Wilkes: "Look," he said, "we're damned hungry. And we don't think you're going to get us any food. We want to come to terms with the school."

Wilkes was stiff-lipped. "All right, you go ahead and give in. You'll still be hungry. I'm going to hold out, like I said."

"But, Wilkes, won't you be banned from school?" Mike O'Laughlin asked.

Wilkes took a long look at Mike. "Yes, I probably will be, if I'm left all alone in this. But I don't care. If you all want to give up, I'm sorry for you, but I won't put in with you."

Again the boys whispered among themselves. It was unanimously decided that they would stay with Wilkes.

The school's first move came in the uniformed personage of their immediate commanding officer, a retired Army Colonel, Theodore Mills. He stood off at the edge of the woods and lifted his clasped hands toward the students in a kind of supplication. The sun hit his buttons and cast darts of silver

28

light into the air. His bearded face looked unusually old.

"Cadets," he called to them, "I aim to speak with you. At once."

With no hesitation, Wilkes came forth from the shelter of the trees. He looked trim and alert in his uniform, as though he had walked onto a parade field. He saluted his officer. "Sir, Cadet Wilkes Booth here."

Colonel Mills returned the salute crisply. "Cadet Booth, where are the other men?"

"Encamped, sir."

"Let me inform you, sir," replied Mills, "that every cadet missing at this time from the school is in violation of our rules of conduct and subject to proper punishment. Accordingly, I demand the immediate response to a roll call of every cadet enrolled in this school."

"Sir, there will be no response. We are on strike against the food served to us at mealtime every day. We'll not return until we are assured that we will be fed decently. We're prepared to starve, if necessary, sir."

"You can't do this—"

"Sir, we are doing it."

"You'll be punished—"

"Sir, there is no punishment more deadly than the food we receive. We'll hold our line here."

"Very good, Cadet Booth. I'll take your word to the board."

"Thank you, sir."

The Colonel returned Wilkes' salute and retreated.

At the end of the second day, before another night came upon them and actual hunger forced even Wilkes to give in, the school met their demands.

Wilkes was carried on the shoulders of his fellow students back to the school buildings where a sumptuous meal awaited them.

Rebellion, as Wilkes saw, was rewarded.

Eight

A brilliant student, Wilkes was ready for college at an age far younger than most young men, and so he was not held back at St. Timothy's, but went on to the university in Charlottesville.

As the school stage swung up the private road, Wilkes leaned out of the window to get a full view of the University of Virginia. There were over a thousand acres surrounding the institution, and everywhere he looked, Wilkes saw the early touch of a blazing autumn upon the land. And as the stage neared the buildings that housed the university proper, Wilkes gazed upon them with wonder.

Ahead loomed the main building, designed by Thomas Jefferson after the Pantheon in Rome—to Wilkes, the magnificent, awesome structure personified the dignity and worth of all Virginia.

The University of Virginia welcomed Wilkes Booth and John Beall into its world. At their request, they shared a room. Though John was three years the elder of Wilkes, they were wholly compatible. They played as hard as they worked and both were extremely popular, having as much fun competing with each other as they did when they were assigned to the same teams in sport.

"You know," Wilkes said one day, "I think there was a mistake made when they were handing out brothers, John. I think I should have drawn you instead of one of those I did get."

John laughed. "Hell, no. If we were brothers, we'd be hard up for friends, wouldn't we?"

The year at the university was almost a perfect one except for a strange event which lingered in Wilkes' mind like a black cloud.

A gypsy woman came to the acres of the university and

camped there for a few days. She made a good sum of money telling students' fortunes, and it was noted that she was uncannily correct in her predictions of the future. When Wilkes and John took their turns at her side, John pushed Wilkes ahead of him. "You go first."

The old woman sitting on the ground was dressed in red and wore a jeweled, gold band around her head. Her hair was long and gray, and in need of a good brushing. Wilkes knelt beside her and extended his right hand.

"Palm up, son, palm up," she instructed. Twisting his hand in both of hers, she carefully traced its lines. She took so long at it that Wilkes dared to sigh. Finally she shook her head and folded his hand in hers.

"Oh, you've a bad hand; the lines are all cris-cras. It's full enough of sorrow—full of trouble in plenty, everywhere I look. You're born under an unlucky star. You'll break hearts, they'll be nothing to you. You'll be rich, generous, and free with your money. You've got in your hand a thundering crowd of enemies—you'll make a bad end, and have plenty to love you afterward. You'll have a fast life—short, but a grand one. You'll die young, and leave many to mourn you, many to love you, too. Now, young sir, I've never seen a worse hand, and I wish I hadn't seen it, but every word I've told is true by the signs. You'd best turn a missionary or a priest and try to escape it."

Wilkes was so affected that he blindly left the woman, hardly realizing that John followed him, not bothering to hear his own future told. "Hell, what does an old crone know about anything? Come on, Wilkes, forget it!"

But he could not; the dire words plagued him all that year. He looked at his hand repeatedly, wondering if a man's fate was really told there.

For days afterward, Wilkes was uneasy, unsmiling, and difficult to be with in work or play. But Johnny Beall finally lifted him out of the misery by challenging him to a cross-country race on horseback. The long ride was the tonic he needed. They came back from the day's ride tired but happy, laughing, and relaxed.

But Johnny could not lose his growing worry about the dark moods that came upon Wilkes without warning. He had fits of temper, too, which included wild interludes of damning the school, his teachers, and his friends; as if Wilkes were fighting an inner devil. There were times when he even seemed to have a grudge against Johnny. But nothing will ever make any difference between us, Johnny told himself. We're friends to the death.

Nine

During the years following his thirteenth birthday, Wilkes continued to maintain an ambivalent attitude toward his father. On a personal basis, their relationship remained aloof and strained. Wilkes simply did not communicate to Junius any of the many thoughts and problems and victories that he had in those years. In spite of every attempt his father made to break through the wall that Wilkes silently insisted on keeping between them, they remained strangers.

But the relationship of master and student was a stronger one and a consistent one. It was impossible for Wilkes not to respond to Junius Brutus Booth, star of the theater.

There was no question but that his father was the world's most acclaimed actor. And Wilkes, often taken to the theater, later went on his own to see his father perform. He was one of the privileged few whom Booth welcomed backstage; he was encouraged to dabble in make-up and costumes and to read the lines of the plays from the very prompt books his father had marked for accent, inflection, and appearance.

During the Christmas holiday of 1851, his father entered his dressing room to find the boy handsomely clothed in a kingly outfit, observing himself in the long mirror. "Good, good! You have the ability to wear costumes as though you *are* a king. And you read Shakespeare with an understanding from the heart."

"Thank you, sir. I'm most grateful for your help." He stopped, squared his shoulders, and said it all: "I want to be as acclaimed as you some day, sir. It's the highest goal I can think of in life."

Tears filmed over the father's eyes, but he knew better than to put out a hand to his young son. He only said, "You'll earn your fame, Wilkes. Edwin is good, too, very good—in fact he is to be my understudy while we travel west this year. I'm proud of him, and of little Joe, too. Your mother tells me he's doing very well in literature and playacting. I am daring to hope I'll have four sons who are stars. But you're the best student of all."

"I don't suppose you would consider letting me travel with you this year, would you Father?" He used the name "Father" unconsciously, for the first time since his thirteenth birthday.

"Oh, no, not yet. You're to stay at school. You may join me in due time, as Edwin did." Junius went to the costume trunk, pulled open a drawer, brought out a bottle, uncorked it, and drank from it. "Besides, this summer you've got to stay home and watch over your mother while Edwin and I are traveling."

"Let Edwin do that, for once." Wilkes began to remove his costume, his face sullen. "I've had enough schooling. I need to learn about the theater now. Edwin's had all the opportunity."

"Well," Junius said as he took another drink and sat down on a stool, "the truth is, you're not strong enough yet."

"Not strong enough, sir?"

"Come now, come now, Wilkes. You're playing coy. Haven't you and Edwin discussed the major part of his chores while on tour with Junius Brutus Booth?"

"No. I don't know what you mean."

"Then I'll tell you, because in due time it will be part of your chores, too." He held up the bottle and the liquor sloshed inside as he waved it at Wilkes. "It's this damn stuff. I drink it too often and too much." He frowned and shook his head. "And lately, mind you, I've even been on stage while full of it. Well, sometimes I don't quite make it home. Or maybe I don't even make it to the theater. That's where your brother comes in.

Yes, sir, he totes me. Home, to the theater. Great part for an understudy, don't you think?

Wilkes tossed the costume into the trunk and reached for his own clothes, staring at his father. "You're drunk right now, aren't you?"

"Oh, no. Well, not really. Just kind of glazed over a little."

"Would it do any good if I took that bottle from you and broke it?"

"I'd find another. But don't worry about it, Wilkes, I'll be all right. Always am."

"Some day that stuff is going to kill you."

"You sound like your grandfather," Junius told him. "I thrive on it, son. I'm going to live to a ripe old age. Got everything to live for. A wonderful family, a beautiful wife I love with all my heart. I'm a success. I love life. Don't worry about me, I'll manage to stick around a while yet to see my sons on stage on their own. Yes, I'll live to be a happy old man."

Then a family scandal stirred Bel Air. Repeating parental history, Junius, Jr., deserted his wife, Clementine, and their daughter, Blanche, and departed for California in the company of a beautiful young actress, Harriet Mace of Boston. The couple traveled to San Francisco where June was to manage the Jenny Lind Theater. A daughter was born to them in the Golden City and they named her Marion.

Not as easily deceived as Adelaide Booth had been, Clementine demanded the return of her husband. June's parents, speaking from bitter experience, wrote their son and told him he must return and face the problem. June brought his new family home with him to Bel Air, and a divorce was immediately instituted between Clementine and June.

His personal problems out of the way, June offered his father and his brothers an alluring picture of the West, and of California in particular. When he extended a contract to his father and Edwin for an appearance at the Jenny Lind, they eagerly accepted.

The news was kept quiet for a time while the divorce took effect. Wilkes was to learn of it only a short time prior to the departure of his father and brothers for San Francisco. Harriet, still unwed, and tiny Marion accompanied them.

Word of their presence swept California, and towns everywhere requested them. Junius and Edwin traveled to Sacramento's old American Theater by riverboat and played successfully before an audience of pioneers, gold miners, adventurers, and cutthroats. The house resounded with applause.

Edwin was exhilarated by the west. "Let's extend our visit," he pleaded with his father.

"Look Ned, I miss your mother. I've had enough of the outdoors to last a lifetime. You and June can come back when you're ready, but this old actor is leaving."

Edwin and June decided they would stay in California for a longer tour of the gold mining towns, but they escorted their father back to San Francisco and said goodbye to him at the Long Wharf.

"Success to you," Junius said, tears in his eyes. "Damn it, I hate saying goodbye to people. I'm just a sentimental old man. Well, you two take care of each other and hurry home."

Junius was robbed of his money sometime during the voyage across the Isthmus of Panama. He fretted about going home penniless, so when the ship reached New Orleans, he arranged to play six shows at the St. Charles Theater. Noah Ludlow, the theater manager who was also his friend, paid him a thousand dollars.

Aboard ship and bound for home once more, Junius caught a cold. As the steamer, the *J. S. Chenoweth*, headed up the Mississippi River toward Cincinnati, Junius developed a fever. He drank some of the river water, which was deadly with raw sewage, and soon after, he was beset with vomiting and diarrhea, and lay in bed in a state of terror. There was no doctor on board, but a man called Simpson knew Junius, realized the actor was missing, and found the helpless sick man in a bunk amid his own filth. Simpson went to work, cleaned him up, and tended him day and night. But on the third day Junius suffered a stiffening of the jaws. When he tried to speak, Simpson could not understand him.

As the ship approached Louisville, on the fifth day of his illness, November 30, 1852, Junius spoke his last words through clenched teeth: "Pray, pray, pray."

A telegram came to Mary Ann telling her that she could claim her husband's body in Cincinnati.

Heartbroken, his sons in San Francisco headed for home,

feeling that they had deserted him.

Prayers were said for him everywhere, and words of praise flowed in from around the world. Rufus Choate set the tone of all the laments when he mourned: "What? Booth dead? Then there are no more actors."

He had not left a will or even an expressed wish that could be faithfully carried out by his grieving widow. Mary Ann, therefore, tried to determine exactly what Junius would have wanted done, and let herself be guided by his vague plans of the future. Junius had promised definitely to take Wilkes with him on his next tour of the theaters; yet he wanted him to complete his schooling.

"He's sharp," he told her proudly. "He understands that acting is an art and that the heart is the instrument to use in that art. He delivers his lines superbly and he coordinates beautifully. He's light on his feet and gives a mighty handsome appearance. I'm afraid he's likely to keep Edwin and Joe in the shade. But he's to finish school."

In the two years following her husband's death, in her bereavement and anxieties, Mary Ann turned for consolation to Edwin, only five years older than Wilkes, but who seemed fatherly in comparison. One summer day in 1854, she called him to her bedroom where she was packing two huge wardrobe trunks with Junius' old costumes. He stood at the window and waited, a little uneasy as he eyed the work to which she was giving such careful and loving attention.

"In just a few weeks now, as you know, your brother is to leave home and try his fortunes. He refuses to stay at the university." She held a silk shirt to her bosom and looked at Edwin, holding his gaze. "I expect you to provide him with a contract, however minor the role, at the Arch Street Theater in Philadelphia. This is what his father had intended to do for him. You have been a star player there, and I am sure you know how it can be arranged, but it must be done at once. I simply can't let him go unless I know he is to be earning a living from his first day. Do you understand?" Edwin wondered what good it would do to speak his mind. "Mother, I've talked some to Wilkes about his debut. Did you know he wants to drop the name of Booth and be known simply as John Wilkes?"

Her face was flushed as she stood very straight beside the trunks. "No. But that's wrong."

"Yet he's insisting on it. He wants to make his own way, he tells me. So I hardly see how I can help him. After all, any contract he might get now, as an unknown, would be based upon his family name. Any manager would want to use the Booth name as a drawing card."

"Yes." She put the shirt in a neatly folded way into the trunk. "I'm sure it's just one of his ideas of the moment. You just ignore him and go ahead and get him a contract to play. He'll come around fast enough."

Edwin went to the trunks and looked down at them, frowning. "I'll talk to Nate Baradorf as soon as I get to Philadelphia. But I'm very much afraid I'll have to do as Wilkes asks. It's up to Mister Baradorf, I would think, but I will encourage him to take Wilkes on under any name. I promise you that."

She touched his cheek. "You know, you're my pride and joy these days, Edwin. Without you I think that I might just collapse."

Edwin looked at the costumes in the trunk and those still waiting on the bed for packing away. "You know, I wish you could see your way to letting me have some of these, Mother. Joe should share in them, too."

"Joe's still in school and you're a star, you don't need them. Wilkes is to have these. It will help him some. His father would want it."

Edwin made one last appeal. "Mother, if I could have just the Macbeth costumes——"

Mary Ann pressed her lips tightly together. It was not that she did not want Edwin to have everything he wanted, if she could help him to get it, nor that she did not love him or recognize his work. It was simply that she wanted Wilkes to have every advantage which she believed Edwin had already enjoyed through working with his father.

"Edwin, my mind is settled." She put a hand on his broad shoulder. "You know I'm very proud of you and that I love you very much," she said. "I'm asking for your help with Wilkes. You know how—difficult he can be. You must take the place of your father for him."

"Good God! Mother, you know I've always found it hard to get along with him. To tell the truth, he seems to have a kind of resentment toward me these days just because I'm where I am in the theater."

Mary Ann's warm hand clasped his. "I ask you, nevertheless, to watch over your brother. You can make it easier for him than he might otherwise find it. Edwin?"

He gave up. Wilkes' arrival had dethroned Edwin as his mother's favorite son sixteen years before. He bent and kissed her cheek, and then said, "Well, our Wilkes may not be the best actor to arrive in Philadelphia, but by God, he's going to be the best costumed. I'll do my best, but you might hint to him that he has a lot to learn. And he'd better leave his rebellious nature right here in Bel Air."

Ten

Philadelphia was like a huge heated brick oven on that afternoon in August as Wilkes Booth walked through Independence Square. Carriages and pedestrians moved slowly through the hot streets. The sunbaked cobblestones gave off a blast of heat which shriveled the passersby and stifled their breath. Shutters and blinds at every window were closed against the glare, but inside the buildings the stale air was moist and heavy. Wilkes, though, was almost oblivious of the heat because he was too interested in his surroundings.

He was walking among the buildings of America which had witnessed the founding of the nation. Awed, reverent, he moved along the streets, trailing in and out of the national shrines, the Court House (Old City Hall), the State House. He stood and read aloud the words on the Liberty Bell: *Proclaim liberty throughout all the land unto all the inhabitants thereof.*

Finally, Wilkes headed toward the boardinghouse a few blocks away, where a room awaited him. True to their mother's wishes, the Booth family was already looking out for Wilkes in his first few hours away from home. Wilkes' attractive sister Asia was engaged to John Sleeper Clarke, an actor, and she had prevailed upon him to secure a room for her brother in the same house in which he boarded. It was a good location for Wilkes' purposes in Philadelphia: Its guests had a view of the upper levels of the nearby Arch Street Theater where Wilkes hoped to make his first professional appearance, if all went as he planned.

He found the boardinghouse with no trouble, and a woman with very light hair and a good but aging figure answered the door. The years had put a knowing look into her pale eyes and a slight twist to her mouth. A few more years and she would be called coarse, heavy, bleary-eyed; a few less and she would have seemed colorless and vapid. But when she opened the door, gazed up at Wilkes with heavy-lidded eyes, and leaned a rather voluptuous body toward him, he became a little excited.

"Well, good afternoon, sir!" she said in a very pleasant voice. "You have got to be John Wilkes Booth. I've been expecting you all day. Come in, come in. Your room is all ready for you." She stepped back to allow him to enter the cool of the dark reception hall and held out a soft hand. "I'm your landlady, Abigail Parsons. The widow Parsons, they call me. Welcome to Philadelphia, sir."

"Thank you, M'am. I'm glad to be here. Is Mr. Clarke in?"

"No, no he's out just now." She looked at him curiously. "You have no luggage?"

"Oh, yes. I've trunks and bags coming. I'd hoped they'd be here already."

"Oh, well, I'll let you know as soon as they arrive and have them brought up. I suppose you'd like to see your room now?"

He took the key to the room from her and followed her up the stairs to a corner room on the second floor which John Clarke had reserved in his name. The view included a glimpse of the Arch Street Theater seen over the rooftops of lesser buildings. The landlady left him alone, closing the door quietly.

Since he had no luggage, he could not change his clothing,

but he removed his coat and shirt and stripped to the waist to wash in the water bowl. Then he stood at the window and let the hot air of the late afternoon dry his torso.

A knock on the door brought him out of his deep contemplation of the Arch Street Theater. It was Abigail Parsons, holding a tray with a glass and a pitcher of ice water.

He looked from her blonde hair which fell loosely to touch her white shoulders, to the rounded bosom which was not all concealed by the scoop-necked organdy blouse she wore. Then he noticed the small waist which gave her too rounded hipline an intriguing accent. My God, he thought, I can have this woman if I want her. She'd let me, she wants me to.

"I've brought you some cold water, Mister Booth."

"Oh. Yes, I see. Thank you very much." He reached for the tray, but she evaded his effort to assist her and put it down on the dressing table. Turning slowly to look at him, she noted the slenderness of the physique, the muscled shoulders, the flat stomach, the sturdy legs. His dark, curly hair and his handsome young face so impressed her, she sucked in a deep breath.

Wilkes looked away from her, somewhat repelled by her boldness, her obvious desire. This was the first woman who had ever dared to openly gaze upon him with an invitation. His lips set in a straight line as he retreated to the dignity of a Booth of Bel Air. "M'am, I'm going out in a few minutes," he said, "to the theater." Moving toward the door, he indicated that she might take her leave.

But she remained where she was. "You're going to be the talk of the town, Mr. Booth. The ladies will all swoon at the sight of you on the stage." She ran her tongue over her lips. "You're a lot more good-looking than your brother, Edwin."

"I'm sorry, M'am, but I do have to go out," he urged her toward the door, rejecting any conversation with her, especially in regard to his brother.

Abigail Parsons nodded. "All right, but leave me your key, and when the trunks come I'll have them brought in here."

The key given to her, a last pulse-catching look from her, and he was free for the moment. He closed the door and let out a whistling breath. How unlike the young women he had met at social events at home and at school! This was the kind of woman he and John Beall had talked and wondered about, but never seen. Once they had planned to go to a district where they knew such women could be found, but when it had come right down to it, each had found some excuse to give the other.

But he forgot her as soon as he entered the Arch Street Theater a half hour later and stood backstage talking to Nate Baradorf, the manager. Curtain time was but an hour away, and Baradorf was extremely busy. He thrust a copy of the contract Edwin had approved for Wilkes into the young actor's hands and quickly briefed him.

"Rehearsals at ten every morning without fail, Mr. Booth. Be sure to study the part. Come prepared to perform. All right?"

Wilkes held the contract and a copy of the play in his hands tightly. "Did my brother explain that I wish to be known merely as John Wilkes?"

"Yes, yes, yes. Very stupid of you, young man, but it is part of the contract. Take a look outside as you go. I have your face hanging there, a very excellent likeness. Now, then, let me go attend to my business, and you go study."

"Study? The part you've given me hardly needs to be put in writing."

Nate frowned over the rims of his spectacles. "Come now, John Wilkes. You're not Edwin Booth. I am not starring you. You don't want to accept the role?"

Wilkes' face was hot. "You pass judgment on my acting after the performance when the curtain comes down. Remember, I'm not trading on my family's name or fame. That's exactly why I requested that you have me billed as John Wilkes."

"I meant no insult. It's only that so much depends upon the cooperation of everyone involved in a play. I just want to make sure that you do know your part, Mr. Booth."

Wilkes wandered out onto the still darkened stage and gazed toward the seats. He observed the arrangements of the seating plan, and tested the acoustics by calling out a few words. These were things his father had cautioned him to do. Never enter a theater to act upon its stage, Junius had advised him, if you are not familiar with its innards. Know what your voice will have to do to be heard in each seat of the house. Be sure to know the size of the interior and the points where you can be best seen by the audience.

After satisfying himself as to the theater's good and bad points, he went outside to look at the posters. For a long time he studied the name *John Wilkes* printed under a large drawing of himself. But, the manager had outsmarted him: There, under his chosen stage name, the manager had added the bold printed words: "The son of Junius Brutus Booth and brother of Edwin Booth."

He reached out to rip the poster off the frame, but then refrained. The damage was done, and he might as well accept it. If part of his fame would always be in the name of Booth, if that was the way it had to be, he would accept it.

John Clarke would have been glad to host him at a dinner following his own appearance in a play that night, but Wilkes wanted to celebrate his first day on his own all by himself. Alone, he thoroughly enjoyed the good food and liquor he ordered at a crowded restaurant. He listened to the northern voices all around him; voices which more than anything else made him realize he was away from home and alone in a strange land.

Suddenly the excitement of the new surroundings and the pleasure he had taken in the meal simply vanished. He found himself miserable and very tired; it was best to go back to his room and go to bed. Though the night air was quite warm, he shivered as he walked the few blocks to the boardinghouse. It was his first day up north, and already he wanted to go home.

He looked for the key in the door of his room, but it was not necessary: The door opened at the touch of his hand. The lamp on the dresser flickered smokily. Wilkes stood in the doorway and stared.

Seated on the trunk which had been placed at the foot of his bed was Abigail Parsons, clad only in a nightdress and robe of a fabric so thin it was like smoke. She was smiling at him but did not speak. Her hands gripping the sides of the trunk, she lifted her feet a bit off the floor, like a child on a swing, her legs extended toward him.

Wilkes shut the door behind him. "What are you doing here?"

"Well, I figured you'd be lonely——"

"Get out!" He moved quickly to the lamp to turn up the flame, but she was beside him, and her hand closed over his.

42

The shock of her touch jerked his face around. "Get out!" he repeated, but there was no real authority to his voice now.

Her hands slid over his shoulders and she pulled herself tightly to him. She looked up into his face. "Scared?"

"Of course not. But——"

"You've never done it before, have you?"

"Don't be ridiculous."

"Come on, lover. Come on."

Wilkes took that which was offered him.

On the evening of his theatrical debut, the sultry weather did not keep anyone away from the theater. In spite of the flimsy evasion of his name being billed simply as *John Wilkes*, everyone knew that he was the son of the late star, Junius Brutus Booth, and the brother of Edwin Booth, whose popularity was soaring. The theater was filled to capacity.

For Wilkes, curtain time could come none too soon. Since his arrival, he had spent little enough time in the theater because Abigail had kept him a kind of willing prisoner, showing him off during the day and shutting herself up with him at night.

Seated in front of the shining mirror of his dressing table backstage, he applied his make-up expertly and grinned at his reflection. John Clarke stood with his back pressed against the door, his arms folded across his chest, his long face sober.

"Wilkes?" John began, not smiling.

"Have you something on your mind?"

"Well, you know, I want to see you do a great job out there tonight. I just wonder, though, if you're as ready as you think you are."

Wilkes smoothed his eyebrows and glanced at John's reflection in the mirror. "Of course I am. That's a hell of a way to wish me luck."

"But you're skating on fairly thin ice tonight. You've missed some of the rehearsals. Nate Baradorf tossed a coin tonight to decide whether to let you go on. You're lucky, that's all."

"Look John, I've known my part backward and forward for days. Why, there are only a few lines anyway."

"Wilkes, there's one other thing I'd better mention before someone else does. Abigail Parsons was backstage to see you a bit ago. She said she just wanted to wish you well. Mr. Baradorf had her escorted out."

"Very nice of her," Wilkes muttered, concentrating into the mirror seriously.

"I know I recommended her boardinghouse; it's clean, and the food is very good, and I find it convenient to the theater, too. But everyone knows what her real business is. She's a notorious whore."

Wilkes stood up and buttoned up his jacket. "I suppose Asia asked you to look after me, but what I do is my affair, in everything." He looked John squarely in the eye. "Correct?"

"Right." John Sleeper Clarke smiled for the first time and gave up. "I'll give the message to Asia, too. She thinks of you as a child, you know."

"I do know. Thanks for paying me the visit."

"Best of luck," John offered as he left.

Wilkes walked on stage on cue. He strode majestically to position, looked at the leading lady, swept the audience with a quick glance, and then deliberately shifted his position so that the patrons might look upon him more fully and less upon the actress who was the star.

The whisper of "Booth" rippled through the theater and was audible on stage. It threw Wilkes off balance. Hesitant, he lost his timing by a fraction of a second and looked in surprise through a fog of footlights at the audience. Faces danced in front of his eyes. A fear such as he had never known possible was upon him.

My God, they knew him! What else would they say? That he couldn't compare to his brother Edwin? That he was unworthy to carry on his father's name? He licked his dry lips, suffocating, and cast a pleading look at the actress near him. She stared back at him, bitterly.

The whispered voice of the stage prompter came from the wings: "Madame, I am Petruchio Pandolfe."

Wilkes tried to speak the words; to do so, he cleared his throat, unforgettably. High-pitched, unnatural, startling himself, he stammered: "Madame, I am Pondolfio Pet—Pedolfio Pat—Pantuchio—Ped——"

The words out, he stood there in the wreckage of his debut, red-faced, weak-kneed, damned. A sound which he could not at first identify broke the awful silence, rolling across the stage like a wave, sickening him. The audience was hissing and boo-ing!

Motionless, witless, Wilkes stared into the great dark well of the theater and saw all the mocking faces. He took a deep breath then, and turned away from the audience to bow to the leading lady. Striding, chin uplifted now, gaze straight ahead, he looked every inch a gentleman as he left the stage.

As he reached the wings, Manager Baradorf grabbed his arm, "This is because you didn't rehearse. This is because you are too great an actor to study your role."

Wilkes pushed the hand from his sleeve, "This is the result of a Southerner trying to win an audience of the North. Yankees are rude and unfeeling. Only my contract keeps me from leaving."

Baradorf's anger was reinforced by practicality. "I'm not sure I'll honor that contract. I don't know that I can ever let you walk onto that stage again."

"Are you going to break the contract?" Wilkes dared him.

"I'll expect you at rehearsals tomorrow at ten. If you are not here, I'll consider the contract broken by your own act. Is that clear?"

Almost as bad as the words of the disgusted Baradorf, was the unfeeling contempt Abigail expressed by withdrawing from his embrace when he reached for her that night. She tried to push him away. But her fear of his intensity became lost in the need he had aroused in her as she struggled against him.

Eleven

As the curtain rose again at the Arch Street Theater on the following evening, Wilkes was sure he would erase the dreadful impression he had made on Philadelphia the night before. He knew that a subdued Abigail sat in the theater, somewhere close to the stage. Tonight she would come to him without hesitation.

Walking onto the stage in full command of his emotions, he moved carefully to the correct position, not trying to take the spotlight from the leading lady.

This time he was on cue, the theater silent. But when he tried to speak, he was stopped by the thunder of mingled cat calls, hisses, boos, stamping feet, and laughter.

Wilkes drew in a breath of air; he attempted to speak his line, even so. But he could not utter a word. He stood on the stage of the theater and curdled. Price, family reputation, personal glory, all fell before the audience. And yet, he stood with head unbowed, gazing helplessly at the pale faces beyond the footlights.

The curtain was pulled across the stage and the leering faces were blotted from his view, but it was Nate's hand on his arm which broke the spell. "Mr. Booth, we need to talk."

In the office, Nate took the time to light up a cigar and to offer one to Wilkes. Waving it aside, Wilkes sat down in a straight-backed chair. The blue smoke of the cigar made Wilkes feel ill, but he said nothing.

Nate sat down at his desk. "Mr. Booth, I want your contract."

Wilkes rubbed his hand over his face, oblivious of the make-up. "I expected that. I'm in no position to argue, am I? I'm sorry——"

Mercifully, Nate ground the cigar into a silver tray and flapped a hand at the smoke to blow it away from Wilkes' pale face. "I'm tearing it up. I want to write you a new one. Wilkes, I'm going to star you."

"This is a mean joke, sir——"

Nate reached out and touched Wilkes lightly on the knee, patting it ever so gently. "I never joke about business, my friend."

A knock on the door interrupted him. "Come in, come in." he frowned.

John Sleeper Clarke entered the room, smiling broadly. "You're looking better, Wilkes. I believe Nate must have applied the remedy we were discussing together just a bit ago out there in a front row."

Nate stood and brought a chair up from a wall for John. "He's still a little dazed by everything, I think. You tell him."

"You're going to be the most famous of all the Booths. You'll draw the ladies in like flies after sugar. We both saw that."

"Look, Sleepy, I won't trade on my father's fame or trot along in Edwin's footsteps, either. Are you anxious to star me just to use the Booth name as a box-office lure?"

"Certainly. That is, if you can handle it. Why settle for supporting roles, minor ones at that, when you can be the star if you use the name you were born to?"

Wilkes stood up and began pacing the room. "Are you giving my acting ability any thought?" he asked. "Either of you?"

Clarke's long-boned face was sober. "There's no question you are a very fine actor, Wilkes. Don't forget, I've seen you in many amateur productions. Tonight and last night, you didn't measure up. You just need to pay attention to your business. Rehearse, learn your lines, know your fellow players. Relax."

Nate leaned back in the chair and nodded. "I saw something out there tonight—*we* saw something—" he pointed his cigar at John, "that convinced us that you can put your brother Edwin in the shade. Perhaps surpass the brilliance of your father." He held up a hand as Wilkes started to protest, "Now, now! Hear me out. I know all phases of the theater; what I don't see and hear and smell, I *sense*. These things tell me that you are to be *the* new star of the American theater."

Wilkes rubbed the back of his neck with a hand that trembled visibly. "But that wasn't applause out there tonight, that was *booing*."

"Male jealousy, that's what it was. And that's good. That's box office."

Wilkes shook his head.

"Oh, yes! But more than that, Wilkes, the ladies love you, every sweet one of them. I took a walk up and down the aisles during the time you were on stage and I saw it. They would pay the price of admission just to come in and look at you. The men know it, so they tried to boo and hiss you right out of their lives, but it can't be done."

"But, hell, I didn't do a damn thing but stand there," Wilkes groped, "like an idiot."

"Precisely," agreed Nate. "Now, think! If you can sweep them off their feet without doing a thing, what will happen when you appear in romantic roles?"

Wilkes sat down again and looked at John. "You don't think I'd be pushing myself too fast? You know the Booths. You know me."

John was very solemn, very sincere. "Wilkes, you've been ready for the stage all your life—it's your natural habitat."

"You know Shakespeare's plays?" Nate asked.

"All of them, ever since I was ten. I can quote you almost any line you want."

Nate enjoyed a puff on his cigar. "After this, you'll get more help from us. Under the new contract, you'll cooperate, every step of the way. You'll take orders from me and behave when you're under the roof of any theater I manage. You do these things and I promise you the next few years will make you famous."

He and John waited, their eyes leveled on the young man now striding back and forth in the office.

"What name would you want me to use?"

"Your legal one. John Wilkes Booth. No other, of course."

"Sir, I'd rather not."

Nate gave a grunt. "I don't give a goddamn what you want. What *I* want is what is going to make a star of you. I say you use the name of Booth and you use it ten times a day, or there is no deal between us. Is that clear?"

"It's clear, but why exactly?"

"Maybe I'm just sentimental. I worked with your father, and I now work with your brothers, both Edwin and Junius. Besides, your father spoke to me of his dreams for you. I know he would want you to use the Booth name, and by God, for his sake, you're going to."

Sleepy put a leg up over the edge of the desk and grinned up at Wilkes. "Why toss away all those beautiful years in the theater which your old daddy gained for you? And your brothers are sort of smoothing the way, aren't they?"

Wilkes' lips tightened. "You know, Sleepy, I'm not at all sure that my sister should marry you. I think you just want to marry into the Booth name." But John only smiled.

"So what's your answer, Wilkes? Do you star or not?" Nate asked.

"I'll want to be sure you allow me some freedom. I will want to travel some. And if I can convince Edwin, I want to appear in a few plays with him in the next few years. And I'll want to tour the South. If you can work all that into our contract, I'll sign it gladly."

A broad smile spread on Nate's face. "I was going to tell you that I believe you must follow your debut here very soon with a debut in the South. I'm certain that the South will claim you as its own. And I'd like to manage an engagement with you and Edwin on the same stage. So we'll keep all that in mind, as we go. Right?"

"Yes, I'd like to appear in Richmond with him when the time comes."

"I'll have the contract readied for our signatures, and then we'll get to work and open within four weeks."

Abigail was not at the stage door as she had promised Wilkes she would be. He supposed she must be waiting for him at the boardinghouse. Wait until she heard the news! Eagerly, he made his way to the room. It was locked, as he had left it. As he turned the key, the door opened into darkness. The lamp from the hallway shone into the room and onto the bed, empty, untouched, cold. He lit the lamp on the dresser and then closed the door. Where was Abigail?

A knock came to the door. He hastily opened it. But it was not Abigail. Standing there was Arlene, the maid employed by Abigail. She was eighteen at the most, shining-haired, sloe-eyed, slender, and altogether appealing. But for all her sweet looks, she was no virgin, as he had heard in his conversations with other young men in the boardinghouse. A thrill shot through him, not only because she was looking at him with bright eyes, but because she was there and Abigail was not.

She handed him a note, curtsying and smiling a little, and turned to go.

49

"Wait a moment, Arlene," his hand touched her bare arm. "This may require an answer."

She waited meekly, eyes downcast, as though she did not know that Abigail's note told Wilkes—with no attempt at apology—that she would be unable to keep their engagement for a late supper.

"Arlene," he said, crushing the note in his hands, "I've something to celebrate. Would you have supper with me?"

Arlene had been waiting for such an invitation. "I'd like to very much, Mr. Booth. But Mrs. Parsons——"

"I have no duty toward Mrs. Parsons." He drew Arlene into the room and closed the door behind her.

"She talks a lot about you, sir. She's been talking to everyone here this evening. She came home from the theater in a regular rage and called you an ass. That's the word she used, sir."

Wilkes laughed. "Oh, she did? Well, I'll wager she comes knocking on my door by one o'clock this morning."

Arlene looked demurely at the floor. "I wouldn't be here, sir, to know if she came or not."

"You'll be here, Arlene." Wilkes lifted her in his arms and carried her to the bed.

Abigail did come knocking on the door, but neither Arlene nor Wilkes heard her. Arlene's dark hair lay strewn over Wilkes' arm and her long-limbed body pressed against him. Abigail went away.

∽

The next weeks rushed past Wilkes in a haze of happiness. The nights were filled with the love of Arlene, and the days were devoted to the play for which he diligently rehearsed.

He had a letter from Edwin, full of generous advice and brotherly concern and pride. Edwin and Nate Baradorf were already busy on future plans for an appearance in Richmond in which the brothers would be co-starred, and he offered Wilkes his affection and his wishes for a brilliant debut in Philadelphia.

Word of Wilkes' coming debut as a star in *Romeo and Juliet* spread far beyond the confines of Philadelphia. He was without question the handsomest of all the Booths, obviously a threat to his brother Edwin. Junius, the elder brother, was a star and considered a most capable actor, but was not spectacular in his career. The interest in Wilkes Booth was only piqued because of the farce he had made of his first two on-stage appearances. Tickets sold by the score to many who were simply curious, or to those who hoped to see him repeat his absurd performance; still, for whatever reason, the theater was sold out.

If there was any fear in the heart of Wilkes Booth when he first appeared on stage that evening, it did not reveal itself. Clad in white velvet, skintight trousers, sporting a waist-length sleeveless cape of matching velvet lined in black silk, paste jewels flashing in the bright calcium lights of the stage, Wilkes' dark good looks and youthful physique caused gasps and exclamations throughout the house. Women were smitten, according to their own admissions, and men were admiring. He *was* Romeo.

When he climbed the balcony and spoke the words of deathless devotion to the lovely Juliet, his career had indeed begun. The breathless females of the audience were spellbound, beyond even whispering to their neighbors.

When the curtain came down, men and women alike were on their feet, giving him a standing ovation; some stood on the seats and shouted, "Bravo, bravo, bravo!"; others tossed flowers to him. As he stood bowing to the acclamation, he caught some of the flowers and tossed some of them back to several of the prettier women standing in the front row.

For the next few months Wilkes felt he had won the world. He was famous, financially affluent, sought after as an honored guest throughout Philadelphia. A social function which claimed John Wilkes Booth as its guest of honor was *the* event to attend. Women vied for his attention, and he had his choice of companions with whom to enjoy everything from the racetracks to the ballrooms to the boudoirs. Through Baradorf's good management, he began to take advantage of the theatrical opportunities in the other large cities to the north; and everywhere he went he was hailed as a star of the theater.

Arlene spent more and more of her nights alone, but Wilkes did not ignore her completely. There were times when he sickened of the scheming, heedless women, married as well as unmarried, who sought to be alone with him. If a woman did not want him for herself, she wanted him for her daughter; he just did not have enough time to take advantage of them all.

51

John Clarke was worried about the reputation Wilkes was fast gaining as a lover, and spoke to him one evening in the dressing room at the theater. "People are talking about your affairs more than they are about your plays. Is that what you want?"

Ready for his cue, Wilkes laughed and pointed to a pile of letters on the dressing table. "John, I don't go looking for affairs. They come to me. I must get three dozen letters a day, and almost every one of them is an invitation. When I throw them away, as I do, the writer comes to see me in my room or here. I send as many away as will go peaceably."

"And the married women? Aren't you afraid of husbands?"

"I've got to admit, the ladies are very indiscreet. I try to protect them. I've burned more letters than anyone will ever know just to save a lady or her family from disgrace."

"You've been seen with a number of young women, Wilkes, at very obvious places and very late hours. What about them?"

A rigidness in Wilkes' expression showed the conversation was becoming irksome. "I've never knowingly deflowered a virgin. If one comes to me, throws herself into my arms, she must take the consequences. Yet I give you my word; when I'm sure she's a virgin, I send her away."

"Well, remember who you are," John cautioned.

"You think so goddamned much of the name Booth, it's a pity you can't take Asia's maiden name when you marry her."

"That's hardly flattering to your sister," John snarled.

"If Asia has any sense, she'll break the engagement."

"Don't worry about me, friend. You're the one with the reputation of false lover."

A long awaited ambition was fulfilled in the autumn of 1856. Nate Baradorf and Edwin Booth had made all the arrangements for a production of *Richard III* in Richmond starring Edwin and John Wilkes Booth. Wilkes was to travel to Richmond immediately and begin rehearsals with Edwin the following week. He was excited and enthusiastic at the prospect of appearing with Edwin; it would be a challenge, too, to act on the same stage. At last people could make a firsthand comparison between the two brothers.

Wilkes had absolutely no regrets about leaving Philadelphia. The place had given him a tremendous success, but he had worked hard for it. And, despite the numerous women he had enjoyed, his heart had never been involved. Not even Arlene had a sentimental hold on him. He spent his last night in the city with her, but it was spoiled by her tears; also, Arlene was showing signs of possessiveness lately. He had never taken her seriously, and she had known this from the beginning.

So his last night with her was a strain emotionally, and his love-making had a little of the brute in it. He was angry with her tears and displeased with her half-hearted response to his demands. If she wanted him, this was her last chance. At dawn he left her and he did not even look back into the room where she stood in a rumpled nightdress to watch him go.

Twelve

In his melancholy, Abraham Lincoln dimly sensed a future preordained by destiny. It eluded him, and so his thoughts grieved instead for the days gone from him. He visited the past often and wrote of it:

> My childhood's home I see again,
>   And sadden with the view;
> And still, as memory crowds my brain,
>   There's pleasure in it too.

> O Memory! thou midway world
>   'Twixt earth and paradise,
> Where things decayed and loved ones lost
>   In dreamy shadows rise,

And, freed from all that's earthly vile,
  Seen hallowed, pure, and bright,
Like scenes in some enchanted isle
  All bathed in liquid light.

As dusky mountains please the eye
  When twilight chases day;
As bugle-notes, that, passing by,
  In distance die away!

As leaving some grand waterfall,
  We, lingering, list it roar—
So, memory will hallow all
  We've known, but know no more.

Near twenty years have passed away
  Since here I bid farewell
To woods and fields, and scenes of play,
  And playmates loved so well.

Where many were, but few remain
  Of old familiar things;
But seeing them, to mind again
  The lost and absent brings.

The friends I left that parting day,
  How changed, as time has sped!
Young childhood grown, strong manhood gray,
  And half of all are dead.

I hear the loved survivors tell,
  How naught from death could save,
Till every sound appears a knell,
  And every spot a grave.

I range the fields with pensive tread,
  And pace the hollow rooms,
And feel (companion of the dead)
  I'm living in the tombs.

Thirteen

Wilkes rode toward a land whose citizens were reflecting the attitudes and convictions of their grandfathers who had risen to rebellion against mother country. The "Don't tread on me" sentiment of 1776 was alive again in the people of the South. The moment was drawing near when the southern Congressmen would voluntarily forsake the halls of the Union. Soon there would be created a new nation whose Constitution would proclaim: "We, the people of the Confederate States . . . in order to form a permanent federal government, establish justice, insure domestic tranquility, and secure the blessings of liberty to ourselves and our posterity—invoking the favor and guidance of almighty God—do ordain and establish this Constitution for the Confederate States of America."

In the South, and in the North, every citizen held precious his heritage as an American. The sight of Old Glory over their heads was held in reverence in Virginia as well as in Illinois. "The Star Spangled Banner," the hymn created by a Southerner, was just as thrilling south of the Mason-Dixon line. Where was the Southerner who would not sicken to think of rejecting Washington as the father of his country?

It was all unthinkable, and yet, Wilkes wondered as he rode south—was this American heritage, with its revered names and its stirring music and its untarnished flag, his *real* heritage?

Or, as the voices around him on the train were declaring, were the Union, the flag, the Constitution itself only cherished symbols of that one thing which stood in the soul of every American citizen: freedom. Without freedom, what did any of it mean? And at what point is freedom lost, when one section of the nation dictates to another? What freedoms must the South give up to the North to maintain the Union, and if it gives up any of its freedom, how free is the South?

Wilkes was warmly greeted by Edwin upon his arrival in their rooms at Richmond's Pohowatan Hotel. "You're too damned good-looking boy!" Edwin complained, "I'm sorry I agreed to get on the same stage with you. No one is going to look at old Ned with you to gaze upon."

Wilkes grinned. "Thanks. Truth is, I'm very impressed with the chance to appear with you. It's not going to hurt me, you know."

Edwin gave him an affectionate slap on the shoulder. "I just wish Father could be here tonight."

"Well, we could have Mother come to the performance."

"I think not. She's content at home just now, and it's best to let her be quiet. The theater is still too much of a reminder to her just now. Perhaps in a few years we can arrange a production with all three of us—you, me, and June."

Wilkes frowned thoughtfully. "Edwin, I heard lots of talk on the train. You know, about things, the way they are, in the country. Do you think it's coming to open war?"

"Oh, I don't suppose they'll let it go that far. Sure, tempers are high, but it's mostly talk. I hope it is, anyway."

"I don't know." Wilkes shook his head. "The North has the idea it can tell us what to do with our property and where we can go with it. They have the idea that the federal government is supreme, whereas it only exists as long as the individual states agree to it. Hell, they can't tell a man where he can take a slave. That's his business."

"Well, they don't see it that way. Of course, what the North is afraid of is that we're going to expand into new territory, taking slavery with us."

"Well, we have as much right to move westward as do Northerners."

Edwin wanted to head off any rise in Wilkes' temper. "Oh, forget it, Wilkes. All our Booth slaves were freed years ago. And we're actors, not politicians or soldiers. We've got enough on our minds without taking on the Congress and the Supreme Court."

Wilkes smiled. "You're right. And this actor is about to bathe. Then let's go somewhere and have a drink."

"Good idea. Afterward let's go take a look at the Marshall Theater and acquaint you with it. We've got a lot to do before opening night."

A week later, the Marshall Theater was crowded beyond capacity for the brothers' first stage appearance together. *Richard III* was a tremendous success that catapulted Wilkes to the very heights of stardom. Long before the scene in which he, as the crusading Richmond, and Edwin, as the evil Richard, battled hand to hand, he had caught the imagination and admiration of the audience and carried them with him throughout the role. The curtain swung closed behind him, sweat bathed his face and his black eyes were brilliant.

Edwin's hand was warm in his and pride choked the older brother's voice as he stood beside Wilkes in front of the thrilled patrons. Then he raised Wilkes' arm up in a gesture of victory. The audience was standing in the aisles to give the brothers Booth a rousing ovation.

Edwin waited for them to stop their cheers and applause. Finally, they gave in to his motion for silence, and his voice carried to every part of the theater: "I think John Wilkes Booth has done well! Don't you?"

The reply was another wild outburst of handclapping and shouts.

Edwin told the critics later: "Wilkes has the genius of my father and is more gifted than I." Because Edwin was not given to easy praise or flattery, what he said warmed Wilkes' heart toward him.

The days that followed the debut in Richmond were probably more rewarding for Wilkes than any that he had ever known before or was to know again, a hero in his own hometown.

Critics noted that Wilkes had a special talent for the scenes of violence and the martial rhetoric which fill the Shakespearean histories and tragedies. The public was fascinated by his lively interpretations of the half-wild, murderous heroes and villains. And just when the critics would write that Wilkes Booth was an actor given to boisterous performances, he would surprise and delight everyone with a quiet, dramatically underplayed role—a technique which became his own special trademark. From John

Wilkes Booth the audiences could always expect a startling portrayal, whether it was performed in a somber mood or in a whirlwind of bravado.

Not only was his acting acclaimed, but so was his amazing agility and daring. He incorporated leaps and bounds into stage "business" with a realism which left his viewers breathless. Lithe and quick, catlike, he was in command of the stage in every performance, a challenge to his fellow actors and a thrill to the spectators. He actually drew blood in many of the sword battles, and had to be cautioned to use less enthusiasm in his pursuits of his fellow thespians.

His fame grew, attracting people from Washington City, Baltimore, and other cities and towns, to see him perform. Just as it had in Philadelphia, his theatrical success spilled over into his social life, and he was constantly sought as escort for the belles of Richmond, welcomed into the homes of the city, wooed and flattered by nearly every girl he met.

He enjoyed every moment of it, of course, and uttered not a word of modest protest over the generosity of the comments daily bestowed upon him by the public and the press. After all, the high opinions of his acting were well deserved: It *was* John Wilkes Booth who was drawing the crowds to Richmond these days; Edwin Booth was being eclipsed by his co-starring younger brother. Wilkes felt a trifle sorry for Edwin, but facts were facts.

Only one truly ominous note spoiled the happy days passing so swiftly in Richmond: Wilkes' country was in dire trouble. Even over the sound of applause, he perceived the angry voices of divided Americans all over the land, shouting accusations at each other across state lines. Now, he realized with a shock, the nation was no longer thought of as an individual whole; even he was thinking of his fellow American citizens in groups: "we" and "they."

Fourteen

In the early fall of 1859, John Beall, quietly handsome in a uniform of the militia of the State of Virginia, brought the word to Wilkes that the time had come for men to react to the events dividing the nation.

Operating with a small army, John Brown—who would free the slaves at any price, and who believed he had been preordained by God to lead the blacks to freedom—had managed one thing in his rampages in Kansas: He had united the South in its determination to not let any man interfere with its right to support slavery. Should his movement ever cross into Dixie, the states would know how to handle him: Old John Brown would hang from the nearest tree.

Up North, John Brown was looked on as a fanatic, but the Yankees were not drilling their militia in case of a John Brown raid. They did not have the slavery problem, of course, but then, John Brown hardly seemed to care where he struck, or at whom, as long as he rode at God's order. The North, however, as well as the South, wanted John Brown hung, proclaiming him guilty of treason. The South proclaimed him guilty of murder.

John Beall was one of the young men who had heard of John Brown and his aim to liberate all slaves at the expense of any white who stood in the way. And as a personal reply to Brown, Beall joined the militia of Virginia. There were rumors that John Brown was traveling south, aiming to trigger an uprising of the slaves. Let him try!

Now John Beall sat with Wilkes Booth and Colonel Aldon Wright of the Virginia Grays at a small table in the bar of the Spottswood Hotel in Richmond. John had brought his two friends together for a purpose: He wanted Wilkes to enlist in the militia and figured Colonel Wright was the one to speak to him.

A fat, dripping candle in the center of the table lighted their faces with a coppery tone. Colonel Wright, his hands cupping a brandy glass and his silvered hair glistening, sat so straight in his chair he might have been at attention on a drill field. He, like John, was completely outfitted in a gray uniform with polished buttons, and had such a vigor to his voice that it was difficult for him to lower it to a confidential tone. "I'll be honest with you, Mr. Booth. I don't think you ought to join the militia. You're a famous man, sir, and you'll have your own way to serve us, I'm sure."

Wilkes gave a glance to John and replied to the Colonel, "We expected you might feel that way. The stage does not have to take all my time and effort. We've talked that over, sir, and in our opinion, I'm qualified for the militia."

The Colonel licked his lips. "I mean this only in a flattering way, sir, so take no offense, but, let me emphasize what I've said. Frankly, I think you've found your career and that you ought to stick with it. I'd say you're too much of a dandy to be satisfied with the military."

John grinned. "Oh, God, Colonel, Wilkes may be the idol of the stage, but he's no dandy. He can outride, outshoot, and outdistance me in every event the field has to offer. You'll never enlist a better man."

Wilkes sat back in his chair and eyed the Colonel coolly. "I understood the militia really has but one requirement these days: loyalty."

"That's it," the Colonel admitted. "Dedication. Every man who signs up is personally pledging himself to the South's interests. We don't want any man who is uncertain in his views. The moment of battle is bound to arrive, and when it comes, we want no wavering."

"That's the only kind of military unit I would join," Wilkes told him.

"Mr. Booth," the Colonel took another sip of brandy before continuing, and he watched Wilkes closely as he spoke: "If it came to it, could you take up arms for Virginia against the Union?"

"If it be demanded of me, I will die for Virginia," Wilkes said without hesitation. "Yes, I will defend the South against the North, sir."

"Then you believe in the right—no, the *duty* of a state to govern herself?"

Wilkes answered slowly, as though actually reaching his conclusion for the first time: "I support the Constitution of the Union that guarantees to each and every state the right of self-government. The right of a state to be free is sacred. I recognize no power in the Union which allows it to hold a state through force. The right to independence is the very backbone of the constitution and the people of the states are only as free as their state governments."

Surprised and pleased, the Colonel glanced at John and there passed between them a silent approval of Wilkes. "Mr. Booth, you've stated our case well," the Colonel said. "I'm sure the Virginia Grays will welcome you." He leaned closer over the table and pitched his voice lower: "Furthermore, I think you ought to become a Knight of the Golden Circle."

Wilkes repeated the title thoughtfully. "I've heard of them, of course. A secret society, working for secession."

"More than that." The Colonel smiled in pride. "I'm a Knight. So is John Beall."

"Listen to him, man," John urged Wilkes. "This is for you, too."

"Tell me about it," Wilkes nodded. He was immediately stirred by the idea of a secret alliance with compatriots; he could actually feel the excitement and intrigue which emanated from the other two as they spoke of the Golden Circle.

Aldon Wright leaned closer over the table and engaged in a very private conversation. "The Knights do promote secession," Wright told Wilkes, "but if the present course of crisis continues, we will do more than that. We will be the nucleus of a Southern army! Further, the Knights are being recruited all over the nation, in the North as well. This will be a war for independence, no matter what the North claims it to be. We know for a fact that many men up north will be ready to fight for the Southern cause within their own states. We expect, therefore, that the Knights will be heavily engaged in intelligence operations during any conflict between the northern and southern states. That's one important reason we are being very cautious in the men we now enlist."

John saw that Wilkes heard the Colonel with a rising spirit of enthusiasm, and was aware of Wilkes' tendency to impulsive action. "You understand, Wilkes? Anyone who joins the Knights is really offering himself as a potential member of the Southern army."

The voices of other men in the public drinking room spread over the table for a moment, and somewhere in the room a glass shattered. Wilkes' voice filtered through the sharp crush of splintered glass hitting a brick floor. "When and where may I pledge myself to the Knights?"

Colonel Wright stretched forth his hand and placed it over Wilkes' on the table, and John reached out and put his own hand over theirs.

In the dark of the Virginia night, Wilkes and John rode side by side, headed toward an open field near a section of woods on the outskirts of Richmond. Stars were brilliant in the frosty sky overhead, and across the fields campfires sparkled in circles. Lanterns flared along a path which led to the fires where men and officers of the Knights of the Golden Circle waited. This night John Wilkes Booth was to be inducted into membership, and all was ready for the ceremony.

Wilkes pulled in on the reins to slow his horse. "John," he called, raising his voice to be heard against the rush of the wind around them.

John danced his horse around Wilkes'. "Not getting cold feet?" he asked.

"Not likely," Wilkes grinned. "Just wanted to say thanks, again. I appreciate what you've done to arrange this."

"Not at all." John's young face was happy. "Truth is, my friend, I've missed you the last few years. Your mother is right, you know. She's always said we're thicker than twins."

Wilkes spurred his horse to ride close beside John. "In fact, she claims that whither thou goest, goest also Wilkes Booth."

"She could be wrong. Maybe it's more like whither thou goes, goest John Beall." He laughed, too. "You want to race me or you goin' to ride that animal like a Yankee?" John spurred his horse and raced away from Wilkes, yelling like an Indian leading a war party.

Wilkes gave chase; they raced across the fields and reached

the campsite at the same time. Laughing and warm from the ride, they swung down from their saddles and tied their horses to the improvised hitching posts of stripling trees.

Uniformed men stood aside to let them approach the campfire where Colonel Aldon Wright stood warming his hands and squinting at them through the firelight. The Colonel's scabbard caught the reflection of the flames and Wilkes looked at it with a shocked remembrance of another sword, years ago, that weapon which had lain forgotten on the hearth of his mother's home—a sword he had believed he would never be able to wield by right. Now, here, in the wilderness of a hidden campsite, he was about to take up a sword in the name of Virginia and the South. He felt a painful thrill in his stomach.

Ground fog swirled around his feet as he moved toward the Colonel. Men were moving around him to the fires to light torches. Smoke stung his nostrils and made his eyes smart with tears.

With a firm clasp of the hand for Wilkes and a nod for John, Colonel Wright greeted them. "I'm mighty glad you got here, Mr. Booth. We feared you could be kept away by the theater."

"Nothing could have kept me away," Wilkes said. He shivered. It was not just the damp air, but the fact that he was wanted and needed. Colonel Wright explained to him that John was to join the other men—fifty in all—for the ceremony of induction and that he would escort the recruit. So Wilkes and the Colonel stood aside to watch as the Knights began the ceremony. Their black-booted feet whispered along the dew wet grasses as they formed a line. And, one by one, each approached the campfire to set his torch ablaze. They peeled smartly away from the fire and under the fluctuating lights of the burning brands held aloft in their right hands, skillfully maneuvered into a large circle. Then Colonel Wright escorted Wilkes into the center of the circle of flaring torches.

Wilkes scanned the circle of men, admiring and envying them. Their silver-buttoned gray uniforms and the heavy belts supporting their swords seemed to be more magnificent than any costume he had ever worn on stage. Now here was clothing worthy of a man! Wilkes was very conscious of the dark riding clothes he wore which tagged a civilian in a land where soon only uniforms would be acceptable. He thought that John, who called himself homely, fit the uniform as though he had been born to it. Very blond, rugged-faced Beall stood with a torch in his hand and winked at his friend.

The ceremony began. Colonel Wright asked, "Sir, what is your name?"

"John Wilkes Booth, sir."

"Are you a volunteer for service with the Knights of the Golden Circle?"

"Yes, sir, I am."

"Will you take the oath of loyalty to the Golden Circle without mental reservations of any kind whatsoever?"

Wilkes' voice was strong and steady. "I will."

"You will abide by all the rules and regulations of this society and maintain its secrets even at the cost of your life, if necessary?"

"I will."

"In case of hostilities between the states, will you support the federal government of the United States of America?"

Wilkes held his chin high. "I would support Virginia, sir, in any action she deems necessary to preserve her independence. Her decision shall be mine."

"Do you believe in the right of a state to govern itself, even though such a right leads to an armed defense against the federal government?"

"Yes, sir. The Constitution of the United States recognizes the right of rebellion against intolerable conditions of government, sir."

"Will you obey the orders of your superior officers and faithfully perform your duties without concern for personal safety or in fear of the enemy?"

"I will."

At that, the Colonel permitted a smile to play on his lips. "Mr. Booth, raise your right hand and repeat after me this oath."

Wilkes held his hand high and repeated the words carefully: "I, John Wilkes Booth, do solemnly swear to uphold and defend the independence of the sovereign state of Virginia against all enemies, foreign and domestic. I will, if necessary, expend my fortune and my life in this cause. This I pledge as a Knight of the Golden Circle."

Colonel Wright stepped forward and attached to the lapel of Wilkes' jacket a gold pin in the form of a circle with a lone gold star embedded in the center. "Congratulations, *Captain* Booth. We are proud to have you with us."

Wilkes fingered the pin proudly as he received the congratulations of all the Knights. There was a new expression in his dark eyes which would never leave him for he was now a man with a cause. The members of the Circle sat on the ground around the campfire, their faces heated by the flames and their backs chilled by the evening fog. Wilkes mostly listened—and there was a great deal to hear. The Knights were well organized and still growing, and he was astounded to hear the details of their work.

There were Knights on missions to the north whose sole duty it was to recruit. Wilkes heard that the Knights were operating in the conviction that hostilities were not more than a few months away. They had already established "castles," or chapters, in Chicago, New York, St. Louis, and other northern cities, with the purpose of bringing many of the enlistees into a Southern army. When war came, the Northerners, as secret members of the Southern military, would be in a position to serve as spies and saboteurs.

Wilkes' rank of Captain held no immediate assignment other than to stand ready should he receive orders of any kind. And, if he received orders, he was to respond at once and without questions.

Riding home beside John, he was exhilarated. "Damn, but I'm glad you got me in on this, John. Just don't go into any action without me. If something comes up and the Colonel forgets about me, you just keep me in mind, you hear?"

"You'll be notified. That's why I brought you into it," John assured him. "Just you stand by, and if we need you, Captain, you come, you hear?"

"What if the militia is called up and not the Knights?"

"Same uniform, same man, same cause. You'll find you're serving two organizations, the militia and the Knights."

"I'll count on that."

Fifteen

A man who called himself Isaac Smith, a cattle breeder who had briefly resided in Maryland after arriving from Kansas (where he was called John Brown) came forth from his lands to invade Virginia, to seize the armory and gun works of the United States of America at Harper's Ferry.

God told him, said he, to arm the slaves and to lead them in a revolt against the tyranny of the white men to whom they were enslaved. He planned to free all slaves in due time, but he would begin in Virginia.

He was operating upon his revolutionary plan as he had detailed it at a general convention of eleven white men and thirty-five black men in Chatham, Canada, on May 8, 1858. The plan of revolution devised by Brown—or Smith—provided for an attack upon the state of Virginia. Brown, or was it Smith?—was elected commander of the liberated area formerly known as Virginia. There was a Declaration of Independence written at Chatham, too, granting the slave population of the United States of America its freedom. And now the old man was enacting the clause which dealt with their liberation, positive that the slaves of Virginia would rise to his call.

At the Kennedy farm in Maryland, Isaac Smith and his brood of sons and their wives, and Mary Ann, his wife, had lived, worked and plotted for a year and more to perfect the old man's ambitious aims.

The women had been instructed in the craft of weapon-making. They honed deadly instruments called "pikes"—long shafts of wood, much like spears, with sharp cutting blades imbedded in one end. They polished the wood until it was smooth and would ride easy in the hand of a man. The pikes were stored away in a shed as they were finished and their number grew with each passing day. There were guns to be

66

stored, too, but the man named Smith had decided to put the pikes into the hands of slaves. Many of them had never used any kind of firearm, and there would be no time to teach them. But the pike was a more natural weapon: A slave with no previous instruction could thrust a pike into the guts of his master.

The time arrived when he figured God wanted him to move. He, as the chosen of the Almighty, must go to Harper's Ferry on his mission to bring the blacks out of slavery. He would first get the arms and ammunition that were stored there by the federal government; he would need hostages, too. Then with his followers he would flee to the Blue Ridge Mountains where, in accordance with Heaven's instructions, he would be ruler of a new government. The blacks then would not bow to any man, unless it be in gratitude to their savior, their leader— Isaac Smith of Maryland, John Brown of Kansas.

He had sent his women folk home to Kansas, away from Maryland beforehand. None of them had wanted to leave, but his word was law and they packed and left.

It was on Sunday, October 16, 1859—a day of the worship of God— that Isaac Smith made his move with a weapon-laden wagon and his band of twenty-one men, four of them black. He rode with his sons and his friends on a rainy evening, along a country road from Maryland to Virginia, traveling a distance of about seven miles. The invasion of Virginia was begun.

And the black people were well represented on that Sunday ride to Harper's Ferry. There rode with him a black man named Shields Green, a fugitive slave who worshipped the man called Brown. When urged by well-meaning friends not to enter into the dangers of the revolutionary plan, he had considered but a moment and then declared, "I believe I go wid de old man." The other blacks were just as determined and ready to ride into battle, wherever it might lead.

John Anthony Copeland, Jr., just twenty-four, a free black from Oberlin, Ohio, was frisky and eager to get the venture under way. He kept just a bit ahead of Brown's wagon all the way to Harper's Ferry.

Osborn Perry Anderson, twenty-nine, had come down from Canada and left his trade as a printer to become a revolutionist at the side of Isaac Smith.

Lewis Sheridan Leary, twenty-four, another free black from

Oberlin, Ohio, was sure the revolution was going to be a success.

Dangerfield Newby, forty-four, a Virginian, a former slave, had good enough reason to try the revolution which would free all the slaves of the Southern state. His young wife and child were slaves not forty miles away from Harper's Ferry. In his pocket was a letter from her begging him to come and free them.

Two of the white leader's own sons, Oliver and Owen, rode with him in the wagon.

Because of its special location and attributes, General George Washington had personally selected Harper's Ferry as a proper site for a government arsenal. It was an important little town in the nook of an arm of the Potomac where it met the Shenandoah. Washington, less than sixty miles away, was easily reached by Baltimore and Ohio trains.

The Harper's Ferry railroad station, just a stone's throw from the arsenal, was partially used as a hotel. All three bars in town were kept well-filled with customers, some of them government employees. The half-dozen buildings of the armory were well guarded, but not well enough.

Isaac Smith and his men were known to the guards for a year now as farmers at the old Kennedy farm in Maryland. Coming over the bridge that Sunday evening, the unsuspecting sentinels hailed them in the usual friendly fashion. Guns thrust at their bellies apprised them of the true situation, but by then they were prisoners. The armory and gun shops of the United States at Harper's Ferry had been seized.

A passenger train came whistling in from Wheeling, on its way to Washington. It was easily stopped by the invaders on the side of the bridge. The engineer was warned, at gunpoint, not to move the train one more inch. The telegraph wires were cut. It was all too easy.

Heyward Shepherd, a free black and the station porter at Harper's Ferry, came running along the tracks to see what was the matter. A yell ordered him to halt. Perhaps Shepherd did not hear the order, or maybe he did not understand it, but in any case he ran toward the engine of the stalled train.

One of the liberators of the slaves aimed a gun and fired at the black man. He spun, grasping his midsection, and fell. Blood gushing between his fingers as he clutched at his wound, he lay writhing at the feet of the men who had come to Virginia to free all the blacks.

"For God's sake, do something!" the engineer demanded. "Send for Doc Starry. This man needs help."

"All right," Isaac Smith said, "Send for Doc Starry." He helped his men drag the moaning porter to the station where they waited for the doctor. Smith kept glancing at the stricken man, and some of the man's pain came into his own eyes.

The engineer asked Smith, "What the hell are you trying to do? Who are you people?" He kept a wary eye on the gun held in the hand of Shields Green which was pointed directly at him.

The eyes of the man called Smith now looked as though they had been ignited by lightning. "God sent me. I am here to free all black people. I am in control of Harper's Ferry. My men are dispersed everywhere and the place is ours."

"You're crazy," said the engineer.

The doctor came and declared that he could not end Heyward Shepherd's agony. Only death would.

Isaac Smith and Shields Green moved down the street and passed through the yard of the arsenal and went into the rugged building known as the engine room. They closed the door. The leader trusted that all his men were at their assigned locations and that the federal arsenal was indeed in their hands; and he was correct.

The train did not move.

At three in the morning, Isaac Smith came again to the bridge and walked with long strides to the train. He told the engineer to take the train out of Harper's Ferry.

"No," replied the engineer. "I ain't goin' to move this engine one foot over that there bridge till I'm most sure you ain't messed around with it none. I don't reckon I trust you. I'll wait till dawn and have me a look. If it's all right, I'll take her on down the line."

"Suit yourself," said Isaac Smith.

"I know what's on your mind, mister," the engineer told him. "You're worryin'. Figure this here train might be missed by now. Someone's liable to come lookin' for us. Well, even so, I'm waitin' till I can see is it all right to go over that bridge. And when we do go, mind you, I'm sendin' in an alarm. You know that, don't you?"

The bearded rebel nodded: "I expect that. Might say, I even welcome it now. I've got the word of God to give this nation."

"Well, you just give it. You're going' to need all the help God will hand out."

At dawn the engineer carefully inspected the bridge. There was nothing amiss; he would risk it. Under his expert hand the engine crawled slowly forward. Safely over the bridge and heading toward Washington, he gave the whistle a long, low blast to warn the men at Harper's Ferry.

When he was able to stop, he wired to the railroad headquarters:

HARPER'S FERRY IN THE HANDS OF INSURRECTIONISTS. ONE MAN SHOT. THEY THREATEN TO ARM THE SLAVES OF VIRGINIA IN UPRISING.

The first workers to arrive at the railroad company office did not believe the message. When their boss arrived at ten that morning, they showed him the alarming words.

The President of the Baltimore and Ohio Railroad took the telegraph seriously and wired Governor Henry Wise that Harper's Ferry was in the hands of traitors.

The Governor immediately issued a call to the militia and wired the White House. President James Buchanan consulted with the military, and Colonel Robert E. Lee of the United States Army was ordered to proceed to Harper's Ferry at once with units of Marines and any other military groups he needed, to retake and secure the arsenal, and to maintain the general peace.

Two civilian wagons rolled into the yard of the arsenal. The lead wagon was pulled by two white horses driven by one of the rebels, Osborn Anderson. On the seat beside the large black man, stiff and angry, was Colonel Lewis Washington, a great-nephew of George Washington. Across his knees rested a family heirloom, a sword that had been a gift from Frederick the Great. Beside him on the seat, in a fine box, was a brace of pistols which had also been in the Washington family for many years. Seized at his home by Anderson and several of the other rebels, the Colonel had been instructed to bring the cherished weapons along.

The wagon following Anderson's carried a dozen black men from the Washington estate. They were free men now, Anderson told them—free to flee with Smith to the Blue Ridge Mountains. All they had to do was help defend Smith and his men, and themselves, against the Union and Virginia.

When the wagons were pulled to a halt near the engine room, Smith went to meet them. "Sir, you are my prisoner," he told Colonel Washington. "Your slaves are freed. You will accompany us to the Blue Ridge camp where I'll free you, but in the meantime you're my hostage."

"You know you can't get away with this," the Colonel said, but he sounded uncertain. To his astonishment, they were getting away with it. He held fast to the sword and the box of pistols.

Smith held out a weather-beaten hand. "Give me that sword, sir. I have won it."

A gun held by Osborn Anderson at his back, the Colonel handed the sword over.

"And now, Colonel Washington, if you please, give the pistols to Mister Anderson."

The Colonel's knuckles were white around the edges as he gripped the box. But the gun prodded his ribs, and the black man grinned with pleasure as the Colonel complied with Smith's request.

"Now Mister Anderson will see that you're made comfortable in a private room in the engine house, sir. And your slaves are about to receive their first weapons."

With the help of a few of his men, the liberator went down the line of the slaves and thrust pikes into their hands. They watched helplessly as their master was led into the engine building. What was happening? Their self-proclaimed benefactor told them: "Stand guard here." And they saw the strange eyes, and they obeyed. At his command, they paced back and forth in that room, the lethal pikes in their black hands, and watched the bearded man anxiously.

The militia had orders to assemble for duty at the depot in Richmond. A train was sidetracked there awaiting the coming of the Virginia Grays who were to be carried to Harper's Ferry. The engineer gave the whistle repeated long, low blasts to help spread the news.

71

Word passed swiftly through the city that there was an attack on Harper's Ferry. No one knew for certain just what had happened, but rumor had it that an uprising of slaves had been armed by abolitionists who had invaded Virginia.

Captain John Beall, in his gray and red uniform, found Captain John Wilkes Booth dressing in his room at the Pohawatan Hotel; Wilkes was to report at the theater for a rehearsal within the hour.

John hardly gave Wilkes time for a greeting. "Man, buckle up! Abolitionists are holding the armory at Harper's Ferry. The militia's been called out by Governor Wise. Where's your uniform?"

Wilkes, his shirt in his hands, was stunned, but John was already back at the door. "I'll meet you at the station. I've got to see Colonel Wright. Hurry it up. Don't miss the train."

"I won't. But I'll have to stop by the theater a minute. They'll have to fill in for me. Just hold that train."

In a half-hour's time, they were both seated in the rear car of the train about to move out of the Richmond station, finding it difficult to sit with the swords belted to their waists.

A thrill of uncertainty was in the air as the train moved past throngs of people who had come to see the militia off. It was as though they were going to war—and perhaps they were. Men, women, and children of Richmond cheered them from the side of the tracks.

Wilkes saw the faces blur and the figures grow small as the train picked up speed. "How did they all hear about it so soon?"

"Oh, it's around. You're about the last man to have heard it. Your trouble is you stay up all night and sleep half the day."

"You think someone's really armed the slaves?" Wilkes said. He could hardly believe that the time of talk and debate in the nation had come to some kind of action.

"That's the word we've got. They say the rebels came in from Maryland."

"Any man who'd arm a slave has to be crazy. But if there really is an uprising there, it can't last long."

"Well, don't push your luck and get nicked," John frowned. "Remember, your face is your fortune."

72

Wilkes grinned and ran a finger under the edge of his jacket collar. "I'm already wounded," he complained. "This damn thing cuts like a knife."

For at least five minutes they rode quietly; then Wilkes broke the silence. "Why in hell can't the abolitionists leave us alone? Those people don't know what they're talking about. Take that Illinoisian Lincoln. He says some of the most damnable things."

"Yes, but he claims he's not an abolitionist, actually. He has some remarkable ideas. Like he says he wouldn't marry a black woman, but he does consider her his equal in her right to earn her own bread and eat it."

"Now he's just going to cause trouble, talking like that. How in hell is a poor black woman going to earn her own bread? Did he ever think of that? We care for our slaves in every way. The women don't have to earn their bread—it's given to them. Lincoln's never had a single black person look to him for anything. Sure, our colored folks need a strong hand, like any simple child. Yankees like Lincoln and their ever-lasting talk encourage things like this Harper's Ferry."

"Well, let's give the federal government due credit. They're dispatching marines under Colonel Lee. According to Colonel Wright, they'll get to Harper's Ferry some time after we do.

"Well, let's hope we have some kind of a confrontation with the abolitionists. It would do a whole lot for the whole country. Might even score a point with Lincoln."

The morning rain was just breaking when the train from Richmond bearing the militia arrived at the Harper's Ferry station. As it slowed to a stop, the young and eager soldiers of the State of Virginia leaned out of the windows and yelled their enthusiasm. The train's whistle blasted, and steam reared from the engine.

The men emerged from the train. There were some five hundred from Richmond and each of them was enthusiastically hailed by the nervous people of the town. They were ordered to fall in for instructions; Colonel Aldon Wright was standing beside the rifles that had been stacked under guard at the station awaiting their arrival. When the men were at attention on the station platform, the Colonel took up a rifle and held it aloft.

73

As their shouts of welcome ceased, the Colonel began his instruction regarding the use of the gun he held for all to see. He raised his voice and was heard not only by the militia but by the gathering citizens of Harper's Ferry. "Each of you men is to be issued one of these. You ought to recognize it. But for those of you who don't, let me tell you it's a Mississippi rifle, the best damn rifle to be had, the same gun made famous by Jefferson Davis and his men. It's been rebored since the army used it in Mexico, but it's virtually the same weapon Jeff Davis found so trusty. You've got to be a man to heft it and use it right. It's a mighty weapon: weight, nine and three quarters pounds; length, forty-eight and three fourths inches. It's sighted for fifty yards, or one hundred and fifty feet. You can count on its accuracy. Now watch closely while I demonstrate how to load it."

The Colonel stood the rifle on its butt and efficiently went through the loading process. He poured powder into the muzzle, then placed a patch over the opening. On it he set a round lead ball, then he rammed the ball and patch down to the powder at the bottom of the barrel. He pulled back the hammer, put the percussion cap on the nipple of the firing mechanism, and aimed as though to fire.

"Now, step forward, one by one. Take your rifle and your ammunition, and then rejoin the ranks."

When each man again stood in line in front of the Colonel, he briefed them on the situation: Militia members from Charlestown had arrived some few hours earlier and had routed the rebels from the bridge, back through the arsenal yard, and forced them to take refuge in the engine house which they now held.

Now and then rebels would fire, and the fire was returned. "We will not do any unnecessary shooting," said the Colonel, "Rather we will try to evade any action awaiting the arrival of Colonel Lee and the marines. The militia is ordered to stand by and not initiate action." They were to be defenders only, but in case of an offense movement, the militia would respond with all necessary force.

Wilkes and John were assigned to a position above the arsenal yard, on a rise of ground which gradually worked back and up to the steep cliffs of the area overlooking the Potomac and the Shenandoah. The military units already on the scene had suc-

74

cessfully cut off any hope the rebels may have had of escaping to Maryland or to the Blue Ridge Mountains. The fight they had been spoiling for would be made at Harper's Ferry.

The clarity of the air following the early morning rain, was matched now by the warmth of the sun in the blue October sky. Nursed by two rivers and guarded by rocky cliffs, the town looked peaceful enough.

Wilkes and Beall were gazing down on the buildings of the Armory. John pointed out the engine house.

"They've trapped themselves. Of course, if they have food and ammunition, they can hold out for a time. But they're doomed."

Wilkes looked to the bridge and the station where people were coming and going. The train which had brought them was on its way to Wheeling to pick up more militia members. Black smoke sparked with hot embers from the departing engine and rose straight into the air. "Sure hope Lee gets here," Wilkes was looking in vain for a train from the direction of Washington.

"He won't be long. Hey, look!" John interrupted himself, "A truce flag!"

They watched without a word as a man came out of the beseiged engine house. Clumsily he advanced to within a few yards of a group of armed citizens who had moved forward from the outer yard to greet him. There was a brief exchange of conversation.

Wilkes, shading his eyes against the glare, was astounded at what he saw. "My God! They've seized the man!"

The rebel taken was William Thompson. The truce flag fell from his hands, and he was escorted out of the yard at gunpoint, a prisoner.

Wilkes and John were outraged that a flag of truce could be simply ignored, and yet their sense told them that anything was fair in this crisis. The arsenal of the federal govenment had to be saved and peace restored to the land. Yet, as Wilkes asked John, "Is it necessary to violate the truce flag? Can't they be taken any other way?"

"Maybe they surrendered," John said.

They were still discussing the pros and cons when the episode was repeated under more tragic results. The flag of truce was carried into the yard once more, this time in the hands of Aaron

Stevens, an enormous-bodied veteran of the Mexican War. He was accompanied by young, slim Watson Brown, a son of the leader of the rebellion. The two plodded toward the citizens of Harper's Ferry.

Shots came, and the white flag fell to the ground with Aaron Stevens desperately wounded. Watson Brown was hit, too, but he managed to stagger back inside the building where he fell into his father's arms. His moans were loud. "Die like a man," his father told him. "Kill me, oh, God, please kill me," Watson pleaded. "I can't stand it." His father lowered him to the floor and prayed for him.

Doctor Starry, heading a citizen's rifle group, stormed the small building on the yard where the rifles were stored, near the engine house, and took it from the rebels, killing two of them.

They seized John Copeland, the black student of Oberlin College.

"Hang him!" the citizens demanded. "Hang him right here."

The doctor held them back, a gun in his hand. "There'll be no hangings here. This black man will have the death he asked for, on the gallows, according to law. Now let him be!"

"Lynching is too good for him, all right," a man in the mob shouted. They dragged him off to the jail.

It was a long, long wait for the federal troops. As the afternoon waned, many of the militia and the citizens, equally tired of the waiting for Lee and impatient for action, took to the bars and drank.

Shots continued to erupt from the engine house, and the citizens, joined now by some of the militia, were spurred to action by liquor and began to return the shots enthusiastically. Stewart Taylor, inside the engine house, was killed by a bullet that penetrated the wall. Then Oliver Brown was shot.

Finally the rebels made a mistake in seeking retaliation. Firing from their fort, they sent a bullet whining into the midst of the citizens of Harper's Ferry; his honor, the Mayor, was struck and killed.

Wilkes and John, sitting on the ground still dampish from the earlier rain, watched with a sense of unreality as the incensed townspeople began the grim business of repaying an eye for an eye.

William Thompson, who had been so easily captured while carrying a flag of truce, was let out onto the bridge for all to see. His struggles were hopeless; his white shirt was ripped under the hands of his captors and pieces of it went flying into the water below. He was shot even while he screamed for life.

They let his bleeding body tumble into the river. For a few seconds it disappeared, rose to the surface, bobbed under the waters, came up again and drifted, blood swirling around it. But the sight was not satisfying enough: Men stood on the bridge above the body and tested their individual marksmanship, and how well they held their liquor, by firing into the floating body. If a bullet made the body jerk, it earned a special shout of praise. The ghoulish tournament was to go on most of the afternoon.

"Jesus," Wilkes muttered, averting his face.

"Let's go get a drink," suggested John. "This isn't a war."

Colonel Lee came at last, accompanied by eighty marines and Lieutenant Israel Green, USMC, and Lieutenant J. E. B. Stuart, USA. At first Lee was inclined to attack at once, leaving the rebels no time to adjust to the arrival of his men. But he decided to wait until the following dawn: he could disperse his troops in the dark and spring them upon the engine house just as dawn came.

Just before the first streaks of light came, Lieutenant Green was ordered forward from the surrounding troops to approach the engine house and demand surrender. He went to the door and knocked as though he were a visitor, and like any good host, the bearded man came to the door and opened it.

"Surrender now," Lieutenant Green said to him.

"No," said the rebel to the officer, "I will not, but I will make a deal. Allow us to go to the Blue Ridge Mountains, a distance of one hundred and fifty miles, in peace, and we will give no more trouble. When we reach our destination, we will free our hostages."

Lieutenant Green recognized the man's determination. There was only one thing to do. Turning at the door to the troops waiting in the dawn, he signaled that an attack would be necessary. The Lieutenant withdrew, the door was slammed shut.

Wilkes and John stood in the ranks of the militia reviewed by Colonel Lee. The orders were not to shoot. The building would be taken without bullets to protect the hostages, one of whom was Colonel Lewis Washington.

"Draw your swords," Colonel Lee commanded. "Heed your orders. The marines will advance upon the enemy, and all other military units shall support them by remaining in the rear. If it can be helped, we will shed no more blood at Harper's Ferry."

The marines, eighty of them, rushed the improvised fort of the rebels. Shots came from the place, but the door gave in under a battering ram. More shots came from the rebels, and two marines fell at the threshhold.

Colonel Jeb Stuart, sword in hand, plunged into the engine room, stepping around the fallen marines. He stood a moment, uncertain, for the early light of day was not sharp in that room.

Colonel Lewis Washington, coming from the shadows of his imprisonment, pointed to the bearded man who was aiming a Mississippi rifle, one of those manufactured at Harper's Ferry, at Jeb Stuart.

Stuart saw that the abolitionist knew him, too. How could Brown have forgotten the young federal officer who had taken him into custody in Kansas a few years prior on murder and other dire charges?

The rebel dropped the rifle—he had fired it at one of the entering marines; it was no longer loaded and therefore worthless—and reached for the sword at his waist, the one he had confiscated from Colonel Washington.

Lieutenant Green, seeing the threat to Lieutenant Stuart, raised his own sword and brought it down hard on the side of Smith's head, stunning him. Still, Smith tried to grasp the sword. Again the young officer attacked, and his old sword fell apart. Isaac Smith went down to his knees, clawing at his adversary, his head bleeding.

Lieutenant Green beat him about the shoulders with the broken sword, wielding the hilt effectively. Smith sank to the floor and lay still, blood spreading over his head and shoulders. The man's sons, who had been called upon by their father to give their all, lay motionless close by, one dead, the other almost gone. Wilkes and John entered the engine room along with other members of the militia. The place reeked with the odor of blood and gun powder.

"It is over," said Colonel Lee. "Our prisoner is not a man named Isaac Smith but an abolitionist named John Brown upon whose head there is already a price. He comes not from Maryland but from Kansas."

Wilkes removed his hat and thrust a hand into his thick curly hair. The air was suffocating. A hand pressed on his shoulder, and he turned to the man who had come to his side from the crowd.

Heavy-lidded eyes were studying Wilkes curiously and there was a smile on his face. "You're John Wilkes Booth," he stated. "I'm Lewis Washington. I saw you on stage in Richmond a few weeks back. You gave me and my guests a very fine evening. How good to see you here——" He laughed, and he gave the place a sweeping glance, taking in all the young officers. "How good to see all of you! It's been an ordeal, a real one."

Wilkes clasped Colonel Washington's hand. "Sir, I'm very glad to be here. We were hoping for a little action, but it looks like all has been done. I'm pleased to see you safe."

"At times I honestly wondered if I would survive." The Colonel looked down at John Brown who was being treated by marines. "Gentlemen, that sword he wears is mine. I'll appreciate its return, when possible. And he also has a brace of my pistols."

"They'll be returned upon the conclusion of our reports to Washington, sir," answered Jeb Stuart.

"Good enough," Washington said as he stooped down and lifted up a pike which had lain near John Brown's left hand. Handing it to Wilkes, he said, "Here you are, Mr. Booth. A little something to take home. He won't mind, I'm sure; he's got quite a supply of them around here."

Wilkes hefted the pike carefully, appalled at its savagery. John Beall fingered it, too, cautiously. "And that damn fool peacemaker was going to arm slaves with these things!" Wilkes blurted.

"Vicious," said Colonel Washington, "vicious! Just show it around, Mr. Booth. Let the folks see what we were up against here today and what has been nipped in the bud."

John Brown, four white rebels, and two black men were escorted to Charlestown and imprisoned, the threat of the gallows hanging over them. Five of his men had escaped the federal troops. Ten lay dead, including his two sons.

The court declared all of them guilty. John Brown was guilty of treason, of murder, of inciting slaves to rebellion. He could have been sentenced to hang three times, one for each charge and conviciton. The date of execution was set for December 2, 1859.

John Brown's reaction to the death sentence was, "Good! Let me die as a martyr on the gallows. Dead, I shall accomplish all that I could not alive. Dead, I shall come back and walk this land; I shall haunt this nation, from one end to the other. The blood of white men and black men will flow in a red river through this nation before the name of John Brown is really buried. Let them hang me!"

His friends, though, wanted to save him and plotted a way to his side in prison. One of them managed to get himself arrested and placed in a cell nearby. "I have come to help you plan your escape," he said to the condemned man.

"No, I do not desire to be rescued. I will die. God's will will be done. I can serve better as a dead man. Do not rescue me. Let me hang."

Brown's beard had grown shaggy and full in the days since his capture. The deep set eyes seemed a shade lighter than normal in contrast to the black hollows under the eyes and the yellowing of the skin that were developing under prison conditions. The bones of Brown's face seemed to be pushing through the skin to the surface, becoming bereft of flesh. He waited for his hanging, obsessed with it.

Sixteen

The Virginia Grays were there on the morning of December 2, 1859. Captains John Wilkes Booth and John Yates Beall stood at the foot of the jailhouse steps to stand guard with the rest of the militia throughout the hanging of John Brown. The militia was deployed around the courthouse square. Lately repainted, the cupola on the ivy covered brick building was a cheerful sight.

No larger crowds had ever gathered for a horserace anywhere in the South than now appeared early in the morning in Charlestown. There were few families who were not represented in full or in part in the town square that day, come to see John Brown hang. Mothers had packed lunches for children who might hunger before they could be brought home; babies were carried in blankets; children scooted through the throngs, eluding their elders who really did not want to be bothered, anyway.

Woman with rouged cheeks and daring dresses mingled with the housewives and the businessmen, flirting openly with the husbands. Sometimes they were lucky, and a man would offer an arm and take one or another off to a tavern, or elsewhere. Young women of good reputation came to watch, too, and engaged in flirtations with the young uniformed men of the Virginia militia. The black people were there, too—mostly young mothers with children in tow, many with the white families to whom they belonged—allowed to come along to witness what happened to any man, white or black, who dared to interfere with the rights of the masters of Virginia. Finally John Brown appeared on the steps of the jailhouse in the custody of armed men.

The militia stood with rifles ready. The jail officials lingered a few moments on the top step with their prisoner as they looked over the mobs of townspeople, searching for trouble, but they saw none. Rumor had it that despite Brown's declarations of wanting no rescue, an attempt would be made. Guns pressed closely around the condemned. John Brown cast his own gaze to where the Blue Ridge Mountains rose above a hazy horizon. He sighed.

Wilkes, standing so close in the ranks to John Beall that their arms touched, looked up at the doomed man. The odd fellow was dressed in an ugly black broadcloth suit, newly pressed, his long-fingered hands holding to the wide brim of a black hat; this thin-faced, bearded man looked as though he had died a long time ago and that his bones might already be rattling in the rough cloth of his suit. Was this person real? Could this strange pious-looking individual really be a threat to the state of Virginia? Wilkes shivered.

The military units moved back from the steps of the jailhouse as the prisoner was led forward by his immediate guards to the wagon which would ride him to the gallows outside of town. John and Wilkes moved with the ranks to take positions behind the wagon.

Boosted into the death conveyance, John Brown stood uncertainly and stared down at the long pine box in the bed of the wagon. A prod in the back from the gun of a jailer invited him to sit down on the box. The wind blew his uncut hair into his eyes.

Wilkes asked John: "Is that a coffin?"

"Of course. They have to put the body in something afterwards."

Three small boys dodged under the guns of the guarding militia and ran for the wagon and got as far as the rungs of the wheels.

John Brown looked at them and shook his head sternly. The father, a young man sporting a beard himself, looked at the prisoner, at his sons, and down the road to the gallows. "Hey, boys!" he yelled lustily, "Come here! And you hurry. We're goin' home."

The eldest son, a rosy-cheeked boy of eight years, freckles splashed across his nose, had a grin of triumph on his face at the excitement he had caused. "But, Pa, we're going' to the hangin'."

The father stepped out of the ranks of civilians, past the

82

militia. He yanked his son off the wagon wheel and carried him upside down back to the waiting mother. The other two boys trotted behind their angry father, wise enough to know when to quit.

The wagon was in motion now. The prisoner was jolted by the rough thrust forward of the old vehicle; he held onto his hat desperately.

The sun was high enough to warm the marchers and raise the dust on the old country road. Moist with perspiration, Wilkes still struggled with the collar of his uniform. He began to think about a cool drink of water. His booted feet scuffed on the stony dirt road and the road dust settled in his throat. The gun he carried, one of those issued to the militia at Harper's Ferry, weighed heavily against his shoulder. Why in hell didn't they just hang the bastard at the jailhouse? Wilkes let out a deep sigh so loudly that John, in stride beside him, turned and gave him a curious look.

In spite of his intention not to look at the man in the cart, Wilkes' eyes were drawn to the figure as surely as nails to a magnet. Damn, but his collar chafed! He looked away from Brown, lost his stride, and bumped into John, who automatically put out a hand to steady Wilkes, shifting his rifle to do so.

The wagon was pitching over the country road like a ship on a rough sea. John Brown dropped his hat to the floor of the wagon and grabbed hold of the edges of the coffin.

The scaffold was just ahead. The creak of the wagon ceased as it came to a halt. The prisoner arose from the coffin and he stood straight, waiting. He looked toward the mountains. "It is beautiful country," he said, as though he were a visitor aiming to please a proud native host.

He was taken from the wagon and walked to the gallows. At the bottom of the scaffold, they halted with him. Did they really believe, he wondered, that his hanging would end the issue between white men and black men in America? He remembered the words he had written and left behind in the jailhouse: "I, John Brown, am now quite certain that the crimes of this guilty land will never be purged away: but with blood. I had as I now think, vainly flattered myself that without very much bloodshed, it might be done."

Wilkes told himself: This man is a slayer of men. I need not feel compassion for him. John Brown has been a cruel and merciless killer of young men. When asked why, he has said: "Well, nits grow up to be lice."

Another group of small boys, tired of the long march and the somber faces of their elders, had taken up a game of hide and seek. One of them ran around the gallows and pushed in front of the old man and the jailers at the bottom of the ladder of the gallows. He would have ascended the steps to the noose, but an alert young officer snatched him away by the seat of his cotton pants.

The colorful flowers and ribbons of the hats of the women in the crowd made a pattern much too lively for the occasion. One young woman, her hat heavy with blue velvet ribbon, looked up at the hatchet in the hand of the black-clothed hangman who would use it to cut the rope. She fainted into the arms of her escort.

A five-year-old girl, shiny brown braids touching her shoulders, leaned against her mother and whined: "I'm hungry, Mommy." The mother threw away the packaged food she had brought along and grabbed the child's small hand and told her: "We're going home where we belong."

John Brown climbed the steps to the waiting noose.

The hangman, jail officials, and a clergyman were on the platform, as well as several members of the militia. The man of religion came forward, a Bible in his hands.

"No," John Brown told him. "If you don't mind, there will be no prayer over me. The only religious attendants for John Brown are those I wanted to help, the bareheaded and barefooted slave boys and girls, and their grayheaded slave mothers." So he had said back in the jailhouse and so he wanted it now.

The minister stepped back and the hangman came forward, a black hood in his hands, to guide Brown to the trap door. "Do you have a final word?"

"No. Just don't keep me waiting."

The hood was adjusted down over the gray head. If Brown's eyes stayed open, they stared in darkness. If he closed them, perhaps he still saw the Blue Ridge Mountains, the sunny day.

Wilkes ran his dry tongue over his lips. God, what a terrible thirst! It was difficult to swallow. There was a pain in his throat. He looked again. It seemed to him the scaffold rocked a bit. Hadn't John noticed? Apparently not: His profile was stern, his gaze steady on the prisoner. Wilkes scanned the calm faces of the other militia officers and clenched his teeth against a sickening in his stomach, a surging feeling within. He remembered that his father had been unable to endure the sight of physical suffering. Had he inherited that weakness; was he going to suffer Brown's punishment with him?

The noose was now in place and the hangman ready. The hatchet swung to open the trap door.

Wilkes averted his head and as he did so, a whiff of his own hair pomade which he had used lavishly after dressing that morning, scented the air he breathed and its sweetness sickened him more. He clutched at John's arm. "I'm sick," he confessed, weak-voiced, dizzy.

John's arm was around his waist, giving him the support he needed. "Don't look!"

But he had to. The trap door let go, the body of John Brown plunged through it and the rope jerked taut. A scream ripped from the throat of a woman.

Wilkes was retching. John hastily maneuvered him past everyone to the rear of the scaffold. The crowds were already moving away from the place. No one really noticed the young militia officer in the shadow of the gallows.

Finally relieved, Wilkes muttered: "I'm sorry." He wiped his sweating face with his handkerchief. "I've never felt like that in my life."

John had placed their rifles against the scaffold. He took them back and handed one to Wilkes. "Don't worry about it," John was pale himself. "You've never seen a hanging before. It must be the worst way a man can die."

Duty over, they made a quick trip back to Charlestown and headed straight for a bar. As they stood together at the counter, Wilkes relaxed and became more his usual self. Wilkes argued: "Brown got what he deserved."

John assented. "Yes, but he was brave. He died well. I'd like to believe I could go as fearlessly if I were in such a situation."

"He seemed lonely up there. I saw him look down the road

to town, like he was hoping to see a rescue coming. It sure must have broken his heart at the last to know he was deserted by the people he trusted."

John shrugged. "A lost cause and a lost man."

Wilkes, elbow on the counter, lifted his glass. "A toast, John. To Virginia!"

John raised his own glass. "Death to her enemies!"

Abraham Lincoln, traveling through the midwest at the time of John Brown's hanging, was giving deep thought to the ultimate outcome of slavery. Thomas Jefferson had stated: "Nothing is more certainly written in the book of fate than that these people are to be free; nor is it less certain that the two races, equally free, cannot live in the same government."

Lincoln found he was sharing Jefferson's view. Yet, was not attaining freedom the first consideration? Hearing of John Brown's assault and capture, Lincoln brought his own feelings into clear words:

"That affair, in its philosophy, corresponds with the many attempts, related in history, at the assassination of kings and emperors. An enthusiast broods over the oppression of a people till he fancies himself commissioned by Heaven to liberate them. He ventures the attempt, which ends in little else than his own execution."

Seventeen

Gradually in the next few weeks Wilkes was able to crowd the hanged man out of his memory. Event followed so closely upon event, both in the national scene and in his personal life, that there was little time to brood.

The long, wonderful theatrical season in Richmond which had brought him such fame and increasing wealth came to a close just in time to permit Wilkes to be best man at the wedding of his brother, Edwin, in New York. On July 8, 1860, Edwin Booth and Mary Devlin were wed in a ceremony held in the parlor of the minister's home. Adam Badeau, another actor, was a witness to the ceremony.

Mary, a tiny, angel-faced actress, was adored by the public as the perfect Juliet to Edwin's Romeo. Their romance and marriage was a thrill to theater fans. Mary was very delicate and her health was a matter of concern at all times. Often after a performance she was too exhausted to do anything but retire to her apartments. She wore a gray dress for her wedding. Wilkes thought it most unbridelike but he considered her a lovely girl.

The wedding dinner was held at Delmonico's. Wilkes was seated next to a woman of thirty, lately arrived from Paris and a friend of Badeau's. Isis had glistening hair which had been tinted in Paris to the shade of a ripe Virginia peach. Wilkes looked into the cool blue of her eyes and thought them like ice on fire.

Emeralds shone around her throat, and the cut of her gown revealed the beauty of that smooth, golden skin. She smiled at him and said: "I've heard of you, Mr. Booth. Did you know your fame has spread to Paris? London? Really, they're very eager to see you perform. You musn't hide away in America forever, you know."

"Paris and London will have to wait. I've a contract in Rochester." He leaned closer to her. "Tell me Isis. Do you plan to visit Rochester?"

Isis looked over the rim of her glass of champagne and gave Wilkes the full flood of her gaze. "Yes," she breathed into the glass, making a tiny ripple on the wine. "I'll be visiting Rochester."

When the bride and the groom made their happy-voiced departure, Isis was able to tell him, above the din of guests: "I'll be at my apartment tomorrow evening, alone. Perhaps we could discuss—Rochester."

Wilkes scrawled her address hastily on a menu.

The next day, Isis welcomed him at the door of her apartment. A dinner prepared by a departed maid awaited them on a small table in the large sitting room. They ate French cuisine in the atmosphere of candlelight, then sat together at the white piano placed against a backdrop of green drapes. Isis sang for him in French and though he did not understand the words, he was warming to the gestures which she delivered with the songs. When he sought to take her hands from the keys of the piano, she eluded him and fled to the white cushioned couch but a few feet away. Wilkes pursued her and once more his hands were on her.

"You are so very American in your lovemaking," she whispered, "In France, we do not rush. We savor romance. It is better so."

Wilkes had her around the waist and smiled into her ear. "All right, show me the French way."

Isis moved closer to him, loosened the silk cravat around his neck, and tossed it onto the floor. She unbuttoned his vest and slipped her hands under his shirt. Slowly, as she willed it, they found their way to that feverish moment when it was no longer her teaching but his. As he drifted off to sleep soon after, peach-colored hair tickling his bare shoulder, he contentedly thought that Paris was right.

Rochester succumbed to his personality as surely as did Isis in his arms. The North now joined the South; such crowds came to see him that many could only be turned away. John Wilkes Booth was hailed by the critics, followed by the stage-struck, recognized and applauded everywhere he went; his magnificent portrayal of King Richard III was the talk of the city.

Wilkes continued to receive indiscreet letters from women of all levels of society. Some were so determined to meet him that they foolishly signed their names, begging him to meet them in privacy. As he had told John Clarke, he gallantly destroyed those letters from women who had no business writing any man, except their husbands. As he reiterated to anyone who accused him of taking advantage of young women, he removed from their correspondence their signatures—which he called the tail where the sting is. Some of the notes so intrigued him, though, as to lead to more than one affair of short duration. He began to suspect that he was not capable of truly loving any one woman, not when so many threw themselves at him. And there was his father's memory: If a man could subject a woman like his mother to disgrace, was there really any such thing as love between man and woman? Passion, yes. Desire, yes. Perhaps even a tenderness and loyalty. But love? He doubted it, and he lived that disbelief through the summer months of 1860, taking any woman who so much as hinted she wanted him, as long as she was pretty, free, and responsive. And there were more than a few such women.

Isis followed him to Rochester and set up an apartment where he often retired after his stage performances. But Wilkes was already wearying of the delicate-haired woman from Paris. What had been a novel experience in New York was a bore in Rochester. He had seen the ice melt in the blue eyes, and a repetition of it now held no new thrill. He would rather seek excitement in new chases, new conquests.

Lying on the big satin-sheeted bed one dawn, he turned to look upon Isis as she slept. He was shocked to see that her hair looked more orange than peach. There were lines around her mouth. She was frowning in her sleep and he found it irritating.

He left Rochester without a word to her but it did not discourage her. By the time she followed him to Albany, Wilkes was already involved in an affair with an actress, brunette Georgia Henry. She was in his rooms at the hotel when Isis had herself announced. Wilkes took the card, looked it over, and handed it back to the bellboy. Seeing his flash of anger, Georgia went to the door quickly and took the card back from the bellboy.

"Tell the lady to come up."

Wilkes shrugged his shoulders, flipped a coin to the servant, and closed the door. He had learned a long time ago that women understand women. Georgia was the boldest woman he had ever known, more brazen, more passionate even than Isis. He wondered what she intended to do to be rid of her rival. Smiling, arms folded across his chest, he stood at the door and waited, eyeing Georgia curiously.

She moved toward the bed where she unbuttoned her dress

and slipped out of it, kicking it toward a chair. She loosened her petticoats, let them drop to the floor in a circle and stood before him in very scanty black lace underthings.

Wilkes feigned shock. "Georgia!"

She came to him. "Are you going to deny to her that you're in love with me?"

He slid his hands down her back, pressed her close, and lowered his face to the curve of her neck and shoulder. The knock on the door broke through their kiss. Wilkes reached to the doorknob, one arm still around Georgia.

In the doorway, Isis' expression turned from anticipated pleasure to terrible surprise. "Oh, Wilkes!" was all she said. But she stepped into the room and took a stand just beyond him, looking as though he had struck her across the mouth. Wilkes slammed the door shut. "Isis, what the hell are you doing here?"

The eyes of Isis blazed, and for just a moment Wilkes wondered if he had ever really touched her. Then Georgia pressed against him.

"Madam," she said, "you are intruding. Would you excuse yourself?"

"Do you really think you can take him from me?" Isis asked coolly.

Georgia cocked her brunette head to one side. "I have taken him away from you. And until I met you, I thought I'd done something!"

At that, Isis moved on her adversary, striking out blindly with her long fingernails at Georgia's face. Georgia ducked the clawing, and at the same time grabbed for Isis' orange hair. Snatching it, she pulled hard.

Isis uttered a scream of pain, lowered her head, and butted at the midsection of the brunette. The unexpected impact drove Georgia across the room and onto the bed.

Wilkes crossed the room, lifted the shrieking Isis off the prone Georgia, and carried her to the door. Isis kicked at him every step of the way.

Wilkes set her on her feet, holding onto her with hard hands and thrust her out the door.

She stood in the darkened hallway, fumbling with her disarrayed clothing and tumbled hair. Even in the dim light, he could see pain in those eyes as she turned without a word and walked away. Wilkes slammed the door once again and locked it.

No sooner was Georgia off the bed than Wilkes had her back on it. His hands on her were the hands of the lover Isis had instructed—gentle, warm, compelling; and then, not so gentle.

✦

When Wilkes was introduced to Henrietta Irving, who was to be his leading lady in a comedy in Albany, he eyed her with a kind of guarded apprehension, taking in her dark good looks, her warmth, and her command of the situation. The actress was his match in sophistication, fame and temperament. He wondered if she would try to steal every scene.

She recognized the look in his eyes and laughed. Impulsively, she pressed against him and kissed his mouth. She would have pulled away quickly from the impetuous act, but he was determined to break her to harness from the beginning. He gripped her and would not free her until she was beating at his shoulders with clenched fists. Then, abruptly, he let her go so that she nearly fell, and it was he who laughed.

There was never any question that they would find their way to each other. In a few evenings' time, in his room at Stanwix Hall in Albany, they shared a midnight supper after an appearance at the theater. It was nearly two o'clock in the morning when Henrietta arose from his bed and declared, "I can't sleep."

"What do you mean?"

She smiled, dressing hurriedly. "Just what I said, Wilkes. I'm very tired and I can't sleep. I want to finish the night alone in my own bed."

He got out of bed and stepped past the supper table, grinning. "You just need attention. Sorry I went to sleep. But I'm awake now."

"No more tonight, Wilkes. I told you, I want to go to my room."

When he ignored her and enclosed her in his arms, she stiffened in his grasp, and with a surprise move she raised a knee and jolted him hard in the groin. Then she picked up her handbag and started for the door.

Wilkes, anger distorting his face, rushed at her and put his arms around her small waist in a vise-like grip. Struggling, panting, furious, falling back a step toward the supper table,

Henrietta reached out blindly to the table, where her hand fell upon a knife. She seized it and with all her strength, slashed at Wilkes' head.

The blade skimmed off his right cheek, and blood spurted. Wilkes stood stunned, his hold broken.

Instantly contrite, Henrietta helped him back to his bed and made him lie down while she tended the wound with wet towels.

He soon regained his composure. "Get out!" he ordered, pale with anger.

She arose from his side, and tears were now flowing from her eyes. "Yes, I'm going. I'll send a doctor. Oh, God, I'm so sorry."

"Just go." He pressed a cloth tightly over the bleeding wound. But hurry with that doctor."

Within five minutes a doctor came and assured the patient that the wound was not a serious one, that it would not leave a scar—and that, yes, make-up would cover it until it healed for stage purposes. The doctor was making ready to go when a knock came on the door. It was the hotel manager, excited and nervous. "Doctor! Miss Irving has stabbed herself with a dirk. Come quickly."

Once again, the doctor was able to assure his patient that a knife wound was not serious, and Wilkes was left alone with her. They both worried about the scandal that might develop.

"I'll deny it all," she told him.

"And so will I." He kissed her gently. "And I think we must not be seen keeping company."

She clung to him. "No! Oh, Wilkes, don't you see? I thought you might die. That I had killed you. I wanted to die, too . . . "

The next day, however, Wilkes left Albany and Henrietta Irving, putting all the distance between them that he could.

Eighteen

Abraham Lincoln, the Republican Party's nominee for the presidency of the United States, was one of four candidates for that high office. John Bell of Tennessee was the choice of the Constitution Union Party, John Breckenridge of the States Rights Democrat Party, and Stephen Douglas, the nominee of the Democrat Party. The day it went to the polls in November, 1860, America was split four ways politically. The voters in all sections of the nation were hostile to each other and sure that their man was the only answer to the overwhelming crisis.

Wilkes Booth was depressed by the prospects he envisioned for the country if Lincoln should win the national election. He began to talk against Lincoln everywhere—in the theater, the public dining places, at social functions and in private drawing rooms. Wilkes' passion for the South's cause of liberty above Union became as personal an emotion as any he had felt for his women. He could not keep silent on the subject and ignored the growing resentment of his Northern associates.

Edwin, who had lately provided Wilkes with a permanent doorkey to his own New York home, cautioned his brother at dinner one evening before the election. "For God's sake, you've got a duty to the public to remain dignified and calm. You're getting a name for loud talk. Be heard on the stage only. You'll do better."

The candlelight deepened the shadows in Wilkes eyes. He saw Mary give her husband a fleeting glance of approval for his remarks, and this made Wilkes even angrier.

"Remain calm? I don't know how anyone can discuss Lincoln's nomination with dignity. If he makes it, this country will be at war with itself in a matter of hours. How can I tone that fact down to polite conversation?"

Edwin patted his mouth with a napkin. "Are you going to vote for anyone?"

"In New York? I'm not going to stand in line to vote with black men. You know that's what you'll be doing?"

"Yes, I guess a free black man has the same right to vote I have. I won't mind taking my turn at the polls. But you might as well know I'm going to vote for Lincoln."

"Why, that's ridiculous!" Wilkes blurted. "You can't vote for that Yankee ape!"

Edwin's inability to argue with Wilkes always left him with a shaky feeling. He gave Mary a glance which she understood.

"Wilkes, if you please?" Mary said quietly. "I'd rather you men argue politics when I serve coffee in the drawing room."

The heat in his eyes receded under her cool voice. "Certainly. I'm sorry, Mary. Maybe I can talk some sense into him before long."

Wilkes was unable to change Edwin's vote, however, and Edwin Booth cast his ballot for Abraham Lincoln. On election night he went with Wilkes to stand in the street in front of the New York *Tribune* Building. As votes were tabulated across the nation and the results were made available, the staff members of the *Tribune* held aloft large signs at the windows with the latest tallies for the public outside to read. The Booth brothers were part of a mob which roared its approval or disapproval of the returns as they were posted.

The front of the *Tribune* was lit almost as brightly as day, thanks to the hundreds of torches and other hand-carried lamps and lanterns.

Edwin looked away from the lighted windows. Wilkes was very pale and the muscles in his jaw taut as he looked up at the signs telling of Lincoln's winning battle. Women fainted; there were fist fights everywhere. The enormous crowds around them seemed on the verge of becoming a frenzied mob. Yet Wilkes Booth, buffeted against his brother Edwin, seemed to be aloof and cool.

Then Wilkes looked at him and Edwin saw a terrible pain in the dark eyes, as though Wilkes had just suffered a physical blow. "South Carolina will be out by dawn. It's begun," he said into Edwin's ear, above the roar of the people.

"The vote isn't final yet," Edwin yelled back.

"Yes, it's final—it's Lincoln. And everything's over—"

His words were suffocated in a booming shout, an ear shattering wave of noise. The enormous sign about the street now read: *Lincoln Elected!*

Pandemonium broke. Men everywhere were shaking hands, slapping each other on the back, shouting hallelujah. They lifted women and children into the air, laughing, stamping. The country was in the hands now of Old Abe of Illinois.

Edwin bowed his head, his eyes closed, and murmured, "Thank God!"

He opened his eyes to see Wilkes looking at him with an expression he could never interpret. "It's war, you damn fool," Wilkes said and pushed past him, leaving Edwin there in the crowd.

Five days before Christmas, a light snow fell on New York. Wilkes walked slowly toward the theater, hardly seeing the decorated windows of the city, with his coat collar turned up against the cold and with his hands plunged deep into the warmth of the big coat pockets.

A shrill newsboy ran swiftly along the sidewalk, expertly vending copies of the special edition to pedestrians. He never stopped his shouting, not even while making change.

Wilkes waited for the boy to reach him, listening in agony to the shouted words: "The South goes out! South Carolina secedes!"

Wilkes tossed the newsboy a penny and took a copy of the paper. The big black lettering seemed difficult to focus. At last Wilkes rolled the paper tightly and held it like a club in his hand as he hurried on to the theater.

The warmth of the small stove in the corner of the dressing room permeating his bones, he flung his gloves and broadbrimmed hat aside and spread the newspaper open on the make-up table. He read the whole story of South Carolina's withdrawal from the Union, in such deep concentration that he did not hear the knock on the door.

Edwin spoke aloud at his elbow. "You've read it, I see."

"I told you, that man has broken our Union."

Edwin was frowning and looked very unhappy. "Wilkes, what about it? Every man among us has got to stand up now for the Union."

"The South has a right—no, a *duty*—to secede, under the circumstances. I told you how the South would feel about the election of that abolitionist."

"Could you fire on our flag? Could you really?"

Wilkes picked up the newspaper again. "I don't see anything about Virginia here. She hasn't acted yet. Maybe she won't."

"You know I'm a member of the Virginia militia. I'm sworn to uphold her in any action she takes."

Edwin was exasperated. "My God, Wilkes! You're under no obligation to a militia oath you took over a year ago. It's a question of patriot versus traitor. You have no choice."

"There's reason to believe Virginia may not go out. Her legislature is divided on the issue, though I can't understand its hesitation at all. But if she stays in, she's placing South Carolina in a very difficult situation. And I can't see Virginia pledging loyalty to a Union headed by Abraham Lincoln. And there lies my loyalty."

"Damn it, Wilkes!" Edwin shouted, "You've but one loyalty and that is to your native-born country."

Wilkes tossed the paper back to the table, ignoring Edwin. If Lincoln had not been elected, there would be no necessity for a man to fire upon the flag he honored.

Nineteen

The next few months witnessed state after state falling away and declaring itself free and independent of the United States of America. North and south, east and west, there were injured feelings and surging shouts for revenge and justice.

Newsmen in the South filed stories through lines of the Associated Press of the Confederacy, reporting the action of the departing states as seen from within their own borders. The legislatures of Mississippi, Florida, Alabama, Georgia, Louisiana and Texas voted, one after the other, to leave the Union.

Yet they were not independent states for long. Within weeks of their separate actions to become free, the secessionist states joined themselves together into a new union. On February 18, 1861, in Montgomery, Alabama, the Confederate States of America was founded by the adoption of a provisional constitution to which its states pledged themselves as one nation. The following day, Jefferson Davis was elected provisional President. Alexander Stephens of Georgia became provisional Vice President.

And still the state of Virginia, where George Washington's body lay in eternal sleep, did not act. The North held that if Virginia could be held loyal, the Confederacy might dissolve and the Union persist. All across the land, Americans looked to Virginia, day after day, guessing, hoping, praying, but none more intensely than John Wilkes Booth.

Virginia was under pressure. There were powerful and good Virginians who ached to set their state free of the North, and each day these men met determined to bring about secession. Yet there were other members of the legislature who, given the wrong push, would throw their political weight to the North. It was a very delicate situation.

It was South Carolina who knew how best to appeal to fellow

Southerners. A representative from that state rose to speak to the Confederate Convention and suggested boldly that Virginia would come into the Confederacy only when Southern blood had been spilled. Then, he claimed, she would not only be a member of the Confederacy, but would lead it in all future action. And, he hinted, the situation was such that blood would soon be shed.

Wilkes waited impatiently along with the rest of the country.

One day President-elect Lincoln, passing from Springfield to Washington, stopped at the venerable Statehouse in Philadelphia for a brief speech and flag-raising ceremony. Wilkes stood not far from the speakers' platform and gazed up at the giant of a man who was taking over the highest office in the Union.

Amid cheers and applause, Lincoln pulled the flag aloft on its ropes and when it stood out on the breeze, the crowds cheered even more. Then everyone listened as the wind tugged at the big man's hair.

Wilkes heard him say: "But if this country cannot be saved without giving up the principle of liberty for all people . . . I would rather be assassinated on this spot than surrender it."

How strange, thought Wilkes. This huge and shaggy man from the North, who would impose his ideas of liberty upon thousands of his fellow Americans, would give his life for his view. And so would I, for mine. I, too, would rather be assassinated than surrender to a demagogue, a traitor to the very principle of freedom he enunciated so appealingly. And how the people loved him for it! How they worshipped him!

Wilkes could not bear the sight of the adoration of the crowd's faces. He turned away and into the arms of an elderly man whose blue-veined hands grasped him by the forearms happily. "Ain't Old Abe wonderful? He's our answer all right, he's our answer."

Wilkes jerked his arms free and told the old man bitterly: "You're a damned old fool." And he pushed through the crowd in a frenzied effort to get away from the presence of Abraham Lincoln.

In the days which followed, Wilkes forgot some of his anxieties in a round of social events. But, even so, he spoke hotly in defense of the South wherever he went.

Along with his increasing popularity as a star, Wilkes was

gaining a reputation among young people of being a red-hot rebel sympathizer. As long as he lingered in the North and espoused Southern views, a moment when he would have to act and not speak was bound to come.

The moment of truth came quite unexpectedly . . .

He was the guest of honor at a ball held in a hotel in Albany. The guest list included the younger representatives of the city's leading families. The ballroom sparkled with crystal chandeliers, candles, and a long banquet table laden with red roses. The young women were in gowns of every color and shade, their bell-shaped skirts like half-opened flowers. It had been an excellent dinner punctuated with laughter and smiles and friendly conversations, and the threat of war was forgotten for a few hours. They thrilled to the sight of the fascinating Booth among them and finally, they started a happy chant for him to perform in some way.

Wilkes did not have to be coaxed long. Leaping upon the banquet table, his feet deftly pushing aside a few empty dinner plates and champagne glasses, he smiled down upon the happy faces and waved for silence.

"How about a song or two?" he asked.

They shouted approval and moved even closer in a large group around him. Wilkes winked at several of the girls as he asked:

"What's your pleasure?"

One or two guests consulted, and called out titles.

"I'll tell you what I'd like to do," Wilkes said. "Tonight it looks as though there may be no war between the States. We're told the South is sending a peace delegation to Washington to see Lincoln. We may all have something to sing about. Why don't we have a few patriotic songs. You all join me!"

Cheers met his words.

"Fine! What should it be?"

The girls turned to each other, their smiles verging on giggles. Before they could reply, a big, dark-browed young man, a champagne glass in his hand and mockery in his eye, pushed to the fore of the group and looked up at Wilkes in belligerent contempt. "Why not sing your own favorite song, Booth? Give us 'Dixie.' "

Wilkes met the moment without flinching. "You heard the

99

gentleman's request, folks." He turned to the quiet orchestra at the far end of the room. "Gentlemen? Let us hear 'Dixie,' if you please."

Uncertain, the orchestra nevertheless did what it was paid to do and picked up its instruments.

While appalled young men and women looked on, music filled the room and Wilkes sang in a mellow voice. Not very loudly, but without faltering, he gave a full rendition of 'Dixie.' In spite of their feelings, the guests kept time with foot tapping to the lilting tune, exhilarated.

As the last note died, Wilkes bowed to the orchestra, to the guests, to the young man who had requested the song. He stood straight for a moment there on the banquet table, the lights of the chandeliers revealing the tears in his eyes, and suddenly the room burst forth with wild applause, a salute to his courage and honesty.

Wilkes jumped down from the table without looking to right or left, and strode out of the room past the young people who continued to applaud him. In a way, it had been decided for him that he could no longer stay in the North. He was a rebel, if that was the term they liked, and he belonged with men and women who were rebels, too.

Twenty

Wilkes' young brother, Joseph, the youngest of the Booths, was a student of medicine who had no desire to act, but like Wilkes, was a Southerner in all his views. And the very day that Wilkes made his decision to return to the South, Joe Booth was already engaged in active military duty against the North, attached to the military units which fired upon Fort Sumter—spilling the blood that South Carolina had predicted.

As Wilkes rode a train over the James River to Richmond on the 17th of April, 1861, his eager gaze seeking the loved sight of the seven hills, members of the Virginia legislature took the long awaited step and voted 88 to 55 to leave the Union. Men on both sides of the vote shed tears openly.

The speaker of the legislature, pride shaking his deep voice, announced that Virginia would accept the Confederate Congress' invitation to establish the new nation's capital in Richmond, and that President Davis and his cabinet would immediately proceed to that city. The legislature forgot its sadness to cheer the announcements. Now all eyes and hearts turned loyally to Richmond and the Confederacy.

They celebrated the new union in the capital of the Confederacy that night. It was the biggest celebration ever known in Richmond As excited mobs roamed the streets, carrying the flags of Texas, Virginia, Mississippi, Alabama, and other states, skyrockets were shot off on the steps of the Capitol Building, flaring over the exquisite structure of the Statehouse which had been designed by Thomas Jefferson. No Fourth of July had ever been so wonderful.

Wilkes walked from the train to the Spottswood Hotel, caught up willingly in the wild demonstrations of the Southerners. It was like nothing he had ever felt before, this elation, this superiority, this victory. Now, he could take up the battle along with all the South.

When President Jefferson Davis came to Richmond, the celebration of the Confederacy's birth gave way to virtual riot. The man who had soldiered alongside Abraham Lincoln in the wilderness of Illinois during the Black Hawk War, who had served in the United States Senate and as Secretary of War under President James Buchanan, came to Richmond boldly, in an open carriage. Flowers were strewn in his path, flags flew everywhere, bands played, women rushed to the carriage to kiss him and take his hands in sobbing welcome.

Wilkes lost no time in seeking his own place in the Confederate army. He wanted a field command assigned to a post where he believed he would be most useful. A superb horseman, an expert shot, and an accomplished swordsman, he was sure

Colonel Aldon Wright would assist him in qualifying for a responsible army assignment. Knowing the Colonel would be on duty at the Armory Building, Wilkes headed there early on the second day of his Richmond visit.

The two-level building, half a block long, was located near the basin area, next door to the Tredegar Iron Works, the largest factory in the South, that worked day and night to manufacture the cannons, guns, and ammunition needed to arm the new nation.

Above the armory flew the bright flag of the Confederacy and the flag of Virginia. In normal times, the armory housed the Virginia militia, but now it was also the center of all military activities of the Confederacy. Through it would be channeled troop assignments for all the South, and its activities had already brought outfits from all the Confederate States into Richmond to await dispersal orders.

Wilkes found Colonel Wright in a small cubicle partitioned off to provide a semblance of privacy, busily checking a list of individuals who had volunteered for duty.

"Wilkes Booth! Captain Booth. How good to see you. I was going to relay a message to you in Philadelphia, if possible."

"A message, Colonel?"

"Yes," replied the officer, offering a chair to Wilkes. "I'm working with Lee to channel our militia and the Richmond Knights into the Confederate army. We have a brief on your personal history here—" he tapped a paper on his desk—"And it shows that you're in a most unique position to be of very special service."

"Colonel, I'm here to volunteer for immediate duty," he protested. "I want a field assignment, without delay."

Colonel Wright stroked his chin thoughtfully. "I believe the President has something definite in mind for you. I'm to notify him of your presence in Richmond. The thing is entirely in his hands, you see. It's very confidential."

"Sir?"

The Colonel smiled at Wilkes' obvious surprise. "Sorry, I really don't know myself what he wants. I only know that he wants to see you at once. Where are you staying, Wilkes? I'll need to notify you about the appointment."

"The Spottswood."

102

"Yes. The President will relay the appointment day and hour through here. I'll let you know immediately."

Their business obviously concluded and the Colonel's desk piled with unfinished work, Wilkes arose. "By the way, Wilkes. Did you know that John Beall is in Richmond?"

"No, sir! But I was hoping he was. Do you know where I can find him?"

"On his ship. He's been commissioned as a privateer. Claims he'll sink the whole Union navy within a matter of hours."

Wilkes was astounded, and his enthusiasm took a new turn. "Say, maybe I can join him!"

The Colonel shook his head. "No, that's not likely. But you better get down to the wharves to see him before he sails. He has two ships outfitted already. His sloops are twins, a regular brace. Very impressive and sea-worthy, I understand."

The Richmond wharves no longer slept idly in the sun, but crawled with activity as men and ships made ready for battle. The *Raven*, a fantastically beautiful black ship, lay close at hand. Rising and falling gently on the water with her black sails furled, she stood next to a long pier; beyond her, anchored in deeper water, was the *Swan*, a graceful and swift-looking white beauty. Wilkes climbed aboard the *Raven* and swung noiselessly to the deck like a cat. John and another man were at the wheel, their backs to him. Suddenly Wilkes shouted, "Captain Beall! This ship is claimed by the Union navy!"

John wheeled around as both he and his man reached for their guns. Wilkes threw back his head and laughed, raising his arms high in the air.

"Why, you no-good Yankee traveler!" John scolded. "You're crazier than I remembered. You should be shot for a trick like that, man! In fact, you almost were."

Wilkes hugged him roughly and slapped him on the back. "What's the idea of giving up land duty for a sailor's life? I thought I raised you to be a soldier."

John looked up at the masts. "Isn't she sweet? I want you to sail with us. Sign on, huh? And then we'll take Washington away from Old Abe. I'll be needing you."

"I'd like nothing better. But I just talked to Colonel Wright, and I'm afraid they've something in mind for me. I couldn't find out much except that I'm definitely to see the President."

"Hell, a man ought to be able to choose his post. Tell you what, Wilkes. I'll shanghai you. We sure aren't going to let them stick you with a desk job, are we?"

Wilkes took a deep breath of the sea air. "No, sir! As a matter of fact, I'm going to ask the President to let me sail with you."

"That's what I wanted to hear. You see, I want you to handle the *Swan*."

"My God, you'd give me command of your ship?"

"Certainly. That's what I've had in mind from the first. I sent a letter to you at Bel Air, but I guess it missed you."

"Anything can happen to mail these days. And then, I've been traveling—New York, Albany, Philadelphia, all over."

"Then, you're not up on the news at all. Wilkes, I've not only got the prettiest sloops in the world, I've got myself engaged to the prettiest girl who ever walked this old earth. Helene Chambers."

"Well, congratulations. I think that's the greatest news I've heard in years. Does she live in Richmond?"

"Yes. I'll arrange dinner for us as soon as possible. She's so beautiful, and I'm so damned lucky."

"Imagine you married. Soon, I suppose?"

"No, not too soon. We feel we better wait and see just how this war goes for a spell." John put a hand on Wilkes arm. "How about you, son? No girl of your own?"

A fleeting frown went over Wilkes' face and his eyes looked quite black. "Oh, lots of women. But I don't think a girl like you mean—like you have—is for me. I can't seem to care about any of them that way."

"You just haven't met the right one, that's all. You can't play Romeo all your life. You've got to find the real thing one of these days, and when you do, it's really going to be worth seeing."

"Well, right now I'm only interested in these two sloops of yours," Wilkes said changing the subject. "Tell me, why the paint? And what do you expect to do with them?"

"Come on, I'll draw you some pictures," John said, leading him to his cabin.

Beall's plan of battle was a daring one, and its very nature struck a responsive chord in Wilkes. It involved a challenge such as few men would issue to the enemy in a war. Beall, a student of Indian warfare tactics, aimed to borrow some of the basic lessons the Indians had provided in their wars against the white man.

Beall had painted the *Raven* black and had given it black sails so he could sail the sloop undetected at night on dark waters or even in the moonlight. He would sail against the enemy in a hit and run method of fighting, surprising the Union ships by apparently arriving on the scene from out of the darkness of the night.

The white *Swan* would operate mostly during the day. It was of the same design as the *Raven*, and both were fast, hard-hitting war vessels. Long and low, they would be able to slide in under the guns of the enemy. "We'll have their ships on fire before they know we're near," John bragged.

"Please, count me in," Wilkes pleaded. "There's nothing I'd rather do than take command of the *Swan*. I'll just have to get clearance from Davis." He brightened: "Look, will you write a letter I can take with me? Tell him we're all set to sail."

"Absolutely! I'll make it a formal request for your services, and I'll make it as strong as I can. Man, I need you."

"Thanks, John. The letter ought to do the trick. I'll take it with me, to save time."

The note from Colonel Wright was awaiting Wilkes at the hotel. His appointment with Jefferson Davis was set for ten-thirty in the morning. Wilkes, mystified, carefully folded the note and put it with the letter he had been given by John.

The President of the Confederate States of America met Wilkes in a second-floor office in the former United States Treasury Building. The old structure was a granite, boxlike edifice across the street from the Capitol Building. The President's office was small, sparsely furnished, and lighted by a window overlooking the capital.

Rising from his desk, stretching forth a long-fingered hand, Jefferson Davis came across the room to meet Wilkes. "This is a pleasure, I do assure you, sir. I'm a most devout Booth patron. Devout!"

Wilkes' hand felt the strength of the President's. He bowed his head and said, "I'm most honored, sir."

"I must tell you that one of my most vivid memories in life is of your gifted father as Hamlet . . . Remarkable, remarkable, sir!"

"Thank you, sir. I'm sure you'll understand if I agree with you; he was a remarkable man and a gifted actor."

The light shining on Jefferson Davis at that moment gave Wilkes a flawless portrait which he studied with interest. Davis appeared stern, except for something in the lines of his face which suggested compassion. There arose in Wilkes' mind the thought that Jefferson Davis and Abraham Lincoln were physically very much alike. He saw that there was an opaque cast to Davis' left eye and realized he was blind in that eye! And so he was, from the time he had nearly succumbed to fever, the same fever from which his first wife, Knox Taylor, had died many years before.

"And now, sir, we must get to our business. Colonel Wright has given me a full report on you, and he's made certain recommendations with which I find myself in total agreement."

The President was moving too fast. Wilkes, fumbling, brought forth John Beall's letter from his pocket and handed it across the desk to the President with no apology. "Mr. President, I've got a letter here from John Beall whom you have commissioned as privateer. Before you reach any final decision affecting my service, may I ask that you read it?"

Turning to get more light on it, the President squinted as he read it, his sharp-boned face impassive. When he finished it, he put it down on his knees and said, "Captain Beall writes a very persuasive letter. It makes it more difficult than ever to tell you what I am asking of you. I see clearly that you'll want to refuse me."

"Sir, if there is a chance I can join Captain Beall——"

Jefferson Davis nodded. "Of course, you may refuse my request, if you wish. But let me say I personally believe you can serve our cause better in the assignment I'm hopeful you'll accept. I'd not ask it if I did not consider it so.

"Mr. Booth, this war will be fought in many ways. One of those ways will be secret, underground, dangerous. A few Southerners can be of a peculiar but enormous assistance to the Confederacy every minute of every day. Through your life as a star of the stage, you can provide us with very important help in the days to come."

106

"You mean, sir, you're asking me to become a spy?"

"Essentially," the President admitted. "But it's both more and less than that. You'd have a task such as no other man, perhaps, in this war." He sat down at his desk. "You do travel freely in the North? You do have many good friends in the Union? You're as welcome there as you are in the Confederacy?"

Wilkes nodded. "Well, there are those who hate me, both North and South."

"There are always a few for every one. But can you, for instance, take a message for us to Chicago or New York or even Washington without trouble? You'd not be suspected or questioned as you travel in the interests of the theater? That is, if you continue your usual routine of stage appearances all around the two nations, you would not be suspected of anything?"

"I'm sure I could continue to appear on the stages in the North without suspicion. My contracts would carry me everywhere—if I were to continue my stage career at all, that is."

"We'd provide you with passes through our lines. Can you get them for the North?"

"I'm certain there'd be no question of that. But, sir——"

The President leaned toward him, pleadingly. "Mr. Booth, you could obtain information, make contacts for us, which we could not possibly obtain in any other way. In traveling freely through the North, at your own pleasure, you'll have access to military information regarding the locations and dispersals of troops, the treatment and whereabouts of prisoners, and many other vital statistics of grave importance to us. Such detailed information has meant the difference between defeat and victory for many armies in the history of this world."

"But, Mr. President——"

Grim-faced, Jefferson Davis shrugged his shoulders. "Of course, if you insist upon service with Captain Beall, I won't oppose it. But remember that in the judgment of both Colonel Wright and myself, you have a very rare opportunity to serve your country beyond the call of duty, sir."

Wilkes hesitated just a moment longer before he stood up. "I'll be honored, Mr. President, to serve as you request."

Davis shook his hand. "Thank you indeed, Mr. Booth. I know how badly you want to sail with Beall but I'm not going to talk about it anymore. I need your help badly enough to take advantage of your good heart in this."

Wilkes did not want to talk about the sailing of the *Swan* either. "What do you want me to do first, sir?"

"First, go to Washington and pick up as normal a routine as possible. Can you contract for a play there?" Davis was speaking more crisply than he had been during the entire interview.

"Yes, sir, I believe so. I'm always welcome at either Ford's Theater or Grover's. If I have to wait for a play, well, that may serve the purpose of a routine as well as anything."

"Yes, good! You'll be contacted very quietly and given further orders on what we want you to do. In the meantime, find a way to get us all the information you can regarding the troops in and around Washington. Let us know any strengths and weaknesses you observe. Your contact in Richmond will be Colonel Wright. See that all your messages are directed to him, unless there is something of such immense importance that you feel I ought to be advised personally. In that event, do not try to contact me any other way than in person. Is that clear?"

"Yes, sir."

"There is one other thing I must ask you to consider. In the event you are ever found out as a spy, this government could not come to your defense. You would be strictly on your own." The President eyed him soberly. "Can you accept that possibility?"

"Yes, I understand." Wilkes smiled. "You know, this assignment may be very interesting, at that."

"I'm sure you'll do well with it," said Davis, offering a hand in farewell. "You know, the Union believes it can dim our lamps of freedom, but I think they're flaring a little too high to be so easily extinguished."

As the two men moved toward the office door, Wilkes stopped to say: "Mr. President, thanks for your faith in me. It means a great deal to me."

"As does your faith in me, my dear sir. We'll see this thing through together—all of us—as long as we share a mutual faith in our cause."

Twenty-One

When Wilkes Booth arrived in Washington, the capital city was under siege. Camps of armed Confederates lined the Potomac, opposite the federal-held shore.

Even so, Wilkes found the city in a mood of elation. It seemed incredible to him that such a difference in attitudes of people could prevail as he saw in that of Washington and Richmond. War had not come in reality to the people of the city except as a sense of excitement, almost of merriment. In the face of a constantly threatening enemy fire, families actually made a holiday of it. Packing picnic dinners, citizens of Washington, joined by sight-seeing members of Congress, traveled to the shores of the Potomac to sit and enjoy their food and the sight of the enemy across the water! Children waded and waved at the Confederate troopers. Men and women chatted casually about the enemy guns, pointing them out to each other.

Fortunately, though, the festive spirit extended to the theater and brought large crowds to see Wilkes. He took every advantage of it and made efforts to increase his popularity with every performance. Made welcome by Washington society, he shortly gained the confidence and friendship of many influential people of the city.

Among them was Senator John P. Hale, of New Hampshire, a man of strong personal convictions who was somewhat pained that he could not always support the ideas and programs put forth by the President of the United States. The increasing result was that Senator Hale was at odds with Abraham Lincoln. Yet between the two men there was a personal respect, probably because each recognized the strength of the other's character and the honesty in which he strove to effect his goals.

Wilkes met the Senator one evening an hour before curtain

time at Grover's Theater. The Senator appeared at the dressing room door in a state of perspiration from the frustrations he had endured in the past half hour. He held his hat in one hand and thrust the other out to Wilkes. His craggy face tried for a smile but it was a failure. "Mister Booth, I'm John Hale." He reached into a pocket and pulled out a card. "My identification, sir."

Wilkes eyed the card, bowed his head, and motioned the man into his room. "Senator Hale, I'm honored."

Then the door was closed, the Senator stood tall and ill-at-ease in the well-lit dressing room smelling of cologne and grease paint. Wilkes was in his dressing gown, his make-up only half-applied.

"No," said the Senator, declining Wilkes' offer of a chair, "I'll only be a moment. Mr. Booth, I'm hoping you can do me a favor, sir. If you can't, I'm lost." He reached into the hat he held and brought forth four theater tickets. "Damn it, man. I bought these for the Tuesday evening performance, but I thought they were good for any evening during the run of *The Marble Heart*. I have a house guest who is very important to me—a friend from New Hampshire. I've promised him an evening of seeing you perform. It seems he worshipped your father as a star, and he's most anxious to see you. Well, now, I want to use these tickets this evening and not Tuesday. Those muscle-heads out front who run this theater tell me they can't help me. Something about being sold out for this performance and tickets not being interchangeable."

"Well, that's true enough, sir. Why won't Tuesday do just as well?"

"Well, blast it all, Mister Booth, I told you. My friend is all important to me. And this evening at dinner when I mentioned that the President and Mrs. Lincoln are going to attend the performance tonight, well, he insisted he be allowed to come to the affair as well. Now what kind of a host, a friend—a Senator, if you please—am I, if I can't have these tickets changed from Tuesday to tonight?"

"And you say the President is coming this evening?"

"Yes, indeed—I thought you'd know. Well, I heard it in his office this afternoon. His secretary, Mr. Hay, I believe, came in to remind him of an early dinner in order that they could all attend the play."

"I'm sorry we didn't have some earlier notice of it. We'd have arranged one of the Shakespeare productions of which I understand he's very fond."

The Senator was impatient. "I'm sure he'll enjoy whatever is played, Mister Booth. But now, about my tickets?"

Wilkes carefully regarded the black-browed politician: Here, indeed, was a potential friend of power within the Union who could be useful in many ways.

"Senator Hale, it will be my pleasure to have you and your party as my guests this evening. You say there are only four?"

"Yes, just four of us."

"I always retain six tickets for my own use for just such occasions as this among my friends. You'll have excellent seats, sir. Just a moment now and I'll get the passes for you," Wilkes moved toward a chest of drawers.

The Senator was overwhelmed. "This is good of you, Mister Booth. I didn't expect to rob you of your own tickets, though. Are you certain you can do this?"

Wilkes had the passes out of a drawer and told the Senator: "Any time at all, sir. And I hope you have an enjoyable evening."

"I'm ever so grateful, Mister Booth," the Senator said, grasping the passes firmly. "If there's any way I can return this kindness, you'll call on me, of course."

"It's nothing, Senator Hale, nothing."

"Mister Booth, would you consider taking dinner at my home tomorrow? Just my family present. We'd be honored."

Wilkes thought of another long, dull Sunday in Washington when everything came to a boring halt, and most of all, thought of accelerating his friendship with the federal official. "That's most kind of you, Senator. I'll enjoy it very much."

"Fine, fine. You have my address on the card, Mister Booth. Say one o'clock?"

They shook hands at the door and the Senator hurried off to tell his family and his guest of the evening of his triumphs.

The lights of Grover's Theater were dimmed and the curtain was raised on a five-act play called *The Marble Heart*, or *The*

Sculptor's Dream. It had been a hit in Paris, and word had come from California that Edwin Booth, starring in it there, had won the city of San Francisco.

President Abraham Lincoln leaned forward in his seat to get a little light to shine on the printed program in his hands. The gas lamps in the theater were too low now for him to be able to read the fine printing but he was able to see that the separate acts were set in "The Dream Scene," "The Artist's Retreat," "A Sculptor's Studio in Paris," "Drawing Room in a Villa," and "The Sculptor's Studio."

"Don't strain your eyes, Mister Lincoln," his wife, Mary, said, taking the program away from him.

John Wilkes Booth, in formal evening attire, came from behind the curtains, bowed, and said: "We're honored, Mister President. And we hope you'll find some enjoyment here this evening."

The audience stood, looked to the President, and applauded. Senator Hale and his party, close to the stage, were most enthusiastic in their applause. The President bowed his head in acknowledgement. With a toss of his hand, he indicated that the show go on.

At the end of the evening, going home to the White House, he told the First Lady: "The play was dull enough. But Booth is not."

What had originally been planned as a small and intimate Sunday dinner for an honored guest had quickly become a social event, an open-house affair. At times the receiving line stalled at the front door as beautifully clad women, escorted by equally fashionable men, took their turns to clasp the hand of the stage star in formal introductions.

The Senator's wife, a slim, graying woman with a friendly smile, a quiet voice and manner, was amazed but hospitable as they found friend after friend at their door that afternoon. "I'm sorry, sir," the Senator apologized, as they stood together in the line of welcome, pitching his voice low so others could not hear. "I had no idea all this would happen. I really aimed to give you a home-cooked meal with my family, a quiet time. But you see, word of your visit has gone out and here we are."

"Don't worry about it, sir. I'm pleased to meet your friends."

He broke off talking and looked—as did everyone else—at the doorway. There stood a beautiful young woman of eighteen years, holding a riding crop in one hand. A riding habit of forest green fitted her slight but feminine figure as well as the glove did her hand. She wore her long blonde hair swept back off her wide forehead and held by a broad velvet ribbon of green. The hair swung as she walked, and her small booted feet made deep impressions in the thick rug of the room. As she approached the receiving line, coming to her parents, Wilkes saw that her eyes were bright blue, innocent, and somewhat bewildered and that she had very black eyelashes, long and curved. Her face had the shine of health, and he saw that she had inherited her broad cheekbones from her father.

She ignored Wilkes and gave her whole attention to her parents, taking her mother's hand in hers even while she gave her father a hug. Those in the receiving line smiled and waited patiently while she spoke to her parents as though no one overheard her at all.

"I'm sorry, Dad. I simply forgot what time it was. It was such a beautiful day and we were all enjoying the ride so much, well—I am sorry." She gave a smile to Wilkes and glanced around the room. "I didn't know it was going to be a party——"

"Now, look here——" the Senator was irritated.

"Elizabeth," said her mother, "please do dress in a hurry. I want you here, darling."

"Girl," complained the Senator, "you're covered with horse hairs and you reek of the great out-of-doors. That outfit belongs in a stable."

"I'll be down in a jiffy," she said, interrupting him. Rising on her toes to give him a kiss on the cheek, and with a final flash of her blue eyes in the direction of Wilkes, she hurried from the room, blowing a kiss to a couple who were just arriving.

The Senator said to Wilkes: "I love that girl, but I'm damned if she isn't a contrary one. I don't think she's ever going to grow up."

"She's beautiful, sir."

The Senator gave Wilkes a sharp look. "Yes, yes, you're right. Still she's only eighteen."

When Elizabeth Hale reappeared some time later, many of the drop-in guests who had come to meet the idol of the theater were departed. The drawing room with its high ceiling and its heavy furniture was clearing out. Her parents were at the front door bidding farewell to several groups of friends, and she found Wilkes giving a parting handshake to an elderly couple.

She gave them her hand in greeting and good-bye, realizing they were the last of the visitors to leave.

She went to Wilkes, who was still standing beside a table where the receiving line had ended. Her hair was still worn loose, but now she held its length with a band of tiny white flowers, and she was gowned in a white dress whose ruffles were ever so delicately interspersed with scarlet ribbons. "We don't need to be introduced, do we?" she held out her hand to Wilkes. "I know you're John Wilkes Booth and you've probably already guessed that I'm Elizabeth Hale. May I ask, do you like to ride, Mister Booth?"

"I love to."

"I like to ride out the Military Road. Have you tried that?" she asked.

"No, as a matter of fact, I've had little chance lately to be on a horse. I'd like nothing more than to do just that, though. Do you suppose we might, later this week, say Monday?"

"That's tomorrow," she told him.

"I know," he replied, still holding her hand.

"Yes, then, Monday," she agreed, withdrawing her hand. "I keep my horse at Merriweather's City Stable. Do you have one, or shall we select you a mount there?"

"I'll need to hire one."

"All right," she assured him, "I know just the one for you. Fast. We'll want to race. I'll meet you at the stable at one o'clock."

"Oh, no, that's much too late. I've got the theater on my hands. I was thinking of the morning——"

"Oh? Perhaps ten?"

"I'm sorry, Elizabeth, even that's late. No, I was thinking of eight o'clock. We could have a ten o'clock breakfast when we get back. Is that too early?"

"No, no it isn't. All right, Wilkes, eight o'clock at the stable."

The parents stepped back in the room. "Have you two introduced yourselves?" the Senator asked.

"Yes, sir, we have." smiled Wilkes.

"We're engaged——", said Elizabeth, putting her hand on Wilkes'.

"You're what?" the Senator gasped. "Elizabeth!"

Elizabeth laughed. "We're engaged to go riding tomorrow morning. At eight."

"You see," said her father to Wilkes, "she's a lot of growing up to do."

"Oh, Dad!" Elizabeth retorted. "We're just going for a ride. We're not eloping."

"Well, all right. But don't speak lightly of engagements, you hear? Your old daddy takes that kind of talk pretty seriously."

"John, don't fuss so over nothing at all," Mrs. Hale scolded.

Elizabeth smiled at her father. "If I ever have one, I'll hang on to it. And I'll let you know, first of anyone."

Twenty-Two

Wilkes had every reason to be delighted with Elizabeth Hale— here was a beautiful young woman of social and political standing in Washington. Surely being her husband would be a stroke of good luck for any man, but think what it would mean to an agent of the Confederacy! As son-in-law to Senator John P. Hale of New Hampshire, a man could move quite freely in Washington and observe and inform himself immeasurably about the military plans of the Union.

Wilkes looked at the girl and he knew what he would do. Wilkes played the game of courtship well—in the two weeks following their first meeting, he and Elizabeth were constant companions as he escorted her to Washington parties and activities that he was glad to be included in through her. He liked Elizabeth very much but was a little concerned to discover that her father had been quite correct in saying that she had a lot of growing up to do. Upon closer association, there was a definite childlike streak in her personality which puzzled him. He had never found a single woman who had ever really evoked an emotional response in him; therefore, a marriage with an adorable girl who was obviously infatuated with him, could hardly be a bad thing. In the meantime, she would afford him the one thing he needed—an entreé to official Washington.

When they were quite alone, on another horseback ride out the Military Road, he suggested a rest under a windbreak of tall trees and when she dismounted into his arms, as usual, he held her close, saying nothing, but gazing very soberly into her eyes.

The wind blew her hair and a silky length of it brushed his face. Leaning down to kiss her gently, he was nagged by the feeling that this woman in his arms was but a child.

Elizabeth surprised him, though. When he took his lips away, she gazed at him for just a moment, and then pulled his head down to give him her lips again in a kiss not quite so gentle. When he could, he asked her to marry him.

She did not answer right away but took him by the hand and led him to a fallen tree trunk where she sat down, still holding his hand. The wind was whipping her hair around again and the color of her face was very pink. "I'll marry you," she said, smiling. "But you haven't said you love me."

He kissed her gloved hand. "You're everything to me."

She put her free hand on his dark hair, twining a curl around a finger. "Well, I love you," she said frankly, as she initiated the next kiss.

"I'll have to speak to your father, won't I?" he asked, locking her fingers within his own, her head resting against his shoulder.

"Yes . . . Wilkes, Daddy's got some real set ideas. He won't like my getting married at eighteen. I'm afraid he'll ask us to count on a long-term engagement."

"Well, I know your family must observe certain social proprieties. But I hope it won't be an overlong proposition." He kissed her neck. "I want my bride."

That evening he was closeted with the Senator in the Hale

116

library. Seated in matching chairs in front of the fireplace, drinks in hand, Wilkes stated his business. The host left his chair and stood at the fireplace, gazing down at his visitor.

"Damn it, Wilkes," he said. "I thought sure you were here to ask for Elizabeth, and I thought I was prepared for it. But it's hit me here," he said, slapping his ample middle. "I guess a father never really wants any man to walk off with his daughter, no matter what," he laughed. "Well, now, that's damned ridiculous of me. I'm proud it's you, Wilkes, very proud. Of course you have my blessings! But look, son, this courtship has been mighty fast, and my girl is very young. And well, you know how every feminine heart beats at the sight of you, or so I've heard it said."

"Well, sir, don't worry. There'll be no elopement, no rushing of her. I give you my promise on that, sir."

The Senator's hand came down hard on Wilkes' shoulder. "Then I guess you and I will leave the rest of it up to Elizabeth and her mother. Let's join the ladies and we'll have a champagne toast all around."

Wilkes left the Hale home a few hours later, a little dizzy from too many drinks with the Senator, his lips still warm from the kiss Elizabeth had given him at the door. He was grateful for the night air's coolness on his hot face, glad to be walking alone in the dark. Wilkes did not feel like a man in love, but like a general who had just planned a battle, fought it, and won.

At the first bar, Wilkes went in for one more drink.

ᔕ

When it was announced that John Wilkes Booth was the prospective son-in-law of Senator John Hale, he was immediately included on exclusive guest lists in high places. Posters of him appeared everywhere, even in shop windows, as his plays were advertised. He was the darling of society now as well as of the theater.

There were many young women in the city who had not yet met John Wilkes Booth, but one of them, at least, had no desire whatsoever to do so. Ella Starr of Virginia, an actress whose own career was still confined to minor supporting roles, had only contempt for Booth: Although he claimed to be a Virginian by choice, he was wearing no uniform, carrying no gun, but merely living a frivolous life amid high society. And, she supposed, he was no doubt a second-rate actor.

The announcement of Wilkes' engagement to the daughter of Senator Hale of New Hampshire galled Ella all the more. How could any Southerner consider marriage to a Yankee? She did not bother to go see him perform simply because she did not want to look upon a Virginian who held no enduring loyalty for his land and his people.

One evening, however, she was a member of a theater party, and did not care to decline just to avoid seeing Booth. Ella came easily by such invitations. Her perfectly formed body did not stand three inches over five feet, and the full effect of the woman was eye-catching. She looked at the world through heavily lashed violet-colored eyes, and her full lips, even in repose, tended to an uplift of the corners, a smile lying in wait. Ella's dark hair was brushed into a shining smooth chignon which was highlighted with pearls. This evening she wore a black evening gown and a tiny strand of pearls around her neck to match those entwined in her hair. She sat beside her escort, Asa Naughton, a doctor on the staff of the Soldier's Home, and masked her dissatisfaction with the evening's entertainment with a brilliant smile.

As the theater darkened, she said to the doctor, "If I swoon when Wilkes Booth comes on stage, will you revive me?"

From the moment the actor appeared, her gaze was fixed on him. Never had she been so lost in the performance of any actor. When the play was ended, Ella rose with the rest of the audience and applauded. But even as she clapped her hands for him, she was swept by personal animosity; as he bowed and bowed again, smiling, she wondered how any man could be so conceited. No one else, she decided, needed to praise his worth. Ego was so much a part of him he couldn't put it aside even when he played *Macbeth*.

In fact, she realized, ego was the thing which made his portrayal so extraordinary. Booth skillfully twisted the real with the unreal to the point where it did not seem that he was playing Macbeth but rather that the character of Macbeth, as Shakespeare had conceived it, was Booth's in real life. There was no quarreling with the tremendous triumph of the result.

But Booth's very ability riled her—he was too handsome, too talented, too adored.

Leaving the theater on the arm of Doctor Naughton, Ella was determined never to see Wilkes Booth again. She knew she had never been so annoyed and yet so thrilled by any performance.

At home she found it difficult to relax and to sleep.

Though she appeared in a play at Grover's Theater for the next several weeks, she returned to her resolve to boycott Booth. Her time was divided between her stage work and long hours of service as a volunteer at the federal hospital on the outskirts of Washington. Increasing numbers of wounded and sick and dying were now being brought to Washington from surrounding areas of battle; there were many Confederates too, toted in from the battlefields. Northern hospitals like this one had a tremendous advantage, while the South was suffering a terrible lack of surgeons' tools and morphine and opium, the federal hospitals had ample supplies of everything. Ella spent as much time tending to the Confederates as she could, but dared not reveal her political feelings too obviously.

She had little enough time to think of the actor. But when she did have fleeting thoughts of Wilkes Booth, it was only to wonder why he should be free of the duties and sufferings which were falling on the real men, both North and South. He could playact a hero beautifully, but he was leaving the actual task to better men.

One inclement night when the wind and the rain were heavy, Ella was on her way home from the hospital in her own carriage, driven by her black employee, big-physiqued, big-hearted, Otto. Otto and his wife, Jane, were Ella Starr's only servants. They had accompanied her from her family's home in Virginia where they too had been born, and their loyalty to her was a continuing comfort. Ella was secure that Otto would get her safely home through the wet streets of Washington, and that when she arrived home Jane would have a hot meal ready for her and her bed warmed with coals.

As the carriage passed the Kirkwood House, where the Hales kept permanent rooms, the rain came down in a sudden downpour, almost blinding Otto up on the driver's seat. He pulled the carriage over to the curb to get his bearings.

Ella looked out at the shimmering lights of the hotel just

119

beyond and saw a man, coat collar up, hat well down over his face, dash from the hotel lobby toward her own carriage. He signaled to Otto to wait at the curb a moment. He shouted something, but she could not understand his words due to the noise of the rain beating on the top of the rig. Before she knew what he was doing, he opened the door, leaped into the carriage, and slid over on the seat beside her, spattering her with rain.

"Look here!" she protested angrily. "This isn't a public carriage. You're intruding, sir!"

Unabashed, he removed his hat. His dark hair was curled in regular childish ringlets, as some men's does in wet or hot weather. His dark eyes looked upon her in surprise, and she stared back. Her unwanted passenger was John Wilkes Booth.

"Ma'm," he said, "I want to ride only a few blocks to my rooms in the National Hotel." He looked out at the street where the raindrops were bursting on the cobblestones. "It's awfully wet out there and there are no other carriages abroad."

Otto, rainsoaked, looked down through the little window and asked: "Miss Ella? Am I drivin' the gent'man somewheres?"

Ella hesitated, then gave in. "Yes, Otto. The National Hotel, please."

"Yes, Miss Ella."

She turned to look at Wilkes. "Mr. Booth, are you always so impulsive?"

His smile was bright, the rain glistened in his hair. "You know me!"

"I should. Your face is plastered on walls from one end of this city to the other. Besides, I'm an actress myself and I'm aware of what most American stars look like. You would be difficult to mistake."

"You have the advantage. Since you're an actress, I should be able to return the compliment of recognition. But I'm sorry, very, very, sorry, I've never seen you before."

She gave him a haughty stare and turned her profile to the window. The carriage already had reached the corner opposite his hotel. "This is as far as you go, Mr. Booth. Goodnight."

Otto pulled the horse curbward, but Wilkes made no move to leave. "Your name?"

"National Hotel, sir." Otto announced opening the carriage

door. "You best leap for it. It ain't rainin' quite as hard as it was."

Wilkes was leaning forward on the seat but gave Otto only a nod. "Won't you tell me your name? Please."

It seemed the only way to get him out of the carriage. "I'm Ella Starr."

"It's a beautiful name." Otto held the door open for him, and once outside he gave her a bow and took off his hat, oblivious of the rain soaking him. Then he was gone into the dark night.

At the hotel desk, Wilkes made a casual inquiry of the night clerk. "Charles, have you ever heard of an actress named Ella Starr?"

The thin-haired man leaned his elbows on the counter and shoved his face closer to speak in the confidential way which he obviously relished. "Oh, certainly, Mr. Booth! Miss Ella's well known in Washington. Really quite among the—famous."

Wilkes was offended by the clerk's manner, but his determination made him tolerant. "Strange, I never heard of her until this evening."

The clerk was smug. "Well, surely you've heard of Nellie Dudall?"

"Of course, who hasn't?" Wilkes expression showed a flicker of surprise. "What has Nellie Dudall to do with Ella Starr?"

"Why, she's her sister! And you know Nellie Dudall operates *the* house of Washington. They say the clientle is practically the official guest list of Washington society. Her *sister*, mind you."

Wilkes felt a chill sweep his body. He picked up his key. He had better get to his room and get some dry clothing.

"Do you know the lady, Mr. Booth?"

"What *lady*, Charles? What lady?"

As he undressed, Wilkes' contempt for Ella Starr gave way to curiosity. What if he were to surprise her and appear at Nellie's the next evening and ask for the pleasure of the haughty Ella's company? Miss Starr was a good actress all right. Her air of innocence, of dignity, of sweetness! Damned if he wouldn't find out a few answers!

Surrounded by pine trees, Nellie Dudall's establishment was set far back on a spacious well-groomed lawn which extended to the sidewalks of Pennsylvania Avenue. Constructed in the days following the War of 1812, the huge residential structure looked like a typical Virginia plantation painted gray, with shining white shutters at all the wide windows.

The evening Wilkes visited, the place was sparkling with the lights of candles and lamps, adrift with the sound of music and laughter. Wilkes dismissed the public carriage which had brought him to the front door; when the time came, he would walk back to his room at the National Hotel.

Gazing at the house, he found it difficult to reconcile its appearance with its reputation. Not just any man in Washington was admitted to the Dudall house. It was operated exactly like a private club by Nellie and her husband. Their policy was that anyone of wealth and influence could gratify his any desire and mood—from the all-night company of a beautiful woman to complete solitude. The famous and the infamous came there for relaxation, passion, gambling—anything or everything. The prices were high, but no one ever complained.

Wilkes banged the gold knocker on the front door. A Negro maid in a white uniform opened the door. "Yes, sir?"

Wilkes cleared his throat, turned his hat nervously in his fingers, uncertain now that the house's warmth, perfumed air, music and laughter, were for him. "I'm calling on Miss Starr." He reached into his coat pocket and brought forth a white card. "Kindly take this to her."

The maid hesitated, took the card, and then bade him enter. The stories Wilkes had heard were not exaggerated. It was a charming place, if the reception hall—richly furnished with a hand-carved table, a glistening framed mirror, and two rose colored chairs—was representative of the entire house. White roses were freshly fragrant in a silver bowl on the table, and a candelabra with white tapers glowing provided the only light in the room.

"Please wait here, sir." The maid hurried up the staircase which spiraled from the reception hall. He began to pace the room, though, wondering if he really wanted to see Ella Starr at all if he had to see her here.

He started for the door, when down the stairs came a middle-aged blonde gowned in black satin and diamonds. Her smooth hair was expertly arranged to offset her patrician profile, and the numerous peticoats she wore under the satin gown gave a purr of a sound as she walked. She held his card in her hands.

"Mister Booth?"

"At your service," he looked past her to the dark-skinned maid who stood now at the foot of the stairs, keeping a discreet distance. "But I asked to see Miss Starr."

"I know. I'm her sister. I'm Nellie Dudall."

Wilkes bowed.

"Mister Booth," she said with a touch of archness, "Surely you didn't honestly expect to find Ella here, in this house?"

"Well, she's your sister," Wilkes blurted.

"Exactly," said Nellie. "My sister—not a paid girl in this house. Mister Booth, do you know Ella at all? Why would you believe that you'd find her here?"

Wilkes was contrite: "I've made a stupid mistake, that's all, Mrs. Dudall. I met your sister briefly the other evening. I learned her name, but failed to obtain her address. I wanted to see her again, and that's all there is to it. I've an apology to make to her now."

"Indeed you do."

"Would you give me her address?"

"Well, now, I'm not sure I ought to do that."

"Well, if you don't feel you should, she told me she's an actress. I'll find her through the theater."

"You don't have to do that, Mister Booth," Nellie smiled. "Ella's home is on a private road called Bay Bend. There's a road sign posted on it, right off Military Road. You'll have no trouble finding it. A small cottage, in a forest of trees."

✎

On a couch in front of the fireplace, Ella Starr nibbled on cookies and sipped hot coffee which Jane had brought her. She tilted the book on her lap toward the oil lamp so that she could read, but her attention wandered. She found she had read an entire page without really concentrating on it.

The house was quiet, as she liked it, the crackling of the fire the only sound in her self-imposed isolation. So when the

wheels of an approaching carriage sounded on the gravel driveway, she heard it with surprise. Well, she was not home to
anyone this late in the evening.

A knock on the door brought Jane from the kitchen. In a
moment Ella heard her protest: "But, Miss Starr just ain't home
this evenin', sir, not to no one."

The Southern accent caught Ella's attention. "Oh, I'll only be
a moment," he said. "You needn't worry."

She looked up to see John Wilkes Booth standing in the living
room doorway, hat in hand. "Good evening, Ella."

He crossed the room in long strides to take a place in front of
the fireplace.

"You've a very bad habit of barging in where you're neither
invited nor wanted." Reddish spots flamed in her cheeks.

Otto was at the door. "You need me here, Miss Ella? Jane
thought you might."

Ella hesitated. "Yes, Otto. Will you bring us fresh coffee?
And take Mister Booth's hat and coat, please."

Otto accepted the orders with a nod of his big head.

Wilkes smiled again. "I was afraid you were going to have me
thrown out."

"I may yet." She smiled back and took a place on the couch.

"I owe you something of an apology, Ella. I went looking for
you this evening at Nellie Dudall's house."

She frowned. "You believed—you didn't! Do you mean you
thought that I was a prostitute?"

"Well, I was told you were her sister, and it seemed a logical
conclusion. I'm sorry."

The smile on her lips changed into a little laugh.

Jane, her fifty-year-old face catching a trace of their mirth,
wheeled a buffet cart in with coffee and plates of cheese, cakes,
and fruit.

Both of them grew more at ease, and their conversation
drifted many ways. Ella learned that Wilkes was a rebel in view,
if not in action; he, that she was a Virginian whose heart would
always be with the Confederacy. Finally she broached the
question she had long wanted to ask him: "Mister Booth, if you
feel so deeply for the South, why don't you fight for it?"

"Oh, I do, in my own way."

124

She was rankled by his evasion, and a slow-rising contempt crept into her words. "When she's at war, there's only one way a man fights for his country. He goes to the battlefield. Of course," she added coldly, "if a man is to become a son-in-law to a United States Senator, it would be awkward for him to fight for the South. Now, wouldn't it?"

"Ella," his voice had an edge on it, too, "you don't understand——"

"No, Mr. Booth?" she said, smiling sweetly. "Well, perhaps I do. I'm told Miss Hale is very beautiful. I'm sure you'll make a perfect match—but tell me, what will she say when you tell her you spent an evening with an actress?"

"Why——"

"Is she the jealous type?"

"Are you?"

Ella arose. "It's very late, Mister Booth. Do you have a carriage outside, or shall Otto drive you to your hotel?"

"I have a carriage, thanks."

At the door he drew on his gloves and commented, "You're the most beautiful woman I've ever seen."

"Well, that's a very generous compliment."

"I mean it."

She took a step back from him. "Goodnight, Mister Booth."

"May I call on you tomorrow evening, Ella?"

Shaking her head, she moved past him to open the door, and he moved toward it reluctantly. "I'm sure Miss Hale must have other plans for you," she said.

He took her hand and kissed it.

"All right," he said. "I'll go. But I'd like to come back."

She withdrew her hand from his. "No."

"I'm not married yet——"

"You misunderstand my reason for not wanting to see you again, Mister Booth. Oh, it's partly that I don't see engaged or married men, but mostly, I don't want to see you again because I think you're a coward and a traitor. Is that clear?"

If she had slapped him he would not have been more shocked.

He turned away from her and walked out toward the driveway and his waiting carriage.

Twenty-Three

Unlocking the door to his room Wilkes stepped into its gaslit snugness and stood quite motionless. In the wing chair directly opposite the door sat a stranger in a dark cape and soft, brimmed hat worn down low over his forehead. The unexpected guest was posed with his hands openly displayed, one on each knee.

"Captain Booth," said the man in a low-pitched young voice, "Don't be alarmed. I'm Lieutenant Chad Barrows: Montreal."

"Richmond," Wilkes replied quickly.

"May I stand, sir?"

"Yes, yes, of course." Wilkes came forward to take Barrow's hand. "It seems to me I've waited a long time to hear from you, Lieutenant. You have my assignment?"

"Yes, sir." The Lieutenant motioned toward the door Booth had just opened. "First, though, Captain, may I make a suggestion?"

"One that is not necessary, Lieutenant. When I came in that door and found you here, I realized that I've been a fool to trust in the ordinary lock of a hotel door. I'll practice better security hereafter."

"In our work, Captain, we have to look to these things constantly," Barrow said. "I could have approached you publicly, but since we don't know who observes us at all times, it is best to meet as privately as possible."

"Agreed. And now, Lieutenant, my assignment?"

"First, by order of the President of the Confederate States of America, I inform you that you are secretly but officially enlisted in the army of the Confederacy with rank of Captain."

"I am honored," said Wilkes.

"You are to understand, however, that your work will be secret and cannot be recognized publicly by the Confederate

126

government. You will be operating without uniform. In case of your capture, you stand at your own peril. No one will be able to help you."

"I understand."

"As far as my instructions to you are concerned, Captain, your assignment is simple enough. You are to report at the Richmond House, Chicago, to Colonel Vallandigham who will give you further orders. You must see him within two weeks."

Wilkes was pacing, his hand rubbing his neck, pondering the order. Then, excited, he whirled to the Lieutenant. "Chicago. Two weeks. That fits! No problems at all. I'll beg off my stage run here by a week, then I'll accept the invitation of the city of Chicago to participate in the Booth Festival they're planning. I was hedging on it, leaving it to Edwin, but it comes in well for us now."

"That's fine, then." The Lieutenant dug his hand into his pocket and pulled out a note and studied it a moment. "Now, there's one more important bit of information Richmond wants you to work with as much as you can, whenever you can."

"What's that?"

"You will assist one of our agents with her work of diverting medical supplies from Washington hospitals to Richmond. In particular, you and she will endeavor to keep a flow of drugs running between the two cities. There's a real need for them in our field hospitals, and the work of obtaining them must receive all the time and attention you can give it."

"Certainly. And the agent is a woman? Where do I find her?"

"Her name is Ella Starr. She lives——" Barrow caught the expression on Wilkes' face. "You know her?"

"Yes, I met her a few days ago. I had no idea——"

"No one knows, of course, who shouldn't. Miss Starr is a very valuable woman who is channeling medical supplies from the military hospital with great efficiency. But she's going to need help from time to time. That's part of your assignment."

"An intriguing job, Lieutenant," Wilkes smiled.

"And a dangerous one," the Lieutenant said soberly.

"Couldn't a man handle the thing in the hospital? No woman ought——"

"This woman is doing a great job."

"No doubt. She's an actress, too, you know."

127

"I believe so." The Lieutenant moved toward the door. "If you have no further questions, Captain, I'll be on my way."

"None, Lieutenant." He took the officer's hand in farewell. "You've made it clear."

"Good luck, sir."

The next morning Wilkes had an early breakfast, ordering food he only toyed with, but he drank several cups of hot coffee. It was the kind of bright sunny summer day which warms gently but never becomes hot. Wilkes walked briskly to Merriweather's stable where he hired a big black horse. The animal was ready for exercise, and once they were on the Military Road, Wilkes gave him head, and made a fast ride from the stable to Bay Bend. He hoped to be there before Ella could leave for the day.

Tying the horse to a post in the driveway, he started toward the walk to the front door, but was met by Otto coming around the corner of the house.

"Good morning, Otto," Wilkes greeted the large black man. "I must see Miss Starr at once."

The servant shook his head, his full round face graced with compassionate eyes. "I'm sorry, sir, but I'm to tell you that Miss Starr is not expecting to see you any more."

Wilkes hesitated. "Will you kindly let her know I'm here? Tell her it's very urgent business which has brought me here and not personal at all."

"I expect I can tell her that."

Wilkes waited there on the brick walk of her home, gazing at the small house and at its flowered yard. He stopped to pluck a yellow flower and was reminded of the fields of Bel Air and the way he and his sister Asia loved to lie flat on their backs and gaze up at the blue sky. This little country home with its deep roof and colorful blue shutters was, in a way, a small version of Tudor Hall.

Otto reappeared in the doorway, smiling and bowing his head. "Yes, sir, Mister Booth. Miss Ella says you come on in at once. This way, sir."

She was standing at the table in the sitting room, a cup of coffee cradled in her hands, dressed for her work at the hospital. A simple white dress with tiny pearly buttons from the throat line down to her toes, was matched with a gray and

128

white cape. A gray bonnet with white trim covered her head.

"Mister Booth. You spoke of urgent business."

"We won't be interrupted for just a few minutes?"

"Oh, we're quite alone. Otto will come though," she warned, "if I ring for him."

"Are you on your way to the hospital?"

"Obviously——"

"Exactly how do you manage to transmit hospital supplies to Richmond?"

She carefully placed the coffee cup on the table and stared up at him. "What do you mean?" she evaded. Relishing the moment, Wilkes explained what had happened after he left her the night before.

"I'm to assist you in any way I can." He reached down and took her small hands in his. "Never mind about the things you called me. You just couldn't know. I'm going to help you all I can," he repeated, "but I'm under assignment to go to Chicago. I'll be leaving within a few days. I'll write you."

She pulled her hands from his. "Miss Hale might not like that."

He stood a moment, uncertain, and then he went toward the door.

She stood and watched him go. The morning light cast a glow upon a bowl of pink flowers on the table. When he reached the doorway, she could no longer bear it. Her voice trembled in the air when she called: "Wilkes!"

Ella ran to him, and he held her in a long embrace. Neither of them remembered Elizabeth Hale.

Twenty-Four

Wilkes left Washington ostensibly to appear at the Booth Festival in Chicago. He dropped Elizabeth Hale a note, speaking of his love for her and pleading he had not received enough notice of his trip to stop for a personal good-bye.

Chicago, an important base of operation for the Confederate underground, was reaping the bitterness engendered there during the rough Republican Party Convention that had nominated Abraham Lincoln to the Presidency. Wilkes took a room at an inconspicuous hotel called Fort Dearborn on Lakeside Avenue, not far from the Richmond House. He dressed carefully in a nondescript suit and topcoat, not wanting to draw attention to himself. He was eager to meet Congressman Clement Vallandigham. The man was a storm center for Lincoln these days, and as such he had already won Wilkes' regard.

Wilkes was the last of the Knights to arrive at the Richmond House for the meeting of the Chicago Castle. When he gave the doorkeeper the password, "Montreal," he was escorted to a room of the Vallandigham suite where, behind a closed door, six Knights were seated around a table.

The fumes from a malfunctioning oil lamp made Wilkes choke a bit as he moved to a take a seat. One of the men tried to dim the lamp to a steady glow, but it continued to flare. "Damned thing," he muttered.

Colonel Vallandigham's greeting was like a rumble. "Sit down, Captain."

Wilkes took the vacant chair next to Vallandigham.

Colonel Vallandigham was a character worthy of a stage setting, his large frame fitting the booming voice. He had long dark hair and a beard. Wilkes knew him to be the nation's most notorious Copperhead, the name widely used to describe persons within the Union borders who were known Confederate

130

sympathizers. Vallandigham boasted that he was the top agitat-
or in the United States and deliberately made speeches designed
to infuriate the Northern authorities and to cast doubt into the
Yankees' minds about the righteousness of their cause.

Constantly threatened with arrest, he challenged the federal
agents to make good their threats. His arrest, he shouted, would
prove that the United States, under Abe Lincoln, was suppress-
ing all constitutional liberties, even including the right of the
people to assemble and speak freely.

The Colonel was terse. "You men all know our friend here is
John Wilkes Booth. Now, Captain Booth, you listen to me sharp
and you'll catch the names of these men." The man on Wilkes'
left was Colonel St. Leger Grenfel, formerly of Great Britain
and one of the world's true adventurers, a soldier of fortune,
going wherever the battle was, or wherever he found a cause
which he recognized as his. He was giving Wilkes a sharp-eyed
study.

There were Charles Walsh of Chicago; Jacob Thompson of
Richmond; and Captain John Headley and Colonel Robert
Martin of the Confederacy.

Walsh, Wilkes learned later, was the leader of the Sons of
Liberty, the organization which was to consolidate the Knights
and the Copperheads of Chicago, and all the other pro-Southern
splinter groups into one immense army which could actually be
called into semi-military service to support the regular Confederate army when the time came.

The man with whom Wilkes would work most closely was
Jacob Thompson, a handsome, dignified, former Washington
official who was a personal friend of Jefferson Davis. Under
President Davis' orders, Thompson had already established
headquarters in Montreal, Canada, for the underground work of
the Confederacy. Rumors of the headquarters were already
spreading within the Union, and it was already being referred to
as "Davis's Canadian Cabinet."

Colonel Robert Martin, one of the famed "Morgan Riders,"
was lean-jawed, black-haired, serious-eyed and close-mouthed.
He was at the meeting in Chicago upon the personal recommen-
dation of the Confederate hero Morgan himself.

Captain John Headley had the reputation of being a man who
fully devoted himself to any task he was assigned. Wilkes

thought the officer looked like a man to whom another could trust his life.

Wilkes was aware they were measuring him and seeing him as an actor of the stage. He hoped in due time they would see him as a soldier, as one of them.

The introductions made, Vallandigham lit a cigar and puffed on it, his cheeks drawing in and out. "First off, I want to be sure we all understand exactly what we're aiming to do. Just to keep our purposes clear, I'll state them simply: We are going to recruit Southern sympathizers of the North into the Confederate armed services. We're going to work at all times at freeing all Confederates held in prisons in the North. We're going to obstruct the recruitment of men into the Union army. And we're going to conspire in every way we can to bring England into the war on the side of the Confederacy. Is that understood and agreed to?"

The men nodded, their faces lit with interest and respectful silence. The mere idea of it fired them with enthusiasm, Vallandigham noted.

"All right, now for specific assignments. We'll start with you, Jacob."

Jacob Thompson would return at once to Montreal and then go on to Toronto where he would establish another headquarters. The Toronto location would be the main point of contact for all the men at the meeting in Chicago. Thompson's office would direct sabotage, infiltration, and spying; he would handle propaganda against the war—a highly important part of his job. Both Montreal and Toronto headquarters would be places of refuge for escaped Confederates.

"Let me emphasize, Jacob,"—the Colonel leaned forward on the table, his cigar pointing at Thompson—"that freeing our prisoners is going to be our toughest work, and maybe the most necessary. We can't afford to have our soldiers locked up in Union prisons. Every one of them must be returned to the battlefields as soon as we can do it."

"I assume we'll have the active cooperation of the Confederate authorities? I'll be needing money and ships, Colonel."

"And you'll have both. Ships will be sent to Canada and held there until you have full loads of liberated Confederates, at which time they'll sail for Richmond. You'll have the money needed to bribe guards in Union prisons and to bring men to Canada."

"The details of my work will be given me in Montreal?" Jacob Thompson wanted to be certain.

"Yes. But I'll add now that you're to place your headquarters and yourself at the disposal of all these men here today. If it becomes necessary, God forbid, you'll give any or all of them sanctuary in Canada and provide them with whatever they may need to return safely to Richmond."

"It's my pledge, Colonel."

Vallandigham nodded and turned to Colonel Martin and Captain Headley. "You two will work as a team for the time being. You'll go to St. Louis, Missouri, to recruit, organize, and outfit into one fighting unit the bands of men who are roving there as snipers and guerrillas. They're pretty wild men, but rounded up from the hills, united and properly controlled, they can become a most effective military organization."

Colonel Martin whistled. "Sir, they're straight out of hell, terrorizing Missouri. Causing the Union a pack of trouble."

"Exactly. But we've got to harness their efforts. Funds will be available to you through your contact in St. Louis. The contact will be made with you at your hotel. I'll have your sealed orders on your assignment, with all necessary instructions, in your hands by dawn. You'll leave tomorrow."

Colonel Martin nodded. "Yes, sir," Captain Headley said.

St. Leger Grenfel was next to receive his general orders. His duty would take him on a tour of the Midwest and the Great Lakes area, in particular, to scout the Union prisons and camps. He was instructed to note their strength and their weaknesses, ascertain the number of men under arms at each place, the condition of the prisons and the men, the supplies available and their sources, and every other detail of military importance; and then report to Thompson in Canada.

At the end of Vallandigham's recital Grenfel asked coolly, "And is there a suggestion as to how I may approach these camp areas, these prisons, without getting myself arrested?"

The Colonel smiled slightly. "As a matter of fact, yes, we've got a suggestion. Your reputation as a hunter and as a wanderer of the world is well known, even in the Midwest. So, you'll be able to shoulder a rifle and take to the fields with no questions asked, and roam where you will. Even if the Union authorities should come upon you in the field, they're just a bit leery of incurring the wrath of any Britisher at this time."

Colonel Grenfel smiled. "But if I have any trouble, I'll know what to do. Right?"

"I'm sure we can trust your superb intelligence, sir."

Charles Walsh was told he would operate in the Midwest in direct cooperation with Colonel Grenfel, assisting him in matters where he was needed. Walsh was to assist the entire program as he traveled with Colonel Grenfel, with special attention given to recruiting sympathizers and directing them to the proper headquarters.

Vallandigham let his gaze fall at last on Wilkes. It was obvious he was doing some mental weighing of the man. Then he shifted his big body in the chair and surprised everyone by talking about himself and his own duty.

"My own job in all this must end in a seeming failure. If I'm successful, I'll be incarcerated in a federal prison. I aim to keep talking, heckling, sabotaging the very devil out of the Union war effort. I'll travel the Midwest and tell the folks they've lost their constitutional liberties. The louder I talk, the more I lambaste Lincoln, the better results for us. I'm going to make the issue *peace*. I'm going to be a martyr. I'm going to scream about the loss of our freedom to speak, to assemble, to petition our government. I'm going to cry about slaying our brethren. I'm going to beg the boys not to go to war against their loving brothers. I'll ask them to let the South go in peace. And I'll be arrested. That's when the hue and cry for peace will rock the Union. There'll be some mighty impressive peace demonstrations on Old Abe's hands then."

He stroked his beard, his eyes bright, and he looked at Wilkes. "Captain Booth," he said, speaking slowly now, more quietly, as though he were a bit uncertain of his path, "you draw a most delicate duty not every man of us could carry off. Your particular position in life—your fame—is a reason for it." Vallandigham's voice seemed to fade out even before his words were finished. He leaned over the side of his chair to lift a small leather valise onto the table. Vallandigham kept both his big hands on it.

"Captain Booth, this bag holds twenty-five thousand dol-

134

lars." There was a little stir of comment around the table. "It was hard to come by. Colonel Martin and a few other Morgan men captured a Union-escorted Red River paymaster. This was a federal payroll for their troops. Men died over this money; it was that important to our cause. It's money which will now serve the Confederacy. You will keep these things in mind, Captain, when you take this bag into your custody."

"Yes, sir," Wilkes replied.

"You're to take it to New York City, and there spend it on the promotion of a people's peace movement. You alone will decide how to use this money to promote whatever plan you determine upon. But every penny of it must be spent in the cause of peace promotion, and every penny of it will be accountable to Jacob Thompson in Toronto. Do you understand?"

"Yes, sir, I understand." Wilkes was proud to have received an assignment which allowed him to depend upon his own initiative: It was an indication of the trust the South had in him.

Vallandigham rubbed the leather valise with his thumbs. "Captain Booth, I'm not asking for any details, of course, but at this moment, what plan occurs to you, if any?"

Wilkes believed his answer was very important. "Sir, after listening to you and learning of our general plans, I believe I'll consider mapping a propaganda plan through the newspapers of New York. You know I'm just speaking unformed thoughts at this time, but I think I'd want to locate a major newspaper in New York which will carry a peace movement plea to the people—an anti-military program if you please. At least it would be a beginning. And such a campaign could be used to stimulate public demonstrations."

"Excellent, Captain!" Vallandigham shoved the bag to a place in front of Wilkes. "Here. Buy yourself a newspaper and a demonstration or two. But I caution you, Captain. Where the men you buy are concerned, be absolutely certain of your enterprise. Don't forget the Union has underground workers, too. You can't be too careful."

"I'll have to stay in Chicago until the festival is over, since I'm an honored guest. But that will give me time to plan, anyhow."

"Don't resent the time taken by the festival, Captain," advised the Colonel. "The theater is the very reason you're so valuable to us. I believe I'll take a look at you on stage myself."

"I'd be honored, sir," said Wilkes.

Despite the sound of the applause, he was extremely anxious to get on to New York. But for a long week he had Chicago enraptured.

One evening became a memorable one to Wilkes. The shellback, open-air stage was set in the great park on the very edge of the shores of Lake Michigan. The festival flags were standing out sharply on the spanking lake breeze. Rows and rows of seats which stretched from the stage to the shadowed reaches of the park were filled with highly attentive people. Because there were more spectators than seats, however, many persons stood throughout the area or sat on the ground.

For the festival, Wilkes had selected highlights from the various roles he had appeared in. Wilkes was a master of the moods of audiences, and knew that they reacted tremendously to the unexpected. He planned his program this evening to play upon their moods through an acceleration of his act by means of constant change. His first appearance was as Richelieu in the "Curse of Rome" scene. Wilkes brought exclamations from the audience when he used the dramatic technique of seeming to grow in stature in front of their eyes. His feet hidden by the luxurious folds of the vivid scarlet robe of the Cardinal, he rose on his toes as the other members of the cast added to the illusion by slowly kneeling before him.

Wilkes performed his scenes in rapid succession, barely giving the audience time to applaud one act before he was engaged in the next.

The curtain was swung down on "Curse of Rome" and raised up again for *Romeo and Juliet* in record time for a change of scene and costume. Now, as Romeo, Wilkes startled the onlookers again. The unexpected color of his blond, close-cropped curly wig caught a ripple of comment. He wore a white velvet outfit, tight-fitting trousers, a long jeweled tunic, and a cape. He climbed the balcony with astounding agility, and received such loud and sustained applause that he had to wait there in mid-air before he could proceed with the lines.

136

Following the "Romeo" scene, he switched tempo again to appear as Hamlet, fencing so realistically with Laertes that some of the women in the audience covered their eyes lest they see blood drawn. When Hamlet, dying of a poisoned wound, fell onto the throne which was rightfully his and was crowned by Horatio, the audience was hushed as though it had witnessed a real death scene.

The next scene was from *Macbeth*. Wilkes drew his sword and threatened the Ghost of Banquo, chasing, stumbling, scared, helpless, lashing out at the nothingness. Macbeth's halting steps, taken in terror and frenzy, were executed with deceptive grace.

Wilkes saved his favorite scene for last, and he gave it his all. As Brutus in the orchard, he very quietly spoke the monologue before a candlelit garden table. The very solemnity of Wilkes' acting held the audience spellbound as Brutus argued with himself over the assassination, deserved or undeserved, of Caesar.

As Wilkes stepped from behind the closed curtains to bow to the cheering audience, men rushed to the stage and lifted him upon their shoulders and carried him down to the people in Chicago. They held him high above the reaching hands around them so that everyone could see him. His clothing torn by souvenir snatchers, he was paraded the length of the theater area, still clad in his Brutus costume which was already ruined. Finally, they took him—disheveled, sweating, protesting, but triumphant—back to the stage and demanded more.

Wilkes, trembling from fatigue, held his arms up for quiet. "Thank you, thank you all. This has been the most wonderful evening of my life. But, really! Please! I beg of you, let me go. No more, my friends, no more tonight."

A large man close to Wilkes feet yelled loudly, "We'll let you go for a song. Lead us in 'The Star Spangled Banner.' "

Shouts of enthusiasm approved the suggestion and the people moved closer to the stage, like a wave from the lake itself. Wilkes held up a hand, backed away from the crowds, and pleaded: "Not tonight, please! My voice——"

Even as he objected, the Stars and Stripes were carried onto the stage by a white-haired, bent old veteran of the War of 1812 who howled, "You sing out, son, just sing out loud and clear."

Wilkes put a hand on the bent shoulder near him. "All right, General. All right, sir!"

The orchestra responded to the call of the crowd, and Wilkes led the singing, straight and motionless beside the flag and veteran. The old man held one trembling hand to his forehead in a salute.

Wilkes sang with tears in his eyes. The sight of the flag that was no longer his, and the words and music of the anthem, unnerved him. For the first time he felt a physical break with his beloved country.

When it was ended, he lifted his hand to his brow in a sharp salute to Old Glory. It was a final goodbye, a farewell. As the crowds cheered him lustily and the veteran stepped aside, he strode from the stage in a hurry. Brutus' cape touched the flag as he moved past it.

The episode had shaken him considerably. With Ed Barbee, the theatre manager, as a captive audience in his dressing room, Wilkes paced the floor as he issued a tirade. The manager, slumped in a chair, watched and listened. He knew all the Booths, and this outburst was nothing new.

"Is there a clause in my contract which demands that I appear as a singer after performing Shakespeare for the evening?" Wilkes was asking.

Barbee shook his head and fanned his warm face with a program. "Nope. No such clause."

"All right, then. I will not be trapped into another songfest. Rather than risk a repetition of tonight's activity, I'll cancel my contract. You can sue me and be damned, but I'll not overtax my voice again. Is that understood?"

Ed Barbee's fat face remained unruffled by a frown. "It was an unexpected happening this evening. We'll be prepared for it after this. We'll make an announcement that you'll be unable to do more than the scheduled performance, and others will close the show with the singing."

"Good. That's settled, then." Wilkes went to the make-up table and wiped off some grease paint from his flushed face. "It was quite an evening, though, wasn't it?"

"Mister Booth," said Barbee, arising from the chair and beaming at Wilkes' reflection in the mirror. "I've lived to see the most spectacular evening in the theater in Chicago, or anywhere else. You were magnificent. I could book the performance you gave tonight for years to come."

The days of that week brought Wilkes new acclaim and celebrations in Chicago. He was a guest of honor at more lunches, dinners, and champagne parties than he had known even in the South. The critics wrote of him in tones which matched the enthusiasm of his audiences.

One day the Chicago *Tribune* carried an article praising him, and in the next column ran a warning to the citizens of Chicago to beware the Sons of Liberty, the Knights, and the Copperheads. Vallandigham had publicly spat upon a copy of the Constitution of the United States, and Chicago was outraged by his disrespect. The *Tribune* claimed that the pro-Southern groups were increasing their strength within Chicago and were now suspected of developing plans to seize federal installations.

As the paper zealously pointed out, the Knights had some 20,000 members in Illinois, and it was high time the government took action against such traitors as Vallandigham and the Knights he led.

Meeting again with Vallandigham in his room at the Richmond House, Wilkes learned more and more about the Knights' penetration into the very citadels of the North. Wilkes watched as Vallandigham roamed the room like a caged lion, a copy of the *Tribune* in his hand. He had the newspaper rolled up like a club and he beat it against the palm of his hand in an angry rhythm.

"You see how long it takes to make these federal people act?" He tossed the paper into Wilkes' lap. "The editor demands my arrest, but I'm still free. Well, I'll force them to drag me out of a public meeting. And when they do—when they imprison me for exercising my right to freedom of speech—they'll have the whole world as a witness that freedom of speech is lost in the Union. They'll have to come for me, and then I will be victorious."

But Wilkes' thoughts were not only of either the war or the theater: He had Ella on his mind. He penned her long letters, which Ella read guiltily, knowing that there was another woman in Washington who was really entitled to the letters she was receiving from Wilkes. And, like a schoolgirl, Ella slept with the letters under her pillow.

But his letters were more than love notes. Wilkes poured all his thoughts, his hopes, and his dreams into them, hiding nothing. His passion for the South came through beautifully to her. She worried about him, prayed for him, and tortured herself with doubts about Wilkes' feelings for her. After all, he was a notorious lover, and another woman did wear his ring and had his promise of marriage. Wasn't it possible that she was just another conquest for Wilkes Booth? And yet, she had believed him when he had said he loved her.

At the end of the week Wilkes was summoned to a lone and final meeting with Jacob Thompson in a room in the back of the Richmond House. The door was securely locked so they would be undisturbed, the transom was tightly shut, making it hot, damp, and even unpleasant.

Thompson, a good host, pressed an iced drink into Wilkes' willing hands. They pulled chairs close to the open window and drew aside the dull lace curtains in order to catch a breeze from the lake.

"Captain," Thompson said quietly, "since our last meeting, I've been advised to take you further into my confidence. We've additional work for you. But first, let me explain some about our set-up in Canada. As of this week the Headquarters of the Canadian Confederate Commission are already established in the Queen's Hotel in Toronto. We've got a bank account there which will be at my disposal to use as approved by President Jefferson Davis and Treasurer C. G. Memminger. I recommend that you open your own personal account there. It's a safeguard that will allow all of us to operate no matter what happens in our home states.

"Captain, I'm instructed to advise you that President Davis and his money official order you to carry messages when needed between Richmond and Toronto. You've been selected for this extra duty because you alone are in a position to travel at will without question."

140

Wilkes was pleased and surprised. "I had no idea that the Confederate government was so well organized outside the South."

"The President depends upon our Canadian effort to a large extent in planning for ultimate victory, Captain. We can't fail him."

A fly circled Thompson's head. He slapped at it, and it bounced away. "Captain, part of our task is to help bring recognition of the Confederacy as an independent, sovereign nation. In particular, we want the recognition of England and France. We're going to send ambassadors to both countries with express orders to bring about an exchange of diplomatic personnel. Lincoln is fighting this with everything at his own diplomatic command because he knows their recognition of our Confederate nation will be a death-blow to the Union."

"Recognition would mean that much?"

"That much, and more. With recognition we could make foreign loans and enter into trade agreements which would give us the ammunition, guns, maybe even men, we need to help us win. We might turn England and France into active allies. And that's exactly what Lincoln fears. Now do you see the importance of our headquarters in Canada?"

"Yes, sir!"

Thompson waved the fly away again. "Captain, to get to you, you'll have a larger sum to take to New York than you now have in your possession. You'll also have a draft on the Toronto bank, signed by President Davis, in the amount of three hundred thousand dollars. Hold the draft in your keeping until you're contacted by a Captain Longmire. He'll take it from you and give it to Mason and Slidell, our goodwill ministers to England and France. Is that clear?"

Wilkes gave a low whistle. "Yes, sir."

"You'll leave as soon as you can, Captain. Go to the Astor House in New York City. Wait there for your contact. He'll come to your room and properly identify himself by giving you the other half of this——" Thompson handed Wilkes a neatly-split half of a pin of the Golden Knights.

While Wilkes was pocketing the pin, Thompson went to a

bureau, opened the top drawer, and pulled out a heavy box. He drew a key from his vest chain and unlocked it, taking out a large envelope.

"Here's the bank draft, Captain. It's your responsibility until you hand it to Longmire."

Wilkes looked it over, and observed quietly, "It's sealed, sir."

"Certainly," agreed Thompson.

"Well, if you please, I'd like it opened. I'd like to be certain that we have the bank draft here, sir."

A light came in Jacob Thompson's eyes which had not been there a moment before. He took the envelope from Wilkes, opened it, then handed it back. "Captain?"

Wilkes drew forth the draft from the envelope, and he took his time studying it. At last, he replaced it carefully in the envelope. "As you said, sir, it's the bank draft."

"Captain," said Thompson, "if you had not asked to verify the contents of this envelope, I was under orders to refuse you the mission." He put a hand on Wilkes' shoulder. "You'll do very well."

"Thank you, sir."

"And now while I reseal this envelope with your permission," he said smiling, "you help yourself to the desk and write me a receipt. Then we'll be in order here."

Wilkes, with pin and draft safely stored in his jacket pocket, lingered long enough to use the mirror to deftly rearrange the cravat he had loosened earlier. He wound the wide brown scarf tie twice around his neck and tied it so the main length of it dangled freely.

"I'll see you in Toronto soon. Good luck, Captain."

"Good luck to all of us, sir," Wilkes said. They shook hands at the door. He left Chicago that evening.

Twenty-Five

Wilkes' room at the Astor House gave him a fine view of New York harbor which he looked at with real interest. Far out, the walls of Fort Lafayette rose from the depths of the harbor. The fort already housed Southern captives, war prisoners of the Union. Every Confederate soldier incarcerated there was a weakness in the link of Southern strength, a loss the South could not afford in manpower.

Wilkes gave thought to his sister, too. If Asia knew he was in New York she would want to see him, and of course he would like to visit her for a few hours—being around Asia always gave him a kind of new strength. But this was a visit he'd have to forego: he would not risk drawing attention to himself on this particular trip.

In the dark of the second night, Captain Longmire came very secretly, almost anonymously, to his room. He would not let Wilkes turn up the overhead gas lamp, so they conducted their business by the light of the oil lamp on the bedside table.

They matched the pin halves, making a perfect circle. Captain Longmire then wrote out his signature. It was exactly the same as the one attached to the bank draft.

The two shook hands, and Captain Longmire left Wilkes' room, the draft in his pocket.

At last Wilkes had time to attend to his original mission in New York City. He had already observed a great deal. The city was a stronghold of Southern sympathy. Violence broke out without warning, windows smashed, fires started. Pictures of President Lincoln displayed in homes and shops were stoned or booed. Union soldiers, marching through the streets en route to trains, were derided by pro-Southerners lining the sidewalks.

The federal authorities were fully aware of the results of the Copperhead groups throughout the nation. The Judge Advocate

General of the United States estimated that the total number of persons in the North affiliated with subversive organizations, armed and led by Confederates, was anywhere from 500,000 to 800,000—an army of considerable size and power should they ever unite.

The Secessionists were so well known to New Yorkers that almost any citizen could name some of them. And so it was with little trouble that Wilkes found his way to Fernando Wood. The former Mayor of New York City was working day and night on his plan to have New York City secede.

As Mayor of the City, he had advised the Council: "With our aggrieved brethren of the Slave States, we have friendly relations and a common sympathy. We have not participated in the warfare upon their constitutional rights or their domestic institutions. . .

"It is, however, folly to disguise the fact that, judging from the past, New York may have more cause of apprehension from the aggressive legislation of our own State than from external dangers. We have already suffered largely from this cause. For the past five years, our interests and corporate rights have been repeatedly trampled upon. Being an integral part of the State, it has been assumed, and in effect tacitly admitted on our part by nonresistance, that all political and governmental power over us rested in the State Legislature. Even the common right of taxing ourselves for our own government, has been yielded, and we are not permitted to do so without this authority. . .

"Thus it will be seen that the political connection between the people of the city and the State has been used by the latter to our injury. The Legislature, in which the present partisan majority has the power, has become an instrument by which we are plundered to enrich their speculators, lobby agents, and Abolition politicians. . . Why should not New York City, instead of supporting by her contributions in revenue two-thirds of the expenses of the United States, become also equally independent? As a free city, with but nominal duty on imports, her local government could be supported without taxation upon her people. Thus we could live free from taxes, and have cheap goods nearly duty free. In this she would have the whole and united support of the Southern States, as well as all the other

144

States to whose interests and rights under the Constitution she has always been true.

"It is well for individuals or communities to look every danger squarely in the face and to meet it calmly and bravely. As dreadful as the severing of the bonds that have hitherto united the States has been in contemplation, it is now apparently a stern and inevitable fact. We have now to meet it with all the consequences, whatever they may be. If the Confederacy is broken up, the Government is dissolved, and it behooves every distinct community as well as every individual, to take care of themselves."

Fernando Wood was harassed and nervous, but proud of his fight for the South and making no effort to hide his views or his work. He believed, he said, in the right of men to choose their own form of government, and for that, he would fight.

Wilkes knew Wood would be able to give him the name of an editor who would join the cause of the peace movement. Wilkes already suspected that editor might be Phineas Wright, editor of the New York *News*, but he wanted to be absolutely sure Wright would be dependable.

The ex-Mayor, no novice at secret work, listened without interruption until Wilkes explained what he wanted. "Mister Booth," he said, "I need time. If you'll return here tomorrow at this same hour, I'll answer your question."

Wilkes rose from the old wicker chair on the summer porch of the old mansion. "Thank you, sir, I'll be here."

Wood merely nodded and watched Wilkes as he went down the path to the street. There were few surprises left in the world any more, he thought, but this was one of them. A young, handsome, successful actor like that interested enough in constitutional rights of the states and of men to involve himself in a very great risk to his life.

All Wood had to do was verify the identity and assignment of John Wilkes Booth and that done, find him an editor. He knew exactly where to go in the city to accomplish both chores.

Twenty-Six

Through the auspices of ex-Mayor Wood, Wilkes Booth met editor Phineas Wright at Wright's desk in the editorial office of the New York *News*. They had agreed to meet at midnight when nobody would observe them to plan a propaganda campaign against the Union war effort in New York City.

The unpolished wood floors grunted with every step they took. Wright groped amid the papers on his desk to find the lamp and cussed a little as he worked to light it. It flared brightly and he adjusted it so that they could see to read. Then he went around to seat himself in the huge leather chair at the front of the desk. The chair operated on a swivel which Wright had invented and installed himself, and it was his pride and joy. As he talked, he allowed the chair to swing from right to left, left to right, ever so slowly, the motion apparently an aid to putting his thoughts into words.

Wilkes was impressed with the level look from the blue eyes, the firmness of the mouth under the broad, silky black mustache.

"This needn't take us over-long, Mr. Booth. Mayor Wood gave me a pretty clear picture of what you want. I'm sure the *News* can handle the entire job to everyone's satisfaction."

"Well, let's be certain we know each other's mind in this. For twenty-five thousand dollars in cash—United States bills, for your convenience—you will plan and execute a peace campaign in New York City which will concentrate on the theme of letting the South go without further bloodshed. You will devote the *News* to that policy, and you'll also promote the peace campaign in any other way you can manage, such as printing handbills and paying hecklers to shout for peace at every opportunity in public gatherings. Is that your understanding, sir?"

Phineas Wright stopped the motion of his chair, and picking up a pen, jabbed it gently at a piece of paper on the blotter. "Right," he said. "The *News* will agitate for peace, pleading that the South has already gone from us and ought to be allowed to live in independence without any more killing of brother by brother. The *News* will demand that the cannons be silenced, the killing halted. Let there be peace."

"Exactly. When will the campaign begin?"

"Tomorrow," said the editor. "Of course, that is, if I have the funds. As soon as the peace issues come off the press, I'll be dropping some paying customers, you know."

Wilkes lifted the valise from beside his chair and he placed it on the desk. "You'll want to count it, sir. And while you're doing that, I'll write a receipt for this business transaction which will be understood in Richmond but no place else. If I may have a sheet of paper and a pen?"

While Wright made sure of the amount he was accepting, Wilkes wrote out a receipt for Wright's signature.

When the money and the receipt were exchanged, Wilkes got to his feet. "You believe you can rouse your readers to demand peace?"

"Yes, and so do you, or we wouldn't be trying. The campaign will have a hell of an effect on the whole city of New York. We're going to give voice to all the feeling there is against this war. We're going to make Old Abe and his force a damned unpopular tribe in this town."

"I'll be anxious to see the first issue." They shook hands over the desk as Wilkes prepared to leave.

"Drop in on me, if you want, although it might be best if we don't meet publicly."

"No, I believe I'll just pick up the *News* like everyone else. But if I feel I need to see you, I'll contact you. I'll be reporting back to Richmond soon and I'll take the *News* with me."

"Well, good luck, Mr. Booth. And if you have any suggestions, get them to me and I'll work them over."

"I'm satisfied to leave it in your hands, sir," Wilkes replied. "But if I have orders myself from Richmond which affect your work, I'll confer with you again."

They shook hands again. Wilkes found his way out of the darkened building and hurried down the street to his hotel.

147

During the next few days he stayed close to his hotel room and eagerly awaited each issue of the *News*. Phineas Wright was performing the job beautifully. War-weary, frightened people were reaching hungrily for copies of a newspaper openly demanding the war be brought to a halt and that the Union take the initiative in settling for peace. After all, wasn't it true that Lincoln and his administration were blocking peace by a cold-hearted refusal to recognize the Confederacy as an independent nation?

Convinced that he need not linger, Wilkes packed his copies of the newspaper in his luggage and headed for Washington. When he arrived he went to his hotel directly from the train and changed into riding clothes. He wanted to see Ella before he made his return to the capital city known to anyone else.

Jane greeted him with a wide smile and ushered him into the sitting room. "Miss Ella just returned from the hospital, sir. I'll tell her you're here. Miss Ella's gonna be that glad to see you, Mister Booth. Yes, sir."

Seated together on the couch, her head on his shoulder, he told her about Chicago and New York. Finally she sat up straight and turned so that she could look into his eyes. "I love you."

"I thank God for it," he admitted soberly as he kissed her. "Ella, we've got to talk about our mutual assignment of getting medical supplies to Richmond. I've got a few ideas on how we can get through the lines." Now he smiled. "Unless you have that problem already solved?"

"No, I don't. Truth is, I'm scared. It's getting more and more impossible to figure out ways to get the stuff through."

"I thought that would be the case by now. Well, I've worked out a system, I think."

"Oh, Wilkes! Are we really going to work together on it?"

"We're under orders, Ella," he said, kissing her neck. Can you get the supplies out of the hospital without too much trouble?"

"Well, of course it's not easy, but it is simpler than getting through to Richmond with them. Seems as though the Yankees are on to almost all our methods."

"Well, you and I are going to figure out a few new tricks for them. First, I want to establish my presence again in Washington—in the theater, that is. But we'll soon set up a regular routine." He was anxious. "Ella, it will mean we'll be traveling to Richmond together. Will you mind?"

Ella studied him silently and shook her head. "No, I won't mind, Wilkes." She sighed. "But if she hears about it, Elizabeth Hale is going to mind very much."

"Yes, Elizabeth." He got to his feet and strode a few lengths, back and forth, in front of the fireplace. "I'm going to see her tomorrow, as soon as I can, and tell her——"

"Tell her what?" Ella interrupted him. "Wilkes, isn't your engagement a help to Richmond—or maybe it will be. Isn't that true?"

"Well, I had something like that in mind, I'll admit, when I became involved with Elizabeth. But she's a wonderful girl, and I——"

Ella put her hand over his lips. "Being engaged to you is a very romantic thing to her. I doubt that she's going to be hurt by it. And if an engagement to her can possibly help the Confederacy in any way at all, then don't give it up. Isn't that part of your job?"

"Obtaining information about the military, yes. But Elizabeth——"

"If I can stand not being engaged to you, I think Miss Hale can stand the opposite." She smiled, then, and added: "An engagement to John Wilkes Booth hardly falls into the category of war hardships."

His hands were hard on her arms. "And you'd travel with me, knowing I'm engaged to another woman?"

Her gaze did not flinch. "I'd travel with you, anywhere, anytime."

Wilkes let go of her and took a step back. "My father didn't marry my mother until I was thirteen. I told myself I'd never treat the woman I love that way. And I won't, never."

"Wilkes——"

"Look, I'm going back to the National now. I want to work out a few ideas on paper."

"But——"

He bent and kissed her. "See me to the door? I'll be back tomorrow. We're going to get to work."

"Wilkes, are you angry with me?"

"No. Not with you. You can't understand. I don't aim to be

like my father, that's all. But, please, forget it. It's all right. We're going to work together, and that's all that is important."

At the door, he took her hands in his. "Ella. I love you."

She smiled, but there was a puzzled look in her eyes. "Then hurry back."

∽

Wilkes' plan of operation proved an excellent one. Under his instructions, Ella set up a clock-like volunteer system of stealing supplies from the woodsheds behind the main building housing the sick and dying of both North and South. Most of the persons who worked with her were black.

There were times however, when discovery seemed close. One day Ella heard a nurse complain to the top-ranking officer of the hospital that medical supplies were being used up in what seemed to her an impossibly brief time. And a chemist reported that there was an unusual amount of morphine being used in the hospital. Fortunately there was neither enough time nor personnel to investigate the shortages, and so Ella and her silent crew were able to continue their thefts with a heavy hand.

In the following few months, Wilkes, working closely with Ella and her hospital contacts, created a smooth line of transmission from Washington to Richmond. The process started in the Washington hospital where Ella built the stolen drugs and instruments into sizeable caches. When each load was ready, she contacted Wilkes who transferred it to a theatrical trunk. He had arranged for short-term stage appearances in Richmond and other southern cities, and was able to pass through the lines with no trouble. But Wilkes worried about Ella more than about himself.

He waited until they were comfortable after dinner in her home, once more on their couch, his arms around her. It was a very cold December night and, in spite of the fire on the hearth, there was a chill at their backs. "Ella," he said matter-of-factly, "I want you to marry me. Right away."

She moved to face him. "But Wilkes, you know, we can't."

His hands gripped her. "Don't you want to marry me?"

No words came from her, only wonder in her eyes.

He kissed her mouth hard. "All right. You're coming with me

on my next trip to Richmond and we'll be married there. We can leave in a few days.

"What about Elizabeth?"

"She'll get over it. Girls have been jilted before."

"But, Wilkes, I'm not prepared."

"Don't worry, we're eloping. Come as you are." He smiled, and she was in his arms once more, greedily accepting his kiss.

They set off for Richmond. They were in Ella's carriage, with Otto at the reins, and a huge trunk strapped to the back of the rig. A strong north wind came blowing up early in the afternoon, and it began snowing heavily.

The Union sentry stood in the barricaded road with his shoulders hunched against the cold wind and snow. His breath clouding the air around his head, he walked stiffly toward their approaching carriage, already eyeing the trunk. Ella slipped her hand into Wilkes' under the lap robe covering their knees.

He looked in the window scornfully at Wilkes who was comfortably situated under the robe in the closed carriage. Without a pretense of manners, the sentry jerked the door open and stuck his head in. "You got passes?"

Wilkes handed him the necessary official passes which certified that John Wilkes Booth and his party were to be allowed passage to Richmond in order to fulfill a stage engagement. The raw-faced man scanned them, gave a long glance at Ella, and handed the passes back to Wilkes. He jerked his hand toward the rear. "What's in the trunk?"

"Costumes, that's all, Sergeant."

"Yeah? Well, I'll have to take a look."

Wilkes was alarmed but he did not show it. "But that will delay us. I have to be in Richmond by six o'clock. Look, it's late, it's cold, and you've seen my passes. Can't you just let us go on?"

"Nope," the sergeant said, shaking his head. "It's my duty to look."

Because resistance would throw more suspicion into the man's mind, Wilkes just had to hope the medical supplies amid the costumes would not be discovered. Getting out of the carriage, he beckoned to Otto to help with the trunk.

Ella watched the proceedings with growing alarm. She knew

that Wilkes was carrying a loaded gun, but if he had to use it and word got to Richmond, neither of them could return to Washington.

Wilkes always packed costumes in the top layer of the trunk as a meager but vivid camouflage of the medicines hidden in the lower half. When the men had the trunk down on the ground and Wilkes reluctantly opened it, a dazzling display of color lit the drab day. He moved back a little, his hand on the gun in his top coat pocket.

In open-mouthed wonder, the sergeant picked up a blue velvet jacket trimmed with pearls and other jewels, feeling the velvet with rough fingers. And now there was respect in his tone. "Say! That's beautiful, ain't it, sir? Whar do a man wear it?"

Wilkes, relieved at the quick turn in his attitude, took his hand from his pocket and smiled. "Why, Sergeant, that's part of a stage costume. I wear it in *Macbeth*."

The sergeant held up the jacket and looked it over carefully. "Why, by golly, now you're that Booth feller. Says so right on the pass, too." He laughed and shook his head. "Say, I'm not too bright today, am I? Seen you act once, sir. Shore did. Like to have scared me half to death, what with leapin' around the stage with witches after you. By golly, John Wilkes Booth." The sergeant put the jacket back in the trunk, rubbed his hands together, and smiled foolishly.

Wilkes pressed his advantage. "Sergeant, how would you like a couple of passes to the theater in Washington? Ford's or Grover's, whichever."

"That would be kindly of you, sir. Guess I'd travel a space to see you act, anyhow."

Wilkes took out a personal card from his carrying case, bent over the trunk and, with a pencil hastily borrowed from the sergeant, he wrote plainly the words that would permit the sergeant free entry to the Ford Theater to see J. Wilkes Booth perform. He handed the card into the sentry's stiff fingers. "That's good any time I appear there, Sergeant."

"Thanks to you, sir."

"How about hurrying us along on the inspection, Sergeant? It's damned cold here for the lady. And I do have an appointment in Richmond."

152

Shoving the card into his pocket, the pacified sergeant pushed the trunk's lid downward. "I reckon you can travel on now, sir. No need to keep you."

Wilkes winked at the shivering Otto and helped him secure the lid of the trunk and pull the leather straps around it. The three men lifted the heavy weight back into place on the carriage. The sergeant flapped his arms against his body to ward off the cold of the oncoming night and watched the departing carriage until dusk and the heavy snow blotted it from his sight.

Twenty-Seven

President Lincoln sat at his desk, studying a mass of notes on a subject he was determined to place before the nation. He tussled with the phrasing of the message he was writing to Congress—it would not do to use one false word; the message would go around the world as surely as though it had been launched from a mighty gun. The subject required his most solemn attention lest it go astray and he be damned as a villain.

The message he had written was really a compilation of his words of the past years, a summation of his beliefs. It dealt with his opinion that the black and white races ought to be separated, and that the separation ought to take place through a colonization of the blacks in an area of the world more suitable to them.

He looked from his notes to the roster of white men who had been enlisted in the ranks of the American Colonization Society, seeing, above all, the name of Henry Clay, his own American idol. There were also Bushrod Washington, Thomas Jefferson,

James Madison, James Monroe, Charles Fenton Mercer, John Marshall, Andrew Jackson, Daniel Webster, and finally, himself—all were devoted to the idea that the slaves ought to be returned to their native land or to a land whose climate would favor them. The Colonization Society believed this was but justice, that that it ought to be done under the auspices of the United States Government in order to protect and defend the blacks in their new land and new life.

Lincoln considered his early words on the subject: "Such separation, if ever effected at all, must be effected by colonization; and no political party, as such, is now doing anything directly for colonization. Party operations at present only favor or retard colonization incidentally. The enterprise is a difficult one; but where there is a will there is a way, and what colonization needs most is a hearty will. Will springs from the two elements of moral and self-interest. Let us be brought to believe it is morally right, and at the same time, favorable to, or at least, not against, our interest, to transfer the African to his native clime, and we shall find a way to do it, however great the task may be. The children of Israel, to such numbers as to include four hundred thousand fighting men, went out of Egyptian bondage in a body."

The President sat back in his chair and mused. Was this really the time to present his plan to Congress? Was the North, any more than the South, ready to let the black people go home with the blessings and unfailing help of the United States Government? He went to the window and looked out upon a city at war.

There were black men and women out there, free persons who loved the American nation as much as did he. He knew many of them as friends. He had personally paid the taxes of his black barber in Springfield so the man could weather a bad financial period.

One wrong step, and all he wanted for them would be wiped out. He went back to his desk, sat down heavily, and wrote to the Congress:

Applications have been made to me by many free Americans of African descent to favor their emigration, with a view to such colonization as was contemplated in recent acts of Congress. Other parties, at home and abroad, some from interested mo-

154

tives, others upon patriotic considerations, and still others influenced by philanthropic sentiments, have suggested similar measures; while on the other hand, several of the Spanish-American republics have protested against the sending of such colonies, for their respective territories. Under these circumstances, I have declined to move any such colony to any state, without obtaining the consent of its government, with an agreement on its part to receive and protect such emigrants in all the rights of freemen; and I have, at the same time, offered to the several states situated within the tropics, or having colonies there, to negotiate with them, subject to the advice and consent of the Senate, to favor the voluntary emigration of persons of that class to their respective territories, upon conditions, which shall be equal, just and humane. Liberia and Hayti are, as yet, the only countries to which colonists of African descent from here, could go with certainty of being received and adopted as citizens, and I regret to say such persons, contemplating colonization do not seem so willing to migrate to those countries, as to some others, nor so willing as I think their interest demands. I believe however, opinion among them, in this respect, is improving; and that, ere long, there will be an augmented, and considerable migration to both these countries from the United States.

Our strife pertains to ourselves—to the passing generation of men, and it can, without convulsion, be hushed forever with the passing of one generation. In this view I recommend the adoption of the following resolution, and articles amendatory to the Constitution of the United States.

The President sat a long time and concentrated upon the articles he was proposing to the Congress. In summation, he called first for the abolition of all slavery in all of the states by 1900, with the states to be compensated therefor.

Article II provided for the compensation for freed slaves of loyal slave owners whose slaves were freed by the chance of war.

Article III provided: *Congress may appropriate money, and otherwise provide for colonizing free colored persons, with their own consent, at any place or places without the United States.*

The President put his pen to paper again and he took his time in the careful writing of Article III:

155

The third article relates to the future of the freed people. It does not oblige, but merely authorizes, Congress to aid in Colonization of such as may consent. This ought not to be regarded as objectionable, on the one hand, or the other, in so much as it comes to nothing, unless by the mutual consent of the people to be deported, and the American voters, through their representatives in Congress.

Twenty-Eight

At the Spottswood Hotel in Richmond, Wilkes signed the register as J. Wilkes Booth and Lady. The two rooms to which they were assigned were connected by an inner door which Wilkes boldly unlocked and opened. "Make yourself at home, darling," he told Ella as she stood amid her luggage.

"You're leaving me?"

"Just for a few hours. I'm going to see President Davis, if I can. I'll come back with a preacher and we'll be married right here."

"Wilkes, is it all true?"

"Every bit of it," he said as he smiled and released her from his embrace.

Jefferson Davis and Wilkes Booth sat alone in the President's Treasury Building office. Wilkes had told the Chief Executive of his immediate marriage plans and, expecting congratulations, was now sitting embarrassed and puzzled, as the President left his desk and walked to the window to look out upon the public square.

The President spoke at last. "Captain Booth, if you marry

Miss Starr, your usefulness as a secret agent of the Confederacy will be destroyed."

Unconsciously, Wilkes bit his lower lip. "Sir?"

There was no softening of Jefferson Davis' tone. "You're a very famous person, Captain. You have no private life. Your marriage could not be a hidden matter, and Miss Starr has made no secret of her sympathy for the South. She knows the federal authorities probably suspect her of being an agent. She is a brave woman, but she may overplay her hand some day and suffer the consequences. If you marry her, the same suspicion will automatically fall upon you. And, because of your own previous attitude—that is, because you were quite outspoken in the early days of this struggle—suspicion could develop into an accusation or an investigation. Captain, your marriage at this time is impossible."

Wilkes said the first thing that came into his mind. "Then, I'll quit the service! I can join John Beall and sail with him."

Jefferson Davis sighed and sat down at his desk. "Yes, you can, if you insist. But—well, Captain, I had a particular task in mind for you. It will be difficult to find anyone else so well suited for the job."

"You're disappointed in me, sir?" Wilkes interrupted.

"Of course not! You've already done a great deal for the South, and if you want to serve in another capacity, I can't find it in my heart to refuse you. Besides, I would be the last man on earth to argue against marriage. I wouldn't trade mine for anything in this world."

Wilkes rubbed the back of his neck, and took a deep breath. "Mr. President, Ella expressed some of the same views. I know that she would ask me to postpone the marriage were she sitting here with us. I can't go against both of you in my arguments. I'll continue my work as a secret agent, sir."

"Captain, are you sure you don't want to discuss this first with Miss Starr?"

"No, sir. She won't be happy with the postponement either, but these aren't days when men and women can decide things without regard for others. I guess we're not alone in that, sir."

Davis nodded. "All right, then, Captain Booth. I'll waste no time. I want you to go to Toronto and report to Jacob Thompson. You'll go by way of New York to check on the progress of the peace campaign."

Wilkes' disappointment with the postponed wedding plans still clouded his face. "And when I see Thompson?"

"You'll be taking him sealed orders from me. The letter I want put into his hands will be delivered by a uniformed officer to your rooms at Spottswood. You're to leave Richmond as soon as you receive it. Thompson will have further orders for you after he reads my message."

The two men parted at the door, the President sending his regards to Miss Starr.

Ella knew as soon as she saw him that something had happened to their plans. "We're not going to be married, are we? The President thinks that it's the wrong time and maybe even the wrong girl for you. Is that it?"

"He didn't absolutely refuse us. He said——"

She took the words out of his mouth. "——that it would be better if we postponed our marriage plans."

His eyes admitted it. She rallied from her disappointment to offer: "We can be married anytime, Wilkes. But tonight we have each other."

He seized her caressing hands and held them in a hard grip, shoving her away from his body.

"No! Damn it, Ella, I'm not going to treat you like a whore. You know how I feel about it. I won't have you as a-, a-,"

"Stop it, Wilkes! It doesn't matter——"

"It matters, woman. Do you think I'd let our son be born as I was?" He had her by the shoulders and he was shaking her. "I'm not going to ruin our lives by taking you now."

She nodded, her head cradled against his chest, his hands pressed into her loosened dark hair. But in her mind there was a sharp pain of jealousy for those women who had lain with her lover and who knew him as she still did not.

Twenty-Nine

Wilkes returned to Washington with Ella and Otto, where he left her to go on to New York. He found the peace campaign a spectacular success, causing Lincoln himself to react.

Its most telling effect was on the ability of the Union to recruit the men of New York. And this was one problem which the South did not face: In the Confederacy, the only recruitment worry was youths in their early teens who were eager to join the battle forces, refusing to stay at home and help tend the growing of food and the manufacture of war goods.

But as the New York peace campaign began to take hold across the North, it became a growing problem to find men to fight. The Union's volunteer system had obviously failed. Lincoln began issuing proclamations urging men to join the army; then together with the United States Senate he enacted a conscription bill.

Every man, North and South, reading the wording of the bill, was astonished. It provided for a draft of all able-bodied men between the ages of 20 and 45. The names would be chosen by a lottery wheel, and all men in the ages defined were eligible and would eventually serve. The draft selection would be made in each congressional district. The system would be inaugurated under a new army official—Provost Marshal General. Every qualified man was ordered to report to his own draft headquarters in May to enroll his name. The name would then be dropped into the lottery.

There was one way to evade the draft. A substitute system was incorporated so that a man could buy his way out of service if he could find another willing to go in his place. A man could purchase a commutation of his own draft order by paying five hundred dollars to the federal government and securing another man not already called. The system functioned as long as the substitute served. If he were killed, or wounded, and out of service, or if he deserted, the man buying the commutation was immediately liable. However, there was no limit to the number of substitutes he could buy. Wilkes would take advantage of the substitute system, and before it was all over three men would have taken his place in the Union army at a cost of fifteen hundred dollars.

In Toronto, Wilkes learned that the message he carried to Jacob Thompson was concerned with the Union draft call. Even before the bill was presented to the Congress of the United States, Davis had a complete file on it. The South saw in it an opportunity to agitate against Lincoln's demands for increased Presidential powers and a larger war.

Wilkes' orders from Thompson took him back to New York City where he was to meet with other Confederates in a new plan to incite riots against the Union. The details would be given him in meetings with officers Headley and Longmire.

Wilkes was in his hotel room writing a letter to Ella when a hard rap sounded on the door. It was Lieutenant Headley followed by Captain Longmire. At Wilkes' invitation they got down to business immediately, speaking in low tones. The draft call for New York would be held on the coming Monday, July 11, in the office of the Draft Commission at Forty-Third Street and Third Avenue. The Confederates' job was to incite riots against the drawings as the first lottery wheel was turned and the names of the conscripted read and listed.

It would not be difficult. The city was crowded with Copperheads, as well as ordinary citizens who saw in the enforced military service system a blue-print for dictatorship, the kind of thing from which their fathers had fled in Europe.

Wilkes acknowledged that he was so well known in New York that he stood in peril of being recognized. However, he declined the chance of another assignment and eagerly asked for his own orders.

"Just give me something to do on Monday."

In a small room in Carter's Restaurant the men held other meetings with those whose help they need. Included in the group were Phineas Wright and another editor, Jonathan Mc-

Donald, who brought his redheaded, pretty daughter, Katie, to the meetings.

The McDonalds operated a printing business in a small office in the basement floor of a building near Carter's. In the rooms behind the office was a virtual Confederate stronghold where pamphlets designed to enrage people against President Lincoln and the Union were printed.

Each of the men had a similar specific area of the city assigned to him for Draft Day. They were to agitate and lure men to the corner of Forty-Third and Third Avenue. There, once a mob rallied, one of them would deliberately throw a stone through the draft window. That should begin the riot.

By then the men in the crowds would be so aroused against the draft that nothing could stop them. The draft riots predicted by the editor of the *Daily News* would sweep the city.

Wilkes asked to be sent to the dock section of the city where he was not as likely to be recognized as he would be uptown.

It was all easier than Wilkes had thought possible. When he reached the harbor area, a mob was already gathering at the end of one pier, their work forgotten on this grim Monday. Idle workers passed copies of the *Daily News* to each other. The paper said they would be drafted unless they could afford to buy their way out. Because they were not rich men, they were to be forced into the army, taken by the government from their families, their homes, their jobs. Moreover, the *News* stated that the Democrats, in political control of the city, were stuffing the lottery bowls with the lists of Republicans!

Wilkes, unrecognized, joined the ever-enlarging crowds and pushed his way to the center of the mob where he could be heard, acting the part of an excited Union draft potential. "Let's get over to the draft headquarters and take a look," he shouted. "I hear there's thousands there. But don't come if you're afraid of a fight. The damned commissioners will probably have us shot at. Get yourselves a stick, a stone, anything, and come on along."

The windows of the draft headquarters shimmered in the morning heat. The lottery bowl, reflecting the sun rays filtering through the window, was placed in view of the window, and several men hulked around it, ready to draw the names of the first draftees. There was a general muttering from the men who watched. The bowl was a symbol of enforced military service of a dictatorial President, a weak Congress, and unwanted war.

The swelling enormity of the crowds began to worry Wilkes. Long before the hour came for the first action by the government officials, Wilkes saw that bottles were being passed from one man to another. As the minutes ticked away, the mob watched and drank and grew more and more restless. Men in their sober minds protesting an unjust law were one thing, but these men were angry, fast losing their sobriety under the heavy influences of too much liquor, sun, and agitation. Wilkes could feel the hate rising around him.

The hour came for the turning of the wheel. The Commissioner of the Draft Board, his hand shaking from the tension, gave the big lottery wheel a hefty turn. Its dizzy spin was the signal to the men outside. An egg-sized piece of marble was hurled over the heads of the crowd to crash against the wheel. Flying glass splattered; the wheel inside was flattened.

Wilkes remained across the street, sickened at the sight. Unthinking, the mob was bent on the destruction of anything in its path.

Pushing, shoving, hauling, they assaulted the office, seized the Commissioner and his fellow workers and beat them senseless, and proceeded to demolish the office. The prostrate forms of the federal and state officials, bleeding and bruised, were strewn with shattered office files. The bowl was dashed onto the floor in a thousand pieces and the names of New York's first draftees scattered like confetti.

The mob started a fire in the demolished draft office, using government records to feed the flames. Within a few minutes, the flames began creeping close to the unconscious men on the floor. The leaders of the mob, feeling a power they had never known before as individual men, moved to the next Congressional District draft office and repeated their actions, destroying everything as they went.

Firemen arrived at the first draft office in time to drag the beaten officials from the intended funeral pyre. However, the flames spread to the next building which had nothing to do with the draft law of the United States. Frightened women ran screaming amid the clanging of the bells of the fire department.

The mob now followed its own course of action, entering stores and public places to take what they coveted and to wreck what they did not. They found new supplies of liquor and made quick work of it, killed any man foolish enough to try to save his property from their grasping hands, and shouted that they would take all New York and hang Old Abe.

Headley had fought against the flow of the mob and had been able to reach the first draft office. Stricken, he and Wilkes stood together and watched the fires spread from building to building. Someone in the crowd began to cuss the "niggers." It was the damned niggers who were to blame for the whole damned war—the niggers and Lincoln.

The mob, still growing, moved toward the nearest black institution, the Colored Orphans' Asylum at the corner of Fifth Avenue and Forty-fourth Street.

Wilkes looked at Headley and without a word agreed instantly on what they must do. Pushing their way through the mobs, fighting some men to make progress, each made his own way toward the orphanage. It was impossible to stay together.

Wilkes managed to skirt around the crowd's edge, panting, sweating, his face streaked with smoke, his clothing ripped by the jostling of the crowds. The sweat on his back and neck was cold and clammy from fear for the children of the orphanage. He had to get there first.

Finally in the clear, able to run, he ran faster than he ever had. His breath was coming in great wrenching gasps as he reached the gate of the institution. The mob was still some blocks behind him, looting and burning as it came, giving him a little time to spare.

The orphanage was protected by a six-foot fence and a huge, well barred, wood gate. Wilkes tried the gate, but it was locked from inside. He banged at it, hoping it would give, but the lock was secure. There was no response from within.

Desperate, he found a foothold in the fancy carving of the gate and climbed. Skinning his knuckles, he went over the gate and peered out to see if Headley was there. He was. Wilkes unbolted the gate for Headley and then locked the bar securely back into place. They ran for the main building.

A black guard in a dark blue uniform was seated inside the door of the building. He stood up, alarmed.

Wilkes wasted no words. "How many children are in this place?"

"Fifty-five littles one, sir. What's wrong?"

Wilkes saw fright come into the dark eyes. He put a steadying hand on the old man's shoulders. "There's no time to talk. Just do what I say. The children are in danger. A drunken mob is coming to burn this place. We'll help you get the children out, but we have to hurry."

The old man was terror-stricken. "Take it easy, old man," Headley said. "We're here to help you. Now let's go find the children and get them out."

"Yes, sir, yes, sir! They're all in the dining room right now. "

Wilkes turned to Headley. "You go out the back way. Stop as many carriages as you can to carry them away from here. Hurry! That damned mob's not far away."

Headley followed the hallway toward the back of the building. As Wilkes entered the dining hall, he ordered the guard to get the cook and her aide and anyone else who might be in the building to leave by the back entrance at once. The two nurses and the administrator were with the children, over-seeing their meal. Fifty-five small black children looked towards Wilkes in surprise, their soup spoons in their hands. Terrified but maintaining her calm, the middle-aged white woman turned to the children.

"Children," she said to the small ones, her eyes speaking to the two black nurses, "we are all going for rides in carriages. Now, you must hurry or we'll miss the rides. This is a race, but we'll be orderly about it. Everyone on your feet, now. Run to the back of the yard, out the back door. Don't push, and wait at the back gate for me. Quickly, now."

Long acquainted with the importance of obedience, the children arose from the long tables and hurried to the door.

Two toddlers, both girls, their baby faces showing their inability to comprehend and their threat to cry, were hurried along by one of the nurses. But their small legs would not carry them fast enough. Wilkes reached down, swept them both into his arms and hurried to the door.

Headley was waiting with a policeman who had helped him stop the carriages. Sober-faced men and women made room on their seats for the children. Wilkes deposited the two babies on the ample lap of one of the nurses who sat next to a white-haired man of apparent wealth who was muttering loudly: "Wicked. Wicked. God forgive them. Now let's get on with these infants."

Headley and Wilkes agreed that the *Tribune* office, where Horace Greeley was god, was the nearest and safest refuge. The last of the commandeered carriages had just left the curb and pulled out into the stream of traffic when the mob battered the front gate down.

Finding its intended victims gone and only their unfinished meals still warm on the tables, they were infuriated. The torches they carried were applied to the building, and the Colored Orphans' Asylum went up in flames.

Headley went in search of his own rest, and Wilkes walked back to his hotel room alone. In a daze, he lifted his eyes to the smoke and glare which hung over the city. What had seemed to be a legitimate war effort had turned into something vile and unbearable. Just as soon as he could reach Richmond, he would tell Jefferson Davis that either he was allowed to fight a war, man to man, on a battlefield, or he would not fight at all.

Night came and still the mobs roared on. Wilkes, weary and horrified, stayed away from his hotel that night. He found his steps taking him to Asia's home. His welcome there was less sure as far as John Clarke was concerned, but that did not bother Wilkes. His sister had provided him with a key to her home and a standing invitation to use it any time he wanted.

She had retired, a servant informed him, and Mister Clarke was not in the city. At his request, the servant did not disturb her, and Wilkes was brought a tray of sliced meats and chilled fruits and water. He did not touch the food but drank a half of the pitcher, then fell onto the couch and was almost immediately asleep.

During the night, Asia came down the stairs and tiptoed to his side. She traced the smoke smudges still visible on his face. Had Wilkes been caught in that dreadful riot? She shivered and placed a cover over him. But when she came down again in the morning, Wilkes was gone.

The draft riots continued unabated for three days of murder, arson, robbery, looting, and beatings. Sometimes the mob would drift back from its filthy work to stand outside the City Hall, to stand there sullen and silent.

Mayor Opdyke came out to stand on the steps of the hall and told the crowd that he had requested Washington to suspend the New York draft until its fairness and constitutional legality could be upheld.

The mob heard him but it did not listen. It went from the City Hall to take up a stand in the street around the *Tribune* building with weapons in hand and torches burning. It yelled obscenities, it cussed President Lincoln and damned the *Tribune* in general.

"Cowards," Horace Greeley had termed them in print, "afraid to fight for their own Country."

And in the *Tribune* building, Horace Greeley, the thin-bodied editor with the sharpest newspaper voice in the country, which he could and would turn on a President or a mob, eyed the mob with cool contempt, but not without preparation for a physical battle.

Lincoln himself, hearing of the threats to the life and property of Horace Greeley, and judging that the crisis in the city would come to a head at the *Tribune,* ordered brand-new weapons—the vicious new Gatling guns which would spray bullets like rain from a cloudburst—delivered immediately under military escort to the *Tribune* editor. Greeley excitedly received the guns and called his staff into meeting.

Every man of the *Tribune* was there, from doorman to the highest paid writer. Greeley, in command of the situation, told his crew exactly what was happening and what was expected of them.

"Gentlemen, the *Tribune* has been under threat of destruction for three days. Now we are ready to shake our fist in their faces. Old Abe Lincoln has sent us three Gatling guns, two of them are now being placed outside my own office and the third is being mounted now on the roof, overlooking the mob below. And each of you is to receive a gun from the army. These men are here to arm you and instruct any of you who need it in the use of the weapon. Now, while you get your guns, I am going out on the roof to talk to the mob."

Greeley braced his hands on the waist-high wall which sur-

166

rounded the roof. He shouted at the top of his voice and waved his arms, demanding silence.

"Now, listen! Hear me well, you cowards. The *Tribune* declares war upon you as of this moment! I am standing beside a Gatling gun and inside there are two more, just in case you try to enter the building without invitation. And every member of my staff—every member!—is armed, ready to kill, if necessary. And this is done with the help of President Lincoln. And there are just two more things I want you to see. Then, if you want war, you shall have it!"

Fearlessly, he turned his back on the mob to motion two men forward. They unfurled a gigantic portrait of Abraham Lincoln and, holding one end securely, they let the canvass unfold over the side of the building and pegged it to the wall so that it could hang there permanently. Then, the two went to the flagpole and attached an enormous Union flag to the ropes.

Standing in full view, armed belligerents saluted the flag as it was hoisted to stand out smartly in the hot July wind. Then without another look in their direction, Greeley left the rooftop, carrying his rifle.

The riots were over. Slowly, silently, sobered for the first time in three days, the mob broke up.

The *Tribune* estimated the number of deaths somewhere between three and five hundred. Over a million and half dollars worth of property was destroyed. But the riots were finished, and the draft was in effect.

Wilkes went to Richmond to ask once more for regular military duty, and once again the President persuaded him to stay in the secret service. From the viewpoint of the Confederate government, the New York draft riots were supremely successful. Jefferson Davis, while sharing Wilkes' personal horror at the tragic episodes involved in the riots, disagreed with him that they could not be classified as acts of war.

Davis congratulated him on a job well done. He also advised him that for a time he felt Wilkes ought to devote himself to his theatrical career with the exception of brief trips to Canada and Washington relative to any business Jacob Thompson might want handled.

"I don't want the public to miss you from the stage. It's best if you concentrate on a few plays for the next months, unless

167

something unexpected happens. In the meantime, you will continue to run medicines into Richmond."

"Don't worry about the public missing me," Wilkes said. "I often arrange substitutes, and so far no one has suspected. Still, there is a chance, of course, that some patron will notice, but if that should happen, I'm prepared to say I was ill and my understudy took over. And if there is a time or place when I can't find a substitute to perform for me, I'll just cancel the show on the plea of illness."

"It sounds as if you've tended to that phase of the problem, then.

"Well, Captain, before you settle into a run of a play you had best go on up to Toronto and check out your work there. If Thompson has nothing pending, I'd still like you to appear on stage just for a time. It's important to us that you keep your public, and I'm not sure your substitutes can act as well as you."

In Toronto, Thompson told Wilkes a major assignment was coming. But he agreed with the President: Wilkes ought to go on tour, observing conditions as he went and reporting back on any Union military operations he believed would interest Toronto.

Ella saw little of Wilkes in the fall of that year, for he made mysterious short trips to Canada, Chicago, New York, accepting stage appearances in many brief runs. The separation was hard for them, and Ella wondered if he would not agree to live with her. But Wilkes remained adamant. Although their longing for each other was becoming more intense, he cooled when she spoke of love without marriage. Could the way he felt about his parents really so affect him that he could not take her in love?

Thirty

On a gloomy November afternoon in New York in 1863 Wilkes, backstage in his dressing room at the Winter Garden Theater, was interrupted as he applied make-up for the afternoon performance of *Richard III*. Edwin, his handsome face flushed with emotion, came in carrying a copy of the *Tribune*. He tossed the newspaper onto the make-up table.

"Wilkes," he asked, "Have you read this speech Lincoln made at Gettysburg a few days ago? Seems to me it's like a poem. Take a look, if you haven't seen it."

Wilkes picked up the newspaper. "Sure." He scanned the front page, but his glance was caught by another story. He read it quickly, shock showing on his face.

"What's wrong?" Edwin asked.

"Listen," Wilkes asked, his voice shaking.

"John Yates Beall, notorious Confederate privateer, and fifteen of his crew members of the dreaded corvettes, *The Raven* and *The Swan*, raiders on the Chesapeake Bay, have been indicted by the Federal Government on charges of piracy. The death sentence is expected to be invoked against all the men.

"Beall and his men were captured after the most comprehensive man-hunt ever instituted by the United States Government. Their capture was made possible when a member of their crew provided the Federal Government with information leading to their whereabouts in return for a lenient sentence for himself. In effecting the capture of the pirates, the Federal authorities used the services of the Fourth U.S. Cavalry, a Negro regiment, six Navy ships and five Army gunboats.

"Beall and the crew members claim to be officers and enlisted men of the Confederate Navy, a claim which the

the Federal Government has ignored in its charges.

"Specific charges against Beall, and the others, include the cutting of the cable of the United States Army in Chesapeake Bay, resulting in failure of communication to the East Shore; the sinking of Union craft; the seizing of Union craft; the imprisonment of Union officers and enlisted men; and the blowing up of the Federal Lighthouse on Smith Island.

"Sentencing is expected to be announced within the next forty-eight hours."

Edwin let out a low whistle.

Wilkes stood up and crushed the newspaper in his hands. "I saw John in Richmond several months ago. He holds a commission as master of privateering in the Confederate navy, a commission given him directly by the Secretary of the Confederate Navy. He's an officer of an independent nation's navy. They can't hang him for piracy." He threw the newspaper into a waste basket. "And just to make it perfect, they let Negro soldiers capture him."

Edwin was sympathetic, but worried—he knew that Wilkes felt a deeper affection for John than he had for any of his brothers, including himself. "Don't worry, if John is a member of the Confederate navy, he'll be accorded all his rights. They won't hang him."

Wilkes grabbed a cloth from the dressing table and rubbed off the make-up he had just finished applying. "No. They certainly won't. I'll see to that." He threw the cloth on the table. "You'll have to use the understudy in my role, Ned. I'll be gone a while."

"Where are you going?"

"Richmond."

"No, Wilkes, stay out of it. You'll just get into some kind of trouble yourself, and you can't help John. It's a military matter."

Wilkes reached for his overcoat. "I'm sorry to give you trouble, but it can't be helped."

On the way to Richmond, Wilkes read more about John Beall. The newspapers were giving the story considerable space, touting his capture as one of the most glorious actions undertaken by Union forces.

The capture came as a direct result of Beall's attack on a Union lighthouse on Smith Island, extremely important to Union ships in the area, and which he and his men had blown up.

The Fourth U.S. Cavalry, a Negro regiment with four hundred artillery men and cavalrymen, was sent into the Bay area in search of Beall and his two elusive sloops. On the waters, the Union navy worked in cooperation with the Union army land forces. Six federal ships of the navy and five army gunboats joined the wide search. All escape routes which the army knew of were thus cut off, but Beall knew the Bay well and eluded the massive search. Moreover, he captured one of the searching schooners in Tangiet Inlet under the very eyes of the federal land and sea forces. Beall then ordered his aide, a big man named Burley, to go ashore to take a look at the military situation facing them. Burley took a small group with him, one of whom, an officer, wandered off on his own and was promptly captured by Union cavalry.

Under promise of a light sentence for himself, the officer betrayed Beall. The Union ships and shore forces descended in overwhelming numbers on Beall's hiding place. Beall, nevertheless, made an attempt to escape even that trap in the captured federal schooner. But the schooner was slow, and Beall lost the race. Now he and his men were in prison awaiting a verdict which the newspapers were already reporting as guilty.

Wilkes met the Chief Executive in the beautiful Presidential office in the Executive Mansion of the Confederacy. Furnished with care and taste by the First Lady, Varina Davis, it was an enormous gracious room overlooking a garden which sloped down gradually from a wide lawn to a ravine-like haven where summer furniture made the place, during the warm months, a popular rustic retreat. Now the garden was covered with snow, the frozen trees and flower stalks taking on fantastic shapes under the white cover of winter.

A fire glowed in the big fireplace and gave a rosy hue to the cream-colored furnishings. The President's desk was militarily neat. A small Confederate flag stood on one end, and beside it, a set of three feathered pens colored red, white and blue.

Wilkes sat nervously on the edge of a chair near the President's right hand. Davis was quite somber in expression this

171

day, and for the first time Wilkes noticed that the President's one blind eye was just a shade or two duller in color than the other. Wilkes could not restrain pushing his plea.

"Mr. President, it's worth a try. The Union won't risk the chance that you don't mean it."

President Davis leaned his elbows on the desk, his long fingers toying with the tiny silk flag. "It's not the kind of thing I would like to instigate, Captain. It could start something none of us could control."

"What is there about any war that anyone likes, sir? This is a matter of saving the lives of men who have fearlessly served you and the Confederacy. Isn't it worth anything the Union may think of us to get those expert fighters back so they can fight again, sir?"

Davis sighed. "You should have been a lawyer, Captain. All right! We'll try it—that is, if my military advisers agree to it. And I warn you, Captain, they may turn it a stone-deaf ear."

Wilkes, his heart pounding, still pressed the case. "But you will recommend it, sir?"

Davis nodded. "In view of the extreme value of these men and in deference to the brave record they have made for us, I'll recommend that we do anything—anything—to effect their release. After all, I suppose this kind of thing is no worse than open slaughter on the battlefield."

Sixteen Union officers were chosen from the long lists of those held in the bleak Libby Prison. Weak and sick from untended wounds and from lack of food and medicine, they were chained to the walls of a cold, damp room often used for prison discipline. A Confederate officer announced that he had an order to read to them.

"By order of Jefferson Davis, President of the Confederate States of America, I read the following to you:

"The Commander of Libby Prison will immediately select sixteen prisoners who hold commisions as officers in the United States Army and hold them in chains until further notice.

"The prisoners will be exchanged with the Federal Government of the United States of America for sixteen military personnel of the Confederate States of America now held by Federal authorities under charge of piracy.

"If the exchange is not agreed to by the United States Government, the sixteen prisoners held in Libby Prison will suffer whatever sentence is dealt to the sixteen Confederate prisoners held by the Union."

But if the Confederate officers' words meant anything to the chained men, they did not show it. The thought of freedom was apparently so far forgotten that they could not grasp the words which told them they had a chance to be free.

The White House in Washington was the scene of an emotional battle between President Lincoln and his Secretary of War, Edwin Stanton. Standing firm on a statement he had made, the President was greatly irritated by his Secretary's defiance.

"Mr. President," Stanton's voice rumbled, "if you allow this uncivilized demand, they'll use it time and again. A retaliatory measure of this nature is repugnant to every decent soldier. I doubt that even the rebels would carry through such a monstrous plan and kill innocent men!"

Lincoln was drawing heavily on his patience. "Mr. Secretary," he said formally, "I've made up my mind. The decision is final. I will not let sixteen innocent men die in Libby Prison for the things John Beall has done. I repeat, John Beall and his men are to be released at once. You will kindly carry out my order, sir."

Stubbornly, Edwin Stanton carried on his argument far beyond the point where the President found toleration possible. "But Beall is a pirate, Mr. President! He has no standing at all which would place him in any position to be an exchange prisoner."

Lincoln's voice could be sharp-edged, and it was now. "Now that seems to be a point of conflict, Mr. Secretary. The claim is made that Beall was acting under orders from Richmond, as a representative of the insurgents. The evidence is that he may well have been, but regardless, he goes free. Now, I prefer that this end the whole affair."

The rebuked Stanton withdrew. "So be it, then, Mr. President. I'll make the arrangements, as you request. But I must say sir, you're much too lenient with prisoners. I dreadfully fear you'll regret releasing this man Beall. I'm afraid more good Union men will have to die at his hands before you see that he's destined for the gallows."

"You may be right. In the meantime, be good enough to get that exchange under way at once. If Beall causes more trouble, we'll catch him again. But my concern is for those men of ours. I hold you personally responsible for their safety."

The Secretary bowed and left.

In Richmond, word of the exchange was tantamount to a major victory. The southern city went wild with enthusiasm for John Yates Beall and his men.

People jammed the railroad station the day the navy hero returned home from the federal prison. Flags waved, bands played, confetti colored the air.

The train slowed to a crawl as it reached the heart of the city, and men, women, and children, ran along beside it, tossing flowers at the smiling faces of Beall and his men, who were leaning against the windows. Beall waved and saluted, as the train began to approach the station.

Wilkes ran beside it, too, and as it slowed, he caught a hold on a hand bar and swung himself off the ground and upon the steps. He leaped over the coupling between the cars and crashed through the car door to find John Beall.

John saw him and left his chair in a bound. Then each threw back his head and let out a shrill rebel yell. They rushed at each other to clasp hands and slap each other on the back.

"Wilkes! You good-for-nothing New York Yankee."

"Johnny Beall. Ole sea dog, got hisself trapped!" Wilkes laughed.

The train came to a halt at the station as hundreds of people peered in the windows.

Wilkes pushed his friend toward the door. "Get out there, you damned hero! Your public awaits."

John reached to pull Wilkes along. "Come on, Wilkes! I want

174

you with me." His smile steadied. "Look, I've had the full word on this action. You put it over. I wouldn't be here——"

Above the noise of the crowd and the blasting of the train whistle, Wilkes spoke close to John's ear. "John, let me go. I can't appear with you. Understand?"

John dropped his hand. "I wasn't thinking, was I? Well, see you later at the Spottswood?"

"I'll be there," Wilkes agreed, and let the crowds take John from the train.

Their reunion in Richmond was of short duration: Both had war assignments which took them in two different directions once again. John Beall was ordered to Canada, and from there was sent on a mission to Lake Erie. He wrote to Wilkes, hinting at what he was doing. Wilkes was highly amused but increasingly curious. What was John really doing up there on the lake?

Ella got as much fun out of the letter as he did, joining him in chuckles over John's word that he was traveling on the lake to help his "nerves." He added that he hoped Wilkes might be able to visit the area himself within a few weeks, as he believed there would be some shipboard amusements which would be a "tonic" for both of them.

"Sounds to me as though Johnny is involved in a caper as interesting as the Chesapeake," Wilkes said.

"But the Great Lakes are protected by the federal navy. What could John possibly do there?"

"I don't know, but I hope I can join him," Wilkes said.

Ella kissed him. "Oh, but Lake Erie is so far away."

"Well, whether I go to Lake Erie or not, I can't spend the war with you. I've received orders to go to St. Louis. The Confederates there are desperate for medical supplies. I'm elected to get some to them immediately."

Cold fear crept over her whenever she knew Wilkes had drawn another assignment. "Sometimes I wish you had regular army duty. On a battlefield, at least you'd know who to trust or mistrust." Wilkes tried to stop her words with a kiss, but she insisted: "Please be careful. St. Louis is such a divided city. You could be easily trapped or betrayed."

As they parted at the door, Ella's eyes were pained: "Are you going to say good-bye to Elizabeth?"

He held her tightly. "No. I'll write her a letter. I think she's become accustomed to having a fiancé she scarcely sees. Just now it's very fashionable to be left at home, you know."

"But she has no idea what you're doing——"

"No, of course not. Well, anyway, I'll see her when I come back——" He touched Ella's face. "——and set her free."

Thirty-One

Before he could travel to St. Louis, Wilkes had to honor a contract to appear in *Pescara* at the Boston Museum. Moreover, he wanted to look in on Mary and Edwin who were now residents of Dorchester, a country community just a few miles outside of Boston. Mary's deteriorating vigor had only lately been diagnosed as consumption, and Edwin had rented a house for her in the country in the hope of restoring her health. He had retained Doctor Erasmus Miller, a noted specialist, and Mrs. Miller stayed with Mary whenever Edwin had to be absent. Mary's baby girl, Edwina, was healthy, however, and for that the family was grateful.

Wilkes wanted to say Mary looked better than the last time he had seen her, but he could not. He wanted to make his fragile sister-in-law smile in hope but the sight of her fevered face and emaciated body shocked him. All that he would have said, ordinarily, in his teasing manner of better days, stuck in his throat.

"We're planning to see you perform Tuesday evening," Mary said. "I'm looking forward to it so much."

Wilkes was happily surprised. "Why, that's great news. You mean you're up to an evening out in Boston?"

She nodded. Her brown hair was long and shining and graced with wide, dipping waves. "Oh, yes. I feel much better these days, Wilkes. I need to get out some. I'm perfectly able to attend the show, really I am."

When they were escorted to their seats, the audience recognized the couple at once. Their friend, Julia Ward Howe, had termed them "The two true lovers" when she first saw them as Romeo and Juliet, and this evening the audience at the Boston Museum applauded them enthusiastically.

Wilkes was so deeply moved by Mary's effort to appear normal, despite the hopelessness of her case, that he felt a strange and bitter anger toward the world, and that evening he gave a performance touched with fury. Edwin later said that Wilkes had given the theater a Pescara "rare enough for the most fastidious beef-eater."

After the closing of the play, Wilkes made a hurried trip to Canada to consult with Jacob Thompson on his St. Louis mission. Then he returned through Boston once more to look in on Mary. He rode fearfully in a hired sleigh to the Dorchester house, the sleigh bells jingling in the cold winter air. Her decline had been so rapid that Wilkes was not sure he would find her still among the living.

Mary was resting on a couch downstairs, a blanket covering her thin body. Edwin was in New York. Mrs. Miller cautioned him not to let Mary become over-excited about anything: "She has no strength. You'll not stay with her too long?"

Mary held out her hands to him and smiled from the pillows but did not attempt to rise. "How good of you to come see me, Wilkes."

Her hand was cold although spots of fever burned in her face. He sat down beside her, trying to keep his alarm out of his eyes. They sat in silence for a moment. Then she squeezed his hand. "Wilkes, will you watch over Edwin when you get to New York?"

They both knew it was the last time they were to see one another. He knew what she meant and he tried to pretend, as she was doing. "Of course. I'll see him as soon as I get there. Would you like to send him a note?"

She saw how it hurt him, so she smiled and gripped his hand

177

harder. "Oh, that's good of you, Wilkes! Yes, yes, I'll send him a little note."

She penned a few lines to her husband, words of love. Wilkes put the finished note in his pocket. Seeing that writing the note had exhausted her, he patted her hands and leaned over to kiss her cheek.

The sound of the baby's voice came to him from the nursery as he strode to the front door. He left the house with tears in his eyes.

He gave the note to Edwin backstage at the Winter Garden. "Get home to her, Ned," Wilkes warned. "She needs you." Edwin waited, though, until a telegram arrived from Doctor Miller: Mary Booth's husband was needed at home, at once. Edwin, who had taken to dulling his terror over Mary's condition with liquor, sobered and wired his ailing wife:

MARY I AM COMING.

At the very moment Edwin's train pulled out of the New York station for Boston, she died in the arms of Doctor Miller. When he was met at the Boston station by a neighbor who had come to drive him home, Edwin held up a trembling hand to halt the man's words. "Don't tell me. I know."

He locked himself in the room with his dead wife for the night. He put a red rose in the pale, lifeless hands and around her neck he placed a locket containing his own likeness. Mary Ann and Wilkes came to Dorchester. They heard Edwin roam the house at night, calling in a pleading voice: "Mary!"

Doctor Huntington spoke the final words at the funeral at Mount Auburn Cemetery in Cambridge. Later, back in the house which seemed so empty, and yet so haunted, Edwin was inconsolable. "Don't tell me all the things people are supposed to say at a time like this. Spare me."

"I only wanted to say—"

"I know, Wilkes. I know. She's in heaven and I'll see her again. You want to tell me that in time I'll forget. My God, Wilkes, do you honestly believe I *want* to? Do you remember how much I loved Father? Yet today I look back on him without so much as a sigh or a tear. Wilkes, I can't even remember what he looked like, really. Can you? If I thought it would be the same with Mary—"

Wilkes left Edwin in Dorchester with their mother.

In time, he heard that Edwin, longing to know if his beloved Mary was near him as he visioned, was consulting Laura Edmonds, a noted spiritualist. The day that would have been his Mary's twenty-third birthday, Edwin took part in a seance held by Miss Edmonds. He saw Mary. She spoke to him and told him many beautiful things, as he was to report later. He came away from the seance with an eased heart and soul. Mary Ann heard of the seance and uttered a prayer of joy. For a long time she had kept her own secret: In the years since his death, she had seen her husband, Junius, come to her in more than one silent visit, standing near her bed.

But there was more personal business Wilkes had to tend to before taking up his assignment. Wilkes accompanied two actor friends, John Ellser and Thomas Mears, to the little village of Franklin, Pennsylvania, to consider investing in an oil strike of major proportions.

The word of the boom had brought large crowds of the curious and interested. One look at the thriving situation and Wilkes eagerly agreed to becoming a partner with his friends in the purchase of acreage belonging to the Fuller Oil Farms Company. They purchased three and a half acres situated one mile south of Franklin and on the east side of the river—land set amid productive wells.

They named theirs the Dramatic Oil Well Company, hired a driller named Henry Sires, and named their well The Wilhemina in honor of Mear's wife. Within a short time it was producing 25 barrels of oil a day, but the partners decided that was not sufficient and determined that they could expect more by blasting a larger hole. But they misjudged, and the blast completely destroyed the well.

Wilkes, not discouraged, responded from Canada by mail when his partners suggested he purchase heavily in The Boston Oil Company, but even his stocks and bonds in oil could not hold his interest long when they were pitted against his orders from Richmond.

Thirty-Two

St. Louis huddled against the double beating of war and a snowy winter, but Wilkes played nightly to overflow audiences. The patrons were not entirely tame. Rough voices were apt to interrupt the stage dialogue, or a rebel yell or a sudden hurrah for Abe Lincoln would pierce the dark. Too, the stage—brilliantly lighted by overhead gas lights and a trough of oil lamps at the front of the apron—was an excellent target for hand-thrown missiles of all kinds. But Wilkes, long ago cautioned by his father to take such disruptions in stride lest they break up the show, paid them no heed and went on with his role.

The young women of St. Louis were as fascinated by him as were the ladies of the South and East. He wrote Ella that he believed he could have his choice of any woman in the city, but that he was content to think of her and to dream.

One day when Wilkes was seated by himself at a small table in a saloon near the theater, a glass of brandy in his hand, a big, bearded man whose long brown hair was in need of a wash, stood at the bar and loudly offered a toast to Abraham Lincoln.

After bragging about the many virtues of the President of the United States, he swayed beside the bar and drunkenly lifted his glass of liquor high—"To Old Abe Lincoln. Long may he live and rule!" The man looked around the saloon. "Ever'one, glasses up!" he demanded, obviously ready to insist upon compliance. Every man at the bar immediately raised a glass, although some with a gleam of resentment in their eyes.

Wilkes, his thoughts elsewhere, did not hear the toast. He was the only man in the place who did not raise his glass.

"An' you, mister? You ain't goin' to toast the President of the United States?"

"What toast, mister?"

The drunk was only too willing to repeat it. "Why, mister, I saiz we're drinkin' Old Abe a toast cause he's the best damn President we ever have us. And cause he's gonne whop the hell out of the rebs. Now, you gonna get your glass up, mister?"

Wilkes sat perfectly still and spoke very softly: 'Mister, I don't drink any toast on the orders of a drunk." The toastmaster pushed away from the bar, his own glass dropping to the floor with a crash, and shoved his shapeless jacket back over his hip, exposing a gun strapped there. He came close to Wilkes. "Drink up, mister," he demanded.

Wilkes gave the room a sweeping glance, estimating the readiness of the enemy and his position. Swiftly, before the man could even guess his intent, the actor was on his feet. He swung the chair up off the floor, knocking the armed man off balance. Wilkes leapt upon the table and drew his own pistols from his gunbelt.

The drunk, stunned by the quick action of the man he had thought was an easy, unarmed target, stood looking up into the muzzles of the two guns Wilkes was aiming so steadily at his heart.

"Come forward, mister!"

Sullen-faced, trapped, the drunk looked in vain at the others at the bar for help, but they kept their positions, watching Wilkes, admiration in their faces. Recognizing his defeat, the giant shuffled to the table where Wilkes stood.

"Now, mister," Wilkes said, "put your gun on the table at my feet, and be quick."

Hatred glaring in his watery eyes, he did as he was told. Keeping the guns leveled, Wilkes ordered him to back away to the bar, arms raised. When the man stood where Wilkes wanted him, he tended to the rest of them: "I'm not anxious to hurt anyone, so let's take this easy. Come forward, one by one, and put your guns on the table at my feet. If anyone wants to try me, I'm willing."

Carefully they came and laid their weapons on the table. When they were all back at the bar, hands raised over their heads, Wilkes jumped lightly down from the table and, keeping them covered, backed toward the door.

As he disappeared through the doorway, the men came to action. Cursing, shoving, they dove for their guns, sorting them out expertly. But even while they damned the stranger later, over their drinks, they recounted his skill and nerve as though they had not all witnessed the episode.

That evening as Wilkes, still in the costume of Hamlet, entered his small backstage dressing room, he found three blue-uniformed Union soldiers armed and ready to seize him. One asked, "Are you John Wilkes Booth?"

A flicker of anxiety passed through Wilkes' eyes as he closed the door behind himself. "Yes, sergeant. What can I do for you?"

"There's nothing you can do, Mister Booth. You're under arrest. You're to dress and come with us to Jefferson Barracks, at once."

Wilkes folded his arms across his chest. "Arrest? On what charge?"

"Treasonable utterances," the sergeant replied. The three Union soldiers exchanged glances. This was really something. John Wilkes Booth, a Johnny Reb?

Wilkes determined that the men would not see him disturbed. "All right, sergeant," he said coolly, "just give me time to change."

The sergeant took Wilkes' guns and the ammunition which Wilkes voluntarily handed to him from a drawer of the dressing table, and scanned the room: no windows, no avenues of escape except the door. He looked into the closet, pushed at the wall in the back of the clothes, and advised Wilkes he would have five minutes.

The prison was damp and water seeped through the split rocks from the river level. The men cramped into the barred room with Wilkes were civilians like himself, picked up on various charges of violation of local or federal laws involving the great national conflict. A man could be seized and kept in jail for endless weeks, forgotten, if the federal government willed it. The right to trial, Wilkes learned, was lost somewhere in the terrible pursuit of war. And there were many who could not be trusted to be loyal to the Union these days . . .

Wilkes had not left a note when he was hurriedly escorted from the theater, and he found that the prison offered him no chance of contact. If a man went to jail, he evidently could expect to stay awhile.

Finally, through promise of money from the theater, Wilkes bribed a jailor to go to the theater manager and tell him what had happened.

After spending a long and uncomfortable night in the chill, basement-like atmosphere, Wilkes was made to wait until the morning was well advanced before the theater manager arrived. Walt Wilkes bore a distinct resemblance to Wilkes' father and was actually a distant cousin who had loved Junius Booth as a friend. The night in prison had soiled Wilkes' clothing and put a shadow of a beard on his face. His hands were white-knuckled as he grabbed the bars: "Walt! For God's sakes, get me out of here."

Walt Wilkes was troubled. "Wilkes, it's going to take cooperation on your part. You have to take the loyalty oath."

Wilkes affected a great sense of astonishment. "What have I done to make them demand that? I haven't said a thing, or done a thing, which should make them jail me or require me to take an oath. What are the exact charges?"

Walt Wilkes tried a little smile. "Well, you threatened an off-duty officer of the United States army with a gun."

"Oh! So the big man went for help from the army. Well, let's do whatever they ask and get out of here."

"You'll take the oath?"

Wilkes rubbed the back of his neck and smiled. "Do I have a choice? As I understand it, there's just one government running this prison, and I'd better like it."

"Still, I thought you might refuse. Knowing how you feel, you know?"

Wilkes' shook his head. "I could spend the next few years in here. Liberty is on short enough rations these days without volunteering to give it up entirely."

Wilkes stood in the court room of Jefferson Barracks, the main installation of the United States army in St. Louis. Uniformed Union soldiers patrolled the room. Seated high above him on a desklike dais which resembled a throne, the judge advocate looked down upon the prisoner in surprise. Wilkes, his hair combed but with no other concessions toward an acceptable appearance, stood before the judge's seat with his hands straight at his sides, proud and quiet.

The judge's voice was loud and well trained. "John Wilkes Booth?"

"Yes, your honor."

"Mr. Booth. You are accused of uttering treasonable statements and of threatening the life of an army officer with a gun. In addition, it is alleged that you refused to drink a toast to President Lincoln."

Wilkes acknowledged the charges.

"Do you plead guilty or innocent?"

Wilkes spoke clearly, as though he wanted to be heard throughout the prison. "I am innocent, sir."

The judge tilted his head to one side as he studied the prisoner. "You did not insult the President of the United States?"

"I did not. The insult was made by the drunken officer. He offered a toast to the President in a public bar while he himself was in a state of alcoholic derangement. I never indulge in toasts made by such men; furthermore, I select my drinking partners. And I never respond kindly to a loaded gun aimed at me by a man under the influence of liquor."

The judge advocate nodded. "I have no witnesses to the entire affair. It's your word against your accuser's. But since he is known to be a heavy drinker, I'm inclined to accept your version of this incident. So, in deference to your own fine standing as a member of the respected and loved Booth family, I'm going to rule in your favor, providing you will take the loyalty oath."

"Thank you, sir." Wilkes bowed his head to the judge.

"All right, Mr. Booth. The Court will now hear the oath."

A court assistant came forward with the Bible and Wilkes placed his hand on it. In accordance with instructions from the judge, Wilkes raised his right hand and repeated the words administered by the assistant.

"I, John Wilkes Booth, do solemnly swear allegiance . . . " As he spoke, a smile of contempt for the oath and for the judge who listened to it lurked in his eyes. The judge did not see it.

Thirty-Three

Wilkes would have left St. Louis at once to avoid any further prying by the federal government, but he had unfinished business. He lingered long enough to make contact with the Confederate agent who would provide him with information on the prison situations throughout the lands of Missouri and Illinois—data he would take to Richmond where it would be fitted together with other details brought by other agents. The South, its soldiers being captured at an alarming rate and growing increasingly anxious for their return, wanted an accurate picture of the prisons of the North.

The facts and figures the agent gave Wilkes were grim. The Union prisons were jammed with Confederate captives, and conditions in the places were deplorable. In Chicago's Fort Douglas, men were kept in outdoor pens, winter and summer, forced to sleep on the ground like hogs. Lacking food and medical attention, overcrowded, understaffed, the prison death rate was ever climbing. The Confederate cause might well be lost unless some of the prisoners could be freed and brought back to fight once more.

"Overcrowded and understaffed"—the words of the report stuck in Wilkes' mind. If that was the worst of it, he thought excitedly, maybe it was also the best of it!

Suppose the silent army in the North—which was composed of the Knights, Copperheads, and, lately, the Sons of Liberty—hit the inexpertly guarded prison camps? Suppose the prisoners were ready, at a given hour, to overcome their guards and open the gates to the rescuing army of civilians?

Wilkes felt inspired. He would get to Jeff Davis as fast as he could, but he would go by way of Vicksburg and New Orleans to see exactly what those places were like since the Yankees had come. It would be a part of his report to the President.

He went by boat to Vicksburg where General Ulysses S. Grant was temporarily headquartered. He would have to obtain a special pass from Grant to pass into New Orleans, where he had an agent waiting for him. The General generously agreed to see one of the famed sons of old Junius Booth whom he remembered seeing on the stage. Besides, the General had heard that President Lincoln thought well of actors and the theater.

Looking at the General, Wilkes wondered if such a man could really be a conqueror of the South? Grant's trousers bagged at the knees and in the seat; his uniform jacket was unbuttoned, unpressed, and entirely too large for him. The General himself looked sleepy-eyed, even listless. Could anyone in his right mind compare this man with Robert E. Lee?

Coolly, almost insolently, Wilkes requested the pass to New Orleans, explaining that he must honor his contracts. He would perform where he was scheduled to appear, even if he had to set up a stage in rubble.

Grant's heavy-lidded eyes flickered at Wilkes in a probing gaze. "You've come from St. Louis, Mr. Booth?" The General's question was routine enough—or was it?

"Yes, sir. I played there for six weeks."

"Were you under arrest there?"

Startled, Wilkes licked his drying lips and came close to stammering. "Yes, sir. I . . . That is . . . Sir, the arrest was a result of an encounter with a drunk."

"You did take the loyalty oath? You did take the loyalty oath to be released?"

"Sir, I took the loyalty oath as the Court ordered."

Grant shifted his gaze for a moment and seemed to be dreaming, his eyes closed. Then he turned in his chair, an unfathomable smile on his face. "All right, Mr. Booth. You'll have your pass."

"Thank you, sir." Again Wilkes began to feel contempt for the Union officer. How could he show such little imagination, such sad neglect of security in his lines?

Wilkes offered the General his thanks and his hand.

"Mr. Booth," said the General, taking the visitor's hand briefly, and dropping it quickly, "You may decide I've done you no favor. I must warn you about New Orleans. I'm sure that in spite of the loyalty to the Union which you have recently pledged, you love the South as she was before this struggle. It would shock any man of the South to see New Orleans as she is now. But it was very necessary."

Wilkes left the General's office with the feeling that his arrival in New Orleans would not be news to the army. He decided to be extremely cautious of his words and actions; his meeting with the agent would have to be held very discreetly.

The paddle wheel of the *Silver Spray* was still splashing the river waters of the Mississippi when Wilkes stepped onto the docks of the great seaport city. All along the river's edge there had been signs of death and destruction, captivity and suffering. Wood huts—the pitiful unheated homes of Negroes who were now free men—lined the shore, and dark faces stared at the passengers as they alighted from the great ship.

How could words describe the devastation of that city? Buildings were crumpled from the guns of Farragut's fleet; bodies still lay in the shattered debris and rubble filled streets, unburied; the stench of death was in the air.

As he walked, Wilkes' hand tightened on the valise he carried. And he knew that General Grant had deliberately wanted him to have the pass, wanted him to see this place. He had not been fooled by the loyalty oath; he knew a rebel would walk the streets of New Orleans. Now that rebel was receiving his real punishment.

Beyond the waterfront, the devastation lessened, the city appeared a little more normal. In the sector where the Union held its headquarters, blue-uniformed men were in control of everything. The Stars and Stripes were flown from every conceivable vantage point, flaunted before the eyes of the conquered. And the conquered, Wilkes noted, were hardly to be seen, gone from the streets, the shops, hotels, sidewalks, and theaters. Now ragged women, pale and silent, went about their daily chore of trying to find food enough to place on their family tables. And there were some bitter-faced men, looking straight ahead, walking captives under the colors of the Union. But there were few young men to be seen. New Orleans was staggered, shattered, its spirit gone.

Wilkes registered at the New Orleans Hotel, one of the few

187

undamaged buildings. After dinner, badly cooked and badly served, he went into the bar, where his drink cost an outrageous sum. He saw that many of the men at the bar were not drinking at all, the price of liquor beyond them, but they had no other place to gather. The little they said was directed in low, unflattering terms toward the Union and all its men.

Scattered remarks traveled up and down the length of the polished bar. Wilkes, his nerves frayed by the walk through the city, by St. Louis, by General Grant, listened until he couldn't stand it any longer.

"My God!" he burst out, "Why don't you fight back and throw the damn Yankees out?"

There was an awful silence. Then a man in a worn gray uniform stripped of its identifying marks, his face haggard in the dim light, stood at the far end of the counter from Wilkes. He took his hidden gun from the inner recesses of his thin jacket and slid it along the counter of the bar toward Wilkes. "There's a shooting iron," the ex-soldier of the Confederacy said softly. "You throw them out. We've been waiting for a hero to show up."

Wilkes handed the old gun back. "I'll certainly do what I can to throw them out of the South," he said. "But in the meantime, sir, you may need this." He saluted, and walked out.

Wilkes passed the night in a frenzy. He paced the floor, then wrote, only to scratch out and re-draft a report to President Jefferson Davis. At midnight the New Orleans agent left his room after delivering a document loaded with more data on Union prisons, and Wilkes went to work on the final paper he would present to the President. A more than factual report, it was a proposed military plan for the seizure of all Union prisons in the Union's northwest states.

Dawn broke the cover of night before Wilkes turned down the lamp and threw himself onto the bed fully clothed.

Thirty-Four

Jefferson Davis found it difficult to comment immediately. He pushed his chair back and walked to the window. He was thinner and much more worried-looking than the last time Wilkes had seen him. The great heart of Jefferson Davis was breaking, but his spirit was not.

Finally he said that he would like to submit Wilkes' proposed plan to his cabinet and to his military advisers. He termed it "brilliant," but said again that he would have to consult with others before reaching a decision. Elated, Wilkes agreed to wait for Davis' summons at the Spottswood, where he wrote letters to Ella, Elizabeth, and his mother.

When Ella saw his words, "I want you, want you, want you . . . Oh, dear God, how I long to hold you," she thought, when he came to her again, it would be all right. He wanted her now.

Jefferson Davis' official family accepted the prison-release plan concocted by Wilkes. The paper he submitted was clear in its wording and so well detailed in plot that there was almost nothing the military experts had to add.

The plan made bold, extensive use of all the secret Southern sympathizers and organizations operating in the North. The civilians would be led, aided, and abetted by as many military personnel of the Confederacy as could possibly be spared. The unique battle plot, was finally to be known as "The Northwest Conspiracy." It was daring in its call for simultaneous attacks on a specified day and at a particular hour, wherever a Northern prison held Confederates.

Jefferson Davis and his cabinet worked for ten days to conceive the last details of how to free every rebel throughout the northwest United States, from Minnesota to New York.

In a final meeting before Wilkes went on to Toronto, President Davis congratulated him again on the plan.

Wilkes asked, "I assume I'm to have a part in it?"

"Yes, of course. You're to carry sealed orders to Jacob Thompson, who'll be waiting to brief you. It's going to take a great deal of careful preparation, but we begin as soon as he can coordinate everything."

The sealed orders were placed in the hands of Jacob Thompson, and the Northwest Conspiracy had begun. Thompson worked night and day, consulting with men in Toronto, sending for others thousands of miles away, gathering and writing new reports, interviewing, assigning, recruiting, dispersing, planning, drafting, buying and distributing arms and ammunition. Always the mammoth, finely detailed map of the Northwest was before his eyes, hanging on the wall opposite his busy desk. Every federal prison camp was outlined in glaring red. It was his almost impossible task to make the whole plan work.

Thompson conferred with Wilkes at intervals to go over the latest reports from St. Louis, New Orleans, Chicago, seeking the best way into each prison. They began to list the names of men inside, Confederates as well as guards. Was there a guard who could be bribed? They had to know and enlist him. Which of the prisoners could be relied upon for leadership at the moment of attack? They had to contact these men. Moving cautiously, they checked and double-checked their information. There must be no weakness in their estimation.

Wilkes' enthusiasm for the plan increased daily as he conferred with Thompson. He sat with the big man as he talked with experts about cities, rivers, railroads, guns, ammunition, and all the other things which had to be figured into the gigantic prison break. And Thompson began to issue orders for the coming day to men who would soon have to be trusted with the actual job.

Wilkes was sent back to the states again, to gather still more information and take secret orders to Thompson's selected men. Wilkes' scheduled stage engagements became more and more erratic and more than once his roles were understudied. Several times the public thought they were seeing Wilkes when the star was actually hundreds of miles away. There was criticism of his acting at such times, and on occasion a comment appeared in print that Wilkes Booth had not performed as brilliantly as usual; there was conjecture about his health. In some instances Wilkes pretended to illnesses, and deliberately let the public believe he was subject to sore throats.

Wilkes disliked deceiving the public, but even his love of the stage came second to his work for the Confederacy. He wrote Ella of all these things, but was careful to cover the facts with a curtain only she could see through in case the letters fell into enemy hands. More and more he wanted to take part in actual battle against the Yankees. Finally in the headquarters in the Queen's Hotel, Jacob Thompson gave him the opportunity. "Wilkes," he yawned, "would you like to see a little action?"

Wilkes poised his pencil over a map of New York.

Thompson was enjoying the moment. "What's the matter?"

"I'm afraid you might not mean what I hope you do," Wilkes said. "You mean, you'd actually send me into the war?"

"Yes. If you want to join John Beall on Lake Erie, I'm here to send you. You know, Johnny is at Sandusky, Ohio. He's the man who will test our plan, really, but I think it only fair that the originator of the prison plot be in on the thing from the start. John's about ready to strike. If you like, I'll send him orders to move on with you."

"When do I leave?" Wilkes asked.

Thompson riffled through some papers on his desk and pulled out an envelope which he handed over to Wilkes. "Whenever you want. The orders are in the envelope. See that Captain Beall gets them as soon as possible."

John Beall's work at Sandusky had been as much of a role as any Wilkes had ever played on the stage. It had taken months to perfect his image, but Beall had carried out his orders perfectly. Aiming to free the rebel prisoners on Johnson's Island, Beall had arrived in the little Lake Erie town pretending to be the fun-loving, idle son of a New York banker, a Yankee who wanted to stay out of the war and enjoy life. He played the part well, making friends of the local citizens and of the authorities whose task it was to administer and guard the federal prison on the island.

Beall was properly supported by Confederate funds to enact the rich youth; he lavished gifts, wined and dined his guests, sometimes in the dining rooms of the local hotel and homes. His extravagance was one of the major reasons for his popularity. Welcomed everywhere he went, he was eventually invited into the federal prison offices, where he made friends with the guards and officials, giving them food, cigars, and even money. The day arrived when he was allowed to give prisoners gifts of tobacco and fruit—a day he had long anticipated. Once the precedent was set and contact with the prisoners was made and approved by the officials, Beall was able to move fast. His fine cigars to the prisoners now carried messages advising the rebels of their expected participation in their own release. The guards themselves passed out the cigars among the prisoners.

Word of the day and hour would be sent them. When they overpowered the guards, Beall and his men would be waiting outside the prison gates with guns and a ship. The prison officials and outside guards would be immobilized one way or another, possibly through drugging their food and drink.

Sandusky lay peaceful in the twilight. Wilkes sat in an old wicker rocking chair, his feet up on the railing skirting the long porch of the Sandusky Hotel. He looked forward to the moment when he could intercept Johnny, who must expect Wilkes to be hundreds of miles away. Yet Wilkes dared not surprise John where others might observe too closely, so he had chosen the porch, dark and deserted at that late hour.

John Beall came striding from the docks to the hotel, his long legs moving quickly. Wilkes waited until John was taking the porch steps, two at a time, before he gave the low whistle known to all Confederates, a few strains of "Dixie."

They stood together, hands clasped; pounding each other's back, hugging each other, laughing. "What brings you, Wilkes? What on earth brings you here?"

Thirty-Five

They waited, though, until they were in Johnny's room before Johnny got his answer. In an all-night talk, Wilkes learned everything about Johnny's stay in Sandusky. Johnny was registered at the hotel as James Roundacre of New York. Wilkes would have to register under another name, too, and they decided he would claim to be Joseph Carson, a representative of the Gatling Company.

Tremendously pleased that they were to work together on the plan that Wilkes had offered the Confederate government, Johnny then revealed his plan of attack upon the Johnson's Island prison.

Johnny's strategy involved the capture of two Yankee passenger ships, one of which would be sunk. The other would be used to seize the United States gunboat *Michigan*, anchored off Johnson's Island to protect it.

Wilkes was worried. "How in hell can you take an armed gunboat? It could blast the passenger ship right out of the water."

"I've got it all worked out to the minute, Wilkes. We'll take it from within. I've got several of our men aboard that gunboat, accepted as chefs. They're going to dope the dinner of every Yankee aboard, and before they get off they'll wreck the engine room, and send off a skyrocket as a signal for us to move in on the island."

The plan depended on team work and split-second timing. Beall's men—twenty of them, excluding Wilkes—were assigned to their tasks. All had been handpicked by Jacob Thompson and had passed under Johnny's careful scrutiny and training.

They would seize the *Philo Parsons* as a Yankee ship on Yankee waters.

Dispersed to the various landings along the lake where passengers embarked, Beall's men would board a large passenger ship in small groups. When night came they were to meet in the cabin that Beall would occupy as James Roundacre, and be given black outfits—much like the skin-tight costumes Wilkes wore in his Shakespearean roles—black eye masks, and black moccasins.

At Beall's order, they would take control of the *Parsons* and sail the ship onto the course of the other passenger vessel, the *Island Queen*. Passengers on both ships would be handled courteously and were not to be harmed unless in self-defense. All would be put ashore on the Canadian side of the lake, then the *Island Queen* would be scuttled to put her out of service to the Yankees. The *Parsons* would be sailed to Johnson's Island to await the signal from the U.S. gunboat that the landing could be safely made.

The success of the entire maneuver depended greatly upon the rebels aboard the *Michigan*. Blond, mustached Godfrey Hyams in his pose as a friend of young Roundacre, had been accepted at Sandusky, too. He also pretended to be a young man of unlimited wealth, and he spent much money in catering to the whims and likes of the Yankees at Sandusky and on the gunboat. He really was acting as a guest chef aboard the boat, and the crew, enjoying the rich foods and liquors he served them, found no quarrel with his idea of fun. Hyams was given the task of wining and dining the men and officers of the United States vessel into drugged insensibility so that the boat could be taken without firing a single shot.

It had been no problem to arrange a champagne dinner party for the crew of the *Michigan*.

Seven of Beall's men boarded the *Philo Parsons* at Sandusky. While the others roamed the decks in apparent idleness, Wilkes and Johnny went to Johnny's cabin to wait and to check out the equipment they had brought aboard which was to be distributed to all the men.

Soon enough, all the men had boarded at their assigned stations, and walked among the passengers, engaging in conversations, in card games, in deck watching. The day passed pleasantly.

When the time came to report to Captain Beall in his cabin, they came quietly and unnoticed by the other passengers. The cabin was crowded now, but there was enough room for each man to dress and take his weapon—a Colt gun and a knife.

Their instructions were repeated, and Johnny inspected each man. Then, assured, he buckled on his own gun, pulled down his eye mask, and looked over to Wilkes, also dressed in the black outfit. "Would you say we're ready for a curtain to rise, Joe?"

Wilkes was grinning under his eye mask. "Let 'er rise, Captain."

Johnny looked at his watch. "It's time." They left the cabin in pairs, slipped silently across the darkened decks, and each went to his pre-assigned post.

Rarely had Lake Erie basked under a more brilliant moon. The wake moving away from the prow of the ship ran golden and light. Music came from the salon where the ship's passengers were gathered for the evening. It was a night for romance and not for war, thought Wilkes. He would ask Ella if she would like a wedding trip aboard a ship.

He followed closely behind Johnny; Burley, the huge man of the crew, moved with them. Avoiding the lights from the cabin, the three of them reached the wheelhouse. Peering in the small window, they saw the Captain standing in conversation beside his helmsman at the wheel. Both were at ease.

Johnny waved his companions on. They drew their guns from their belts, opened the door to the wheelhouse, and stepped into the cabin, leveling their guns at the two crewmen.

Johnny's soft voice was raised to a higher pitch than usual. "Sir, we take this ship in the name of the Confederate states. You and your crew are prisoners."

The old sailor's blue eyes were wide with shock. "Are you men," he sputtered, "you men . . . are you rebels?"

Johnny's pride trembled in his voice. "We are Confederates. Tell the helmsman to turn that wheel over to my aide. Now!"

The captain did not mistake the mood of the rebels. "All right, do it."

The helmsman removed his hands quickly and Burley came forward to take it into his own huge hands. The *Parsons* responded to his touch, and the ship continued downlake undisturbed by the change of command. After Wilkes and Johnny tied the prisoners to chairs with rope from the ship, Johnny went to the cabin door and gave a low whistle to notify the others that the wheel was in Confederate hands. It was also a call to active duty. Others of the group began knocking the crew members of the *Parsons* unconscious so that no one could aid the imprisoned captain and helmsman.

Leaving the two prisoners secured in the cabin and Burley at the wheel lustily singing "Dixie," Wilkes and Johnny were joined by those who had been called by the whistle, and went to the salon where most of the passengers were located.

The first realization the passengers had that there was trouble aboard was the sound of Johnny Beall's ringing voice from the top of the stairs. The people turned, alarmed, to look up at the masked men in black who stood on the stairs and aimed guns at them.

"We are Confederates and we have just taken command of this ship. You are prisoners of war. Ladies and gentlemen, stand still!"

The reaction was not totally unexpected. Several women screamed in terror and one fainted. Her husband caught her, lowered her into a chair, and fanned her white face.

Wilkes saw that the passengers were desperately afraid, and he knew that panic brings its own troubles. He whispered to Johnny, and Johnny nodded in agreement.

Leaping to a table where he could be seen by everyone, Wilkes held up restraining hands, pleading for attention to quell the rising hysteria. "We're not going to harm anyone. We're going to put all of you safely ashore within a few minutes. Now, be calm, stay quiet, follow orders and you don't need to be afraid."

Johnny touched Wilkes on the knee, motioning to him to bend low so they could confer. Remembering St. Louis, he wanted Wilkes to direct all the male passengers to come forward, one by one, to place their guns and knives on the table. Several pistols and a dagger were laid on the table at Wilkes' feet and were promptly carried off to John's cabin. The passengers were left under the watchful eye of three rebels and once more advised to keep quiet until their transfer to shore. Anyone resisting orders would be shot. They whimpered and fussed, but kept calm enough and made no overt move.

The conspirators took to the deck again, and Johnny and Wilkes led the work of clearing the decks for action. For its maneuver against the gunboat, the boat had to be lightened as much as possible and, although they did not expect it, they had to be prepared for any chase which might come their way. Johnny had learned his lesson on the *Chesapeake*.

In the wheelhouse where Burley was still enthralling himself with a rendition of "Dixie," Johnny Beall found a cash box containing $80,000. This prize of war was immediately sent to the cabin for safekeeping. It would pay for a lot of ammunition in the great Northwest operation.

They headed the *Philo Parsons* for Middle Bass Island, knowing that somewhere near there they would find the big steamer, the *Island Queen*, which maintained a route between Sandusky and Detroit. Beall's men lay flat on their stomachs on deck where they could scan the night waters. The ship sailed in a strange silence; there was no more music from the salon.

And then suddenly they saw the *Island Queen* moving along through the gold-touched waters. They could not chance the possibility that their craft had been sighted by the *Queen*, off course and without its usual lights ablaze. They would have to attack before she took warning. Burley received Beall's order, and the *Parsons* was swung around to come across the path of the unsuspecting steamer.

"She's close enough to touch!" Wilkes observed.

"Watch Burley now! He'll bring us around to board her."

The *Parsons* came around to cut off the forward progress of the *Queen*, whose crew only partially realized what was happening. The steamer was at the mercy of the *Parsons*' mammoth grappling hooks which flew through the air onto the *Queen*'s decks. The Confederates pulled on the ropes, the hooks held, and the two ships were bound together.

Guns in hand, Johnny and his men boarded the *Queen*. Again each man knew his job. As soon as the crew was standing with raised arms, Johnny and Wilkes and several others raced for the wheelhouse. The door to the captain's sanctuary was locked—a defensive measure taken too late. The rebels kicked the door off its hinges. Once more Johnny faced a Yankee captain. "Sir, I have just taken your ship in the name of the Confederacy. I warn you, sir, don't try to resist. Your men are prisoners on deck. You and your helmsman will do as I say."

The captain of the *Queen* took a puff on his old pipe. "The ship is yours."

Aboard the steamer were passengers who brought smiles to the faces of the Confederates—thirty-five privates and officers of the 130th Ohio Infantry Regiment on their way home to Toledo, all of them unarmed. Herded like sheep, they went below the decks under the prodding of the Confederate guns and there they stayed until their release on shore.

Johnny took a particular delight piloting the captured steamer to shore. Wilkes was beside him, enjoying every second of the fast trip. They put the Yankee soldiers, the crew, the skipper, and the helmsman ashore, and saluted the stranded men with a rebel yell.

The captain shook his fist at Johnny. "Some day someone will find out who you are behind the masks. And that day, I promise you, you'll be punished for this piracy!"

Johnny took his mask off and said: "Remember my face well, sir. We may meet again some day."

The passengers and crews of both ships now ashore, the two vessels, lanterns out, were sailed out side by side into deep waters. Johnny could not allow such a valuable ship as the *Queen* to remain in the active service of the Union. He remained silent, his hand on the railing, as his men went about scuttling the ship. It was not the kind of thing a man of the sea liked to do.

Burley stood by the *Parsons*, holding her close to the doomed ship. As water rushed into the hold of the *Island Queen*, the rebels hastily retreated to the *Parsons*. As the paddle-boat moved away from her, the great *Queen* began to founder. The waters were beginning to swirl around her; the decks were awash. The beautiful ship was quickly gone from sight. The sinking, so fast and so silent, depressed the men's spirits.

At about eleven o'clock they sighted Middle Bass Island, still a half-mile distant. Approaching with reduced speed and without lanterns, the only sound that of the paddle wheel on the water, the rebels lined the deck to look for the gunboat. Their target rode at anchor dead ahead, lantern lights glowing, rocking ever so gently on the midnight waters. Beyond her, looming big in the dark, touched on its high points by moonlight, was Johnson's Island.

The *Parsons* drifted lazily, anchor up. The rebels had to be ready to move in the moment the sky rocket exploded overhead. The signal was to come by exactly midnight, and even though they had less than an hour, the wait was endless.

At twelve midnight, all were crouched shoulder-to-shoulder on the deck, waiting. First the signal would come and then the seizure of the *Michigan* would begin.

The only light in the sky came from a frosty moon. They waited another minute, two, three, five... No rocket came. The *Parsons* drifted on the backwaters. They waited far beyond the time of hope. Had something gone wrong?

"Give Hyams more time," Wilkes urged.

The anxious crew began to whisper to one another. If Hyams had been discovered, maybe the *Michigan* was just waiting for them to move in. She could open up with her guns and blast them apart!

Up there on the island, behind those ugly prison walls, those men who had relied on John Beall were waiting. By now they must be sick with dread.

Wilkes could not tolerate the thought of failure. "Johnny, are you sure we can trust Hyams? Is there a possibility he would betray us? I don't see how else this plan could fail."

"He came to us from Jacob Thompson. I'd have trusted him with my life. But now, I just don't know."

When the watch came to the second hour after the deadline, Johnny was trying to remember everything he could about Hyams. "He was once a prisoner on Johnson's Island," he told Wilkes. "He escaped and got to Jacob Thompson."

"Well, that certainly ought to keep him clear of working with the Yankees," Wilkes commented. "He'd hardly want to betray the men of Johnson's Island."

"Could he have fooled all of us? Maybe it was all set up by the Yankees."

"Well, look, we can go ahead. We can stand off the men of the gunboat and get to the prison. Once we get to the men, we're all right."

Before Johnny could consider Wilkes' words, his crew had

come to stand near them at the railing. Johnny turned to them in surprise. "Who released you men from your posts of duty?"

One of them made himself spokesman for all. "Sir, we're sorry but we're not going back to our posts at all. It's no use watching any more. Sir, we want to get out of here right away. We figure our plan is discovered and that we stand now under the guns of the *Michigan*."

Johnny's voice had the crack of a leather whip. "What in hell are you talking about?"

"There won't be a rocket sir. It's obvious we've been betrayed or discovered. If you keep us here, the *Michigan* will surely fire on us. It would be suicide to stay, sir."

John looked from one face to the other; the moonlight on their faces showed him the look of mutiny. "We'll attack the *Michigan* at once," he shouted to Burley. "Signal the engine room, sir."

"Sir, if you attack the *Michigan* it will be without our help and without us at all. We'll go over the side and swim to shore before we'll take any part in any action as foolhardy as an attack on the armed gunboat."

Johnny finally reached the question which any commander dreads to ask. "Are you men refusing to honor the order of your commanding officer?"

"Yes, sir, if you want it straight. That's the way it's going to be. We're refusing to commit suicide or to follow an unreasonable order."

Wilkes and John stood alone, except for Burley. They could not attack the *Michigan* under such hopeless circumstances. John gave an anguished glance to the gunboat, to the island, to the shadowed prison. "All right," he said. "We'll turn back. But I command each of you to sign a paper admitting your treachery and cowardice here this night. I'll report each of you to Toronto for punishment.

"Proceed to the ladies' salon. It seems appropriate for the occasion. You'll sign as non-fighters of the Confederacy."

While Johnny went to the wheelhouse to confer with Burley and to change the course of the ship, Wilkes accompanied the men to the salon.

Daintily furnished, the place was an incongruous background for the black-clad, armed men. Johnny returned from the wheelhouse, went to the hand-carved writing desk, and turned up the wick on the lamp. He reached for a pen, bottle of ink, and writing paper and wrote rapidly in long, strong language. When he finished he handed it to Wilkes.

"You want me to read it to them?" asked Wilkes.

"Yes, please do."

"On board the *Philo Parsons*, September 20, 1864. We, the undersigned crew of the boat aforesaid, take pleasure in expressing our admiration of the gentlemanly bearing, skill and courage of Captain Beall, as a commanding officer and gentleman. But believing and being well convinced that the enemy is informed of our approach and is so well prepared that we cannot possibly make it a success, and having already captured two boats, we respectfully decline to prosecute it further."

Wilkes saw the men were greatly relieved to hear that the document was not nearly so critical as it might have been.

The men signed, and Johnny put it into a piece of oil-skin he had brought from the wheelhouse. "We'll take the *Parsons* to deep water on the Canadian shore and burn her," calmly he told them. "You'll all have to swim for the beach. From there, go your own way. I'm no longer responsible for you."

The *Parsons* ablaze, Wilkes and Johnny made the dive together. After reaching shore, they sat on the sandy beach to rest, their backs to a rising wind. Shivering in the pre-dawn, wet and miserable, they watched the wreckage of the Yankee ship sink beneath the waters.

"It's a bitter defeat," Johnny managed to say at last.

"Look, man. War isn't all victory. Besides, you've sunk two Yankee vessels tonight, and the gunboat may have a wrecked engine room. We can't be sure."

Johnny was not easily brought around to a better frame of mind. "We'll never have another chance at Johnson's Island. The surprise element is gone now, and so is the method of taking the island. We'll be lucky to get out of those woods alive. By now the whole area must be awake with reports. They've seen the flames. They'll be out hunting for us, if they aren't already."

"We'd better start moving, man. It's a long way to Toronto."

Thirty-Six

Both Wilkes and Johnny appreciated the warmth in the Queen's Hotel as they sat down to confer with Jacob Thompson. Of their trek from Lake Erie, they had been able to travel by horse only the last twenty-five miles, getting the loan of two from a farmer who finally took their word that he could pick up the horses and receive his money at the end of the week.

Thompson watched them settle back in comfortable chairs, cigars and liquor in hand. "Gentlemen, I suppose you'd like to know what happened aboard the *Michigan.*"

They leaned forward in their chairs, surprised. "You know?" Johnny gaped.

"I've had word. Your work was well done, Captain Beall; it was mine which failed you. Our friend, Godfrey Hyams, had me fooled, and don't think that doesn't rattle me to the core. I've even wondered if I should continue in this work. He gave your plan of attack to Captain Carter of the *Michigan.*"

"Then the gunboat was ready for us?" Johnny was appalled.

"Not exactly, no. Hyams was late in getting his information to the captain. I don't know why, maybe he lacked the proof he needed until the last minute. Anyway he didn't warn anyone soon enough to save the two boats from you. And he didn't warn the captain in time to prevent the crew from being knocked out with drugs in their food and drink. The other two men you had aboard the *Michigan* did their job very well. Why there was a slipup in Hyams' timing, I just don't know. But your two agents were even able to wreck the engine room of the *Michigan* as you ordered. The ship was not able to move, but the guns were turned on you at the last minute."

They discussed the Lake Erie venture for an hour and were disturbed not only by the failure of the mission, but by the realization that Godfrey Hyams had undoubtedly identified John Yates Beall to the Yankees. Once more they had a cause against Johnny. Wilkes worried over that more than anything else.

Restless and concerned, Wilkes paced the room, tossing out impractical suggestions. Why not return to Lake Erie and rescue the men at the prison, after all? The Union would not expect them to strike again on the very heels of the abortive attempt. The surprise element could prove successful.

Both Beall and Thompson rejected the idea. There was no hope of surprising the federal forces in the area again. The guard duty was already doubled, and the island was a fort. Any further raid attempts would only work against the prisoners, who were already being subjected to harsher treatment and more rigid restrictions. The unhappy Wilkes was prevailed upon to sit down and listen to his own next assignment.

Within minutes Thompson had fired Wilkes and Johnny with new enthusiasm. The date had been set for the Northwest Prison Plan: Election Day in the United States, November 8, 1864. On that day the major cities of the Union from Minnesota to New York would be set afire, the locations of the fires making it necessary for civilian officials to pull men away from the prisons and arsenals in order to fight the numerous fires, quell the public panic, and keep the peace. Then, while the authorities were kept busy, the rebels would storm the prisons and release the waiting Confederates.

All over the northwestern United States, barns and homes were already being stocked with guns and ammunition, horses, boats, carriages. Even trains were being brought in as close to the prisons as possible so the escaping men would have every possible chance of obtaining transportation. Men everywhere, even in the prisons, were being armed.

Camp Douglas, in Chicago, was expected to yield the greatest number of prisoners. Nine thousand rebels were there, including the famed raider, Morgan, and his men. As the buildings of Chicago burned, Camp Douglas would be attacked from three sides. The extremely important assignment was in the capable hands of St. Leger Grenfel, Felix Stidger, and John Hines. Carefully chosen prisoners were already working from the inside for the day when they would rush the guards from within and help open the camp to the rebels.

But before the day arrived, additional money was needed. It was taking an appalling amount to finance guns, ammunition, transportation, hiding places, bribes, travel expenses of agents, the paying of civilians. Thompson reported that there just did not seem to be enough cash at any time. Funds would have to be raised some way.

Shaking the ashes from his cigar into a silver tray at his elbow, Thompson looked at John. "You're going to the State of New York, Captain. There you're to organize and lead raids on federal payroll trains carrying gold for federal troops."

Though the assignment took him from sea to land, John nodded his approval. Seizing a train and taking its gold sounded like an interesting mission. He looked at Wilkes and they shared a thought.

"Let me go with him," Wilkes requested.

Thompson shook his head. "Your assignment is for New York City. Right away. Johnny will work the raids all during the Northwest operation. I'm sorry, but I can't let you two work together this time."

Wilkes and John were to take a day of rest in Toronto and then proceed to their new posts. Twenty-four hours later, astride newly purchased horses, the two said good-bye in front of the Queen's Hotel. Leaning forward in their saddles, they grasped one another's hand in a firm lock.

"Take care, Wilkes," cautioned Johnny. "I don't want to hear of any harm coming to you."

"I'm going to miss you, Johnny."

Strangely, the half-joking banter which had passed between them since childhood did not come easy this time.

"Well, watch yourself, Wilkes."

"Watch out yourself. I'm not sure Old Abe would be willing to exchange you again."

"Hell, if the damned Yankees catch me again, I'll just sit and take it easy until John Wilkes Booth comes to free me!"

Wilkes was grinning too. "Just rattle your chains and I'll come running."

John laughed, stood in his stirrups, pulled his horse around, and with a wave of an arm, was racing down the street. A block

204

away, he pulled the horse up, stood again in the stirrups, snatched his cap from his head, and waved a last good-bye.

Spurring his horse on again, Johnny rounded a corner and was gone from view.

Wilkes, a lump in his throat and a terrible sense of loneliness upon him, rode out of Toronto, feeling that he should have insisted on his right to be with his friend in the battles of their country. It was all he could do to keep from pulling his horse around, to race back down the road which Johnny had taken.

Thirty-Seven

The Northwest attack plan was perfected; the hour, the date, and targets all set. Jefferson Davis decreed that on Election Day, November 8, 1864, at high noon New York time, under the guidance of the military personnel of the South, the Confederate govenment's secret army—now given the name of the Sons of Liberty—would effect a simultaneous attack.

Wilkes, according to his orders, met with Colonel Robert Martin in New York. A room in the Fifth Avenue Hotel became their headquarters.

In the meantime, also at the suggestion of his superiors, Wilkes made arrangements to join his brothers, Junius and Edwin, in a play. The three famous brothers agreed to make the New York appearance for charity. Wilkes, however, found it difficult to concentrate on the play and even harder to get along with Edwin, who so often hurled anti-Confederate remarks without thinking. But Wilkes could not afford to speak out now. The plot to burn New York and release the prisoners held in the harbor in Fort Lafayette, where the stern General Dix was in command, held Wilkes' real attention. His meetings with the Confederates, stolen from hours of his stage work, meant everything.

Nor did blonde Katie McDonald, working hard in her father's print shop, resent a minute of the time she gave the job. Wilkes thought her tall, willowy figure and shining-haired beauty were worthy of the stage, but he did not say so. She was a devout rebel of strong character and a disarming frankness of manner.

Seated next to Wilkes at the first meeting in Carter's Restaurant, a look in her blue eyes, a rise in her color, told everyone at the table that Katie was not immune to Wilkes' appeal. Katie's hand brushed his as she reached for a cup of coffee, her gaze lingered too long on his face, her voice mellowed too quickly when she spoke to him. There was no doubt in his mind that this girl of great intelligence, high spirit, and Irish blue eyes, would follow him anywhere he might beckon.

Wilkes was greatly tempted. Katie McDonald would be a joy to any man. To watch her undress, to see her naked, to make her eager, to take all that she offered, would be to know moments of violent ecstasy. And a few years earlier, Wilkes would have done just that, night after night.

Now, though, Wilkes recalled the day he discovered his mother was an unmarried woman, and all desires went from him. He would not be like his father and dishonor the one woman he loved. Katie McDonald might as well have been just another conspirator. Her wild infatuation, however, grew with every meeting. As night followed night, she realized that Wilkes Booth had no intention of even holding her hand.

The conspirators met together in a small room at the back of Carter's Restaurant on Election Eve for the final checking of their plans. Two dozen Confederates sat at the large table, including Wilkes, Captain Headley, Colonel Robert Martin, Captain Longmire, Katie McDonald and her father, and the leaders of the Sons of Liberty, the key men of the plot, who would disperse throughout the city at dawn for the purposes of leading others into action.

Colonel Martin, who did most of the talking in a low pitch so that no one outside the room could hear, went over the details of the national plan. Chicago's Camp Douglas, he said, was to be attacked from the river as well as from the land. The prisoners, supplied with weapons ranging from stones to Navy Colts, would storm the gates from within at the precise moment the Sons of Liberty arrived outside. It was anticipated that Camp Douglas, most of its military personnel withdrawn to help control the raging Chicago fires, would fall with little resistance under the guns of the riverboats and the double attack upon its guards and gates.

Haunted by the betrayal at Lake Erie, Wilkes could not let the Camp Douglas attack plan stand without questioning it.

"Colonel," he asked, "can we be sure that the federal authorities aren't aware of our plans? On such a wide scale, with so many hundreds of people involved, it hardly seems possible that some of the things going on in the city haven't aroused their interest."

Colonel Martin nodded. "Oh, yes, indeed, Captain! The federal authorities are aroused. They most certainly do suspect something, but they're helpless. There's no break in our lines. We stand solid, and they haven't been able to determine a thing."

"But if they suspect," Wilkes worried.

"Captain, we're taking every precaution. The suspicions of the Chicago authorities arise only from generalities: They know the city harbors many pro-Southern men. *The Chicago Tribune* has been stirring up the situation, campaigning to make the citizens act for their own protection, calling upon them to set up their own home-grown army, to organize a home guard unit. The Mayor of Chicago has worked with the *Tribune*, and now the citizens are being armed to patrol their own streets in the event of what is termed an 'uprising.' " The Colonel smiled. "What the good Mayor and the *Tribune* don't know is that most of the men they have armed are the Sons of Liberty. Their cooperation has helped us tremendously!"

Wilkes sat back. If the local authorities armed Chicagoans, they could hardly suspect that such action suited the rebels most handily. "What about St. Louis? What's happening there?"

"St. Louis is under control. The boats and docks are getting special attention. Fires in that area will draw away the guards from the arsenals and prisons, and the entire attack will operate on schedule, as in Chicago and here."

"And here in New York," Wilkes stated, "we're relying on

the Sons of Liberty, too." He paused, looking at the civilians of that organization. "There's no way they'll fail us?"

"Fail us?" Colonel Martin looked from Wilkes to the man seated next to him. "Would you like to tell us what the Sons of Liberty will do tomorrow in New York?"

George Leander, a citizen of Rochester, arose from his chair. He looked at Wilkes, giving him a curt nod.

"Captain, tonight, a few hours ago, in this city, twenty thousand Sons of Liberty met in convention. Twenty thousand men, all armed. The convention is still in progress, and I've got to get back to it right soon. If I may review briefly——"

The Sons had arrived in New York from all over the nation, each state setting up its own activities and then subordinating them to the overall plan. The main aim of the plot would be the capture of Fort Lafayette and the prison, a feat approximating a total victory on any battlefield.

The Sons of Liberty, all twenty thousand, all armed, would march down Broadway, ostensibly in an Election Day convention in support of the Presidential candidacy of General George McClellan. Actually, they would march to the Sub-Treasury Building on Wall Street, a property of the United States government, take the building, and hold the federal officials in custody. The next target would be police headquarters on Worth Street which would be seized with the help of police officers who were also Sons of Liberty.

Next on schedule was the Federal Courthouse, with all its federal officers and officials; and finally, Fort Lafayette. The strike from armed prisoners inside would come at a pre-set hour as soon as the Sons of Liberty were on the grounds. General Dix, commander of the fort, would be the first man seized, and he would be held until he issued orders for the guards to release all the Confederates and open the fort to the Sons of Liberty.

The fires that Wilkes and the others would set throughout the city would coincide with the actions of the Sons. After the fires were burning, Wilkes and the others would get to Fort Lafayette to help hold General Dix and his men so that the prisoners could escape out of the harbor. When the last prisoner was out and away, the rescuers would follow—it was expected there would be enough available boats to accommodate everyone.

Still, Wilkes was not completely convinced that every phase

of the immense operation was being handled with all due secrecy. All evening he was uneasy.

"Colonel Martin, there's something else that bothers me. Do you know that the Confederate Associated Press is all but decorating us? Richmond newspapers are actually carrying stories—rumors—of our plan to seize all the prisons in the North. They're boasting that we're going to burn New York City. Of course they aren't identifying us, but my God, the plan is right on their front pages!"

Martin nodded. "Well, it's too bad, of course, that there's any speculation. But don't let it worry you too much, Captain. The Union authorities consider it bravado and nothing more."

"But I don't see why they printed it——"

"Look, Captain. If the Union officials believed the story, they'd at least have set up some kind of defense in all these cities. But now it's only a matter of hours until we strike. It's too late for them to do a thing."

Wilkes gave up. There was no time now for anything but concentrating on the job ahead. He was to help set fire to half a dozen of the big hotels, then get to Fort Lafayette.

That night, he persuaded himself that everything was all right after all. Gossip and rumor carried a certain element of danger, of course, but they were not military facts. The shouts of the Sons of Liberty in a torchlight Election Eve rally kept him awake for a long time, and he got out of bed several times to stand at the window as the mob paraded past the hotel.

New York City was jammed with wide-eyed, celebrating, noisy people, many of them strangers. General George McClellan, the Democratic candidate for the Presidency of the United States, was carried on the shoulders of his admirers, the Sons of Liberty, his ears almost deafened by shouts of acclaim. Here was a General not afraid to talk back to Abe Lincoln, a man after their own hearts—and their votes.

The mammoth Copperhead parade proceeded through the streets in a holiday mood. The Southern sympathizers carried their man past the *Tribune* building where the giant portrait of Abe Lincoln hung, decorated this night with red, white, and blue bunting. The crowds, with their General hero in tow, stopped there long enough to boo Lincoln in a mighty roar.

General McClellan looked away from the portrait of his

commander in chief who had caustically asked of him if he might "borrow" McClellan's army in the field if McClellan were not going to use it.

And when the noise of the parade abated, Wilkes closed his eyes. The morning would soon come. He stared at the ceiling a long time, though, and even in his sleep, his fists were clenched and he was restless.

While he slept, trains bearing federal troops slid into the New York station. The trains not only brought armed troops, but men to lead them, and the man in charge of them all was General Ben Butler.

Quietly and efficiently the famed officer moved into the city where he dispersed his troops, hundreds of them, throughout the vast area. They went to the United States Sub-Treasury Building, to the Courthouse, the police stations, the federal offices. Especially heavy reinforcements, armed to the teeth, went to Fort Lafayette.

General Butler himself went to the Fifth Avenue Hotel and was assigned an entire floor, his own room directly under the rooms occupied by Wilkes Booth, Colonel Martin, and Captain Headley.

In their convention hall, the Sons of Liberty were in the very act of distributing weapons when word was brought that Butler was placing his men at every point of the city where an attack had been planned!

Utter confusion ripped through the convention hall. Leander banged and banged on the table for order. Some of the men did not wait to hear him. Word was that Butler had set up cannons everywhere. The secret attack was no secret and would be met with military resistance! Hundreds of men bolted for the doors of the hall, running for their hotels, their carriages, their homes, and to the station.

After consultation with men as pale-faced as he, Leander shouted into the hubbub that the convention of the Sons of Liberty stood adjourned. And then he, too, found the nearest exit and beat a hasty retreat to Rochester.

Before the sun rose on Election Day, Wilkes was awakened by a quiet but insistent knocking. Instantly, he knew something was wrong. He opened the door to let in Colonel Martin and Captain Headley, both fully clothed, their faces grim with shock and disappointment. Wilkes stood back and mechanically reached for his robe. The alarm in their faces flooded into his heart.

"My God!" Martin exclaimed, "It's all over. Do you hear, Wilkes, it's all over."

Wilkes buttoned the robe with fingers that shook. "Make sense, man! What are you saying?"

"General Butler's here. Came in at midnight. He's got the city. Declared martial law. He's got all the targets covered with men and cannon."

"And that's only part of it," said Captain Headley, "The Sons of Liberty have deserted. They can't be found."

"It can't be," Wilkes groaned. "Everything is lost for the South if we don't free our men. Don't you understand?"

Colonel Martin put a hand on Wilkes' arm. "It has happened, Captain. We're all through. Here, at least."

Wilkes went to the window and looked out with bleak eyes at the sight of the federal troops far below, pacing the streets of New York. "How did they know?"

"Maybe they don't actually know anything, Wilkes. But as you kept worrying about it last evening, maybe they have been taking stock in rumors. What does it matter? They're here." Colonel Martin sat down wearily on the bed and looked at the other two blankly.

Wilkes turned from the window. "Maybe the Sons of Liberty are through, but we're not."

Colonel Martin's spine straightened a little. "What do you mean, Captain?"

"We have Longmire, McMaster, McDonald, Ashbrook, Kennedy. And others, real Southerners. And we can go right on with our plans. We don't have to depend on anyone else. We'll concentrate on Fort Lafayette. We'll blow the gates apart with gunpowder and grab Dix outselves. All we really need is Dix. With him as hostage, we can demand and get anything we want. We'll make General Butler talk terms of exchange. All the rebels for Dix. Lincoln himself would order the exchange."

"It could be done," said the Colonel. "With some changes, of course. There are things to be rearranged you know. But, by God, maybe we *could* do it!"

The next day public reports came to them from all over the Northwest. Every newspaper carried the story. The Northwest

Conspiracy could be summed up in one word: rout! Stunned, Wilkes kept to his room, unable to eat.

Chicago's Camp Douglas had been the worst disaster of all, the very worst. There the attack had been anticipated, and the leading conspirators were picked up by federal authorities before they could even get to Camp Douglas. Felix Stidger—long a member of the Knights of the Golden Circle, high in office in that group, beloved in that office even before the shooting began at Fort Sumter—had proved a traitor to the Confederacy. He had been working for the United States government all along and it was he who had alerted General Butler and other Union officers.

In hearing about Stidger, Wilkes had to be grateful that their paths had never crossed and that Stidger did not know of Wilkes' work for the Confederacy. But he had known about many of the other agents, and had given all his facts to the Union.

All the next day, and for days to follow, tales came to Wilkes of the collapse of the Confederate plan. The Union had not only triumphed, but had taken more Confederate prisoners. True, a few rebel prisoners had managed to escape, but they had been deliberately allowed to do so by the Yankees, who followed them directly to the plotters' hideouts. More men were thus captured as they gave sanctuary to the fleeing prisoners.

After the first terrible shock, Wilkes rallied quickly to plot anew the capture of Dix and the freeing of the prisoners at Fort Lafayette. The idea took hold of him completely and he had little tolerance for food, sleep, or conversation. He lost weight, and in his face there was a new grimness which was strange to see.

One evening after he failed to appear at the McDonald home for dinner as he had promised, Katie McDonald went to his room. She found him at work on a map of Fort Lafayette. She put a gentle hand on his back. "Wilkes, this is no good. You've got to take time to eat and relax."

"I'm not hungry. Look, we've got to pull this thing off. I don't see how anyone can eat or rest until we've liberated those poor souls in that prison."

Katie touched Wilkes' dark hair, wrapping a curl of it around her finger. "Come on, please. Let's have dinner."

212

"Goddamn it, Katie, get out!" he bellowed, turning his back on her.

She was very sober and calm. "There's someone you love, isn't there?"

"It's more than that. I can't possibly make you understand, Katie."

"Well, she's a lucky woman, whoever she is." She smiled a little. "I'm ashamed of myself, Wilkes. But I do have an excuse. I'm very much in love with you."

Wilkes shook his head. "No, Katie, you aren't. Infatuated a little, I think. But it will pass. And you'll find the right man one of these days."

Katie was at the door. "Oh, I'm in love with you, all right. Katie McDonald is not a woman to misjudge her own heart."

She opened the door and gave him a smile. Then she was gone.

Thirty-Eight

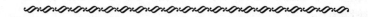

The new plan to seize Fort Lafayette and its commanding officer was based on the same general plan of operation that had been scheduled for Election Day. But this time there was only a small group of proven veterans, each man known to the other without any possibility of a betrayal. This time Wilkes was confident the prisoners would be freed, and his enthusiasm burned more brightly each day.

He was even able to show a genuine interest in the play which he was to do with Edwin and Junius. Edwin had been increasingly worried about the extreme moodiness Wilkes had displayed in the past weeks, he was unhappy about the many mysterious trips Wilkes was always making. Lately, Edwin had even pondered a serious question: Could Wilkes be engaged in any Confederate activities? So it was with relief that Edwin witnessed Wilkes turning to a more lighthearted, agreeable mood. Edwin credited Wilkes' change in attitude to the production of *Julius Caesar*. Not only were all three brothers to be united on the stage for the first time, but their mother was to be in the audience. The production was a real family occasion, and Wilkes seemed to be giving it his best efforts.

Edwin was cast as Brutus, Wilkes as Mark Antony, and Junius was Cassius. Wilkes had wanted the role of Brutus, his favorite, but his mother had requested he play Mark Antony for her, and he could not go against her. The play was scheduled for the Winter Garden Theater, and it was to be a benefit performance with proceeds going to the Sanitary Commission, an organization which was dedicated to helping victims of the war.

Not until after Wilkes and his group had selected November 25 as the day for the second attempt on Fort Lafayette was the date for the play chosen. The theater management also chose November 25! Upset, Wilkes tried to get Edwin to change the date. "I've got a very important engagement on the twenty-fifth," he complained. "This just doesn't suit me."

"Wilkes, be reasonable. There must be several hundred people directly involved in the scheduling of the play. It's too late to expect a change. The tickets are being printed, the advertising is being circulated, everyone's contracted. Tell the young lady you'll have to cancel."

Wilkes gave up arguing. He never did get anywhere with his brother Edwin. Had they ever seen eye to eye on anything? But neither could he change the date of the second attempt at Fort Lafayette.

The conflict began to be a challenge to Wilkes' sense of timing, calling for the mental and physical dexterity which enlivened him. Every moment, every movement on November 25 would have to be handled with all the precision of a watchmaker at work. The McDonald place was to be their operational headquarters. From there they would disperse to burn the hotels and public buildings. Wilkes, however, would begin setting fires in the hotel he occupied as a guest. In the evening, Wilkes would have time to leave the burnings, and rush to the theater. He would appear on stage while the fires were under way, then leave the theater immediately after the performance and get to the McDonald basement with his fellow conspirators. The diversionary fires would be at their worst at the time the theater emptied, and every available man would be brought from the fort and the police stations to put out the fires and to calm the public. That was when Wilkes and his men would proceed to the fort. Fire bombs and guns and ammunition were stored at the shop, where Katie and her father stood guard over them.

As the men in the shop talked of their plans, Katie simply watched Wilkes, hardly caring about anything that was said. Still, she knew her job. The fire bombs were cached in the back room of the McDonald premises, and Katie had the key.

Wilkes, with a gun, ammunition, and a suitcase full of firebombs, registered at the Astor House under an assumed name early on the afternoon of November 25. He sat down in his hotel room to wait. All over the city, his friends were similarly employed. The great hotels of New York—the United States, the Hoffman House, the Fifth Avenue Hotel, the St. Denis, and the Astor House—were hosts to men who had come to set their rooms afire at sunset.

As the winter sun reddened the windows with its last rays of the day, Wilkes went to work, his gun strapped around his waist now. He took the suitcase from the closet where he had stowed it earlier, opened it, and laid a fire bomb on the bed. Then he pulled all the drawers out of the bureau, snatched down the drapes and piled them on the drawers stacked in the center of the floor.

Opening the door, he stepped into the hall and saw that no one was in sight. He put the suitcase in the hall, and leaving the door ajar, went to the bed and got the fire bomb. With another glance out the open door to be sure no one was coming, he hurled the fire bomb at the mound in the center of the room. Flame spurted and a feather of smoke curled upward.

The fire was still in a smoldering state when Wilkes left the hotel, suitcase in hand. The clerk at the desk gave him only a glance. Wilkes had paid for the room in advance, and the clerk was not interested in his departure. The guests' rights to come and go was unquestioned. Soon, though, the odor of smoke would alert other guests, and the clerk would realize that the young man had good reason for leaving the hotel in something of a hurry.

Night had fallen and Wilkes was in make-up at the Winter Garden Theater before he heard the first faraway clang of the fire bells. Knowing a satisfaction he had not yet felt in his war efforts, he went on stage.

The next day, the New York *Herald* would tell the world that "No playgoer has seen Shakespeare presented with attraction more likely to draw and charm the true lover of the drama since the days when Shakespeare himself appeared in his own plays. Three parts in the tragedy of Julius Caesar were personated by actors of first merit—a thing that can hardly be seen in any city but ours. Only English cities could hope to rival us in this; and England does not now possess three tragedians, or even one, comparable to any one of the Booths. Moreover, if there were three men of such ability on the British stage, audiences would hope in vain to see them together in one play."

When the blue velvet curtain came down on the final act, the Booth brothers appeared in front if it, hands joined, bowing to a tremendous ovation.

The playgoers gazed upon the brothers with an attitude of adoration. They looked from one to the other, bewitched by them. There was Edwin, still in the costume of Brutus, a black toga trimmed in silver, strutting to the footlights to motion his two brothers closer to the people. Junius came to stand beside him, dignified in a purple garment with gold, and took his bows grandly.

But the attention of the audience wavered to the younger brother, John Wilkes in a toga of white, his bare, muscular legs wound around with silver straps rising from the white, soft shoes. He timed himself just right, moving slowly forward to join his brothers, thus deliberately centering every eye on him. A huge medallion hung from a wide gold chain around his neck, and the lights made the jewels of it sparkle. He stood just a little apart from his brothers, gave the patrons a low, sweeping bow, and flashed his brilliant smile.

The women in the audience uttered a sound: one scream, one pitch. So unanimous was their vocal reaction that it brought

216

smiles to the brothers. They exchanged winks, perfectly content to let their young brother win all the hearts this night.

Having paid their respects to the audience, the brothers turned to look up at the box where sat their mother, and sister Rosalie. Edwin motioned to the two women to rise so they could be seen by the audience.

Rosalie, as excited as a child, put a loving hand under the aging Mary Ann's arm and helped her to her feet. It was a moment they both would remember all their lives. These were Mary Ann's sons, hers and Junius'. Her love had not been wrong, after all. They were the Booths of Maryland, they shared an honorable name. She loved them dearly.

The brothers bowed to her, and Wilkes blew her a kiss, heedless of everyone. He saw the tears flowing now, the trembling of her lips, the kiss she delicately tossed back to him, and his throat almost closed.

Softly crying, she sat down amid applause and admiration. Rosalie held her hand, murmuring to her. The patrons were thrilled. This had been an added show, something very special.

Suddenly, the theater was filled with the sound of firebells just outside. Gone was the atmosphere of a moment before as everyone listened in terror.

Wilkes, the only man there to know what the bells meant, stepped quickly to the footlights and held up his arms, indicating that the audience should stay seated. He threw a worried glance at the box where his mother and Rosalie were rising to their feet and motioned to Rosalie to be seated and to get their mother back in her chair. He was almost sure the fires were not in the neighborhood of the theater.

"Don't panic!" he shouted above the murmuring and the bells. "Keep your seats. You'll be hurt if you stampede. There's no smoke here, and there's probably no fire, either. The ushers will kindly find out what's wrong and report back. Everyone in here remain seated and we'll keep order."

Edwin put his arms around Wilkes' shoulders in a brotherly fashion, and this act in itself brought a measure of calm to the audience. They kept their places, casting anxious glances from the stage to the doors.

A fireman came down the aisle, followed by several of the ushers and the theater manager. They stood in the pit and held a consultation with the actors who leaned down to them from the stage.

Wilkes stood up. "There's no fire here, folks, no danger. The fire department is checking as a precautionary matter only. Fires have been set in some parts of the city this evening, evidently by rebels, but they are mostly under control. You're safe, but it will be best if you leave now. Go quietly, there's no need for hurrying. Goodnight to you all."

The place was evacuated in an orderly manner. The brothers, still in costume, saw Rosalie and Mary Ann to a cab which would take them to spend the night at Asia Clarke's home.

"You're a darling," his mother told Wilkes. "So brave. You know you stopped a panic in that theater."

Later, swiftly changing his clothing in the dressing room, Wilkes felt a stab of remorse. How innocent his mother was of all that he was doing! But this was war and he would do his duty, no matter what form it took.

It was not true that the fires were under control. They were burning furiously in most of the places where they had been set, with the exception of the Astor House, where, much to Wilkes' disgust, the clerk had responded to the alarm spread by other guests. The fire in Wilkes' room had been doused before it could spread.

But the other buildings burned, some of them to the ground, and firebells sounded the whole night through. Hoses ran dry, fire fighters were choked, blistered and fatigued, and not very successful. A pall of smoke hung low over the city, adding to the gloom of winter.

Wilkes walked as fast as he could to the McDonalds' in Union Square. Now that the play was over at last, he thought, he could go about the real business of the day. Hurrying, he went down the steps to the basement shop of the McDonald establishment with a bounce. The window which opened up onto the steps, built high in the wall of the room below, was flooded with lamplight.

As he reached the second step down to the basement, he saw Katie move the lamp to the table in the center of the room, where she put it down and dimmed it. This plunged the steps into darkness, and Wilkes stopped still, uncertain of his footing. He looked through the filmy curtains again.

Katie stood quietly at the table, her hand still lingering on the lamp. Her father was with her, in conversation with a man who stood with his back to Wilkes. Katie turned her head ever so slightly in the direction of the steps, and ever so slightly she shook her head. She had been listening desperately for the sound of his feet on the steps, and had taken the lamp away deliberately so that he would have to pause outside.

The stranger talking to her father turned to look at Katie. Wilkes recognized him to be Godfrey Hyams, the man who had betrayed John Yates Beall at Lake Erie.

Wilkes moved noiselessly back up the steps and stood on the sidewalk, the odor of burning wood sharp in the air. He tried to think. If Hyams had found out about the McDonalds' work for the Confederacy, he probably knew, too, about the plot to seize the fort and General Dix. Hyams had probably found the fire bombs hidden in the back room of the McDonald shop.

Wilkes fought down the impulse to return to the basement and beat Hyams to death. There would be other federal agents in that shop, probably still in the back room. It wouldn't do Katie any good to go barging in there himself. Hyams wanted every rebel he could lay his hands on. He probably had the place watched, too.

Wilkes hurried away to Carter's Restaurant and the room which was kept available for his group's meetings. Perhaps Hyams was only suspicious of the McDonalds. If anything could be done, Katie would do it—he had to rely on that. And if the plan was lost, surely the others would report, as he was doing, to the private meeting room.

Martin and Headley were waiting for him. Katie had warned them off too.

One by one, the conspirators came in to sit down in weary dejection. The last man to come reported that he had arrived at the McDonald shop just in time to see Katie and the old man taken away in custody of federal officers.

That was the word that Wilkes had dreaded. His fist came crashing down on the table, and he pounded it again and again. "Damn, damn, damn!" There could be no attack upon Fort Lafayette. If there were any action now, it would just go harder on the McDonalds. There was nothing to do now but split up fast and get out of New York.

The cup of coffee in Wilkes' shaking hands went cold, and he stared vacantly into the black depths of it. The conspirators sat together a little longer.

Wilkes was thinking mostly of Katie, in the prison at Fort Lafayette! Katie, who had gone to prison but who had not betrayed them, Katie who had wanted his love, and all the other prisoners at Fort Lafayette, doomed. The South was doomed.

Or were the prisoners lost? Wilkes put the cup on the saucer and looked at the dejected faces around the table. He straightened his posture. A new thought was flooding him, bringing him alive. . . .

"We're not through——" he announced.

Colonel Martin lifted haunted eyes and shook his head. "Come on! Now, you know Lincoln won't even permit the normal exchange of prisoners. He knows every man we get back means the South will fight that much longer."

"Exactly! Lincoln knows how important the release of our prisoners would be to the outcome of this war. But we can beat Lincoln on this issue."

"How? We've tried everything."

Wilkes smiled, but there was no humor in his eyes. His look put a chill into the heart of Colonel Martin. "Our mistake has been in trying to operate on too large a scale. This time we won't need more than half a dozen men."

Colonel Martin shook his head despairingly. "How you can be sure of anyone, I don't know. This time we don't even know which of us informed Hyams."

"Well, I know I've got the solution. But I won't go into it now. I'll be going on to Canada in the morning to talk to Jacob Thompson about it."

Colonel Martin said it for all of them: "Captin, you're overwrought. It's all been very difficult, but there's no more to be done regarding prisoners. The best we can all do now is ask Richmond to put us into field duty."

"No, it's too late for that." Wilkes was adamant. "The Confederate army has got to be re-supplied with its men or there won't be field duty for anyone. Don't you understand, Colonel?"

"You're wasting your time, Captain. Jacob Thompson won't approve anything now."

Wilkes was calm. "Well, if he won't, I'll go see President Davis."

Thirty-Nine

Jacob Thompson was opposed to the new plan Wilkes offered. No more attempts would be made to release prisoners, Thompson told him. Wilkes must content himself with the knowledge that every effort had been made. Now they must all turn their minds and hands to the work that could be done. Wilkes was to return to Washington by ship, taking with him medical supplies from Canada.

Wilkes spent the long, gloomy shipboard hours mulling over his plan which he still had not dropped from his own mind, despite Thompson's bad opinion of it.

In New York State, John Yates Beall was pursuing his own idea for releasing a small band of Confederates. He had received definite word that the Union was transferring Confederate officers from Johnson's Island to Fort Lafayette. A train carrying federal gold and prisoners was going to pass an isolated area of land near Buffalo, near his own hideout.

It looked as though a rescue would be fairly simple. John immediately sent word to the New York conspirators, and Colonel Martin and Captain Headley and Ashbrook responded. He had hoped that Wilkes would be among the men coming to him from New York City, but to his immense disappointment, he learned that Wilkes was already en route to Toronto. The plans had to proceed without him.

Beall and his men would lay iron rails across the tracks just four miles outside of Buffalo to derail the train. Then Beall and his riders would board it, free the prisoners, grab the gold box, and make the passengers change clothing with the rebels, guaranteeing the men a proper disguise when they reached Buffalo. Beall and most of the others rode their own mounts, but two of the men were assigned to drive sleighs which would be used for the escaping Confederates.

It was snowing heavily as the train pulled into sight, and the iron bars on the tracks were already lightly covered with an icy crust. The engine's speed was not such that the impact of derailment would be too severe.

The train slowed, plowed into the rods on the track, and came to a clattering halt, still on the tracks. The railroad personnel aboard the train, from conductor to engineer, were fully armed and under the orders of Union soldiers riding the train in reinforced numbers. The soldiers, guns in hand, swung out and jumped down to the frozen ground, charging toward the horsemen and sleighs.

Completely surprised, John Beall and his men raced away. But the sleighs were slow and the ground slippery. The Yankees seized Anderson, a young conspirator who had fallen onto the icy tracks. He lay there, pleading for his life as Yankee guns nudged at his ribs. For information, they would spare him. He identified the leader of the rebels as John Yates Beall, probably headed, he told them, for Toronto.

John Beall had run out of luck. Waiting in the station house at Niagara Falls for a train to take him to the safety of Toronto, he was suddenly surrounded by Union soldiers. He pulled his gun from his pocket and considered shooting it out, but there were too many women and children about. He would have to make his break for freedom in some other place. John handed his gun to a Yankee. Handcuffed, brutally shoved along, he was escorted under arms to Fort Lafayette in New York Harbor, where he was put in chains and placed in a dungeon to be held for trial.

He was accused of numerous crimes, including the violation of the laws of war, of pirating and burning the *Philo Parsons* and the *Island Queen*, of an attempted attack upon the U.S.S. *Michigan*. He was accused, further, of spying in Ohio and New York, with the implication that he was one of the instigators of the attempted burning of New York City. And, finally, he was accused of the attempted derailment of a federal train. Word of Johnny's capture spread like fire on land, but Wilkes, aboard ship, had no news of it.

As soon as the ship docked in Washington, Wilkes hurried to Ella's cottage. She opened the door herself, staring up at him in disbelief.

He was looking at her with such love and longing that she gave one cry of joy and was in his arms. Big feathery flakes fell on them as they embraced on the steps of the cottage.

As soon as they were inside the house, she assisted him in getting out of his wet topcoat. "Did they let you see Johnny?"

"Johnny? Why, no, I haven't seen Johnny since he left for Toronto. I wrote you about it, Ella," he reminded her, puzzled.

"Oh, Wilkes! You don't know? But everyone knows about Johnny! Where have you been?"

"You mean something's happened to Johnny?"

"He was captured at Niagara Falls, trying to get to Toronto. He derailed a train, hoping to rescue some of our men. He's imprisoned at Fort Lafayette."

"My God!" His face, which had been reddened by the cold, became very pale.

He let her draw him into the sitting room, warm from the heat from the fireplace. She moved to him and put her arms around his waist, but he pushed her away, holding her firmly by the arms.

"Tell me what you know about Johnny."

"There isn't much more, Wilkes. Except that he's to have a trial very soon. And General Dix has said that he will hang."

A clammy sweat broke out on his face. "No one's going to hang Johnny. I know what to do. I've got to leave. I'm going to Richmond."

"Oh, no! Oh, please, don't go away. Darling, you just came home to me." Ella was almost in tears.

"I'm sorry, Ella," he said, taking her hands in his and kissing her briefly. "But I've got to help Johnny. I'll be back as soon as I see President Davis."

She kissed his hands. "You can't even spare me an hour?"

"God, woman, Johnny's in prison! They're threatening to hang him! How can I do anything but work on rescuing him?"

*

President Davis arose from his desk to greet Wilkes as he entered the Presidential office. Wilkes was alarmed at the Chief Executive's appearance: He looked very tired and thin and there were blue smudges under his eyes. Had he been sick? Wilkes excused himself for intruding on him so late in the evening, on the plea of emergency. "I fear I'm imposing on you, sir."

"Not at all, Captain Booth." The President was cordial. "I am tired, though, and grieved. We lost our little son, Joseph. He—fell to his death from the balcony of this house, while at play."

"I'm terribly sorry, sir. What can I say? I hadn't heard——"

"No, it's all right. There's too much these days for everyone. A child dies. A nation . . . " The President left the words unfinished, glanced at Wilkes and indicated a chair.

"Sir, I want to go about another plan for the release of our prisoners. And, specifically, for the freeing of John Yates Beall."

President Davis gave his visitor a penetrating look and shook his head very slowly, from side to side. "That's impossible. I'll hear what you have to say, Captain, but before you go on, it may save you time and trouble if I tell you how things are. Our military situation demands that I give it all my time and attention. There is nothing more I can do where our prisoners are concerned at this time."

"Mr. President, this plan is simple. Just give me a dozen cavalrymen, the best we have, and I guarantee you the freedom of John Yates Beall and all our other prisoners! They must be excellent riders, good shots, and close-mouthed."

The President stroked his chin and his eyes glinted in the lamplight. "Captain, how would that be possible?"

"Sir, with a dozen men riding at my side, I can seize the President of the United States and bring him here to you as a hostage to be held for the exchange of every Confederate prisoner, including John Beall."

The elder man's face was suddenly blotched with color. His fist hit the desk a resounding blow, and his voice was distorted with fury. "By God, sir, that's a damnable suggestion! How dare you make it to me?"

Wilkes drew back. His eyes guarded. "Sir, I don't understand your aversion to it."

The President spoke slowly. "The Confederate States of America are composed of civilized people honorably engaged in a struggle for survival as a free nation. We live by law and order, as we did under the Union. We do not function as a band of lawless people. We're fighting hard, on battlefields, to gain our independence and freedom, our status as an honorable nation

224

among men. We recognize the independence and sovereignty of the United States of America. We respect the elected officials of the Union, though we may be enemies. And we aim to treat that nation with all due respect and lawfulness. In this way we can hope to take our place beside her as a nation worthy of the same kind of respect and honorable treatment. We shall not descend to the level of cutthroats, Captain; we'll not resort to kidnappings and blackmail."

Wilkes tried once more. "Mr. President, I respectfully remind you that the United States, in refusing the exchange of any prisoner of war, has stooped to cutthroat methods. And blackmail. And now it holds John Yates Beall, the hero of the South, bragging it will condemn him to hang even before he is tried. General Dix has declared it. Is that the action of an honorable man and an honorable nation?"

Jefferson Davis was not moved. "The action of the United States is to be regretted, and is a blot on its own history. But it doesn't mean that we must commit similar crimes. Indeed, it is our particular duty to appear before the world as men of honor."

"Sir," Wilkes was tight-lipped, "there's another fact involved here. Lincoln serves as commander in chief of the Union army, the highest ranking soldier in the federal government. He goes to battlefields and places himself in the line of bullets. If he considers himself a soldier, why do you choose to spare him the risks that any soldier takes? Why is his life any more valuable than John Beall's?"

"Captain, you have my opinion. That's the end of it."

"But that means that—" Wilkes could not put his thought into words.

Davis' face softened with pity. "I'm sorry," he said, "I'm desperately sorry, and if I could rescue that brave officer, I would. But there is nothing I can do."

Wilkes was trembling. "You're saying we're lost. You've given up?"

"No, we haven't given up. We'll continue to negotiate for the release of our men, for the life of John Beall."

"And if we can free our men, the North will never be victorious."

The President looked at Wilkes. "Well! It's no use dwelling on dreams, Captain. Now we must be practical. There's not time for anything but hard military planning."

"But without the release of all our men, can we carry on this war, sir?"

The President turned from the desk and looked out into the night. His voice was that of a very exhausted man. "Our chances for success go from bad to worse with every passing day. But we're not yet defeated. We will fight on, if we have to. We'll never surrender."

"But, sir——"

"Captain! I've made myself clear. I appreciate your visit. I'm aware you've contributed brilliantly to our efforts. I'm thankful for your devotion. You will return to Washington, Captain, and await any orders there."

Bitterly disappointed, Wilkes asked, "And John Beall? He is to hang?"

Jefferson Davis saw the anguish in Wilkes' dark eyes and tried to halt his frenzy with another dash of cold facts. He spoke roughly: "Captain! Control you emotions. John Beall is one of the most cherished men in the Confederacy. We have done the only thing we can do. We've tried to impress upon the federal government that Captain Beall is an officer in our navy and not a pirate. The plea has failed. Now, much as I regret it, I must tell you again that there is nothing we can do to help John Beall. As for you, sir, you shall return to Washington and wait there until you receive further orders."

Wilkes took the reprimand; as he quietly shook hands with the President of the Confederacy, his mind was already running ahead to Washington. He thought about the last time he had seen his friend in Toronto, and remembered Johnny's laughing words telling him that if he got caught he would expect Wilkes to ride to his rescue. Rescuing Johnny was one burden he would take off the shoulders of the weary Davis.

Forty

Wilkes was aware that time was the enemy in the battle to save Johnny, and kidnapping Lincoln would take more time than there was to spare. Since he would have to handle whatever plot there was entirely by himself, even to the recruitment of his men, the enterprise had taken on a new dimension. He determined to grow a mustache, figuring that it would help disguise his face later on. The growth came in easy and dark.

The thing he must do before he could proceed was to see Johnny, and the one way he could manage that was to ask Senator John Hale for his assistance in getting Wilkes a pass to the prison. He did not even think of working through Elizabeth in this matter. And, he remembered, the Senator had once said he owed him a favor. Well, this was the time to collect.

Senator Hale came to the door of his private office. Wilkes was waiting in the outer room of the Senator's suite. "Wilkes! By God, stranger, it's great to see you!" He gave him a powerful handshake. "Come in, son, come in. We'll just get some brandy here and warm you a little. You look cold as hell."

Wilkes shook his head and he remained standing. "Senator, if you don't mind, sir, I'd like to get on with my business. I have very little time."

Senator Hale put the bottles back on the table. "Oh? What's wrong? What can I do?"

Wilkes was twisting his hat in his hands. "I need your help, sir." Businesslike, the Senator moved to his desk. "You know about John Yates Beall?" Wilkes asked.

"Certainly. Who doesn't?"

"Johnny and I are friends. We've known each other since childhood. We were roommates at the University of Virginia."

"Is that so?" The Senator was amazed. "Well, I can imagine

your feelings, then, on hearing of his capture and imprisonment. I'm sorry."

"Sir, my feelings are concerned not only with Johnny but the effect his trial and sentencing will have on the South. He's a hero there, you know, and I think he deserves to be treated as a regular officer of the Confederate navy."

"Well, Wilkes, he's been charged as a pirate of sorts. That makes it difficult to defend him."

"Senator Hale, all I ask of you is a pass to permit me to see him in prison. I want to talk to him and get his story and offer him my friendship."

The Senator sat back in his chair and rubbed a finger over his lips. He nodded. "Yes, I believe I can do that for you, Wilkes." He smiled. "You have every right to see your friend, if they are allowing him visitors. But there's a chance they will refuse, you know."

"Not if the President requests it, sir," Wilkes dared to suggest.

"Well, we'll see what happens. Even the prison authorities must expect to be petitioned by their prisoners' friends and relatives. No, it will be fairly routine, I'm sure. If necessary, I'll request the President's good word, but don't worry about it."

"It won't cause you any trouble?" Wilkes asked, not really caring if it did.

"No, I think not. Check back here tomorrow about this time, and I'll have the necessary paper for you."

Wilkes offered the Senator his hand over the desk, smiling, "My thanks, sir. It means a great deal to me."

The Senator beamed. "You know, the President has asked me to serve in the capacity of next Ambassador to Spain, and I'm very excited about it. Have you heard from Elizabeth on it?"

Wilkes frowned. "Sir, I'm afraid Elizabeth has had no chance to advise me of anything. I've hardly seen her in the past months, and I'm a poor man at writing. I'm not even sure she still considers our engagement in a happy light. I'll be visiting her on my return to Washington from the prison. Perhaps we'll settle things then." He paused, edgy under the shrewd look of the Senator. "Congratulations on the appointment, sir. Spain is fortunate to be receiving you as an ambassador."

"Thank you. Yes, I believe if I were you, son, I'd get things settled with Elizabeth. It will be a time yet before we go to Spain, but if there's to be a marriage of my daughter first, we'll have plans to make."

"Of course." Wilkes was turning his hat around in his hands. "Well, sir, until tomorrow, then? Please give my love to Elizabeth. And her mother." Wilkes was backing to the door, anxious to get away.

"I'll do that, Wilkes. Take care of yourself now and get some rest. You look done in."

The pass Wilkes obtained from Senator Hale led him to a subterraneous cell of the Fort Lafayette prison. When the guard first opened the door the terrible odors which rushed out stopped Wilkes at the moment of entry. The guard gave him a slight nudge into the place, saying, "You got five minutes, sir. No more."

After the glare of the snowlighted world outside, the dim light of the airless little room took some getting used to. A shadowy form sitting on the narrow shelflike bed which was attached to the damp stone wall with chains, moved, and the prisoner was on his feet; the chains he wore clattered.

Wilkes had only to take a few steps. He held Johnny in an embrace and neither man could speak. Wilkes was sobbing, wiping tears away with the back of his hand.

Johnny patted him on the shoulder. "Wilkes, we only have a few minutes. Do you know anything about the trial? What are they saying? I have to sit here and guess what's going on."

Wilkes had control of himself now. He took a deep breath. "You have a defense attorney, don't you?"

"Yes. But I'm not allowed much of anything, not even advice. But they're going to hear what I've got to say."

"I'm not paying much attention to the trial," Wilkes told him, speaking fast. "I figure they're going to give you that much, anyway. The truth is, General Dix says they're going to hang you."

Johnny groped for the bed and sat down. "I figured the verdict was in."

"Well, Johnny, they're not going to. I've got something I'm working on. You just hold on."

"Wilkes, the things you and I plan don't often turn out so well."

"I wouldn't play with your life, Johnny."

Johnny looked up and gave a faint smile. "If you say you'll get me out of here, you will."

"Johnny, how are you standing it? Do you get any kind of food you can eat?"

"Well, I eat it. I'd say I've dropped thirty pounds so far." He laughed bitterly, and sweeping his hands at the room, said, "But don't look at my housekeeping!"

Wilkes reached into his pocket. "I dropped by a restaurant and had them fix up a meal of bread, cheese, and meat. I'm sorry, Johnny, it's the most I could get into this place."

Taking the package, Johnny said, "Thanks, Wilkes. This is one meal I'm not going to share with Yankee."

"Who's Yankee?"

"The biggest, sneakiest, most greedy rat you ever did see."

Wilkes grinned. "I wonder how come he got his name."

The sound of the guard approaching brought their smiles to a halt.

"Remember, Johnny, I'm going to get you out of here. Just hang on to that and I won't worry too much about you."

Johnny took his hand. "I'll count on it."

The guard opened the door, and Wilkes hurried out in order to keep the guard from seeing that Johnny had a small package in his hands.

When the trial came, Johnny's testimony was a vivid account of his life as an officer of the Confederacy in contradiction of the prosecution's claim that he was nothing more than an outlaw.

On February 8, 1865, John Yates Beall stood before the judge in the court room of Lafayette Prison. Still in chains, the captured Virginian heard the judge's voice as though it came from a long distance away. But Johnny held his head high and kept his back straight in spite of the chains which pulled at his shoulders and arms and the iron ankle cuffs which had rubbed his shins raw a long time ago, leaving open sores. Johnny presented a dignity and a courage not to be denied by his captors. There was no fear in his face.

The judge looked down upon him and asked: "Is the prisoner ready to hear the sentence?"

The prisoner replied: "I am."

The judge advised: "John Yates Beall, you have been declared guilty by this court on six specific charges of violation of the laws of war."

A faint smile touched Johnny's lips, as he remembered the events behind the charges. "Yes, sir."

The judge was irritated at the rebel's spirit. "Are you ready to hear the sentence of this court?"

"I have said that I am, sir," Johnny told the judge with definite amusement in his tone.

"John Yates Beall, you are sentenced to be hanged by the neck until dead. Until the time of execution you will be placed in the dungeon of this prison in chains. The execution will take place at Governor's Island at two o'clock, the afternoon of February 24, 1865. And may God rest your soul."

As soon as the death sentence was known, Wilkes rushed to Senator Hale. "The President can recommend clemency. He can save John Beall's life!"

The Senator was very somber. "Wilkes, others want Beall spared too. Many feel it will work against the Union to hang him. The truth is, there has already been an appeal made for clemency by some very highly placed persons in Washington. I had hoped to have good news for you on it, but it's no use. Lincoln has replied that General Dix has complete jurisdiction over the prisoner, and that he has no right to interfere. Further, he point out that John Beall has been brought to justice for acts of grave injury to the Union. No, the President is not sympathetic in this."

"Lincoln is said to be concerned with saving lives," Wilkes insisted.

The Senator shifted his position in his big leather chair. "Well, we could try once again. I hold with the opinion that every man on both sides of this conflict should be saved from a death such as this one. It's the kind of thing which will bear bitter fruit."

The Senator called his secretary and, with Wilkes listening, carefully dictated the wording of a petition which he would personally circulate for his colleagues' signatures:

"Your petitioners respectfully represent that John Yates Beall was arrested on the 16th day of December last and tried

*by a military commission upon charges of 'Acting as a spy,' and
after a hasty trial was found guilty. As it is admitted that the
said Beall is a Captain regularly commissioned in the rebel
service and that Jefferson Davis by a manifesto assumed all
responsibility for the acts and thus publicly asserted that the
several acts were done under his authority and direction, we
therefore respectfully recommend, Mr. President, a commutation of the sentence of death pronounced against him."*

Wilkes left his chair to grip the Senator's hand. "I'm very
grateful."

"I've not always seen eye to eye with the President but, still,
I'm hoping this time we share the same opinion. Just don't set
your heart on his answer, Wilkes."

Before the Senator could open the door for Wilkes, Elizabeth
Hale stepped into the office. The two faced each other in
mutual surprise. Then Elizabeth, smiling, gave her hand to
Wilkes in greeting. "John Wilkes Booth, isn't it?"

Oblivious of the Senator who backed away from them unnoticed, Wilkes held Elizabeth's tiny hand and looked down
upon her with a searching gaze. "It's good to see you, Elizabeth.
I'm sorry. I've just been so busy." He gave a short, guilty laugh.
"That sounds pretty lame, even to me," he admitted.

"Don't worry about it," she told him, pride chasing the
laughter out of her face. "I'm just glad to see you, really. I
wouldn't have wanted to go to Spain with my family without
seeing you. I think we ought to part as friends. It's what I'd
like, Wilkes."

"We are friends, Elizabeth," he took up her lead. "I'll always
cherish the knowledge."

"Thank you." Her gaze was steady and her smile genuine.
Impulsively he bent and kissed her cheek.

Then when he was gone, Elizabeth turned to her father.
"There goes the most handsome man in the world."

The Senator put an arm around his daughter. "The most
handsome, probably, but I think a little mad. Too emotional.
I'm glad he's gone out of your life, my dear."

She sighed. "Totally charming. Absolutely unpredictable. I
never could have made anything at all of a marriage with
Wilkes."

232

"Well, he's loyal to his friends, I can tell you that." He frowned. "So loyal, indeed, that I'm involved in circulating a clemency petition for one of them. And I'd best get at it."

President Lincoln refused the petition, repeating that the matter was in the jurisdiction of General Dix. The hanging of John Beall would take place on February 24, 1865, as set by the court.

Ella came home from the hospital toward dusk on the day the President turned down the written plea. Wilkes was waiting for her in the sitting room. He had dismissed her servants when he came in, telling them Miss Ella would not need them for the rest of the day and evening.

Crossing the darkened room, knowing without being told that something was wrong, Ella seated herself beside him and saw tears glistening in his eyes.

"Wilkes?"

He did not say a word but he took her in his arms.

"Lincoln ignored the petition." There was no fight in his voice. "He disregarded it completely. He won't do a thing. For God's sake, Ella, tell me what I can do to help Johnny!"

Ella's concern over Wilkes gave her an idea. If anything in the world could make President Lincoln change his mind, it would be to see Wilkes in his agony. "Go see the President yourself, Wilkes. No one else cares as much as you do. No petition could be half as effective. Oh, darling, surely the President would react to your own grief."

Wilkes looked at her for a long, long moment. Then he kissed her full on the mouth, joyously, and was on his feet. "That's it, Ella! I won't leave the White House until I have his promise to save Johnny's life, I swear it!"

At the door Ella put a restraining arm around his waist. "Wilkes, are you sure you can see President Lincoln without anger?"

Wilkes laughed. "Ella, today I have a real fondness for Mister Lincoln. He's going to save Johny's life. I'll get along with him just fine."

Once again Senator Hale assisted Wilkes. The appointment with the President was made for four o'clock the following afternoon, and Wilkes began to suffer a kind of stage fright.

Never had any stage performance been so important to him as was the appearance he was to make before the President of the United States. The life of John Yates Beall depended upon his ability to win the heart of President Abraham Lincoln.

Alone in his hotel room, he concentrated on what he must say to the President. What would be the best approach? He tried to remember all the things he had heard about President Lincoln. All the stories of prisoners he had saved. What touched his heart? Wilkes could not sleep. He waited for the dawn.

Forty-One

Janet Beall, pale but dry-eyed, greeted the Confederate officer in the parlor of her Richmond home. He had come, she guessed, with an answer to an appeal made directly to the President of the United States in her behalf. He stood before her with an unreadable look on his face, bowing formally over her hand.

"Am I to see my son?" she asked, pleased that there was no tremor in her voice.

He handed her a folded paper. "Your pass, Mrs. Beall. The President of the United States has declared that you shall be escorted to New York, to Fort Lafayette prison, under a flag of truce. It will be my privilege to take you to the Union lines where you will there come under the protection of the truce flag as raised by the President of the United States."

Janet Beall closed her eyes briefly in prayer, holding the paper to her heart.

The Union cavalry escort was ready for her with a handsome black and silver carriage. Above the side lantern near the door of the rig was attached a white flag which stood out taut in the winter wind.

The Union newspapers were highly critical that the President should have allowed the mother of a murderer, a traitor, a pirate, to see her imprisoned son. She was not welcome in New York, they said. The hanging could not come too soon.

It was a bitterly cold day, the wind lashing at the harbor waters, as they took her along the icy walk to the dungeon. The flag of truce was stiffly carried ahead of her in the gloved hands of a young Union officer who walked fast, without looking right or left. He knew she was behind him because he could hear the tap of her shoes on the brick flooring. At every cell window ahead of him were the white faces of prisoners, but he would not turn his head toward any of them.

Janet Beall walked the prison corridor with a sense of growing panic. She looked at the staring white faces of her son's fellow prisoners as they gazed at her from their small, barred windows. Dear God! John could not live in such a place.

At the door of John Beall's cell, the officer was met by an armed guard whose face was sullen and almost as pale as the prisoners he guarded. He saluted.

"Corporal," the officer's voice echoed down the corridor, "open the cell. By order of the President of the United States of America, Mrs. Beall is to speak to her son for a period of five minutes. You will stand guard with me."

The other prisoners strove to see what was happening as the cell door was hauled open and Janet Beall entered the small closet-like space.

A shadowy figure stood there. She held out her arms, and John was there.

She kissed him and held tightly to his hands.

"You shouldn't have come here, Mother. It's no place for you, not even for a minute."

She put her fingers over his lips. "Don't waste our few minutes scolding me, darling." She lowered her voice to a whisper, glancing toward the small window. "Your friends are all trying to get a Presidential stay of execution. But if it fails, if President Lincoln refuses, can I reach some of your men?"

"Mother, don't. Please." He squeezed her hands hard. "I

don't want you to grieve over this. If I die here, it's no more than could have happened to me on a battlefield or on shipboard. It was a chance I took from the beginning."

"Well, now, Johnny, if the President does not save you, then your friends and I shall. Make up your mind to that."

Johnny soothed her. "I know. Wilkes was here. Mother, don't despair, and don't get involved in this thing. Wilkes is capable and he knows all my men. I trust him. I just want you to go home and stay there. Take my love to everyone and be happy. And know that I always love you."

She held to him. "Oh, darling! This is so terrible——"

"It will pass, Mother. I spend my time remembering happy days. You do the same. Please."

There was a knock on the door, a warning. Time was almost gone. Reaching into her bag, she brought forth money and said, "Here, Johnny. Maybe you can buy yourself a few things in this hell, if you have this. It's Union money, so it's good here."

He took it quickly. "If you can spare it, I can use it. Thanks."

Once more she plunged her hand into the bag and pulled out a small box. "And this is chocolate fudge. I made it myself, the way you like it."

"I'll parcel it out to myself slowly," he said, "It's quite a gift."

"I thought about bringing a gun. But I decided it might just cause you a lot of trouble. I know you couldn't get out of here with just one gun. They'd kill you, if you tried."

"It's all right, Mother. I'm sure I'd have tried, if you had."

The key was in the lock of the door again, and it was turning. She kissed her son again. He held her close for a moment.

The officer standing in the open doorway said, "Time is up, Mrs. Beall."

At the door, the gray light of the corridor falling upon her, she turned to say, "John, God is with you."

"I know. As He is with you, Mother."

The door was closed and locked and Janet Beall followed the flag of truce back down the drafty corridor. From the cells she passed she heard the voices of doomed men.

"God bless you, Mother Beall."

"Give the Yankees a spit in the eye, m'am."

"To hell with 'em, m'am. They ain't fit to shine his shoes."

"You're a brave woman."

"Say hello to our friends in Richmond."

"Bless you, little lady, bless you!"

Tears washed her eyes then, but she kept on following the flag of truce without a falter in her step.

Forty-Two

The President's secretary had kept Wilkes waiting only a minute in the outer office while he went in to announce his arrival. At the appointed hour, Wilkes walked alone into the office of the President of the United States.

President Lincoln stood up at his desk and extended a big hand of welcome, smiling. "John Wilkes Booth"—he measured out the entire name grandly—"I'm pleased to see you."

Wilkes hurried forward, took the President's hand, and was impressed with the warmth and strength. "Mr. President."

"Sit down, Mr. Booth, sit down," the President invited. "You know, Mrs. Lincoln and I attended *The Marble Heart* several years back and we enjoyed your performance no end. Still, I felt a bit cheated, seeing a Booth in a comedy. I hope to see you in a Shakespeare play before long."

"Thank you, sir." Wilkes was obviously pleased. "As soon as possible, I'll arrange a Shakespeare play in your honor."

"Good! Let it be *Macbeth*, if you will. They say you do a leap of twelve feet in that play. That's pretty agile, Mr. Booth. I expect I've got to see that."

"I'll be honored, sir."

The President studied Wilkes candidly. Then he saw the actor *was* a trifle embarrassed by his open curiosity. "I'm sorry, Mr. Booth, I'm staring, am I not? Well, it's this way. Molly will be asking me all kinds of questions about you—like the exact color of your eyes up close, things like that. And I'd best know!"

Wilkes smiled. "I'd be honored to meet Mrs. Lincoln, sir."

The President folded his arms across his chest and leaned back in his chair. "Well, you shall, soon enough. But I believe you've come here on a matter of some urgency, according to Senator Hale. It concerns John Yates Beall?"

"Yes, sir. I'm here to ask—beg—for your help to save his life."

The President's face shadowed. "I'm afraid the matter is out of my hands, Mr. Booth. I don't believe there is anything I can do—or ought to do."

"You have shown mercy for others, Mr. President. You've granted clemency many times," Wilkes dared to remind him.

"Yes, and I could now if I were convinced that it would be right and proper. But this affair involves a verdict of a military court following a just trial."

Wilkes could not remain seated. He stood at the President's desk, his knuckles white on the rim of his hat. He remembered the appeal he had decided upon during the night. "Please, sir, there's more in the case of Captain Beall than you may realize. He's a hero in the Confederacy. After the war ends, John Beall could work with you for the reunion of this nation; you'd find him invaluable. But if he dies at the hands of the federal court, he'll become a martyr, and his name a rallying point for further resistance."

"I'm sorry, Mr. Booth. I just can't interfere with the sentence given John Beall on any such grounds." The President stood.

Wilkes, felled by the words, dropped to his knees, grabbing the President's hands in his own, which were cold and trembling. Gone was the Booth pride, gone from his mind were all the fine arguments he had formed all during the long hours of the previous night. "Don't let him die! For God's sake, Mr. President, don't let them hang Johnny!"

Abraham Lincoln reached down in compassion and helped Wilkes Booth to his feet, steadying the younger man with a firm hand. Tears stood in the President's eyes. The deepening, graying lines in his face had been etched there through such emotions as the President was now experiencing. How long must he

238

give orders that broke the hearts of men? How long was he to bring men to their knees? Oh, God, how long!

He could not bear it. "If John Beall is worthy of such grief as this, he deserves to live. I'll recommend clemency."

Wilkes tried to speak but words would not come.

"I will do no more than ask that the death sentence be revoked, and it shall be," the President continued. "But John Beall will remain in prison until such time as this nation of ours is again at peace."

"God bless you, sir!" Wilkes finally found a way to speak, but it was only a whisper, husky and choked.

The President went with him to the door. "I'll see that the order is sent at once."

"Thank you, Mr. President." Wilkes was finding words again. "I'd like to telegraph the news now to his mother. Would it be all right to do that?"

"Of course. She needn't wait for the news." He gave Wilkes a pat on the back as he opened the door. "Perhaps some day when this is all over, you'll bring Captain Beall to see me," the President smiled. "You may not know it, Mr. Booth, but Captain Beall has had a way of causing me considerable trouble over the years, and I fear I'm not clear of it yet. When Mr. Stanton hears of this, he's going to fuss and fume like an old steam engine."

"Johnny will want to pay his respects to you, sir, after the war. You'll find you've saved a fine man."

"I'm sure he is. Well, now, Mr. Booth, you'd best get on and spread the word to those you know will be personally interested. But, until it has been handled officially, let's keep it as quiet as we can."

"Yes, Mr. President, I wish there were some way in which I could thank you, sir——"

"No, no! I'm grateful for your visit. It gave me the courage to follow my own sentiments in the matter. I'll only be doing what I wanted to do all along."

Wilkes left the White House filled with strange new emotions and a mind with new thoughts. He had always heard the talk that Lincoln was the most unusual man to ever sit in the White House—they said it seemed as though the giant man walked under the guidance of a Heavenly Hand, and that any man who

239

walked with him could feel that hovering influence. Wilkes knew now what they meant.

Lincoln, the blessed savior of John Yates Beall, was not the same person Wilkes had visioned the President to be. The Lincoln he had met today was the enemy of no man. Wilkes remembered the things he had said about him in the past, the things he had believed of him, and he was astounded.

After sending a wire to Johnny's mother, he rode a swift horse to Ella's house. He burst into the house, shedding his hat and coat and tossing them onto a chair, and caught her, whirled her, lifted her in his arms and kissed her soundly. "Ella! He's saved! Lincoln's actually saved Johnny! It's all right! I feel as though he's spared my life, too!"

Wilkes had not looked like this in months. She broke into tears.

"Hey, now, what's this?" he asked, wiping at a tear with his finger, tenderly.

"Happiness," she told him. "Oh, Wilkes, do you know it's been weeks since you've even smiled, really smiled?"

He grew solemn. "Of course Johnny's still in prison."

"Well, that will end, too," she said.

Wilkes wondered what he'd have done if the President hadn't saved Johnny. He would have tried anything to free him, that he knew. Now, though, he could relax, and think about something else. He could even forget the war itself until he received new orders. Wilkes was suddenly content to let events take care of themselves. Johnny was to live.

In his desk on the third floor of the War Department Building at Pennsylvania Avenue and Seventeenth Street, Secretary of War Stanton stared unbelieving at a note from the White House, asking him to advise General John Dix at Lafayette Prison in New York that the President was granting clemency to John Yates Beall.

The clerk who had brought the message stood waiting for a return message to the President. The Secretary frowned. There were times when he bitterly opposed the President. Once he had refused to carry out a Presidential order regarding rebels, and he had been so angered by the President's mildness in the matter that he had dared to call him "a damn fool."

"There will be no answer," he told the clerk.

Secretary Stanton hesitated, his fingers smoothing out the folded note. He pushed his glasses up onto this forehead and rubbed his eyes. If he let Lincoln reverse the court's decision there would be national hell to pay. If he sent the message on to General Dix, as the President asked, justice would be a farce in the nation. When it was over, the Secretary would explain that he had ignored the plea on the ground that the verdict had been a military one and that the hanging fell into the authority of the Secretary of War. Oh, they'd have a round or two, but what was new about that? Justice would be served, and the Secretary of War would continue to function as the strong man of the Lincoln Cabinet.

Ultimately Lincoln would see that it had been the right thing to do. And, the Secretary told himself, he was within his own rightful powers: As Secretary of War he had every right to deal with the matter—the prisoner was in his jurisdiction. Secretary Stanton put the paper in the drawer and slowly shoved the drawer back into place.

The next week passed swiftly for Wilkes as he went about in a glow of well-being. He was returning to a normal routine, at ease with the world and Ella was constantly amazed at the change in him.

The Fords wanted Wilkes to appear at their Washington theater, but he was still uncertain of just what play he wanted to do. Thinking about the President's request for *Macbeth*, he refused the Fords' offer to appear in a comedy. He wanted to be certain of the vehicle he chose for his return to the stage.

The Fords appealed to Ella to get him to reconsider their offer, and she promised she would try her luck at changing the star's mind. Finally Wilkes compromised—he would accept a Ford Theater engagement of *The Apostate*, and make plans with them for a presentation of *Macbeth* later in the spring. They agreed and worked out a schedule for rehearsals for *The Apostate*, which would be presented after the Easter holiday.

Forty-Three

On February 24, a tugboat landed at Fort Lafayette to transfer John Yates Beall to Governor's Island.

Blinking against the light of day, hands bound behind his back, legs chained so that he could only shuffle, Johnny was led through the prison yard. The clothes he wore were scarcely recognizable as jacket and trousers, so torn and dirty were they from his two months in the dungeon. He was thin, and his awful pallor was partly hidden by the growth of beard.

At Governor's Island, they led him toward the gallows, through a prison yard. Word of his coming had carried from guard to prisoners, all rebels.

As he was escorted across the yard, he looked at the faces of his fellow Confederates. Their voices were stilled by their imprisonment, their blank-expressioned eyes had the look of the condemned and the hopeless. Their once cherished gray uniforms hung from their starved bodies like rags. They were like dead men, but the sight of their hero, John Yates Beall, reached their spirits, long dormant. As he was moved forward toward the scaffold, every man of the Confederates in the big desolate prison yard moved defiantly closer, in a semicircle around him.

The guards brought John's walk to a brief halt as one of them stooped to straighten out a slight tangle in the chains which was making it almost impossible for the prisoner to proceed. John turned and saw the men at his back who had raised their bony hands to their foreheads in a farewell salute to the Acting Master of the Confederate Navy. As Captain Beall touched his brow in a return salute, the faces of the prisoners came alive with hope and courage.

Then Johnny was pushed forward again. He almost stumbled into the dust but he went on, head up, When he approached the bottom steps of the scaffold, passing the coffin in which his body would be laid, the drums began their death roll.

Five hundred Yankees were present for the long-awaited hanging. Twisting in the grasp of the guards and against the chains, Johnny looked back at the Confederates there in the prison yard, and before the guards could stop him, he tossed his head back and let out a wild rebel yell that drowned out the muffled drums and shook the scaffold.

Then they took him up to the rope. He stood calmly as a lieutenant stepped forward to read the charges which had brought him to the gallows.

When the *Philo Parsons*, the *Island Queen* and the U.S.S. *Michigan* were mentioned, Johnny grinned, remembering how Wilkes and he were willing to attack an armed gunboat with nothing but their Navy Colts. God, how hard this day would be for him. Johnny uttered a little prayer for his friend: "Dear God, let Wilkes Booth understand that everything's all right. Help him to live with this day. Let him understand that I'm about to have the biggest adventure of all. I'm not afraid."

He wondered what Wilkes had tried to do to free him. Knowing Wilkes, he had tried something. Johnny hoped it would not mean trouble, whatever it might have been.

The lieutenant droned on with the charges. Determined to show his contempt again, Johnny reached out a chained foot and managed to hook a chair with the toe of his ragged shoe. He dragged the chair clumsily forward in one movement and seated himself precariously. Below, Confederates grinned and looked at each other. There was a man!

He was yanked to his feet. While the reading of the charges continued, the guards removed the chains from his ankles. And then the reading was finished. The lieutenant carefully folded the document and retreated. Johnny eyed the proceedings with a nonchalance which was not entirely feigned—death held its terrors, but he had faced them before, many times. He had a faith in God which a mere hanging could not destroy. A man had to die, one way or another, sooner or later.

A Presbyterian minister came to his side and read a prayer from the Bible. "I'm gratified to see you have no fear, sir," the minister added.

Johnny shrugged. "As some author has said, Reverend,

we may be as near to God on the scaffold as anywhere else."

The drums rolled. Johnny looked up and the rope was lowered over his head and around his neck.

The minister, holding the Bible tightly, stepped back, and the hangman sprung the trap door.

Forty-Four

Wilkes and Ella finished dinner at the cozy small table in front of the fireplace. Jane, perhaps with an intuition, had prepared a meal which could not have been surpassed by any kitchen in the mansions of the antebellum South. Chicken baked in real butter and cream was side-dished with potatoes whipped to a feathery lightness, peas in sugar sauce, apples in cinnamon, biscuits with honey. And wine and coffee, both superb.

They were settled on their couch, wine glasses in hand again, watching lazily as Otto removed the dishes.

"Imagine me," Wilkes said, "actually planning a play just to please President Lincoln. As a matter of fact, I'm enjoying the work on it more than anything I've ever done on the stage."

Ella started to say something, but was interrupted by Jane who entered the room wide-eyed and an envelope in her hands.

"Miss Ella, 'scue me. The man said this is mighty important. For Mr. Booth. From the President hisself, the man said."

She handed the note to Wilkes, whose own expression was one of surprise. The Ford Theater personnel had sent the messenger to Ella's home with it after being told that the President wanted Wilkes Booth to receive it at once.

Ella smiled. "You really ought to open it, Wilkes," she suggested.

He smiled too, and opened the note, but then his face blanched and the letter fell from his hands. Staggering a few steps to the fireplace, he grabbed hold of the mantel for support.

"My God, what is it?" Ella asked. Wilkes seemed not to hear her. She reached for the letter at her feet.

Fear so gripped Ella that she could not focus on the paper in her hands. The words steadied and she read the note. President Lincoln couldn't write to Wilkes that Johnny Beall had been hung that day! Johnny Beall couldn't be dead!

"Oh, God, no!" Wilkes cried.

She turned to him and was stricken at how he changed. In that one minute, John Wilkes Booth had become transformed. He had to lick his dry lips, work his powder-dry tongue, before he could moisten his throat enough to get out his words: "Damn Lincoln! Damn him to hell!"

"Wilkes——"

"He'll pay for this murder. Johnny Beall doesn't die this easily. They'll all pay for it!"

"But, Wilkes!" Ella was terrified. "The President says Johnny was hung contrary to his orders."

Wilkes seized the note from her hand and threw it into the fire. "A lie! A lie, Ella. Oh, God! I told John to count on me. My God, I've betrayed him. I believed the worst enemy Johnny had!"

"Please, you've got to take his word. There's nothing you can do now."

He pushed her hands from his arm. "Oh, but there is! It should have been done a long time ago."

"Wilkes, you're not thinking of that kidnap plan again, are you?" Ella could feel the beat of her heart.

"No more Confederates are going to hang in federal prisons. No more rebels will be held prisoner. I'll capture Lincoln and take him to Richmond. I'm going to do it in Johnny's name."

Ella was close to screaming. "Wilkes, you can't! They'll hang you if you make a move toward the President. For God's sake, Wilkes!"

Fiercely he took her by the arms and held her motionless. "Are you with me or against me?"

"President Davis doesn't want it done."

"It was a mistake to ask him. Of course he had to reject it, in his position. But if I get Lincoln to Richmond as a prisoner of the Confederacy, do you really believe Jeff Davis won't ask for an exchange?"

"I don't know."

He shook her. "I asked you a question. Are you with me? I've got to know."

"I love you, Wilkes. I could never be against you."

He pulled her into his arms, crying. "Help me!" he groaned, "I see him, Ella, I see Johnny hanging!"

"Hush." She was crying too now, her arms around him, rocking him a little.

The revived plan progressed rapidly. It was a plan which Wilkes held with a tight rein—there would be no mistakes, no betrayals. Wilkes recruited his band of men mostly from persons he had known all his life. Some of them were successful, and some not. Some were his childhood friends whose devotion to him had been long established and was unbreakable. They had loved Johnny Beall, too. Only a few of those he gathered were strangers to him, but these he checked out and rechecked and even tested with acute strategy, giving them false plans to spread, if they would. All proved loyal.

There was Samuel Arnold who had gone to school with Wilkes at St. Timothy's and ridden with him in their childish games of war at Bel Air. He wanted the Confederacy to win the war, but he was born lazy. After he was wounded and mustered out of the service, he did nothing but loaf until Wilkes contacted him.

Sam Arnold was a little older than Wilkes, but he was not overly intelligent and was always content to follow the younger man. He listened eagerly to the plan of capture; the adventure of it appealed to him. Because Sam was unemployed, Wilkes gave him money on which to live, not wanting Sam to desert because of lack of funds.

Another friend of long ago who joined him in the plot was Michael O'Laughlin. Dark haired, dark-skinned, dark-mustached, Mike had also been a Confederate soldier. After release from the service, the only job he could find was one as a clerk in a government office, and in order to get the job, he had to take the oath of allegiance to the Union. He was enthused with the plot to kidnap President Lincoln, and warmly thanked Wilkes for allowing him to participate in the capture of "that damned Yankee who hung Johnny."

Beardless, and freckle-faced, David Herold, only eighteen years of age, was looking for a steady job when Wilkes ran across him in his recruitment effort.

Wilkes had known Davy's father, who had worked for the navy and had an excellent record as a top clerk at Washington Yard. Wilkes' offer to David came at the right moment—the elder Herold had recently died and left a widow and eight children with very little to live on.

Lewis Payne was a fanatic whom Wilkes had known slightly for several years, the son of a Baptist minister of Florida and a Confederate veteran who had, in fact, fallen wounded at Gettysburg. His brothers were killed there, and Payne took their deaths very hard, even viciously. Recuperating in a Baltimore hospital, he aimed to get well just so that he could return to the battlefields and kill as many Yankees as he could in personal battle. Payne became an expert male nurse at the hospital, and the hospital considered him a hero for his work in putting Confederates back on their feet.

He returned to battle and killed until he was sickened by the sight of bloody, torn, dying Yankees. One day he simply threw his rifle on the ground on a battlefield and went home, through with war. But approached by Wilkes, he saw another way to avenge his brothers.

George Atzerodt was the old man of the group at thirty-six years of age. Born in Germany but raised in Maryland, Atzerodt was in business for himself, with his brother, at Port Tobacco, a center of smuggling mail and general supplies to Richmond. George ran a boat himself, carrying contraband materials back and forth. His reputation as a smuggler for the Confederacy was well known to Wilkes who had, on occasion, been able to use his services in sending medical supplies to Richmond.

Tall, skinny John Surratt, just twenty-one, wore his hair long and boasted a small goatee and a mustache. As a government employee in Washington, he was a familiar face in federal buildings. He was well known in Richmond, too, as a courier for spies. Expert at delivering messages, John Surratt had an argu-

247

mentative personality, always capable of arousing controversy if he were so inclined. He lived with his widowed mother and sister Anna, in their boardinghouse on H Street. In the days of their planning, Wilkes found it convenient to meet with his men at the Surratt house, figuring, too, that the constant stream of young men who left or entered the old boardinghouse was an excellent cover for his meetings.

Wilkes refused to use Ella's home for any of the meetings with his band of men, telling her he would not allow her to become involved. Her concern over Wilkes' plans came to be centered on Wilkes. Seeing the change in Wilkes since Johnny had hung, she began to blame the President, too, whatever his excuse. She had shared Wilkes' agony, and she rationalized that Lincoln might suffer the indignities of a captured man, but he would not be hurt. Besides, the South might be helped, perhaps even to a negotiated victory.

John Surratt's mother, Mary Surratt, a devout Confederate, offered the use of the one-time family inn at Surrattsville, thirteen miles south of Washington, as a storehouse for the arms, ammunition, and food which the conspirators would need in their flight to Richmond with the President of the United States as prisoner. If all went on schedule, it would not take many hours, but they had to figure on having to hide out for a time, and so they stored ample supplies. At the inn, the President would be transferred from his captured White House coach to a faster carriage. After burning the Presidential vehicle in a field, the fast carriage, carrying Lincoln, would race to Port Royal where a boat readied by Atzerodt would be waiting. From there, Richmond was in easy reach.

Wilkes dedicated himself relentlessly to the mission. He cancelled his stage engagements, pleading that his doctor had ordered a rest period for his voice. Actually enduring a new hoarseness, he convinced everyone of his story.

He then put a twenty-four hour watch on the President of the United States to learn the daily schedule of the Chief Executive. Wilkes and his men observed as the President took unguarded walks from the White House to the telegraph room of the War Department. For a time, Wilkes considered seizing the President from the sidewalk, but decided that the risk was a little too high. He intended to risk nothing this time.

The trips the President made to the hospital near Ella's home interested Wilkes. The curved, lonely road from Washington ran from the city's edge through a wilderness before it opened into the hospital clearings. Carriages seldom passed one another, and any vehicle coming or going was plainly visible—with the exception of one wide curve, in the wildest section. A grove of trees grew beside the curve, and the underbrush was heavy; from that point the road could be watched by observers hidden in the brush. It afforded an excellent ambush position: From it the conspirators could ride to seize the reins of the Presidential coach which traveled the road without any guard.

Leaving absolutely nothing to chance, Wilkes made a trial run over the course, all the way from the road to the hospital to the boat at Port Royal, bribing people he thought might be necessary in the case of any emergency as he went. He paid heavily and promised much more, knowing they would not betray him. Because all were Confederates desperately in need of money, he was sure none of them would so much as speak to a Yankee.

Following the trail along the regular Underground Confederate Mail route, through Surrattsville, Beantown, and Port Tobacco to the boat and so across the Potomac into Virginia and Richmond, Wilkes treated the first trial run as he would a dress rehearsal on stage. From the pursuit and capture of a carriage similar to the President's, to the placing of the "prisoner" aboard the boat, it went off without a hitch.

But Wilkes made a second trip over the route, checking those he had bribed, reviewing the plans all the way. After he had completed the purchase of a swift horse in the village of Bryantown one Sunday morning, he went to the church for consolation. Bright, springlike weather, such as blessed the countryside that day in March, reminded him of the days he and Johnny had enjoyed so much as boys.

Dr. Henry Mudd, a tall, sandy-haired, blue-eyed man, only thirty years of age, was introduced to Wilkes by a man called Queen. Because the Mudd family had seen him on stage several times and thought him a marvelous actor, the doctor was very pleased when Wilkes accepted his invitation to Sunday dinner.

The doctor's wife was a pretty young woman, the dispenser of pleasant smiles and pink-cheeked excitement. Obviously thrilled, she blushed like a schoolgirl when Wilkes took her hand in greeting.

After dinner, Wilkes entranced the three children with military songs and the recital of beloved poems. When he stopped, they squealed for more.

"How have you escaped marriage, Mr. Booth?" Dr. Mudd questioned.

Wilkes smiled over the soft-haired head of one of the Mudd youngsters. "I'll marry one of these days, Doctor. And I'll have children like these. As soon as the war ends. This is not the time for it yet."

The Mudds insisted that Wilkes stay the night.

The upstairs room they gave him was large and neat, furnished with a big feather-mattressed bed, probably a family heirloom. The springtime weather of the day was gone, and the night was cold, but there was a fire on the hearth.

Wilkes lay looking up at the ceiling where the dying embers of the fire traced moving shadows, and reached out to the bed table for the letter he had taken from his coat pocket when he was undressing, a cherished letter Ella had written during the time he was in New York.

The next day when Wilkes had long departed, the doctor's wife found the letter under the pillow as she took the bedding apart. She started to put the letter in her apron pocket. She must send it to him. And then, absently, she looked at it and saw the signature, "Your lonely Ella."

Wasn't Wilkes Booth engaged to marry a daughter of a Senator? Why, yes, that's right, she remembered. Miss Elizabeth Hale. She looked at the signature again and read the letter in spite of everything she felt about anyone reading another person's private correspondence. She was shocked by such open avowals of love. She hadn't imagined that any woman could express such thoughts to a man. Her face burning, Mrs. Mudd threw the letter into the fire. She could never tell anyone about it, not even her husband.

On March 19, a cold, clear day, President Lincoln was scheduled to attend an afternoon performance of a play to be presented before convalescent men at the Soldier's Home hospital. Wilkes learned that at approximately one-thirty he was to

250

travel to the hospital in a carriage manned by only one driver. Things would never be more ready. The time had come.

Davy Herold was waiting at the Surratt Inn for the arrival of the Presidential carriage, the transfer rig ready. George Atzerodt was ready with the boat at Port Royal.

Wilkes kissed Ella good-bye at the door of her cottage. They had no idea how long they might be separated this time—it would depend upon what President Jefferson Davis wanted when Wilkes got to Richmond with Lincoln.

"He may ask me to handle the negotiations for the prisoner exchange. I could carry on the negotiations through Senator Hale."

Ella was much more frightened than she dared to admit. Feeling her anxiety, he said, "I'll be back, Ella, I promise you."

And then he was gone, astride the big black horse he had purchased at Bryantown. In his pocket was a black mask which he would wear over his eyes, around his slim hips and waist was a gun belt heavy with ammunition and two pistols, and in his upper coat pocket was one of the twin derringers Ella had given him at Christmas. He had fallen in love with "the beautiful toys," as he called them, and almost always carried one of them on his person these days. The other he insisted Ella keep in her bedroom for her own protection. Wilkes, John Surratt, and Lewis Payne rode to the bend in the road and hid in the brush among the trees. All dressed in black from the broad-brimmed hats to the masks and capes, they waited patiently in the grove for the sight of the Presidential coach. They would let the coach get ahead of them on the long road and then race after it. After Surratt grabbed the reins and brought the carriage to a halt, Payne would climb to the driver's seat, overpower the coachman, and toss him into the ditch. Wilkes would leap from his horse to the carriage and force his way inside even before it had stopped rolling. He would hold a gun on the President while Surratt and Payne took over the carriage and turned back along the road to the cut-off to Surrattsville.

In case of a challenge anywhere along the route, they were prepared to don Union clothing, salute their challengers, and ride like the wind, their guns ready. Wilkes impressed upon his men something he had learned as an actor. Act like the loyal personal guard of the President, he told them, and no one would have the nerve to challenge them until the President was actually reported missing. They had several hours before that would occur, and until they were stopped by bullets, they would bluff their way.

They were not kept waiting for long before the White House coach came down the road. The black, closed carriage was drawn by two horses, their coats glistening in the glare of the afternoon sun. The driver, seated on a high perch, looked neither to the right or left. There was no other vehicle on the road. The conspirators slipped their reins loosely in their hands, ready to ride. The coach passed the grove.

Exhilarated by the coming chase, Wilkes let out a rebel yell. The others howled, too, and they spurred their horses in fast pursuit of the unarmed carriage.

Surratt caught the reins on his first attempt, pulled back on the leather straps, and brought the rearing horses to a balky halt.

Lewis Payne, his dark hair falling forward on his knobby forehead, grabbed for a hold on the coach, found it, pulled himself up out of the saddle to the swaying driver. Without compunction, Payne swung a fist down hard on the skull of the frightened man who slumped on the seat, blood oozing from the scalp. As the carriage stopped, Payne lifted him down to the ground to tie and gag him.

Swinging from his horse to open the door of the coach, Wilkes slid swiftly inside, gun in hand. He pressed the pistol into the passenger's side at heart level. But the man in the Presidential coach was not Lincoln! Wilkes sat staring at the man he had never seen before. Disbelief, shock, struck him dumb.

Backing out the door Wilkes jumped to the ground, slammed the door closed, and called to Surratt who was still holding the reins, and to Payne who had just finished his work, "We've been tricked! Let's get out of here!"

Without question, they swung into their saddles and raced away, following Wilkes blindly back to Washington. There was no time for explanation. As they rode, they dropped their masks and capes along the way, and they slowed their horses to canters as they rode into Washington, where they separated.

Wilkes went to his room at the National Hotel. If he had been observed and followed, he had no intention of leading anyone to Ella's home. He spent several hours alone in the room before he dared to venture forth.

She knew that the venture had failed as soon as she saw him. "Why? Ella, why?" he begged. "Everything I do is doomed."

"Who betrayed you? Do you know?"

"No. It must have been Surratt's contact in the White House, but we'll probably never know for sure. Maybe Lincoln just changed his plans and sent someone else to represent him. If we had been betrayed, surely they would have had troops out there. No, it must have been just bad luck."

"Darling, you've got to be content to know you've tried. You've done so much for the South. Let it be."

"There's got to be something I can do. If only Johnny were alive——" his voice broke. "Damn it, I'm going to make them sorry they hung him. I swear it." It seemed to Ella that he was talking to John Yates Beall now and not to her.

But for the next days in Washington, Wilkes felt lost and hopeless. He wanted desperately to do something which would yet help the Confederate cause and he wanted to avenge Johnny's death, yet no idea came to his mind.

He was in the bar of the National Hotel when shouts of "Hallelujah!" greeted the news of the fall of Richmond. Men slapped each other on the back, filled glasses full, sang, danced, laughed, shot off guns, and yelled. Grant had taken and burned the capital of the Confederacy. Nothing was left of the rebel stronghold, they said, and Jeff Davis was an exile, running for his life, hunted by Yankees in blue coats.

And that wasn't all. A drunk sputtered the news happily into Wilkes' face that "Old Abe Lincoln walked hisself right into Richmond. Sat hisself in Jeff's chair, too! How about that for a man!"

Richmond, fallen. No! Wilkes could not accept that. The drunken Yankees were lying. Richmond stood and Jefferson Davis sat in the chair at the Presidential desk. The South would win. God bless her!

Rebels everywhere believed that Jefferson Davis and Robert Lee would rally the cause and the Confederacy would survive—

until six days afterward, when General Robert E. Lee gave all his forces into the hands of General Grant at Appomattox Courthouse.

Ella tried to talk to Wilkes but he seemed not to hear her. He moved like a sleepwalker. She knew only that he was meeting again with his friends at the Surratt boardinghouse. She supposed it was natural that they should gather together in each other's company—men who have fought and sacrificed for a lost cause have only each other in their moment of defeat.

The evening of Lee's surrender, Wilkes went with the crowds to the White House to listen to Lincoln. Standing amid the mobs of Yankees, a military band playing Yankee songs, Wilkes looked at the tall figure on a White House balcony accepting cheers of the people.

Lincoln's youngest son stood with his hand in his father's and grinned and waved. The President's face was now dim, now bright as the torches of the crowds bobbed and swayed. The White House's windows reflected the sky rockets bursting overhead. Every federal building was gleaming with lamps in every window, and flags were flying and bunting wrapped the capital.

Then President Lincoln spoke about the new South, about Negro voting to come, of the new Southern state governments and the new brotherhood of all men, black and white. As Wilkes listened, he grew pale and rigid. The fires of Richmond were dimmed this night, but in John Wilkes Booth's heart they were flaring high.

Abraham Lincoln turned to the nearby military band and requested: "Mr. Bandmaster, let us hear "Dixie." I believe it is a song properly captured!"

The Yankees went wild as the song of the Confederacy was heard as a spoil of war on the grounds of the White House. Remembering the way he and Johnny had happily whistled its bars as a signal to each other time and again, Wilkes put his hands over his ears. He could not keep out the terrible noise of hundreds of Yankees lifting their voices in a raucous rendition. "My God!" he shouted. "I no longer have a country!"

He went back through the celebrating crowds to the National Hotel, not even noticing that the coals in the burner in his room had no fire. The sound of skyrockets resounded every now and then, and somewhere downriver a cannon was being fired. But

Wilkes heard none of it. After turning up the wick on the lamp on his writing table, he wrote a long, long letter addressed to "My Countrymen."

Forty-Five

For years I have devoted my time, my energies, and every dollar I possessed in the world to the furtherance of an object. I have been baffled and disappointed. The hour has come when I must change my plan. Many, I know—the vulgar herd—will blame me for what I am about to do, but posterity, I am sure, will justify me. Right or wrong, God judge me, not man. Be my motive good or bad, of one thing I am sure, the lasting condemnation of the North.

I love peace more than life. I have loved the Union beyond expression. For four years I have waited, hoped, and prayed for the dark clouds to break and for a restoration of our former sunshine. To wait longer would be a crime. My prayers have proved as idle as my hope. God's will be done. I go to see and share the bitter end.

This war is a war with the Constitution and the reserve rights of the state. It is a war upon Southern rights and institutions. The nomination of Abraham Lincoln four years ago bespoke war. His election forced it.

I have ever held the South was right. In a foreign war, I, too, would say "My Country, right or wrong." But in a struggle such as ours (where the brother tries to pierce the brother's heart), for God's sake choose the right. When a Country like this spurns justice from her side she forfeits the allegiance of every honest freeman, and should leave

255

him untrammeled by any fealty soever to act as his conscience may approve.

People of the North—to hate tyranny, to love liberty and justice, to strike at wrong and oppression, was the teaching of our fathers. The study of our early history will not let me forget it, and may it never. I do not want to forget the heroic patriotism of our fathers, who rebelled against the oppression of the mother country.

This Country was formed for the white, not the black man. And, looking upon African slavery from the same standpoint held by the noble framers of our Constitution, I, for one, have ever considered it one of the greatest blessings both for themselves and us, that God ever bestowed upon a favored nation. Witness, heretofore, our wealth and power; witness their elevation and enlightenment above their race elsewhere. I have lived among it most of my life, and have seen less harsh treatment from master to man than I have beheld in the North from father to son. Yet, heaven knows no one would be willing to do more for the Negro race than I, could I but see a way to still better their condition.

But Lincoln's policy is only preparing the way for their total annihilation. The South is not, nor has it been, fighting for the continuance of slavery. Their causes for the war have been as noble and greater far than those that urged our fathers on. Even should we allow that they were wrong at the beginning of this contest, cruelty and injustice have made the wrong become the right, and they stand now before the wonder and admiration of the world as a noble band of patriotic heroes. Hereafter, reading of their deeds, Thermopylae will be forgotten.

When I aided in the capture and execution of John Brown (who was a murderer on our Western border, and who was fairly tried and convicted by an impartial judge and jury of treason, and who, by the way, has since been made a god), I was proud of my little share in the transaction, for I deemed it my duty, and that I was helping our Common Country to perform an act of justice. But what was a crime in poor John Brown is now considered (by

256

themselves) as the greatest and only virtue of the whole Republican Party.

Strange transmigration! Vice to become virtue, simply because more indulge in it. I thought then, as now, that the Abolitionists were the only traitors in the land, and that the entire party deserved the same fate as poor old Brown. Not because they wished to abolish slavery, but on account of the means they have ever endeavored to use to effect that abolition. If Brown were living, I doubt whether he would set slavery against the Union.

Most, or nearly all the North, openly curses the South. If it is to return to the Union, will it retain a single right guaranteed to it by every tie which we once revered as sacred. The South can make no choice. It is either extermination or slavery for themselves, worse than death, to draw from. I know my choice, and hasten to accept it. I have studied hard to discover upon what grounds the right of a state to secede has been denied, whether our very name, United States, and Declaration of Independence, provide for secession.

But there is no time for words.

I know how foolish I shall be deemed for undertaking such a step as this, where on the one side, I have many friends and everything to make me happy, where my profession alone has gained me an income of more than $20,000 a year, and where my great personal ambition in my profession has been a great field of labor. On the other hand, the South has never bestowed upon me one kind word; a place now where I have no friends, except beneath the sod; a place where I must either become a private soldier or a beggar.

To give up all the former for the latter, beside my mother and sister whom I love so dearly (although they so widely differ from me in opinion), seems insane; but God is my judge. I love justice more than I do a Country that disowns it; more than fame and wealth; more (heaven pardon me if I am wrong) more than a happy home.

I have never been upon a battlefield, but, oh! my Countrymen! Could you all but see the reality or effects of this horrid war, as I have seen them, in every State save Virginia, I know you would think like me, and pray the Almighty to create in the Northern mind a sense of right and justice (even should it possess no seasoning of mercy) and that He dry up the sea of blood between us which is daily growing wider. Alas! I have no longer a Country. She is fast approaching her threatened doom.

Four years ago I would have given a thousand lives to see her remain as I had always known her, powerful and unbroken. And now I would hold my life as naught to see her what she was. Oh! My friends, if the fearful scenes of the past four years had never been enacted, or if what has been had been a frightful dream, from which we could now awake, with what overflowing hearts could we bless our God and pray for His continual favor.

How I have loved the old Flag can never now be known. A few years since, and the entire world could boast of none so pure and spotless. But I have of late been seeing and hearing of the bloody deeds of which she had been made the emblem, and shudder to think how changed she has grown.

Oh! How I have longed to see her break from the mist of blood and death so circled around her folds, spoiling her beauty and tarnishing her honor. But no, day by day, she has been dragged deeper and deeper into cruelty and oppression 'til now, in my eyes, her once bright red stripes look like bloody gashes on the face of heaven. I look now upon my early admiration of her glories as a dream. My love is for the South alone, and to her side I go penniless.

Her success has been near my heart and I have labored faithfully to further an object which would more than have proved my unselfish devotion. Heartsick and disappointed, I turn from the path which I have been following into a bolder and more perilous one.

Without malice, I make the change. I have nothing in my heart except a sense of duty to my choice. If the South is to be aided it must be done quickly. It may already be too late. When Caesar had conquered the enemies of Rome and the power that was his menaced the liberties of the people, Brutus arose and slew him. The stroke of his

dagger was guided by his love for Rome. It was the spirit
and ambition of Caesar that Brutus struck at.

'Oh that we could come by Caesar's spirit,
And not dismember Caesar!
But, alas!
Caesar must bleed for it.'

I answer with Brutus, he who loved his Country better
than gold or life.

Wilkes reviewed the letter carefully, making sure that he
cleared his family and the South of any personal responsibility.
There was no hint of his work under the orders of Jefferson
Davis, no suggestion of family approval of his views. His only
reference to Ella Starr was in his lamentation about giving up a
happy home.

He signed his name then and put the letter in an addressed
envelope to John Coyle, editor of the *National Intelligencer*.
Then he put the envelope back on the table and stared at it,
flexing his fingers for they were cramped from the long writing.

The knock on Ella's front door was loud enough to awaken
her at once. Grabbing a robe, she called through the house to
Jane that she would answer the knock herself. She was sure it
was Wilkes.

He was standing there in the midnight dark, quiet and apolo-
getic. "Forgive me, coming here like this, so late. I just needed
to be with you for awhile."

They sat together on the couch, gazing into the fire which
was the only light in the room. When he kissed her mouth it was
with a tenderness which surprised her. He seemed to be drained
of emotion. She thought she understood: The fight was over,
the cause lost. But it took only a little while before she realized
that far from being serene and hushed, he was highly nervous
and excited. He stammered when he began to talk. "Ella, if
I . . . Ella, if I tell you—there's something——"

It wasn't over, then. Oh, God, Wilkes was still fighting the
war! She was afraid to hear more. "Wilkes?"

The look in his face which had first appeared the day Johnny
had been hanged was still there.

"No!" Ella pushed herself to her feet and stood apart from

259

him. "No more. Do you hear? No more plans." She beat at his chest with her fists. "You can't do anything any more to help the South. Don't you understand, Wilkes? The South is gone."

He closed her within his arms and he stroked her hair as she sobbed.

"Ella, don't be afraid. Don't worry." He lifted her tear-stained face so that he could look down into her eyes. "Look, I came here to talk about us. But it's very late and you're very tired. So am I. Why don't we just sit here by the fire a little longer and then I'll be on my way."

She knew that he lied, but she let him. She simply could not face any more talk. She let him change the subject. Wilkes suggested that they be married soon after Easter and wondered if they might not find life in California, or Spain, or some place away from the torn South and the victorious North a good thing. He told her of Lake Erie and the moonlight on it and how he had thought he would like to take a shipboard cruise. "Edwin and my father thought San Francisco was an exciting place. Maybe we could sail for it after Easter." She listened to him dreamily, and all her fright of a moment before vanished.

It was nearing dawn when he got up to leave. He walked to the door with his arm around her waist. Then he kissed her, his mouth lingering long on hers, and smiled. "I love you," he said quietly. Once outside, he turned at the gate to look back at her, and she blew him a kiss. He waved and started walking, striding fast, not looking back.

Forty-Six

╭∽∕∽╮

Wilkes was very busy the next few days. On April 14 he met with his men at the Surratt boardinghouse and was reported at the Ford Theater several times. He was later said to have been seen at the Navy Yard Bridge, talking to a uniformed man, and—it is claimed—near the telegraph office of the War Department. Someone later remembered seeing him in front of the White House. In time, another would testify that Wilkes was in a barbershop, expressing loud sympathy for the South. It was said he was in the Petersen house, that he left a calling card in the rooms of the Vice President of the United States, that he walked and rode the streets of Washington that day in endless trails.

Wilkes covered a vast amount of territory, talked to many men, passed bills from his pockets. He was directing the final attack upon the Union. Even though the Southern Army had surrendered and President Jefferson Davis and his staff were in flight, he aimed to strike down the leaders of the Union and create such chaos and loss of federal authority in the capital that a rebel uprising could result in its seizure and bring victory to the Confederacy.

He did some very effective work. For one thing, the telegraph wires of Washington, especially those carrying messages to the nearby forts, were set to be cut. And during the day his plans expanded: The deaths of Stanton, Seward, Johnson, Lincoln would leave no one to take over the reins of the government, no one to calm the people. Grant was removed from the death list when he left the city—he would be too far away to be of immediate aid in the crisis which would grip the nation's capital that evening.

The day passed in a rush of activity, but as the hours went and the fateful moment drew closer, Wilkes became coldly calm. He stopped thinking and reacted to his own planning.

He spent some time at the Ford Theater, talking to the carpenters who were decorating the box which the President of the United States would occupy that evening. The workers were always glad to see Wilkes, a friendly young man not given to conceit like some of the other actors. He helped them drag a big heavy rocker into the box in which the President would be seated during the evening.

Wilkes inspected the seating arrangements, sat in the rocker, and went to the hall door at the top of the stairs. He fitted a wedge of wood, left by the carpenters, between the door and the wall; the wedge would hold against any attempt to open the door from the outside. He hid the wedge back in the far corner of the hall, near the Presidential box, and then drilled a hole large enough to look through in the door of the box.

He went back to his hotel room and rested on his bed for a time, flat on his back, staring at the ceiling. He went over every detail of the day's activities in his mind, reviewing his men and their assignments.

Later, he took great care to dress for the evening: He wore a pleated linen shirt, buttoned up the back, and a wide silk black cravat, wound twice around his collar and tied in a soft knot, the ends hanging loose. The black brocaded vest, the tapered black trousers, with loops at the bottom to fit over his foot, were all part of an outfit which was smart in detail and dramatic in style. He fastened a pair of silver spurs over the riding boots that reached halfway up his calves. The spurs jingled pleasantly as he walked around the quiet room. His hat was flat-topped, wide brimmed, black, shadowing his face.

Opening a drawer of the dresser, he took out a dagger and the little gold-plated derringer Ella had given him. He looked at the cutting edge of the dagger critically, turning it so that the engraved words *America, Liberty, Independance* were clearly visible. He smiled at the misspelling of the last word and slipped the knife into his belt. Finally, taking the envelope addressed to editor John Coyle, he put it in his pocket.

Some other items were already in his suitcoat, including a small packet of pictures of his mother, Ella, Asia, and several actresses. He debated leaving them behind, but decided he wanted them too much, and so put them in his pocket.

He took up the derringer and scrutinized it with care. The hammer screw was broken off, but it did not matter. He clicked the gun several times. It worked smoothly enough. He picked up the bullets from the dresser and inspected them——remakes, like most ammunition at the end of the war. It did not matter, either. Being so poorly made, the bullets would probably shatter on impact and make an awful wound. That did not matter, either—a man was lucky to be shot instead of hung.

After slipping the loaded gun and the bullets into his coat pocket, he looked into the mirror. The black of his clothes made him look even paler than he was.

Now he was ready. He would not be coming back to the National this night, but he left the gaslight with a little glow so inquisitive people might believe he planned to return.

And in the White House only a few blocks away, Abraham Lincoln had finished dressing. The carriage with the President and First Lady and their guests of the evening proceeded along its way to the Ford Theater. The family gone for the evening, the White House lamps which had flared so brightly in the early evening were dimmed.

Wilkes went to Pumphrey's stable to get the bay mare with the white star on its forehead. Riding down Tenth Street to the stable behind Ford's Theater, he was admired by passersby. One remarked to his companion: "There goes Booth, the most handsome man in America!" They watched with a tinge of jealousy as the actor rode past, straight-backed, firm-chinned, eyes direct, as proud and easy as a general.

Turning into the Ford Theater alley, Wilkes met John Matthews, an actor he had known for years. He reined up the horse and took out the envelope addressed to Coyle. "Will you do me a favor? If I don't come by for this by tomorrow afternoon at one o'clock, will you take it over to the office of the *National Intelligencer*? I want it delivered to the editor in person."

Matthews looked at it curiously. "What is it? 'Booth's Travels Through Darkest Africa'?"

"No," Wilkes said, managing a smile, "but I think they will print this quicker."

Matthew put the envelope in his pocket, and Wilkes thanked him and moved on. Spangler, the stage hand at Ford's, held the horse for Wilkes while he went inside the theater. But Wilkes was gone too long, and Spangler soon handed the care of the horse into the hands of a half-witted stable fellow named Peanuts.

Wilkes entered the theater as intermission was under way: The second act of *Our American Cousin* was already finished. He was right on his schedule and hoped the others were following through to the minute on their assignments. This was the last chance for them and for the South. Satisfied, he left the theater to go to Taltavul's, the bar next door, where he liked the brandy. He ordered it but he did not drink it, gazing out the window at the dampish street. Washington had been threatened with a rainstorm, but it had not amounted to much. Now the clouds were lifting.

Back in the lobby, he watched the audience go to their seats. Some of the people recognized him and paid their good evenings to him. He spoke a few words about the weather to the doorkeeper, and the curtain rose on the third act.

He wandered down the dark aisle into the theater pit at his leisure and looked the audience over. He scanned the box where the President and his party sat. The front of the box was bright with red, white, and blue bunting. A portrait of George Washington hung in the very center of the draped flag.

Slowly he went back to the lobby and the stairs which led up to the boxes. He went unchallenged along the outer row of seats of the dress circle now, his feet light and soundless on the carpeted floor. The small door which led to the corridor of the boxes was just ahead. No one was there at that door to stop him. The guard had left his post.

Wilkes opened the small white door into the corridor. He got the wedge of wood from its hiding place and quickly jammed it between the door and the wall. It held securely. The corridor to the boxes was now cut off from the main part of the theater.

He leaned down and looked into the Presidential box through the hole in the door. Mrs. Lincoln had just finished some remark to the President; he nodded attentively.

Wilkes opened the door, stepped quietly inside, and stood a moment in the dark recesses. The box was gaily decorated with ruby-red hangings and matching red carpet and red velvet chairs. Lace curtains hung with the velvet portieres.

No one in the Presidential box saw Wilkes as he stood there, but the President must have felt a presence, for, suddenly chilled, he reached for his shawl and pulled it around his big shoulders. He had been under a heavy sense of foreboding the past few days, and could not shake the dream he experienced in which he had seen himself lying dead in the White House.

Major Henry Rathbone, holding the hand of his fiancée, Clara Harris, was unaware that anyone had entered the box. Completely engrossed in the play, the young woman at his side did not notice a thing. Mary Lincoln was concentrating on the play, too, and saw nothing else. Abraham Lincoln sat with his hands clasped together, smiling a little at the comedy being enacted below.

It took only three paces to bring Wilkes directly behind the President's rocker. He lifted the derringer a little higher in his hand and placed it close to the back of Lincoln's head. Wilkes hesitated. Here, within a few inches of the gun at his head, enjoying life, sat Johnny's murderer.

Wilkes squeezed the trigger. The explosion was not loud, but Lincoln's head fell forward, instantly, wordlessly. He slumped a little to the side, toward his wife.

At the sound of the shot, Henry Rathbone arose from his chair, uncertain, alarmed. Mary Lincoln turned to her husband and gave a terrible scream. Clara Harris sat and stared, her eyes wide in fright.

Rushed by the Major, Wilkes dropped the gun to the floor and reached for his dagger. The sharp-edged knife cut through the sleeve of the Major's uniform to the bone. As blood ran down the whole arm, the Major stepped back in shock. Taking advantage of the Major's faintness, Wilkes leaped to the wide rim of the box railing, holding onto the velvet curtains. There, balanced precariously, he raised the bloody dagger high and shouted, "Sic semper tyrannis!"—the motto of the state of Virginia, the birthplace of Johnny Beall, the heart of the Confederacy, the place where he hoped to raise his own family. Wilkes then shouted the translation: "Thus ever to tyrants," and looked down on the stage where the actors and actresses stood stunned. Laura Keene looked up at him, recognizing him. Faint with terror, she put her hand to her mouth.

Wilkes took a quick look back into the box. Lincoln was still slumped in the rocker, Mary Lincoln bending over him. Major

Rathbone was moving toward the stricken couple, holding his bleeding arm helplessly. Clara Harris was rushing to kneel beside Mary. They had no time for him.

Wilkes was balanced perfectly on the railing and, as he so often had done on the stage, he leaped into space. The jutting spur on his left boot caught in the folds of Old Glory which was draped at the front of the box, and he had to jerk his foot free as he fell, throwing himself off balance. He landed on the stage with his left leg twisted under his body. Excruciating pain blacked out the world for a split second, but desperation drove him back immediately to full consciousness. Above him Rathbone was waving a bloody arm to the audience and was shouting: "Stop that man! He has shot the President!"

Laura Keene put out her hands to him in a feeble effort. In shock she knew only that he was John Wilkes Booth, a friend with whom she had often shared a performance. She did not yet understand that he was a murderer, only that he was a fellow thespian and he was hurt. But Wilkes was not to be stopped now—he shoved her aside, not really seeing her.

The orchestra leader ran at him, responding to the shouts from the audience to stop him. Wilkes pushed away from him, slashing him with the dagger, and the man fell back. Limping badly, Wilkes ran across the stage.

When he got to the alley, he leaped upon his horse, and spurred the mare to a fast gallop. Away from the theater, down F Street, past the Herndon House, the Patent Office, Judiciary Square, the Capitol Building, to Pennsylvania Avenue, to Eleventh Street, to the Navy Yard Bridge that would lead him to Surrattsville, Beantown, Port Tobacco, Port Royal and—finally—Richmond and Ella Starr.

Forty-Seven

A young sergeant, his rifle ready, halted Wilkes at the bridge.

His mare danced in circles, as lively and excited a horse as the soldier had ever seen. The guard asked the stranger his name. The answer came honestly and quickly, but the soldier was not acquainted with the name Booth and needed more information. He wanted to know where Mr. Booth had been.

"I've been to the city."

"Where are you going?"

Mr. Booth claimed he was going home. He had a small place outside of Beantown.

The sergeant thought maybe the rider was trying to jest him. "I never heard of a place called Beantown."

"What? Come now, Captain! Surely, you've been to Beantown."

Not certain that he was being treated seriously, the guard became curt. "There's a law says you can't cross this bridge. Nobody can."

"I had not heard of that law. I haven't come to town for a long time."

"Why didn't you start for home earlier?" After all, it was nearing midnight.

Mr. Booth looked up at the sky where blue-rimmed, yellow-bellied clouds drifted across the moon. "I deliberately delayed going home so that I would have the benefit of the clearing weather and the light of the moon."

"All right, then. Pass."

Taking no chance that the guard would change his mind, or that a message might arrive from the city, Wilkes sped over the bridge astride the frisky mare.

On a hill beyond the bridge, he met a terrified Davy Herold. Lewis Payne was not there, though. Herold's young face was

267

white and he was over-talkative, nervous, almost hysterical. "I skipped, Mr. Booth! They got Lewis, all right, I think they did. I heard an awful big ruckus in that house. That man Seward got him. I had to get out o' there, Mr. Booth. I had to leave Lewis No use both of us getting caught, was there?"

Wilkes looked down the hill to the bridge. There was no sign of any other rider. Davy was right: Lewis Payne was not coming. They would have to travel on without him, and fast. The Yankees might make Payne talk, if they had him.

"It's all right, Davy," Wilkes tried to reassure the frightened youth. "You did right. Maybe Lewis got away. Anyway, we'll have to go on without him."

The pain in Wilkes' leg was becoming unbearable. He bit his lip hard and tasted blood. Davy was all concern: "Mr. Booth! You're hurt. Is it a bullet?"

"No. I fell. I'm afraid it's broken. I feel sick." He sat up straight in the saddle, suddenly remembering. "But I shot Lincoln, Davy. I shot him. I think he's dead."

Davy Herold looked at his companion in wonder. Wilkes Booth had actually shot the President of the United States. There was a real fearless man for you!

They spurred their horses. There was no time to rest, and not much time to think. But Wilkes wondered if Washington was in chaos, if Lincoln and Johnson were dead. If Seward had been slain . . . and Stanton. If so, would the rebels in the city rise to their chance and seize the city? He prayed so.

They headed for the Surrattsville Inn which loomed dark and big off the road. Wilkes was not able to leave the saddle. Davy dismounted quickly, under Wilkes' orders, and banged loudly on the door. Davy and the proprietor of the Inn, John Lloyd, conversed hastily at the door and then Lloyd went inside and came out quickly with a bottle of whiskey and two carbines and ammunition.

Davy handed the bottle to Wilkes. "Drink the stuff, Mr. Booth," he urged. "It will make you feel better."

Wilkes tipped the bottle high and swallowed enough to make him choke. He put the bottle, capped, into his coat pocket and reached down for the carbine.

"I'm all right. Let's travel," he ordered, reluctant to lose any time at all.

From Surrattsville they rode five miles to the town of T. B. Wilkes hesitated at the fork in the roads—one would take them to Beantown, as scheduled, and the other toward Dr. Mudd's home. Bleary-eyed with pain, swaying in the saddle, he decided he must have medical attention. "We'll turn off here," he told Davy, "To the Mudd farm. I have to have help. Doctor Mudd can set the bone. We'll tell him I fell from my horse. You understand, Davy?"

"Yes, sir! You got to have a rest."

They reached the Mudd farmhouse at four in the morning, now thirty miles from Washington. Half-faint, Wilkes stayed in the saddle while Davy Herold went to the door. The whiskey had turned to flame in his stomach and was spinning his head. Every foot of the long ride had been agony. The slightest move of the horse was almost more than he could endure. Dawn was just faintly breaking in the east.

Doctor Mudd came to the door at last, a lamp in his hand. His night robe was flung loosely over his flannel nightdress and he strode toward Wilkes Booth in amazement. John Wilkes Booth here, at this hour! And drunk?

The doctor helped Davy Herold, half pulling, half sliding Wilkes from the back of the mare. Together they managed to assist him into the living room and stretched him out on the sofa.

Mrs. Mudd, accustomed to having the doctor called upon at all hours of the day and night, nevertheless felt a sense of alarm. She hurried into the room to find her husband bent over the man on the couch while a scarecrow of a youth stood awkwardly beside them.

Wilkes looked up at her and smiled. "I'm sorry to cause you all this trouble, Mrs. Mudd, but I'm in very great need of the good doctor's help."

"Wilkes Booth!" She could not hide her astonishment, and she pulled her robe closer around her neck.

The doctor stood up. "Mr. Booth has injured himself in a fall from his horse. I believe there are broken bones. My dear, I shall have to cut this boot from his foot. Would you fetch a kitchen knife?"

The boot removed, Wilkes' leg and foot were exposed to the doctor's scrutiny. He shook his head thoughtfully. "There is a break, Mr. Booth. Perhaps several small bones, just above the ankle. Let me do what I can to ease the pain. I'll improvise splints and bandages for tonight, but tomorrow morning I'll take you by carriage to the village. There we'll attend to the proper treatment."

"Do what you can to set it now, Doctor Mudd. I must be on my way in the morning. There's a contract I must meet."

"Leave without proper setting? That would be foolish, indeed, Mr. Booth. You have a bad break there, and if it is not set right it will cause you serious trouble all your life. It could cripple you. And, left this way, there is the danger of blood poisoning."

Adamant, Wilkes closed his eyes against the racking pain. "Please, Doctor! Set it—bind it. I can't stand it much longer."

Doctor Mudd and his wife exchanged glances. There was something strange about the whole business, but what? Still, there was nothing they could do but offer the injured man their help and hospitality.

Wilkes did not lose consciousness, but he came close to it when the doctor set the bones and wound bandages around makeshift splints. Finally the doctor handed him a glass of brandy. "Here, now. This will help."

Wilkes drained it in a gulp, and then the doctor insisted that he get some rest. Wilkes was too exhausted to argue. The doctor and Davy left him alone on the couch to sleep and went to the barn, where they worked together on fashioning a pair of wooden crutches. Mrs. Mudd, acting as nurse, looked in on Wilkes many times. He was sleeping well.

Forty-Eight

As Wilkes Booth slept a dreamless sleep, thirty miles away, in Washington, President Lincoln died at 7:22 A.M. It was April 15th.

On Davy Herold's plea that Booth would want to be awakened, Mrs. Mudd went into the living room at two in the afternoon and stood over him.

He smiled at her and said, "You found my letter, didn't you?"

The color in her face deepened. "Yes, I did! I destroyed it."

"I was hoping you had it for me. But it's all right, Mrs. Mudd. I shouldn't have been so careless. I only meant to tease you."

She reached for a glass of water for him from the tray on the table. "I apologize for reading it, Mr. Booth. I've never done such a thing before. It just happened."

He took the glass, but before he put it to his dry lips, he said solemnly, "I love her, Mrs. Mudd. We're to be married."

"I hope you'll be very happy, Mr. Booth, and that you have a family as beautiful as I do. You must be very hungry by now. I'll bring you a tray."

As soon as Wilkes had finished his meal, he practiced the use of the crutches in the yard, the doctor helping him. He went away with the warning that if the leg was not treated properly it could develop into a dangerous condition. Wilkes told the doctor he would stop at the first town and locate medical help. Doctor Mudd watched him ride away, shaking his head silently.

They went on into the land of the marshes and swamps near the Maryland side of the Potomac and took time to rest, hidden by ground fog. The desolation was frightening.

Wilkes' physical condition was worsening. He was suffering increasing pain, and his leg was rapidly swelling, bespeaking the blood poisoning the doctor had feared. Davy helped him dismount, letting him lean heavily on him. Davy propped him against a fallen, decaying log in a half-sitting, half-lying position. Wilkes sank against it, grateful for the support but aware that Doctor Mudd's warning was accurate: The splints had loosened in the riding and the bandages were now but dirty rags. The leg was already badly infected and its color was becoming purple.

When dark came that night, Davy Herold went in search of food and medicine—anything. Wilkes began to concentrate on a drink of brandy. If he could have just a small glass of it, he could endure the pain, get back into the saddle and ride out of the stinking swamps. He wondered what was happening in Washington. Was it in the hands of Confederates? God, don't let this all be in vain! He hungered not so much for liquor as for news.

Davy came upon a farmhouse. The odor of a dinner cooking in the huge brick oven drifted to the hungry youth. He went boldly up to one of the Negro hands and begged for food for a sick man and for himself—two men traveling home from the war, he said.

The Negro hesitated, and while he tried to decide what to do, the master of the house came out of the kitchen door. The word of the flight of the assassin of the President was widely circulated now. "I turn no man from my door hungry," the sharp-eyed farmer told Davy Herold. "Bring your sick friend. We will feed you from the kitchen. Then be on your way."

Davy managed to get Wilkes back into the saddle and led the horses through the swamp to the farmhouse. The big Negro was at the kitchen door with plates of hot food and meat, but when Wilkes sniffed the food, his stomach revolted. "Brandy!" he begged. "Give me brandy."

The farmer came out of the kitchen in time to hear the plea, and disgust filled his eyes. "Take the food and get off my property. Keep traveling! I have no liquor for such as you."

Through sheer willpower and pride, Wilkes sat up straight in the saddle and looked down at the man in scorn. Then, reaching into his pocket, he drew forth the leather case, and took out two and a half dollars—every cent he had—and threw the money at the feet of his reluctant benefactor. His words were almost slurred with pain: "Sir, there is all the money I have. Take it in payment for this poor dinner and for your hospitality. Little

272

though it may be, it is still more than your offerings are worth. I couldn't turn a dog away from my door in such a condition as you see me, sir, let alone a fellow citizen of Maryland!"

Wilkes pulled on the reins of the mare and turned her around. He fought to retain consciousness as he rode away, stiff-backed, head high, his feet well placed in the stirrups. Only when Davy had led them back into fog-shrouded swamps did Wilkes faint. Davy caught him as he collapsed in the saddle and he lowered him from the mare's back to the ground.

When he awoke hours later, Davy was kneeling beside him. "You had a real good sleep, Mr. Booth. I reckon you needed it, all right. How's it feel now?"

With Davy's help, he sat up. The leg was stiff, but it seemed there was less pain. Wilkes was feverish, though. "Davy, is there any water?"

Davy handed him a flask. "Drink all you want, Mr. Booth. I'll get more, if you need it."

Wilkes drank. He patted the shoulder of the young man. "You're a good friend, Davy. I'll never forget."

Davy grinned. "I got a newspaper for you, Mr. Booth. Got it while you were asleep, from that colored fellow. He took it from the house for me."

Wilkes grabbed the newspaper but he could not yet read it in the pre-dawn light. They dared not build a fire. He would have to wait.

With the first gray light of dawn, he read the newspaper. Lincoln had lingered all through the night after being shot, but had died at about seven thirty. Lincoln was dead. So was Johnny.

Wilkes scanned the other news hurriedly. The other men who had been targets of the assassins were alive. The rebels in Washington—so many of them!—had not seized the government. The Union endured. Ella, Johnny, his mother and family, his future, his country, all gone for nothing!

His tortured gaze went back to the news columns. The government offered a reward of $20,000 for the capture of John Wilkes Booth, dead or alive. Wilkes looked at the story for a long time. It said that the Booth family was being taken into custody, one by one.

Another column revealed that President Jefferson Davis was

accused of conspiring with John Wilkes Booth to murder President Abraham Lincoln, as was Jacob Thompson. Edwin Stanton had put a reward price of $100,000 on the person of Jefferson Davis, who, it was said, was in flight from justice. Find the man who once was President of the Confederate states, demanded Secretary Stanton. Bring him to Washington and collect a huge reward!

Wilkes bent over the newspaper, no longer able to read because of the blinding tears in his eyes. He had made a hunted man of Jefferson Davis! Throwing the newspaper aside, Wilkes groaned aloud: "God, what have I done?"

As Davy picked the newspaper up, Wilkes looked at it again and his glance fell on a story which brought him to a sitting position. He snatched the newspaper from Davy's hands without an apology. The story said that an actress named Ella Starr had attempted to commit suicide in her home. She had gotten chloroform from the military hospital and used it expertly, but she had been discovered in time. Found unconscious on the couch in her living room, a portrait of John Wilkes Booth under her pillow, it was believed that Miss Starr had tried to take her own life in an act of grief over the murder committed by her lover.

Wilkes fell back onto the ground and bit into the knuckles of his hand to stop the cry which came from within. At the last, in spite of all that he had wanted to spare her in the way of scandal, in spite of his honorable intentions toward her, the newspapers had destroyed her reputation and her life. Wilkes turned over onto his stomach and threw up.

Davy patted his back awkwardly. The friendly touch was too much for Wilkes. He pushed himself up and pulled his good leg up a little so he could put his arms on his knee and he bent his head to his arms and sobbed.

Forty-Nine

For seven days more of hell, Wilkes Booth and Davy Herold were alone in that wilderness. Hunted, wet, cold, and sick. Toward the last, when it was really too late, Davy was able to get a little help from a Negro who hid them for several days near the plantation on which he lived, bringing them food which Wilkes could not keep down.

Davy finally had to shoot their horses because the noise of the animals was a constant threat to their hiding places. Wilkes put his hands over his ears, but even with the gun muffled by clothing, the reports sounded loud in his ears. Wilkes tried not to think about the animals. It was too much. Bloodhounds, held in leash by armed men, followed their trail, closing in always, day by day. Federal gunboats plied the Potomac, scanning the shores for signs of the escapees who had definitely been reported by witnesses in the area. The United States Cavalry was everywhere, beating the countryside, talking to farmers, black people, school children. Little by little, their route was becoming pegged down. The gunboats drove the weary pair away from the waters back into the swamplands—the dismals, as they were so rightly called.

Back in the depths of the miserable hideout, Wilkes was no longer able to sleep. Fevered and all but delirious, he wrote constantly with stiff fingers in a thin-paged diary. He wrote no word of regret, hoping that it would be published in full. But everything that he wrote, probably including a message to Ella, was never made public. A limited part of the diary was to be seen eventually, but the Secretary of War, demanding that the diary be brought to him personally, found it necessary for the good of the nation to tear out some of the pages. Wilkes might as well have saved his strength.

When he finished writing, Wilkes dropped back exhausted

onto the ground and went into an uneasy sleep, the first in several days and nights. Davy Herold put his own coat over him and sat close to him in a grim vigil. He looked at the book in which Wilkes had been writing so often and he picked it up to read it, as much for companionship as for anything else.

"Tonight I try to escape the bloodhounds and the gunboats once more. Who—*who*—can read his fate? God's will be done. I have too great a soul to die like a criminal. My God spare me that and let me die bravely. I bless the entire world, have never hated or wronged anyone—this last was not a wrong, unless God deems it so, and it is for Him to damn or bless me. And for this brave boy with me, who often prays, yes, before and since, with a true and sincere heart. Was it crime in him? If so, why can he pray the same? I do not wish to shed a drop of blood, but I must fight the course. 'tis all that's left me."

Davy put the book back in Wilkes' knapsack. He looked at the leg, the bandages, soiled black and waterstained. There was nothing to do about it. If he tried to change the bandages, the bones would shift again to tear anew at the flesh. Young Davy could do only what he had been doing. Kneeling, he clasped his hands together over the sleeping form of John Wilkes Booth, and prayed. "Dear God, kindly take this suffering from him."

On April 22, they crossed the Potomac with the help of a Negro who rowed them across himself. He even found a wagon and a horse. Wilkes lay in the bed of the wagon, and Davy drove on toward Richmond.

On that road they met half a dozen Confederate soldiers, returning to their homes in Virginia. Captain Jett brought them to a halt as the wagon approached them.

"Well, sir!" the captain greeted Davy. "What's your trouble? Hungry, like the rest of us?"

"Sir, I see you're a Confederate like ourselves." Davy looked back into the wagon. "My friend, he's in a bad fix. He fell from his horse. We need help."

Captain Jett spurred his horse forward and he looked into the wagon in horror at the ragged, dirt-covered, odorous, skeletal man. The thin face was hidden by a heavy growth of beard. The captain swung from the saddle. "You do need a doctor, sir!"

Davy, on the driver's seat, turned to the captain. "He's got a real bad leg."

The captain started to reach for the bandages, but thought better of it. He had seen such things in the war. The odor told the story: gangrene, a very advanced case. too. Jett had seen many men with less horrible infections unable to stand the pain, and was sure the poison had spread throughout the man's body. He could not live long, but still, he ought to be made as comfortable as possible.

Jett gave Davy explicit directions on reaching the Garrett farm down the way. The Garretts were good people and they would help.

William Garrett, a Virginia farmer and a Confederate still, came to the wagon, led by tired Davy and he looked at the man lying in it. "You're John Wilkes Booth."

Wilkes motioned Davy away. "It's so," he said, weakly. "Will you turn me out?"

"Hell, no," said the farmer. "You'll come in for tonight, but I ain't going to be stupid, either. You'll have to help me think of something to get you elsewhere tomorrow."

He and his family tended the ailing man as best they could. They carefully removed the stinking rags, and some of the rotted flesh came with them. After a washing of the leg which made Wilkes shriek in pain, they rewrapped the leg, ever so gently, and then he fainted. Later he managed to eat a little food, and finally he had his glass of brandy.

"We're going to bed you two down in the barn," farmer Garrett told them. "It's safer. We've had the Yankees here before, often enough, in fact, looking us over. I'll fix you up comfortable on the hay and you'll sleep well enough. Tomorrow morning we've got to think about what to do with you. It's a hanging offense, I guess, to be hiding you here."

"I'm grateful, Mr. Garrett." Wilkes stood on his crutches. "Not just for what you're doing for us. But because you're a Virginian who can still tell the damned Yankees to go to hell."

"Well, Mr. Booth, you did wrong—the good Lord is witness to that. But I can't lift my hand against you. I'll pray for you, sir."

"Thank you, sir." Wilkes balanced himself and offered his hand. The farmer did not hesitate, as Wilkes half expected he might.

"Goodnight, Mr. Booth. My son will see you two down to

the barn. Now be as quick as you can, and stay as quiet as you can. If you hear any riders, don't make a sound."

Fifty

They were comfortable in the hay, the carbines they picked up at Surratt's Inn close at hand. Wilkes lay flat on his back. He was no longer thirsty, no longer hungry. The pain was still atrocious, but the little bit of liquor he had been able to down had helped.

"Do you think we'll make it, Mr. Booth?" Davy whispered.

Wilkes put his hands under his head. "I don't know, Davy. Mr. Garrett says the Yankees are all around this farm." He sighed. "We'll have to see, Davy. We'll fight the course, whatever it is."

"Sir, I'd like to go with you, if we get out of here. You know, I mean, wherever you go, I'd like to go along."

Wilkes spoke softly. "Davy, you're a brave boy. I brought you into this."

"Don't matter, nohow, sir." He hesitated, then cleared his throat.

"Yes, Davy?"

"You ain't sorry? About the other, I mean. About killing *him*? Do you think it was right?"

"It was not wrong unless God deems it so, Davy. It's for Him to judge. But, no. I'm not sorry. Not about that, anyway."

"Yes, sir." Davy was satisfied.

Silence took the barn, and then it was Wilkes who spoke.

"Davy?"

"Yes, sir?"

"I've heard you pray, sometimes."

"Yes, sir."

"Davy, would you pray for me? I've prayed, sometimes, but I'm not sure I ought to, just now. I think God might hear you, though."

"Pray for you, sir?"

"Well, Davy, not really for me. But for the people I love. I know I've wronged them."

"You want I should pray for Miss Ella?"

"Yes, for Miss Ella." Wilkes bit his lip. "And for my mother. My family."

Wilkes closed his eyes and went to sleep with the sound of Davy's words of simple prayer in his ears. Davy Herold did not finish his prayers because he was too tired to stay awake long enough to say them all.

At midnight the United States Secret Service arrived at the Garrett Farm in a detachment twenty-five strong, led by Lafayette Baker, Chief of the Secret Service, and Lieutenant Colonel E. J. Conger. They had rousted Captain Jett and his men from beds in a tavern not far up the road. The captain made a valiant but futile effort to deny that Wilkes Booth was anywhere near.

The sound of creaking saddle leather, the tinkle of spurs on boots, the hushed voices of men, awoke Wilkes abruptly. He knew at once what it was—federal troopers! He reached out and touched Davy and clapped his hand over the boy's mouth so that he would not speak out loud as he awoke. Davy sat up, alarmed.

The loud voice of Lafayette Baker roared in the night: "Booth! Come out of there, hands raised! You're surrounded by the United States army."

The two in the barn sat quiet. It was easy to hear what was happening up at the farmhouse. The Garretts were ordered to come out of their home, hands up, out on the porch, where they were vainly searched for weapons. They were told to consider themselves under arrest.

Hefting their carbines, Davy helped Wilkes to his feet and handed him the crutches. Wilkes hobbled forward and looked out through cracks between the planks of the wooden door to see the Garretts, father and son, being pulled toward the barn under the urging of rifles. Wilkes lifted his carbine a little higher

279

and peered out again to the yard. Lieutenant Baker was standing now beside the Garretts, an easy target. But Wilkes did not pull the trigger.

The Yankees were dispersed entirely around the barn. Baker and Conger faced the barn door, the Garretts between them.

"Booth!" Conger shouted, "we're going to open the door. Come out with your hands up!" Davy pressed close against Wilkes.

"Stand back, Davy! Stay way back. They may start shooting right through that door."

"Booth!" Conger called, "we're sending Billy Garrett in to talk to you. If you harm him, you'll die at once."

Wilkes and Davy, carbines raised, whirled to face the door. At the quick movement, Wilkes' leg pained him so that he almost dropped to the floor. He held the gun as much for support as for defense.

The door opened from the outside, the farm boy stepped into the barn, and the door was closed behind him. Billy Garrett eyed the trapped men in compassion. "They say it will go hard on us, Mr. Booth, if you don't come out at once. Please, sir, surrender. You can't get away."

Wilkes shook his head. "I'm sorry, but it won't be any worse for anyone if I make my stand. Go back. Tell them I'll never surrender to any Yankee. And Billy, you thank your father for me. He's a fine Confederate, a real man."

Billy went out of the barn alone to his father, tears rolling down his cheeks. "He's going to fight it out with them, Pa. He doesn't have a chance. Not a chance in the world!"

The elder Garrett brushed his hand over the boy's soft hair. "I know. I know. There's worse ways to die than to go fighting for the things in which you believe, right or wrong. It takes courage. He's not afraid, son. Don't you be for him, that's not fair."

While the federal officers conferred on their next move, Wilkes turned to Davy. "They'll be coming in for us. I want you to get out of here, first. It won't be much better out there for you, but at least you'll have a chance to plead for your life in a court."

"No, sir." Davy stood his place. "I want to stay with you, Mr. Booth. Like I told you. I'll go wherever you go."

"Booth!" Baker's voice boomed forth. "We're going to burn you out. Do you hear? Come out right now or be smoked out."

Wilkes pushed Davy toward the door. "Go, now. Do me that favor. Do what I want. Please."

Davy wavered. He handed his gun to Wilkes who put it against the wall. Davy's eyes were glistening with tears. "Mr. Booth?"

"It will be all right, Davy," Wilkes told him.

"Yes, sir."

"Davy Herold is coming out," Wilkes called.

The door began to creak.

"Thanks for all you've done, Davy," Wilkes said.

The door was opened, and Davy left the barn very quickly. The troopers grabbed him roughly and dragged him to a tree and tied him so tightly that he could hardly breathe.

"All right, now," Conger yelled again to Wilkes, "it's just you, Booth! Come out or we start the fire."

Wilkes moved toward the center of the barn, away from the walls. Standing alone, without his crutches, he held the carbine in his hands and he put Davy's carbine at his feet.

"Captain!" he bellowed. "Give me a chance! I could have killed you half a dozen times tonight, but I won't murder you. Give a lame man a show. Let me fight you all—one by one!"

"We came here to arrest you, not to fight you, Booth. You have your last chance to surrender."

Wilkes listened to the men running, to their voices as they ignited the hay all around the barn's exterior, to the crackle of the flames. Smoke began to fill the barn. Still defiant, Wilkes moved toward the door.

Sparks were flying everywhere. Burning bits of hay exploded in all directions. The walls would soon fall, the roof crash. He would have to make a run for it, carbine ready to take the first man he met.

Something stung his neck as he moved forward, but before he could put his hand up to it, he fell. The bullet from the gun of Sergeant Boston Corbett had lodged in his upper spinal column, paralyzing him. Wilkes lay on the floor of the burning barn, and the gun slipped from his hands.

They dragged him out, stretched him on the porch of the Garrett home and searched him, removing his few belongings.

He cried out: "Water!" Farmer Garrett's young sister came to sit beside the dying rebel and bathed his face and moistened his lips with water. Wilkes' pain-wracked eyes saw his diary, his pictures, in the hands of the enemy.

When they gazed upon the photograph of Ella Starr and they passed it from hand to hand, the appeal in his eyes reached the heart of Miss Holloway. Cradling his head in her lap, she spoke to Lieutenant Baker: "Give me that picture, sir! Mr. Booth wants to look upon it."

The officer hesitated.

"Sir, a dying man's last request?" she prodded.

Lieutenant Baker gave her the photograph.

She put it in Wilkes' hands. Even though his torso and legs were stricken with paralysis, the gift of life was still in his weak hands, and he was able to lift it up to look at it.

Miss Holloway stood up, crying. William Garrett took his sister into his arms and tried to soothe her. "Child, cry for men who die without a cause. Be sad for men whose spirits are conquered in life. Don't cry for such a one as this!"

She looked down and saw that Wilkes was trying to speak. Quickly she got to her knees, leaned over him, and took the photograph from his hands.

Her long hair brushed against his face. "What is it, Mr. Booth?"

Wilkes gazed searchingly at the palms of his hands. Overhead, a scarlet sunrise was tinting the new day, and the light of it fell upon his hands, and he saw the lines in them, blackened by smoke and accentuated by waning vitality.

Before those hands fell lifelessly, Wilkes cried out with his last breath, "Useless! Useless!"